The Itinerary of Beggars

The Iowa School of Letters Award for Short Fiction

H. E. Francis

THE

ITINERARY *of* BEGGARS

UNIVERSITY OF IOWA PRESS

 IOWA CITY

The previously published stories in this collection
appear by permission:
"The Frog Lady," *Prairie Schooner* 30 (1956).
"The Woman from Jujuy," *Southwest Review* 57
(1972).
"The Fence," *Prairie Schooner* 28 (1954).
"The Man Who Made People," *DeKalb Literary Arts
Journal* 1 (1967). Reprinted in *This Issue*, The
Magazine for the New Creative, Book One, Number
Three.
"One of the Boys," *Southwest Review* 51 (1966).
"All the People I Never Had," *Transatlantic Review*
21 (1966).
"The Moment of Fish," *Southern Review* 7 n.s.
(1971).
"The Deepest Chamber," *Four Quarters* 15 (1966).
"3," *Virginia Quarterly Review* 44 (1968).
"All the Carnivals in the World," *Southern Review*
5 n.s. (1969).
"Don't Stay Away Too Long," *Southwest Review* 54
(1969).
"The Rate of Decomposition in a Cold Climate,"
Southwest Review 53 (1968).
"The Game," *Georgia Review* 16 (1962).
"Going West," *Transatlantic Review* 28 (1968).
"The Transfusion Man," *DeKalb Literary Arts Journal*
4 (1970).
"Where Was My Life Before I Died?" *Southwest
Review* 56 (1971).

Library of Congress Catalog Card Number: 73–80957
University of Iowa Press, Iowa City 52242
© *1973 by H. E. Francis. All rights reserved*
Printed in the United States of America
ISBN 87745–039–0

FOR
ANTONIO SANCHEZ-BARBUDO
HENRY MANN
AND
EVELYN VERITY, MY MOTHER

Contents

Preface

A HUNDRED and fifty of us here in Iowa City make up a community known as the Writers Workshop which likes to believe writing is the most difficult and the most important line of work a man or woman can pursue. We also like to believe that this town, although no longer capital of the state, holds just that relation to the writer's territory which reaches wherever the American language is read.

Whatever is myth in that notion, there is none in Iowa City's being a writing town where for better than thirty-five years people have come to write and to share their ideas about writing.

So it is natural that trends which affect writers are discussed here and when they are deemed harmful, countermeasures are devised and sometimes taken. When the reluctance of commercial firms to publish short story collections by new authors was noted and deplored here a few years ago, reflective, resourceful people acted. They proclaimed that whatever the public taste and the inclination of publishers, the short story remains the first and truest test of a writer's craft, and thereupon established the Iowa School of Letters Award.

This is an annual celebration of the short story which sees one collection into print and its author richer by a thousand dollars at least. The Award is four years old now and hope is strong that it will continue as regularly as the coming of spring and at least unto doomsday.

This year the thousand-dollar sum is provided by the Iowa Arts Council and it goes to H. E. Francis, a Rhode Islander who for nearly a decade has divided his time between this country and Argentina. His stories reflect an enviable ability not just to absorb an alien culture but to make it persuasively his own. Nor is this Mr. Francis' only virtuosity. His stories preclude comparison with those of other writers. Their mood is strange, often brooding and monstrous, and yet they are reassuring too, for they are never without the glow of the author's compassion.

John Hawkes, who made the final selection of this volume from among two hundred forty-five candidates, describes Mr. Francis as a writer who speaks in new, surprising ways about "the oneness of all things," about the individual who contains within himself the entirety of life in all its power and beauty.

John Leggett
Director of the Program in
Creative Writing
The University of Iowa

H. E. Francis

A NATIVE OF Bristol, Rhode Island, H. E. Francis has published many stories in the United States, Argentina, and Europe. He has received four Fulbright Awards—one to Oxford and three to the Universidad Nacional de Cuyo in Mendoza, Argentina. He is Professor of English at the University of Alabama in Huntsville, although he has taught creative writing and literature at several American universities. He is founding editor of *Poem* and poetry editor of *This Issue*.

9

The Frog Lady

At FOUR one Monday afternoon the yellow door of Jamiel's clothing store, which had been empty and so much waste for many years, was opened. Everybody who saw the big red letters SEE THE FROG LADY —TEN CENTS stopped, and most of them got so curious they had to see for themselves then and there. Nobody in town, after all, had ever seen a frog lady, or even believed, in fact, that such a thing existed. Outside, Donnie Matthewson himself hesitated. For he had waited at the door, looking at the red sign, then at the thin dime in his hand, dwelling on the risk of loss. He knew what a dime was, but what was a frog lady? And a dime went fast if she was just a fake—he knew that much.

So he stood outside with his idiot stare (everybody knows he has scarcely an ounce of sense, because he was born without the equipment) . . . he stood with that stare at the door and every time someone came out he'd ask, "Is it a real frog? Is it?" But they got fog in their faces and didn't answer or were filled with sadness or laughter which had a dirty sound—like snickers. You know the kind. And after a while he couldn't stand it any longer and handed his dime to the keeper, a man dressed queerly with colors men didn't usually wear like that: red and yellow and green all in a wide, striped ribbon shouldered and across his chest, then banded about his waist.

Inside, the arrow pointed immediately around the corner; and he could hear her singing the minute he got into the store. He stopped and the wild flutter of his eyes stopped too as if he saw something thrown up from deep inside him that was not really anywhere but just inside him. Whatever it was it made his face full of a look. He rarely had a look before. His face sags with a lapjaw, loose and uncontrolled, and his eyes droop into his cheeks—one of those faceless faces never explained, expressionless maybe because there's no learning held behind to mould it. I've heard his aunt say, "Poor Donnie's face wasn't even as good as the dead clay." At least you can take that in hand, lifeless as it is, and make it a form and control it. And when you look at it, you can even get emotion from the sight of it, but what feeling can you get from Donnie himself?—though his aunt got some, because she'd cry sometimes. But that was long ago. She got over that. At least if she still cries, it must be inside.

Anyway he was inside the store, and he was stopped. It was the singing, it seemed. Or the song. You couldn't tell. But he went toward the sound with his head bent, a stealth in his steps as if he'd got a bird trapper or a thing in the bush the least shiver would scare off. He moved into the crowd around the voice. It was loud and nasal, growing in a big surge and falling, but always loud—

> *Let me call you sweethearrrt . . .*
> *I'm in luuuuuuuuuuvvv . . .*
> > > *wiiiiiittttth . . .*
> > > > *youuuuuuuuuuu.*

She was sitting on an empty showcase, a huddle of flesh in a mound with her neck pushed into her shoulders; and her breasts hung into her belly indistinguishably. And it all sat on weighty thighs that seemed to stop at the knees where there were little knobs of toes on flat-bottomed fleshy pads that were her feet. But she stretched her head up into the air out of the flesh and sang—clear, loud, toneless—and her mouth wide like a fish after air. . . .

> *Let me hear you whisperrrr*
> *That you luuuuuuuuuvvv . . .*
> > > *meeeeeeeeee . . .*
> > > > *toooooooooo.*

Tight around her, holding her bulk in, was a green satin cloth out of which her arms hung like her legs, only narrower, but with the same stubby knobs of flesh for fingers. He could not see her face, only her profile. When she ended her song everyone applauded, but he stood there and gaped. After, she took up a darning bag and pulled out blue yarn and needles and began to knit with two very busy hands. At that everyone applauded again. So she smiled and nodded thanks. She smiled all the time anyway, with lovely white teeth. Then she set the knitting aside and spoke:

"I am Erna. I am called the frog lady. I am twenty-seven years old and one of seven children; all the others are normal. I have ten toes and ten fingers (she directed the gazes to her feet, then held out her hands demonstratively). I move about without help. I can cook and sew and I make my own clothes. I made this dress. We have been traveling for four years. Twenty-two states have seen me. I can sing and I read and write."

It came out fast and all without a breath between, like a speech learned. Finished, she held out a little tray the color of her dress; and without even knowing it, Donnie found himself looking straight into her face, with his hand on the tray. Still he didn't move; and catching the unexpected stillness, her gaze fell over him, held by his own. And her face blanked, disarmed, the smile went like a veil in the wind, leaving her face its nakedness only—like a reflection of the boy's face. But something else too . . . for the first time that night there was feeling: because she saw something, and it made sadness and warmth in her—

But the jolly crowd wanted more. The silence was not right for it, and a voice prodded her to sing again. Everyone laughed and egged her on: "Yes! Yes, sing!" Quickly she was caught up in their spirit and responded, laughed herself, but there was bleakness in her. Then she did her great feat—always made them applaud—took her needles, held them between her toes, and knitted. They loved it, gasped, sighed with awe and admiration, then pitied in relieved laughter. They forgot the boy. And at last she sang, still and smiling, the same song, in the same loud monotone among the giggles and people coming and going and the clinking of coins. And she sang loud with a wide smile and still eyes as the boy went out of the store back into the dying light of day and blinked, for he had seen the frog lady, and he didn't have a dime anymore, and he did not know what he had at all. . . .

The sign said: ONE WEEK'S ENGAGEMENT.

"When is the week?" he asked the barker.

"Saturday night—that's the week. Five more days before we shove, Sonny."

The man looked at him, sizing him up, and chuckled to himself.

"Besides, we gotta get out for the big p'rade," he said. "There'll be nothin' doin' here for us with a convention in town. It'll be here, come Saturday. They'll be movin' too—men and animals all over the place."

"Animals?"

"Yeah," he said, "horses, lots-a horses." Donnie nodded. "And maybe others, the dog show," the man added. He nodded again, held by the man's talk. *Animals.*

"How old're ya, boy?" the man asked, suddenly studying him shrewdly. A good-natured feel of his hand rubbed encouragingly on Donnie's shoulder.

A long time he looked at the man. But he said no more about the animals.

"Aw, come on, kid—what's the age? I ain't meanin' no harm. How *old're* ya?"

Agnes had told him to say it, but maybe it was the hardness in the man's asking or that he was still thinking of the frog lady he was going to see for the second time that prevented him. He wanted to go in bad now and he didn't want the man to stand with his bright stripes in the way.

"Ain't talkin', hey?" The barker was piqued. "I got no one to talk to all day," he said, " 'cept her, and she ain't good for much when it comes to talkin'. I as'ed ya becuz it was somethin' to say. Oh, what the hell!"

"My name is Donnie Matthewson," he said, blunt, "and I live on Hope Street and my mother's name is Agnes Matthewson and I'm twenty-six." *There!*—now he'd said it by rote like Agnes always told him to say it if he was asked.

The man sullened a bit, looking hard at Donnie's smooth, unhaired skin; then he got back, getting the point, coming out of his denseness.

"Yeah," he said. "I guess ya mean it. Twenty-six. Well, whattaya know!"

Donnie could not understand what the man's look and tone said. Maybe he heard what was not right in the sounds, because there were some that set him all wrong and uncomfortable like hairs turned down the wrong way, and made twistings in his feelings so tight and uncomfortable; so he escaped, pushing past the man anxiously dropping his dime in the box, and went in.

—and there she was, sitting on the showcase as if she'd never left, encircled by a crowd thicker than last night's. He edged up close but someone cut in front of him, curious for a look at her limbs, and he ducked off and hung back farther with a silent waiting in him. From there he could hear her little speech just as well, and the *Let-me-call-you-sweetheart* number. That's when his head cocked, his eyes large on her, unmoving and unblinking . . . that tone shivering in him like the long sound of a new chord never heard before in all the world. . . .

After the song the crowd thinned quite rapidly. Still he waited, walking around the room, coming nearer, then standing by the last man, listening to his questions. And as the man turned finally to head out the door, Donnie heard him talking to the barker, but not their words, because he saw her, and saw her smile fade, and her one automatic hold on the public gone. At his approach the tenderness came into her and maybe he felt some of the fluttering and throbbing in her as she looked at him. Because she held out her stubbed hands, and he could not resist it, the drawing of them. He went close and did not know what he was feeling. Taking his face between her hands, she looked long into it, over it, and touched it and pushed back his hair then to see all his face. But who could tell why? There was something between them, she knew that. Only she couldn't stand the restlessness of looking at his face anymore; she fidgeted at his hands, dropping her eyes. . . .

When the barker came in a few minutes later he found her holding Donnie's hands, and there was a sound like quiet sobbing.

Christy, the barker and proprietor of the enterprise, had suddenly got a problem, though he didn't realize it instantly. Only when Donnie came back the next two nights and sat with an unregistering face until he heard her sing, did Christy see the drawing come to life. *And wasn't Erna getting different, now he thought of it? Why the hell didn't he see it before? The kid had* sent *her maybe.* But when he told her that, she let him have a spiel about sick-and-tired of the racket.

"You're no fake, are ya? Then how the hell's it a racket?" he attacked her.

But she fretted. She looked out of their room into the bleak dark of the town she didn't know, except its name, Bristol, and she said in a longing, "It's like the town I come from, it's near the water and the air smells salty." She told him she could see the sand even. "You never seen wild roses, Christy?—pink, wild roses of the hot summer growing in the sand?"

What the hell did he know about pink roses, huh? He was a businessman. If he thought of pink roses, where the hell would they be?

Maybe he was thinking *Where are we anyhow?* because he scowled at himself questioningly.

But she answered him: "I would be back there."

"It's your own fault—*you* wanted this 's well as I did. Was *my* idea, yeah, but you had nothin' to lose either. Ya only wanted to get out of that house where everyone was all right but you, that's all."

And it was true, she confessed it: *I went to him, I told him yes, I welcomed him like he was a church for shelter.*

"Yes," she said aloud, with a nod, weak and unable to fight anymore.

In her simple way she knew she had gone down the glamor path in his mind, all because he had come in a whirlwind, high pressure and clear vision set in his words. It told her dreams could live. And she left the old lady who blamed both her and the old man for what Erna was—a freak. But they didn't know that a freak can think, she's got nothing else to do but think. She let Christy undress her down to this green satin piece and let the world see her for money.

He got a nice place in a town up-island, not far from Brooklyn, but in a few weeks he exhausted the possibilities. They set up in another town, then another, spending too much on fares, food and bed, not making enough. Drifting. They became irritable; then it would be right, calm. . . . The feeling of skulking came over them as they began hiring dinky side-street stores, ex-shoeshine nooks, anywhere under the sun that he could perch her on a box and him stand outside where people went by. Sitting there, she saw her life, a headful of faces without meaning—only laughter sometimes; she could give them that at least—though sometimes hatred too; a headful of faces and dives, low joints—one-night stands, a week in a small town, a week in a big town sometimes, lucky. . . . And the thick odors of people jamming close around her.

He left her in dirty rooms, calling her his sister who couldn't be separated from him—except when he went out, sometimes to get drunk and all the time to drink a little. Maybe the drinking explained the dirty rooms. Soon she was a burden to him, but he put up with her.

At least he was smart, she was his bread-and-butter, she was useful anyhow. Everybody had to do something useful, didn't they? Well . . . ?

In the dirty rooms she sat with her knitting, making sweaters and socks for Christy; and more and more she looked out the window, on the dark days especially, when the clouds thickened and the wind was a desolate blowing; and she forgot her knitting. Then it was that there was a big bleak dark space inside her, bigger than the day, too big for her, and she couldn't do anything about it. She sat, and looked into the vast sky, and she forgot her knitting. . . .

But on the fourth day in Bristol she stopped knitting in her spare time.

"What the hell'd you quit for?" Christy asked when she told him she'd put it away for a while. Maybe so she could go on sitting in a slummy room on Thames Street, looking into the harbor. . . . And sea gulls flew white into the gray November sky. A smell of sea came in, lingering, and grease from the restaurant downstairs. But she didn't say all that.

"I don't know," she said. "I can't, I don't want to."

"OK! Forget it," he said. He let it go at that, because her glance was heavier than before, though all the time he was thinking about how it shouldn't make any difference anyhow if she wanted to knit or not off the job. Only he couldn't hold back, asking testily:

"Only you'll knit on the job?"

"Yes, on the job," she said, comprehending, but already she was caught in the graceful swoop of gulls outside and that was the end of their talk, until the fifth morning . . .

. . . because something had happened.

It was happening last night all the time he was out front yelling SEE THE FROG LADY. ONLY TEN CENTS, ONE THIN DIME in the only language he knew, over and over. He couldn't see it even when he was standing inside, watching the bastard little idiot again and watching Erna, because he didn't know where it was going on. But even she and the idiot boy didn't know that. Maybe it was because Christy couldn't see it that he yelled louder and walked up and down faster and glanced back and forth into the store and then walked some more. He smoked fast, twice as many cigarettes, and stomped and ground on them, heavy. For something was in the whole room and he did not understand what.

It was worst of all when she sang, because it was the same monotone but the voice was different or the measure or . . . what was? Word about the frog lady had spread fast. There were more people tonight than ever. He should be happy as hell about business being so good. But he wasn't; he couldn't get through this feeling. It had nothing to do with the crowd in the room or the thick tobacco smoke he couldn't see through. But he felt a thickness there that filled the room and made no room for him in it . . . and he did not know, that was the thing. . . . O, what the hell!

SEE THE . . . FROG . . . LADYYYY, he yelled, *TEN*-CENTS, calling it loudly down the long main street, knowing it was barren at this hour.

From the door he watched her shadow cast on the wall, its shapeless mass, its arms raised above the heads. He saw her through part of her last performance, then went back out to smoke in the cool air. The customers came out noisy and went down the sidewalk into the streetlights. Now he had to tell her it was time to leave, she could pack up.

"You go now, huh?" he said to Donnie, who looked blankly until Erna nodded *yes,* making him actually smile. Then he went out the door.

"How come ya not waitin' for me?"

While Erna put her knitting and her change-plate in the carrier, put a tam on and threw a heavy coat about her, Christy paced impatiently. He offered to help her down but she had already slid to the floor and seized the bag herself. She didn't even ask him how much money they made tonight. And her walk was settled and firm.

"Erna . . . ?"

She halted, thrusting her head boldly back, with no effort to turn herself. She was inquiring coldly. Not like Erna. *Well? What is it? I'm waiting.* . . . She waited while he blew smoke, then turned indifferently away.

"Where you going?" he said in a voice of almost-not-being-able-to-take-any-more.

"To the room," she said, "where else?"

"How come ya not waitin' for me?"

". . . ."

"What're ya doin'?" He plagued at her, begrudging the silence. "What're ya thinkin' a-doin'? Whatta ya think *I* am—nobody? I'm Christy. *Christy,* ya hear?" But her silence made him feel pushed aside.

"What'd *I* do?" he said. "Ya mad—well, what'd *I* do?" He paced up and down, flung his hands out at her, asking her *what'd he do?*

"It's that kid!—that God-damn blitherin' idiot comin' here three nights straight!"

"He's not an idiot, he talks sense when he wants, he talks to me fine." What was the difference in her voice? Filled. What was empty didn't sound empty anymore, but even soft and it surprised him so he couldn't say without stuttering or something.

"Erna—"

He saw her stiffen with protection or anger or indifference perhaps —he'd never know—but she got herself away, and he swore as she went to the door.

"Wait," he called after, "I'll take ya home."

He pulled out his watch, scanned it anxiously, telling her it was too late for her to be in the dark by herself, she might fall, they might not open tomorrow night, he'd better see her safe. He put the watch back in his pocket, thinking *why didn't he let the kid stay, all because of the kid! Damn!*

"No," she said.

"What's the matter with you?" Now his bungling made confusion and rage in him. "I'll take ya home."

"No," she said. She pushed the door out and the cold night came in. "I am not a gold watch," she said disdainfully and padded heavily out into the street. And the door came closed between them.

And that's what had happened; but for a minute before he left the store he stood there realizing that it had happened, and he still did not know what it was. . . .

In the morning she went out early—rare for her who usually slept late—and did not show up until lunch, and then only briefly. Never before had she left without telling him where she was going.

But Christy knew small towns and the corner gab. He knew the simple trick: you talk around until you get to the immediate point, which at first you made seem the remote point. So everything is an accident; and nobody is blamed for telling. . . .

—the two were seen walking across the Common under trees bare in the dead cold, their voices crystal clinks and their steps scrapes on the echoing ground. They didn't mind the cold, walking close, talking: nobody ever heard Donnie talk *that* much before. At the waterfront they stood on rocks, hearing waves and the windbeat, and watching the seaspray and holding hands. They came back into town along Hope Street with indifference toward everyone. And this time she walked him home.

That is what the town told Christy. What he couldn't know without her telling it was their other two meetings while Christy was drinking, or how they'd agreed to meet, right in front of Christy himself, when Erna had nodded *yes* to Donnie last night. Or he couldn't know about Donnie's mother waiting for Erna; or of the woman's own warped love. For Mrs. Matthewson knew about the meetings. In a clarity baffling even to her—coming from his head as it was—Donnie had told her.

"She is a frog lady," he had said.

Erna held out her hand that was not even like a hand and said, "Hello," clearly and forward without shame. That pleased Mrs. Matthewson, who had been made an outcast from the town by its pity, the thing she hated and grieved over as their most merciless sin against her. But Erna came, not knowing this, so it gave the woman a rare warmth for the girl.

At last Mrs. Matthewson told Erna what she had hoped.

"I've watched him all week," she said. "He tells me what he can, you know. After the first time, I wanted very much to meet you, Erna. Did you know I went downtown and stood in the crowd to see you because the first day he talked so of you?" She did not tell of the first hurt of seeing Erna, because it was a small thing to the pleasure the girl brought to Donnie and her, his mother, at seeing it in him. Not only that, but she feared Erna's leaving town, because she never could know Donnie's mind or what it would make him do. But they must talk it out. Rather, she talked it out.

"It is scarcely a rash judgment, Erna. Fast, yes, but we have short lives, we must grasp the right things when they are here. I've a good bit of money and I'll do anything to make Don happy. And you, Erna—can you live this life of wandering to maintain yourself for long? If something should happen to you or to your partner . . . but, of course, that is too unpleasant to think of.

"I have this big house and I'm a lonely woman. . . ."

And Erna could not say. . . . Her hands. Floundering.

"He is my whole life, Erna," the woman said. Above all things, she loved him, glancing at her whole fragment, "and he is so fond of you already. He's never really been fond of a person before, you know. Oh, you could make us very happy and we would both try very hard to do the same for you. I think we would succeed, Erna."

And in the tremendous awe of it, Erna did not know what to do, only say *Yes! Yes!* it was all so wonderful that it hurt. Yet she did not comprehend everything until she was outside and the meaning came clearly: it meant change, and no Christy, and the goodness of the woman, and the house, the lovely house, and she could help someone at last— Oh, that above all she wanted and so desperately that she could not do without it now—ever. But how could that come suddenly in five days? How could life change so? How? But there was only the quiet of the late afternoon darkness. . . .

By the time she returned to Christy she was talkative, with a nervous animation, and a plan she feared—the first she'd ever had—but she did not get to tell it to him—not yet. For she had to sit through his rantings—*her showing herself to the whole town free! How the hell could they make any money? Who'd come to see her now—and what were they supposed to do, starve? She trying to get down with a cold or something? Did she know what she was doing? What got into her anyway? And them leaving in two days and never coming back anyhow—*

Then she spoke out:

—but she could never come back, she said, she was not leaving, you see. . . .

"Whatta ya mean!"

So she told him what happened in that house this afternoon.

"O, please, don't be so mad, Christy," she pleaded. "They're only meaning to be kind."

"And that's what kindness is—huh? Does a man out of a job!"

"Please, Christy!"

"'*Please, Christy! Please, Christy!*' That all ya got to say after all I did for ya? Is it? Well, *is* it?"

"For me . . . ?"

"Yes—*you!* An' you used-ta say we got everythin' we need—what more we want *You*—not me!"

"But we haven't any more, it's not the same now, I got more."

"What? *What?* I ask ya. Tell me what ya got now you didn't have before. A house? Ya want a house, is *that* it?"

". . . ."

"Well?"

"I don't know."

"There! What'd I tell ya? You're not in love with that—"

"Love . . . ?" Her face questioned curiously as with discovery.

"—idiot!"

"Love. . . ."

"Now what's the matter?"

"That's what I have," she said. "I didn't have that before, Christy. Never. . . ." They had said the word she could never say, the word she could only sing but never say.

"Have what?"

"Love," she said, rolling it softly. Because at last they had said it, what was hid, and she knew.

Filled with the sound of her own self thinking it, she scarcely heard him, and her quiet infuriated him so that he broke into shouting she couldn't do that to him.

"Ya got responsibility, ya don't let people go like that. We got somethin' together—yes, *us!*"

He was close with a mad look she had never seen in him. She held up her stumped hands . . . "Christy!" It bunched out, she couldn't find words, only that one over and over. But he only stood by her. She rolled then, deep-breathing on the bed, as he turned to the window, not knowing anymore what to say. And their hard breathing made a heavier silence that held them as if they couldn't move anymore.

Worn out, yes. But what could she do? It was time to have a bite, to go back to the store together, for him to yell and her to sing: and the evening would come down slow and long and heavy between them.

All through the evening, she knew he was watching. He barked less and if she looked she could see his shadow on the front panes, walking. She went on singing and talking and watching the shadow. But after, it was Donnie who walked her to her door and told her not to forget tomorrow at his house.

In the room she couldn't get the house out of her mind; she sat with all her clothes on in the bed, rolled over—the warm cozy house, the woman like a mother, and Donnie. . . . In the darkness his face came to her and she heard how Christy always said the word *Donnie,* to make her sick inside because it brought the boy's face back and her feeling as she saw it on Monday in the crowd; that she would like long fingers to reach out with and stroke that face into movement—because it looked like a plate, empty, and it stared; because it did nothing, like her own body, and herself, nothing. Ah . . . she knew that so well, so she would like long hands to touch him with and to make him feel. For he had done that to her, deeply. Now Mrs. Matthewson would make it possible for her to do something, for she had never really done anything for anybody before. . . .

When Christy came in—ranting again—she was already so filled with thought she could not listen to the words. She lay unresponsive and felt no connection with anything. She was Erna alone now, the first time she knew who she was, and she thought, trembling, the first time she was a woman and could make a decision. . . .

Sometime deep in the morning dark she woke from a doze and rolled her head round toward the window, the barely visible frame. And there was the red cigarette and Christy's face faint when he puffed a glow. At her movement, the glow rose and she heard his steps back and forth in the room, and she could discern the black, moving Christy, a shadow too. . . . She tried to doze again, but it was a long night, and thoughtful; and she figured how Christy was a shadow on her, how all people are shadows on each other. . . .

In the morning she found him in the chair asleep, still dressed. When she put a blanket over him, he twitched, looking at her with eyes red from lack of sleep and staying out half the night and not sleeping the night before. They were tired and not Christy's, she thought, but they were not different either. How could that be? It had not occurred to her before, but she had never seen them true, never looked really. But he had her hand and said: "You can't go. You gotta stay. We're no good alone, 'specially me," and he dropped her hand.

"That's not so—" she said, not sure now, never sure now with the night gone. "I can be something to them. I'll make them happy. I can do it, Christy, she said so. *I* can make them happy." Her voice rose, frenzied. She wanted to beat him and make him know she could make them happy. She wanted to beat it into him until he said *Yes! Go . . . go!* and admitted she could do it and gave her a reason for going. But his head rolled drunk-tired. Her hands fell, nothing came out of her, but his words were unexpectedly sore in her, burnings. . . . "Erna. . . . I need you, Erna."

Why did he have to say *that* again?

She panted down the stairs, holding tight to the bannister, and went into the cafe.

"Cold, 'ey?" the Italian said. Because she didn't reply with her usual cheer that he liked so well, he went behind the counter and waited. The entire meal was like that—him waiting and Erna sitting and eating quietly. Finally she left silently, leaving him puzzled.

Outside, the chill was good, made Erna alive in it as perhaps she'd never been before. Mrs. Matthewson expected her early. As she walked she grew happy with the strength of her decision. She could not yet believe a week could make a life so different. There was early morning noise in the town, quickening because the holiday was coming. It all made her laugh audibly. But near the house the joy went, she became upset and strange, and when she saw Mrs. Matthewson she did not have the conviction that had come over her partly in bed, then wholly at breakfast, so she sat in a tremble and maybe from fear or shame began right away speaking, jerky.

"Why, Erna dear, what is it? You must be more plain than that," Mrs. Matthewson said. "Whatever are you trying to tell me?"

"I don't know what it is," she said. "I thought if someone liked you it was easy. You could like back and that was all and you could go anywhere or do anything. Like Donnie—because I made him happy and it made me happy to do it, see—? And I thought: that's all there is to it. But it's not. It's just he woke me up and I never was awake before—see? It made me be so strong. I never was before, I mean. Oh, I *want* to stay—more than anything—with you and him, but that's wrong 'cause what would I do then, huh? Well, that's what I *thought* would be so nice and it *would* . . . but then it would hurt too, because I got what *I* want—and where's Christy then?"

"Erna . . ." The forlorn world inside the woman returned. She saw the foreboding *no* in the girl, gently given, but still *no*. And she knew the old truth—out the window was the town and it could be no different out in the world—that it was only the girl's excitement after all and her own, that they must grow slowly and they had had their life with one another quickly in a few days, and that was no whole growing.

"You have changed your mind, yet it would have been so good for all of us. But you must think what might happen—"

"That *is* what I thought. Only Donnie's got you to look after him and I'd have you too. See?—I thought I'd help—and I would—but you don't need it bad as Christy does now. And it's something else too: life—it's not being easy-living and warm and with always the sure thing behind you—"

She was close to the woman, she talked excitedly and fierce power came in her: that she could be the cause of this. Donnie. Or Christy. Both of them in need. And one would be unhappy—and she the cause. For a moment there was a strangeness in this new thought: *it is me who was nobody, nothing to nobody—me, Erna.*

But Mrs. Matthewson could not know what she was thinking. She had her arm about the girl, smiling.

"How you have *seen* things, child," she said, rising, going to the window. "We'll be very sorry. We'll miss you."

Missed. But she could not stand it all at once—all the joy or what it meant, love, the power, the discovery too big for her.

"So you are certain you will not change your mind?" It was her last attempt, hopeless, she knew. *"Are* you certain, Erna?"

She could say *no*. But there was Christy lying in the chair, Christy's red eyes and desolate voice, and their long, weary, sweating drag into everywhere and together, that had not ended. Oh, she was wise: it would never be love that she could have, but she had a right, hadn't she, to a kind anyway. What he said . . . need.

Rising, she felt tall and caught at her fingers, feeling for a minute they were long like the ones she wanted to soothe Donnie's empty face looking at her. But of course they weren't. No matter. They didn't matter at all now.

She felt the towering in her. "I cannot tell you," she began. And she could not, because she didn't know the word for all that: giving up the woman and the boy, yet towering in the joy of it. . . . She tried to understand. "When you give up something you want, you're supposed to be sad. . . ."

Yet she smiled, waving to them both—to Donnie behind, a kiss.

She knew the woman understood, as she went out into the crisp, clear air. . . . And there was a happiness in her because she could look back—perhaps no one would ever miss her again, but already she could say: *somewhere I am missed, I made someone care, they want me to come back.*

She trudged down the street, glad because she would be with Christy, she had made him need at last. Somehow it was very right, that was a kind of love; and they both knew it, she felt. . . .

That evening after closing, while the Saturday night bonfire in celebration of the coming holiday blazed in the sky, she and Christy stood waiting at the railway station, two black figures against the orange glow the other side of town. Erna laughed into the flaming sky, thinking how she was with Christy because he needed her and he might change at last; and how Donnie would be sitting in that house, lonesome for her. . . . Beside her, Christy sighed deeply with relief, setting down the bags, thinking how clever he was he'd got her to stay, maybe he'd stash a little cash away for later on, but just now they had lots of time, why not a drink before train time . . . ?

And close to the bonfire Donnie roared with a nondescript gurgling laughter as he warmed his side joyfully and watched the mascot goat brought for the Monday morning parade. It wore a colorful American Legion patch on its back, and Donnie reached out his long hands to pet the goat with all the tenderness of new-found love.

The Woman from Jujuy

THROUGHOUT the province she was famed for her infamy. She was shameless and everyone shunned her. She moved among them like an object of fate, indifferent. Her eyes seemed a perpetual black night in that dark face. Her thick mass of hair was blacker than crow, never washed or combed. It hung in matted clusters. In the wind they leaped up like a riled nest of snakes about her placid face. She had no possessions but the black dress, the torn black shawl, ashen with dust and dirt, which she draped loosely over her back and arms, black cotton stockings, the dark blue *alpargatas* torn and breaking on her feet, and always over one arm the enormous patched burlap which served as a mattress on hot days, as a blanket on cold nights when she stretched out at full length to sleep on the pavement.

You might see her at the most crowded noon on the main street, San Martín, ambling among the hundreds dodging around her in and out of stores, or standing in the midst of traffic pouring out of the Mercado Central on Las Heras, or strolling along the wall of the *zanjón* that cuts across the city, staring into the canal water. She sat wherever it occurred to her, with her hand out. She was not like the other beggars. They mouthed and trembled, wore easily moulded pain on their faces, and stealthily counted their gain. They had friends and families, a place to go, and made profits. But she held out her hand as if expecting nothing but accident or grace: to eat, no more. When anything came her way, she simply pocketed it. Her eyes—aimed at the end of the street, far above the passers' heads, or through them—were always clear and peaceful, her face easeful, often with the faint shadow of a smile. You might see her sitting against Gath y Chaves, on the sidewalk near the Cine Radar, by Casa Heredia, in the *parquecito* by the Teatro Gabriela Mistral, eating—as if even the pedestrians did not exist—

from an opened tin of tuna or potted meat, her gaze too filled to include them.

What was she doing in Mendoza?

"All the beggars end up in Mendoza," people said, "because it is rich and there is much sun and no rain, they can sleep anywhere."

She was thirty but she looked ageless now.

She was from the far north, a *jujeña* from the province of Jujuy. She was from a house of children, thirteen, fourteen—she was not sure —nor did she know her father. She lived in an isolated hut by the river, crowded in with those who were left, and did whatever they told her—pounded meal, picked herbs, set traps for now and then a *liebre,* but mostly went for twigs and fuel and stole whatever food she could to help the family keep alive. And when the time came, she worked in the field with her mother and her mother's man and the children old enough.

That's where Lucas first saw her.

She did not see him. He saw her. She was fifteen. She was so pushed with tasks by her mother and her mother's man and the children that she had not yet lifted her eyes to men, though she knew the fumblings of children, laughs and jokes and gropings in the night, playthings of little animals. And she did not think. There were things that happened. What did not happen she did not know.

But Lucas happened. "Your name?" he said, working in the row beside her. She looked up at him. He was tall and made her feel small. She had never felt small before. His face was sweating, and his shirt all wet, and the hair where the shirt was open. Even his white teeth were so wet they seemed to be sweating, and his tongue in his open mouth. "Lucía," she said, and he threw back his head and she saw how red his lips were, and thick, when he laughed, and how his chest swelled, and she felt strange so she looked down, and when she looked back up, she felt stranger because he was looking at her but not laughing now, so she crouched down, bending her head to the earth, dizzy with the smell of it and the plants, not daring to look up until he said, "I see you tomorrow, Lucía," laughing that laugh she did not yet understand, and watched him down the furrow, tall and thin-hipped and straight, his buttocks firm under the loose trousers. Then her eyes gripped the furrow; she wanted to laugh, to cry—she did not know.

She was glad when the others called "Lucía!" because it was getting dark.

He worked fast. He far outstripped her. He was furrows away by the end of the first hour of the morning, and she did not look again. But twice in the morning he called "Hola, Lucía!" and flagged her. She nodded, but did not flag—she could not make her hand move—but she felt red, her whole body felt red and she wanted to cry. She went down on her knees, tearing roots up hard all day. The baskets filled. In the afternoon he said, "Leave your baskets. I'll help you when the time comes." Her eyes widened. She always carried her own baskets; she did not even think if they were heavy. She did not speak now. And when he came, at dark, and the children were calling "Lucía!" he said to them, "Go. She'll be along," and carried her baskets to the end of the furrows. She walked up and down behind him.

With the last one he said, "Come, Lucía," and took her hand. She could hardly keep up, he was so tall. He stopped by the willow and turned to her and took her shoulders and dropped his hands over her breasts and arms and waist and drew her up off her feet and suddenly she could not breathe, she felt his sweat hot and burning, it made her burn, and so fast his hand came down over her breasts and tore down her dress she knew she was going to die. His hard beard burned over her face and neck and breasts until she wanted to scream with it and when he opened her legs she did cry out but with such a groan of pain and pleasure together that her hands could not hold him close enough, could not, and he said, "Sí," and she felt how hot the ground was, for the first time the smell of earth came into her, he was gripping the whole earth, she was the whole earth, she came up to meet him, and suddenly for the first time the sky tore her eyes open, it came in, she had never seen it, blue—and red with the sun burning far.

He left her there. She did not move for a long time. She did not want to move. She watched the blue die and the red die, and the dark grow and slowly turn to moony night with a glow of silver. She listened to the soft flow of river, the thinnest rush of wind, the plants, the earth in soft breakings, and herself—the brush of her skin, her breath moving, the quiet river in her, and the sky. The others were calling "Lucía!" again. She rose. She was covered with dust, twisted, her dress torn and stained; she clutched the stains, holding him in them—and smiled. It had happened. It seemed the first thing that happened, and the last. It was not a dream. It was more real than dreams. She did not want to dream any more.

In the morning he was gone. The work was over. He was a migrant worker—he went from province to province: there were *palmitos* by the jungle, peanuts, avocados, sugar cane south in Tucumán, artichokes, grapes in the *viñas* of Mendoza, wheat in the *trigales* and alfafa on the pampas—it did not matter.

She followed him. When they were all asleep, she stole her mother's black shawl and slipped away—taking the highway south to Salta, where others moved as the days grew hotter. She never spoke to anyone, simply followed the movements of small groups going south, not even thinking it was a miracle when—perhaps because she was young or quiet or apparently confident or stoic—people gave her bits of bread, cheese, salami, some *fideos*. Sometimes she stood on the edge of a field and, seeing her, someone offered her work, rare and unexpected since mostly entire families were contracted for the harvest; or invited her to share; and more and more frequently—she came to know the look—there were men's sly offers of a night's rest which gave her a taut stomach and she went on, not comfortable until the clean moon whitened the barren flats and the far mountains, without a soul on the horizon. When occasional cars passed, a truck or one of the buses, she tried to duck, make a rock or a bush, until it had disappeared. This way, she worked from place to place. She was alive now, she would not die. He was somewhere ahead—she did not even know his name yet.

It was not long—ten or twelve weeks—before she saw him for the first time. From Salta she had gone the logical way: to Tucumán and the canebrakes. She grew used to the road. Her life was dust and heat. In one of the *barrios* of Tucumán, when she felt near lifeless with hunger, dried out from thirst, she happened on an open doorway, an old house with a rich tiled patio overlapped with vine leaves, filled with palms and geranium and garden, and an old woman eyed her. *"Hambre,* eh?" The face was stone but the voice soft. She dropped her eyes. "Come. . . ." The woman stretched her hand, but she would not let her touch her. She would let no one touch her.

She stayed over two months, doing all the chores, not abused but with a motion which allowed her perhaps two hours in the afternoon when the old woman, Doña Melinda, took the siesta. It was then she made the rounds of the *cañas,* first one, then the other, never duplicating. With a kind of instinct, she moved systematically over the zone. And then one day, standing at the edge of a *cañaveral,* motionless, she turned slowly—with a habit she had developed of letting her eyes trace from one side of a field to the other, encompassing it all bit by bit —and she saw the familiar form straighten up. She would have recognized it anywhere, the same long black hair falling off the right side, the wide shoulders, the narrow hips, that loose blue shirt opened nearly to the waist and the loose gray trousers strapped about with a wide brown belt, and the black *alpargatas.* She sat down and watched him. She felt a fierce flow come up as if from the earth and pulse through her.

He did not see her sitting distantly at the edge of the brake that day or the next, but on the third day he looked several times as if curious and before the afternoon was over he had even ventured down the brake to stand and from a good distance look at her. At first she was not sure he knew her, but after a while she was convinced that he had satisfied himself because he turned away, then stopped, looked back, and laughed loud, shaking his head, then went back to work. That day she did not return to Doña Melinda's but sat there, and every day throughout the season, until the fields were clean. He did not again come to her and look and laugh, though she knew each morning he had seen her arrive and take her place.

Nobody knew why the strange girl was there. They saw her, they said what they would no doubt, but she listened to no one.

When the harvest was over, he was gone again. She expected it now. There came a quiet rhythm of drift in her. She knew that he was ahead somewhere, with the sureness of inevitability. If she moved thus far day after day, even if she missed him in one place, fortune was such that tomorrow she would cross him at another. There was no doubt to it. It was the same to her as the movement of the sun and the moon and the stars. She also knew she had to follow their motion. It was inside her as it was in them, and it impelled her as they were impelled, and she wanted that—because always at the end of that motion he would be.

After so many months, she knew he too expected her, though he seemed never to have mentioned her to anyone else, even when they commented on the stranger like a dark bird at the edge of the field or orchard or even, when he went into the canning factories, outside the plant. She saw, when he arrived—if she was early—that he checked, assuring himself that she was there. Perhaps he thought it was uncanny at first—how she found him; how miraculously within a fairly brief period after his arrival on a new job, as if by sorcery, she materialized. Then it was evident that he could gauge the period between the beginning of a new job and her appearance and that he had accepted but ignored her.

She made no overtures to speak to him or anyone who knew him. There was no gesture of harassment, no reminder that they had ever met—except the ritual of her apparition. She came like an embodied spirit. Only once in the first three years did he speak to her—and then as if he did not actually know her. He must have drunk too much wine because he railed as her mother's man used to—crying out in a fury that broke his words, a mixture of swearing and anger and no sense and some anguish: ". . . bitch, go back to your other world . . . black bird, eats out the heart and sucks blood . . . never again, no . . . with my own bare hands kill, yes, next time kill . . . vulture, never to let alone nobody, not even when I close my eyes, that black thing there, in the dark night, yes, witch. . . ." She understood nothing except that he really did know her, it had to be. As certain as the pulse of blood through her, she knew too that one day he would speak—not such words as these, but other words—or what was that first afternoon for? She was alive. She did not know that before. Something would come. She did not know what, but she would wait. She believed the moment was always there just ahead, so she did not need to speak. It would come.

In time her face and arms and hands had changed color; they had become darker, browned deep so her eyes were quick with light in her head, her arms and hands stronger from work in the fields, in this house or that pension, from washing and scrubbing, sometimes lugging buckets in a factory, sometimes other menial tasks; but her face, oily and dark, did not dry out. Something in the life began to accustom her body to so little food that in the periods when she had more than enough merely to subsist, she even gained weight, her face round. Later her body widened a bit as if the hips balanced better for walking, her legs planted farther apart by habit.

Bits and snatches of cloth, clothes, burlap—thrown into refuse—she saved, replacing so the change was almost unnoticeable the things she came away with, weaving dirty threads, cord, string into the shawl, hoarding the burlap so that whenever she worked for anyone she could sleep nearby. But less and less frequently as time went on was she given work, because she did not keep herself up, her body knew no water, her hair was matted and dusted, and so conditioned was she to her own odors, never anyone else's, that she recognized no need. In Jujuy they had never washed—only once or twice she had gone into the river, but so long ago she must have been four or five. So she became an unchanged image, recurring as persistently as a sign in one province after another. When people passed her, there was an almost imperceptible recognition, as of a malignant sign fortunately grown no larger, and a shift of eye which negated her presence therefore. Occasionally, in the cities, now and again someone dropped pesos into her hand. She never said like the beggars *"Que Dios le bendiga,"* for she knew in some way food would always come; she did not even look into her hand. When she passed the market she bought what the change would buy and sat wherever she was to eat a small portion of it. She wrapped the rest in the burlap.

They lived forever in the warm seasons, he moving with the sun and growth, she behind . . . Buenos Aires, Rosario, Córdoba, Mendoza, San Juan, San Luis, Tucumán La Rioja, Jujuy, El Charco. . . . She knew all the *barrios,* the streets, the *centros* as if by some primordial memory, though she saw nothing, she talked of nothing—she had no one to talk to, perhaps no voice left, for she never muttered even to herself and for her few purchases she pointed. It was only her eyes that spoke. They looked far.

After the first months—and for all the years she traveled—the men, perhaps because she was so unkempt and dirty, no longer tried to take her. Nor did people try to get rid of her overtly. There were many beggars since Perón's betrayal of the República. What could you do?

He did not stop. He did not marry, though there were many women. She did not care. She knew he had recognized her, he expected her. He would have sent her away otherwise, though she knew that too was impossible. When the sign came, she would know it.

She waited fifteen years.

It came in March during the *Fiesta de la Vendimia,* the annual grape harvest—the greatest event in all the province of Mendoza—when wine

runs in blood-red spurts from the public fountains, free, and the ritual
of the grapes is offered: blood pressed from the grapes, from deep in
the earth, the pulse, and into the mouth; and the ancient dances and
song fill the air and the blood. Sometimes she saw him dance the *gato*
and the *cueca* and laugh and sing so alive, and a remote stirring from
the field of Jujuy came into her and she felt she was very close.

Often those years in Mendoza she went for rest to the old ruins of a
church on Fray Luis Beltrán Street. Green grass grew in the shades, and
vestiges of marigold and *enamorados del sol;* it was cool against the
stones, and night made a roof over the fallen church. Nobody bothered
her there. The neighborhood too was accustomed to the emptiness of
the ruins. He knew she stayed there—she had found the place not far
from the pension he usually stayed in, near the plaza, farther down the
street. That building was old and crumbling now; they would con-
demn it soon surely; but to her it was the same as always, as he was:
though he was weathered and his eyes tired, and thin, but still not
forty, and young, to her he was the unchanged youth in the field of
Jujuy.

That afternoon the bishop blessed the vines on the Plaza Independencia with an enormous crowd around. The week of joy and holiness
had begun. At night she walked the several kilometers to the Greek
amphitheater, *el teatro griego,* to see the panorama of dances and song
under lights that went into the mountains as far as God. After, she
went down into the city. There was dancing on the plazas and she went
where, always, he would be—and watched for a long time. She had a
seething inside her from so much joy around her. Once she crossed his
gaze—he looked long at her—and for an instant she felt this must be
the moment, but his look was filled with anger and hatred, not the first
time, and she told herself that did not matter, she was used to it, it was
to be expected, where there was such hatred there was feeling. She
knew his feeling—she remembered. Almost she spoke. But when she
saw his look, she turned away and went back to Luis Beltrán to curl up
against the great overshadowing column where she liked to lie on such
warm nights on her burlap.

The three boys were there—she knew them on sight; they must hang
about as always, but she ignored them. She did not fear them because
once she had overheard one tell the others, "She must smell like that to
keep us away and stay pure." She pretended not to hear. It made no

sense to her. She knew only her own body now. She stretched out to sleep. But in a minute they were standing over her. She had not expected that. She bolted up, sitting, curious, startled. But before she could speak she was booted in the neck and side, hauled up by her arms and struck in the face and stomach and breasts—and then remembered nothing more. They must have dropped her in the corner, thrown her burlap over her, because when she woke she was covered, she could scarcely move, she felt broken, she wanted to scream; but she could not, dared not, move, the slightest breath tore like fire through her. She thought she was blind, but there was sun through the burlap, though she could not raise her hand. She felt paralyzed. She did not know how long she lay there, she never knew, but she felt a burning over her, more in her side than anywhere else; and when finally after long effort she moved, she felt her hand tear with a terrible pain from her side, she felt herself in her hand as if she were holding her body in it. For the first time she smelled herself, a stench she could not bear, worse than rotting fish. She wanted to speak but she could not, her mouth was taut, and even the sounds in her throat ached. When she remembered the first kick, her throat felt as wide as her head. She fainted and in spells came to, but she could not remove the burlap, she could scarcely get her breath.

Then it was she had the dream—for a moment even fell into it as if she *wanted* to dream: someone tore away the burlap, the sun poured down over him so quick and full and bright that her eyes pained, needled. She wanted to cry the name she had heard shouted in the fields, that thousands of times ran over her silent tongue, *Lucas!* But no sound came and she felt dry even to dying. She was not dreaming; surely she was dying. But his voice broke. "Lucía!" he cried. She felt the voice in his hands; his hands were on her, burning, breaking her body till she wanted to cry out, scream, but in joy too. Her name! He remembered, he spoke her name. She wanted to scream *Lucas* before the vision disappeared. And then in an instant when he released his hands and stared at her unbelieving, with a glitter like tears in his eyes, all the pain came back, her body racked with so many pains, she knew it was real. She opened her mouth to speak to him, but it would not open. *Lucas!* She wanted him to know she knew him. Still she looked—she would not close her eyes—but suddenly he vanished. She must have fainted because when she saw again, he was still there only

talking to her now fast, fast, words she could not even understand.
". . . years, and me, for *me*. . . ." He was tearing at her clothes. She
felt now his hand over her side, and she moaned. He heard it, he *did*,
and he touched her and she knew she would die now. The blood in her
burned. She never knew such joy though the pain was too terrible,
more terrible when he himself shouted with a look of pain and terror
and thrust his face down against her, against her side, where she could
see now the terrible mass; and he clutched her, sucking at her, licking
like Rubio's little dog in Jujuy, licking; and she screamed *No, Lucas,
it's all right, I can die now,* feeling the whole pulse of the earth come
into her so that she could not stand the burning pain and joy; and his
head sucking at her deep putrid wounds touched her hand and his hair
fell between her fingers. . . .

He carried her to the *zanjón,* which was empty of water except for a
narrow meander in the center, and washed her wounds, put water in
her mouth, and laid her on the burlap, under a footbridge.

In the night he brought her food. "Listen," he said, "it's dark. I'm
taking you now into my pension, but you must not cry out, no matter
how much I hurt you." She could not fathom the despair of that man.
She wanted to tell him nothing mattered, she had had her sign, but she
could not speak, only to make a sound even she did not recognize from
her own body. Maybe she would die. But she did not want to leave him
alone. Maybe now, after all the years, he did not want to be alone.
Maybe she had been in him all those years. She nodded.

He carried her stealthily into the pension, across the patio to his
door. Everyone was sleeping. She knew he would have a hard time
keeping the secret. On the bed she went to sleep or fainted at once. She
never knew how long she slept, but when she woke it was to the
shouts of a woman, the *patrona,* screaming, "No filth in here! Look at
the rot! I'll have bugs! You filthy *puta,* getting beat up and kicked out
of any man's bed. Left you here and didn't come back, eh? Get out!
Out, you filthy bitch! Joaquín!" They pushed and kicked and thrust her
out, despite her shrieks of pain, and dumped her by the gutter, the dry
acequia. Painfully she sat up. She held onto a tree root, leaned her head,
gasping, against the tree. Where was he? She crawled to the plaza
across the street and stretched out on a bench. In the morning she
tried to walk. She sat on the plaza with her hand out.

Where was he?

After, in the five days that followed, every day she went back and sat before his pension, farther off now because of the fury of the *patrona*. She watched the same *pensionistas* go in and out, but never Lucas. She would wait, if need be, until he returned. And then on the fifth day she went closer. Perhaps from long experience, sitting as he did in a front window, one of the old men knew who she was. He crossed the street and strolled about the plaza as always—it was as if each time he went round he was coming closer, like the sun and the moon and the stars and something in her own blood. She waited. "You . . ." He seemed not to know how to say, or what. She dropped her eyes, her head. "Lucas . . . ," he said. Instantly she raised her head. The sound of his name from someone else's lips maddened her. "He died—yesterday," the man said, "in the *villa miseria,* near the park. The boy, there—" he indicated the pension, "told me. At Alonso's house, in the *villa miseria.*" She could not fathom it: they were words, a nightmare. And then she moaned, she could not stop moaning. When a crowd gathered at some distance, she pulled herself up. . . .

Lucas!

She went to the *villa miseria.* A wind came up, a sea of dust rose over the park, the *viento sonda* was coming, the *villa miseria* was thick with rolls of dust, it poured down between the mud huts. Children kept playing everywhere; outside, in some doorways, women were cooking; rags fluttered over all the window holes. She stopped a little girl. "*Hija* . . . ," she said. Her own voice struck her with fright, a phantom's. She did not recognize the sound. Her throat resounded, hollow. "*Hija* . . ." The words pained her: "*La casa de Alonso?*" "*Allá,*" the girl fingered. She turned. The blown *tierra* burned her eyes, her lungs ached. "Lucas?" she said in the doorway. An old woman came close: "*Muerto,*" she said. "Where? Where's Lucas?" she cried. "Dead—there, in the Hospital Emilio Civit. Poison." "Poison?" she said. "What from?" "Who knows? Poison. I told you," the woman said, dropping the curtain. *Poison? From her?* "Lucas!" she cried, as if she had regained full power of her voice. It thrust up like a stone scraping harsh and terrible. She shouted in fury, raged, as if her arms themselves flagging the shawl bellowed against the sand and air and mountains and the invisible sky beyond.

"Lucas! I killed you, *I*, Lucas!" The children gathered, men and women came from their *chozas,* they stood in the smiting sand listening, watching her beat her breasts and wail.

"Ay, Lucas, I waited for the sign all the years, I knew the sign, but I did not know—Ayyyyyyyyyy!" She screamed, she fell, her fingers dug the earth, her face pressed into the dirt. But even when she fell and they thought she could not get up, she rose to her knees, she turned to them, she shouted, "You see what a man is! He saved my life— *mine.* For me, who hounded him, he died. And who else would suck the wounds of a beggar, I ask you! Such a man! Ayyyyy, Lucas, you saved my life, yes—" But her rage rose, her rancor knew no limit. "But you left me here, you left me *here,* you, you—I curse you, Lucas, I curse you. Ayyyyyyyyyy." And now she stretched full, her arms rose, the black shawl blew. And she cried out, "Lucas, I swear, I swear before God and these witnesses—all my life I will do penance. You *hear* me, Lucas? All the life left to me I will follow you still—" But the wind blew her words, the sand smote, the people went back in, the children laughed at her and threw clods. Dust filled her mouth.

She went down through the park to the city. For a while every night she went back to Luis Beltrán to sit before the pension. He did not come.

Around the ruins of the old church they put a high iron grating to protect them or to keep vagrants and children from danger—who knows? So she took to the streets again, stopping whenever she was tired—sometimes on San Martín in front of Casa Muñoz with her arms stretched out on the flagstones, stiller than a nun, staring up at the sky she first really saw fifteen years before, indifferent to the people passing, sometimes during siesta on the shady side of La Rioja Street, or Salta, or San Juan—it made no difference—crossing her arms over her breast, letting the deep blue sky come down into her quiet eyes.

The Fence

Even on the truck Anna Skivsky watched for the woman. Her eyes rolled like wind over the pickers moving down the furrows to the trucks, dragging their potato bags. They kicked up clouds of dust that rolled in behind, low-lying and drifting. . . .

"Anna!" Old Sophie called through the thick brown air, breaking Anna's search for the dark woman.

". . . eh, Sophie? What you want?" she grunted with weight, her big fast-moving arms reaching to pull Sophie up onto the truck.

Sophie's face was coated. Her gray hair, dust-grayed heavier, clung to sweated skin. Ends blew out around her. Standing, she was big in the sky so blue with nothing behind. A woman, Anna said in herself, a good woman with an emptied womb, like should be all women . . . a good woman, Sophie, with nine children living in the world, and not just the one young boy like in her own house.

"I don't see Stanley nowhere," Sophie said. "He don't work today maybe?" She spat dirt, wiped it with the back of her hand off her mouth, and stroked it clean on her pants.

"No, today he is with men," Anna said. "He goes for crabs."

"—by the crick," she added.

"Eh?"

"I say—he crabs. *Crabs!*" she shouted hard in the mounting wind.

Anna's eyes sagged a minute, not seeing. For they were at the crick, Stanley and the men, bringing in crabs, for eating and selling. Now in her head she could see how their backs were bending, picking with the nets' lightning-strokes at the softshell crabs, and hardshells. At times Anna herself did netting too. It was best then. She liked to show how her heavy arms shot net out, exact, like arms hungry for bread and not missing. And on the oilstove hardshells cook fast, make quick orange colors with boiling, and they eat plenty, the three, at one meal. . . . No, not three— Two. Is gone, Big Stanley. . . . So now, no sitting long with talk over empty hardshells and cleaned-off plates, and beer bottles swigged empty.

"An . . . naaa!"

"Eh, Sophie?" She watched Sophie's flagging arm, held straight-out into the far furrow, and she was still. . . . Her—Geebo Hannibal's woman. Tight on her head with the hair hid was the green cotton, dirtied good but bright yet in the sun.

Heat from the burning ground came up in Anna's face with the wind, like thick resentment quickening. Sweat came, and the burn and tingle. She itched up an anger.

Aaaah— Why she don't work with spics and niggers on back road! No—she got come like Poles! She got pick like white woman—get big, sit like queen! You got pick potatoes with Pole women. Yaaa—you chief's woman, dead Geebo's woman. You un-stan me?

She looked, as if talking to her.

You un-stan me? Aaaa . . . you un-stan nod-ding.

Anna sat down in the forward end with her back against Sophie's. They talked over their shoulders, glancing sideways. The pickers crowded tight around the edge of the sideless truck, their legs dangling.

Then the figure came in her eyes: proud she saw her, and up straight, with no jaunt like the one that made Anna's whole fatness move everywhichway. The woman came gaunt and lean (even with the fleshless bonespread of age), with no shoulder moves, just level, and no bobbing, only the slight hip-sway, regular and regular . . . down the furrow. In her walk was the girl even then left in the woman. But no hurry was in her blood. She moved almost still, like the hot afternoon sun of the day she first came to town. Like in a parade, on a float, she sat in Anna's head: she who sat with pride beside her Geebo had come in a wagon, with her head wrapped colorful, and her body too. There were big silver earrings in her ears and her hands were long and dark on her knees. Behind her was the baggage—one big wood trunk set beside the bolt of bright yellow cotton, and the rooted twigs and stubs wrapped in burlap (they were to come scarlet and tea and bachelor-button-blue, and sunflower heads of yellow through Anna Skivsky's wire fence).

"Geebo Hannibal's got a nigger wife!" went up and down the street like vine and in all houses. She had sat proud, Mrs. Geebo Hannibal, welcomed in the town, wife of a Setauket of Long Island.

So when she descended straight from the wagon, the news had already reached Anna Skivsky making blackberry jam out back. Over the boiling jars she saw everything, for her backyard ran right into Geebo's, a hard, unseeded patch of land that pushed into the rich garden of the Indian. And right away her boy Stanley, almost five, was helping with the bolt and burlap bundle, while Geebo lifted the trunk into the house.

Now Anna watched her boarding the truck and remembered how the woman had stood and looked at the house stretched out low over the lot, needing shingles and paint and sagging on the left bedroom side, and almost head-low so you had to bend into it where the last addition went on. It looked as if running sloping into the ground. And behind was the wobbly shed, pushed almost into Anna's own yard. But there had been no sound of voice or change of face in the woman when she saw it, just followed the trunk inside. Yet it was plain she'd accepted the sight and the living in it with Geebo as if there had been no change. Maybe in her poise Anna had read that—her coming on that wagon, all color and proud and straight.

"Ready back there?" the driver yelled out.

The truck started. The woman sat. From her place Anna sat staring at the back of Geebo's wife. . . .

Down the highway the cool was good, blowing around. Anna felt the other workers stretch close, listened to the girls laughing, whispering, then the laughing that broke out boisterous when Una called *pig* to Big Kate. Anna stuck her foot up under Una and they laughed harder, and Una turned on Anna and filthy words she shrieked at her.

Anna wiped her nose on her hand. Dirt smelled so strong and stinging-clean that she drew in deep breaths of scent from the air. The truck first stopped at Stowolsky's farm to let Pete off, then at others, and when the truck slowed, the air died and sweat came back stinging in her nose like pee under the bed at night. She was glad when the truck went again.

The girls giggled together, making wedding talk—that of Una and Teddy Ulsky's youngest, Joe. Wedding talk was good. Cheerful and white Anna saw the bride. It was weddings she liked. Una was slim but full with tight, small waist—like Anna's own when she—

Anna poked her toe up wiggling under Una. "You skinny," she said.

"You fat!" Una mimicked, blowing her cheeks out, cuddling in her chin, thick, until she made a chorus of jibes.

"You got man keep you warm. I got fat, no man." Anna said in quick, jolly tone. But the smile was only flesh turned. She felt her face flatten, her eyes hang loose and bleak, her heart sink deep down. The girls knew the black on Anna was for mourning. But they knew more —that always in the back of his head old Makovsky, who had long since lost his wife, had prized Anna, and that already three weeks Big Stanley was dead now. . . .

Death had cried her out good. But what was out, that was gone. Then you got live. Anna Skivsky was live woman, and cold bed is no good, no bed. A woman got think of her one boy, growing big, still needing father. . . .

And she would not be alone in the world—never. Not when much depended on her. And there was deep the need—it was not old Makovsky, not Stanley gone three weeks, but now . . . Ah . . . . She looked at her thick flesh. Her hands sagged, big. A woman could not choose, always. For now she was a woman thick with weight of years. But there was more—there was want and desire and need, all hid in these years of flesh around her. And how could she tell *them*, those women? One day—far maybe—but one day they would know what it was, this inside. Not just warm of arm around you, but there was a feel in the walls, in the kitchen and the cellar and in the toilet, and even the look of a house outside said, *yes, a man is here*. And in a woman the movement was different then. Things grew together. Like her—Anna Skivsky. So what did they expect, eh? So she went—*plunk!*—all to pieces after—yes! For she was not even whole without . . . Ah, but life could not die because pride kept one back. . . .

"Anna's got no man, eh?" In Una's mean talk was an undulation of mockery, teasing.

"No man," Anna said, and knew her voice did not hide the dejection in her quiet brooding, or the little wave of anger that they did not understand about Makovsky and her need and Stanley her boy.

Geebo's woman looked back at Anna, whose bleak eyes stared for a moment. There was a soft melt in the dark face. The brows raised gently in understanding sympathy.

She try say something to me? She try speak to me, that woman?

Anna wondered, wavering, with a hand-fidget, a slight forward swaying with inside pain, seeing quickly: the woman had lost her man too, yes. Ah, she was woman, she lost man. . . . And she sat there straight and proud, yet there was—no one. Then inside Anna indignation rose hot as flame at the thought of Geebo Hannibal's woman alone but *proud,* coupled with the thought of herself, Anna Skivsky, and old Makovsky, and already three weeks gone. . . . But that woman was too proud, she get no man now. . . .

Still, Anna turned her face away.

"Anna?" It was Sophie talking over her shoulder. The truck was slowing. Ahead was Sophie's. "Tomorrow, Anna?"

"Ya, tomorrow," she said as the truck stopped.

Now she knew it would be this way: every day it was Sophie's getting off that left her alone with Geebo's wife, last on the truck because they alone lived in the village. Now they sat so one's back was to the other. But sometimes they sat not avoiding face-to-face. And each time Anna said to herself, it is good it is only season work, over soon. So the truck would stop and the two turn away from each other at the corner, each going in the opposite direction, but always to houses that faced each other from behind. . . .

When Anna came home she was tired and sat awhile, taking her shoes off, for always after the fields she walked around the house and yard in her bare feet, a slow, heavy clomp.

She pulled herself up, holding onto the kitchen sink—old iron, but it had a faucet, just new, that Stanley himself put in and that now he was not here to use. The window looked into her backyard and into Mrs. Geebo's garden, where everything came fast-growing and rich green out of good fertile soil with the care of a green thumb that Hannibal woman had. Anna liked it when the corn grew tall and flagging in the wind so the woman could not see her. Then they would not always be looking into each other's eyes when they hung clothes or made jam, or when she worked sanding or painting in the yard.

There! That woman! Already she was in the garden. Always she came home from the fields and went immediately without eating into the garden for an hour anyway. She was bent waist-over in the peas now. Sometimes she weeded, or picked green beans, pulled radishes or onions for her meal—often in great clumps, more than she could use. Then there was painting to do. Or from the long hollow where the wind skimming over the flats broke rustling in the elms, came the sound of the lawn mower. That woman with her energy, with her forever doing something! Aaaah . . . it made Anna tired.

She could scarcely gather up energy enough to unpack the goods left there on the table. How little she bought in the three weeks since her Stanley had died! Those neighbors gave everything—great quantities of food in jars or fresh—when it was the funeral; then on days when they were visitors; and even on the doorstep when she was out, they left all kinds. So the closet was filled, and it was good to have them. Still . . . working she did, cleaning now, laundry, and picking. Money she needed, and though she did not fear, she worried a little. There was the story of the five thousand and the little fish and bread, but that was long ago. . . . She smiled: a good story, that. And a good priest too. She should hear him more. Ah, she had not been to church again since Stanley . . .

At times like this, thinking of Stanley, she did not like to walk close to the front room. When she passed the door, she turned her head as if he were in there looking at her, and she had strange fear for a moment in her thought of Makovsky—and somehow of Mrs. Geebo out there in the garden. . . .

Oh, where was Stanley? He should be home from crabbing—long now. She glanced quickly again out the window as she washed over the potatoes. The swell of resentment came, filling her breasts massive with air drawn-in hungrily, angrily. How could she have one minute's feel for that woman—like in the truck? Aaaah . . . An-naaa, you big fool, that's all—you great big fool. *She* get no man, no—

She watched outside where the brown hands worked rapidly, flicking green sprigs from the radishes, and her own hand clumsily peeled too-large strips of potato. She began cutting them closer. There must be no waste now, with no man. She dared not turn round—it left her thinking: two women, no men. This was a net always over her, like squeezing cuts into her, tight, when she thought of it. Yet, each had no man. And woman got to have man, close, good. And was Anna Skivsky like that woman? But right off, their color was different. Wasn't that right? But Stanley, he said no, she's no nigger, Ma, she's white like us too.

Because it is one day from the yard, with that woman standing in the corn straight as a stalk herself, that Anna screams to Stanley her boy: "Eh! Stanley! You come here, you got come here. *Now!* You leave nigger woman lone. Hey you—Stanley!"

But there was something: that word *nigger* made no jolt in the thin, dried stalk of woman browned like potato dirt. Then, like a sway, the hand moved to Anna, up only a few inches, with its saying she could not understand. Perhaps because Geebo in his love learned *her* words, and she only some of his, there were no words the woman could then give that Anna would know. Anna sensed what the woman felt—that she could not say anything to her. Then Stanley ran. It was a strange run—not an answering run. He was not running *to* her, he came *at* her, and stopped on the woman's land, on Geebo's land.

He said, "Ma, she's *not* black. She's white like us. You know, Ma—she's white, like *us*, Ma!"

Something in his eyes startled her. But it was not new. She had seen it working into him in the years. She had seen it when he and that woman played side by side laughing. It came upon him whenever Anna came near them. My boy, this is my Stanley, she said, and even when her hands did not reach out to embrace him, it was the memory of Big Stanley gone that made her say to herself, my boy; and it was Stanley who was part of Big Stanley that said to her, "not nigger!"

But she did not answer. Then, still and proud the dark one moved, as if the wind carried her gently along with her long black skirt pushed out before her. She stopped behind Stanley, and with it darkening and her coming out of the corn and standing in the short radishes, she seemed to grow tall in her straightness. Though her words were different and Anna could not have understood them, her eyes were wide and intelligent looking. They moved rapidly and Anna felt them move over her and talk to her as understanding her gestures. Her skirt fell as she stopped; it hung loose and straight into the ground. Her raised hand almost touched the shoulder of Stanley by her, when she detected Anna's eyes on her moving hand—and she let it go out, held toward Anna.

"Soy *puerto-riqueña*," she said, "*puerto-riqueña*," smiling, and with her two hands trying to make Anna understand.

"She can understand you when you say *nigger*, Ma. She's *not* black, she says so. She comes from a country we learned about in geography and it's Puerto Rico and they're not black there. They're like Mexicans —see, Ma? She's not black!"

Geebo's wife smiled, nodding *yes*. This she can understand, *this is what I mean to say to you* was in her nod. Gold teeth were in her mouth and they glinted. Even that made Anna fill with anger.

Not looking at the woman, she said to Stanley, "You come. Time to eat now." And she turned her big flesh round to the house. But the mumble of the Puerto-riqueña to Stanley came to her—that familiar sound, an old habit of Mrs. Geebo as she worked in the garden. Sometimes, even in the fields, Anna heard the jangled whispers of words she couldn't understand come down the furrows like distracting winds blowing seeds that grew in Anna's head.

She carried her anger back to the house, irritated to a sore in her. She rubbed her belly as if soothing it, and called without looking back, "Stanley!"

It did not matter now if she was black, Anna told herself. It did not matter that she was straight and thin, not like Anna; or even that such energy was in her; or that she could make the yard neat and clean with flowers and plentiful with vegetables, though the house was warped some and not all painted, yet with much green growing around and over to cover it. No, these did not matter. For pride was what the woman had—and worse that was. You get no man, with pride, no Makovsky. . . . And there was the likeness again, the woman was with no husband; so always it came to this: Anna sat and thought of the two funerals . . . and that *she* was a Puerto-riqueña, but—how was her Geebo buried?

For the mourning was not just quiet with solemn visitors to stop in dressed drape at a coffin like her Stanley's. But this was great ceremony, and though the Puerto-riqueña was sad, the visitors were filled with severe joy in their ritual. Even the governor of the state had come. And after the long living snake of color and movement that bore Geebo along, not the sadness did the Puerto-riqueña show, but she sat straight; and it was the pride in the burial of her Geebo that Anna saw in her— and at such a time!

The governor had said a short but strong speech, and had gone back to the city that same day. Anna herself had gone home and sat in the front room. There she thought about the two funerals.

And in the morning Anna saw her up with the sun, working in the garden as if nothing had happened. Soon after, it was a shock to Anna in the fields to hear the mumbles down the furrow, to look up at the

Puerto-riqueña quiet and steady picking potatoes. Then, because she was no citizen in Anna's eyes—even married to a Setauket chief—it was an insult, that last thing she learned: the woman received a government pension to live on.

Aaaah! Her eyes fell on the woman now, and on the long, gleaming strands of wire. . . .

For it was the Saturday of that week of Geebo's funeral that Anna Skivsky put a barbed-wire fence to separate the land of the Puerto-riqueña from her own.

The water slurped into a screech down the drain. She grunted, setting the potatoes on the oilstove. Fumes tickled her nose, pungent. She set the dishes out in a clumsy pattern on the table. Then another pot filled with water she set to boil for the crabs Stanley would bring from the crick. Weary, she sat heavily, and dirty too—the sweat smelled. She thought of the crabs. A good catch, maybe. Plenty, maybe.

Voices came through the screen lightly and clearly, tossed out to her in the lap of the curtain blowing. She rose gruntily and went back to the window, though she knew there were Stanley and the Puerto-riqueña standing in the radishes. The woman was, clearly, listening to his story. Anna saw him lunge his two hands out, and knew he was describing, with an invisible net, the action of catching crabs. The woman laughed down at him, sharing his joy. Though she almost always had the soft curl at the ends of her mouth, it was not often she broke out in loud laughing with the big smile which, Anna knew, showed her gold teeth. . . .

Watching gave Anna greater annoyance—that they stood so long in talk, like mother and son in the dusk, against the darkening sky. The Puerto-riqueña laughed. Until she had learned to understand English, it had happened seldom. Then she laughed more after she came to speak more and more words, until she did not have even the difficulty of Anna herself (who had not yet received papers for this country). Especially when she was mad, Anna could not even think in this hard-to-master English. So when she saw Stanley was not understanding her big shaking arms that were so angry, she broke into Polish and he had a string of words at him that were easy for her. And *those* he could understand, that boy. No, there was nothing he could not understand when she spoke *that* way. Clear were the words of English the Puerto-riqueña was speaking now. . . .

"—and good help to mother, Stanley. That boy good who is help to mother. They don't forget, *nunca,* the mothers. . . ."

Aaaah! *Good help to mother!* What she know, good help to mother!

This good talk annoyed Anna. It was right talk but it was wrong from that woman to *her* son!

Anna pushed her unkempt head into the screen and held her blowsy self up to the sink, tight.

"Stan . . . ley!" she yelled clear out. "You come now, Stanley!"

He did not answer except in a turn toward her—and the woman turned too. He waved the hand with the invisible net. Then he said more words to the Puerto-riqueña. Anna could hear sounds, but not what they said. When he picked up the bucket, straining to one side, he pushed it along, resting its weight on his leg. At first the Puerto-riqueña made a gesture to help, but as if thinking better of it, she stood unmoving again.

He came to the fence and slid the pail under at a place where the wire drooped slack because he had pulled it out of shape from crawling under so often—and why did she put fence if that is what he is to do!

"Stanley!" she yelped, quick-cut in exasperation. "Hey—Stanley!"

"I'm comin', Ma!" he called. He climbed over the first strand of wire, carefully avoiding the barbs, and jerked the bucket half-dragged across the yard into the back door. He had on old sneakers that squelched with the sucking sound of water, and his pants were rolled up high, wet right up to his fly, almost to his belt in places. It was getting cool. The wind was blowing hard through the kitchen screen.

"You wet. Take off clothes before get cold—and keep off fence! What you think I put fence for—eh? You keep off fence!"

But the eager-tired face could not get angry, just hurt, so he said, "Yeah, but I didn't feel like goin' round," and went into the bedroom. Yet what he said was clear in tone. Anna felt it.

See—if she could know how to say to him with a voice like she meant was in her head, it would be different when she said, *Stanley, I want talk to you.* But always wrong she spoke, because it is speaking right in right sounds she must yet learn; then she can to Stanley speak with right meaning and in English. Only when it was with Polish she could make him feel it—soft when it is soft and hard when it is hard. So with the Polish she spoke, and so did not learn English good. But was he not American and in a good school?—and how could she ever know him *inside* if she could not say. . . . Aaaah—think! When he is older and she is not yet speaking good in English, what of his friends and would he then have shame for her? But she *must* learn. For the Puerto-riqueña—*she* had learned. And Anna heard them laughing together again as a few minutes ago, only now in her head, where she kept all these things in a closet, like that of the kitchen, where she packed all things and saved them together.

Watching the crabs left her chuckling suddenly at the fun of tempting them to bite the finger dodging out just faster than their quick claws. She let them run slipping on the smooth sink-metal, then scooped a few hardshells up into a pan and poured the wildly-scraping claws into boiling water, listening to them scrape sounds into the room. . . .

The thud of Stanley's shoe in the next room clouded her head with the sound of Big Stanley's shoes dropping by the bed when he came drunk from Front Street, late of night always—times when she lay heavy on the bed, raspy-breathing in her tiredness. But she had never said words to him, because he was good, Stanley. When resentment was sick-sore inside her, only with a grunt without words did she show him her broad back to ignore him. So, without questioning, he slept. But if with good humor, forgiving him at once, she did not turn from him. Well, yes—sometimes there *were* words, but those she forgot quickly.

Stanley came from the front, dressed in dry clothes. In his hands he held two jars of preserved tomatoes. He gave them, smiling.

"They're sure red and beautiful, huh, Ma?"

She held them out far, turning them.

"Ah," she said.

"They were on the stoop—out front," he added.

And still cold, with a deep-cellar coolness that felt good in her big hands. And in jars like those sold in the supermarket downtown. They were good people to her with no man, a good neighborhood when something happened. Then people came out of dark houses and tried making things bright for you. That was good. It filled the heart.

She sniffed thick crab odor, strong and heavy, that made fast saliva in her mouth.

"Stanley," she said, draining the water, "come now," and heaped the crabs on old newspapers. She set them down on the bare oilcloth with a separate paper to pile empty shells on. For a while there was the crack of breaking shells, and between long noisy sucks, Anna talked of the fields. She talked to him as if he were Stanley the man now, for if she did not, then Big Stanley was in her mind when she looked at the place next to her son, where he used to be every night and every morning after. It was not just that Big Stanley was not sitting there, but in the place that was a man's place there was no one. For young Stanley that was not good. For her—Anna Skivsky—that was not good either. A boy and a woman needed someone. And she grew strong, a fortress in her quick feeling. In a hurry in her mind was Makovsky.

She ate faster as her thought pitched faster. For in his logic her husband had known. To him it had been like a plan: there should be man and woman and neither ever alone; there should be for the woman, and always for the boy, a family. In the young days they had talked of this at night, lightly. And that young Stanley himself must work young because, though he would stay at home, pay he must and make for himself a part in this house that would be his by his own hand someday. That was just. In the end he would thank them that he was taught how to be a man.

So in Anna's head again was Makovsky. . . .

"But it is Sophie calls," she said to him, "and at that Mrs. Geebo she points finger—" Like *this*, Anna was showing. And Sophie had missed Stanley in the field picking, this day. Anna set out the field-talk, on and on. . . . But when she saw the many crabs left and only a few empty shells the two had picked meat from, Big Stanley came again. And when she looked, there were no beer bottles on the table. . . . Her eyes bleaked. She noticed, too, as every night when she talked of the field, that Stanley was silent while she talk-talk-talked until his silence struck her. Why didn't he speak more—like with his father, like with the happy minutes with the Puerto-riqueña? What did they talk of? Maybe . . .

She rose, with no desire to sit longer with him, only to escape the discomfort. It was not tiredness, not thought, not even anything in her sight, but there was a feeling. . . .

In the sink the still-living crabs clawed at the smooth sides, trying to escape, then lay still as if resigned to the wall fencing in their world. Anna watched. When she picked them up, it was with care, knowing that in this momentary quiet of helplessness it is the nature to strike out to the last for escape. Carefully she grasped each from behind, chuckling because that way they could not bite her, and dropped them one by one into the bucket.

"You sell crabs," she said to Stanley. "Take to Art White's—for bait." She flung her hand out to indicate the *Bait Shop* down on the dock, knowing that he knew where. He had gone often lately, and though it was not much, it was money. She spoke her thoughts out:

"Not much, but money. We need. We got no pension, like some—"

Her face turned out into Hannibal's garden, grumbling what Stanley could not hear, but in the mumble her meaning was clear. She held the bucket out. He took it. His look was—she did not know—different? Yes, but—how? Still he did not go, looking at the crabs, and at her—long. It made her turn, roll the empty shells in newspaper, saying, "Wait—you take these too, for trash."

The back door slammed. Hearing the clump of shells dropped into the trash, Anna went to the screen to watch him, a shadow down the darkening road. The bucket rocked in his hand. The sound knocked rhythmically a long way down the block.

Mmmmm. . . . Again she felt the weariness return, something she did not quite know so well, so often, before. A wash—that would do it. For she smelled her armpits—strong. But she was so tired. She sat. Long ago—three weeks only, but it seemed long—there was the good sound of the knock of a hammer; the saw, maybe; the scrape of sanding or the strong smell of turpentine, good stinging in her nose, a deep-breathed smell like kerosene that she liked so much; or the sweet-bitter odor when Stanley was calking the boat in Geebo's yard. But the air was empty now, and the quiet was not soothing. The only sound that comforted came when the wind heaved weight down over the unprotected flats so it sounded worse than it was, blowing a gale up with no end, and fierce. And even that was so often that it was no longer noise to her. Only the others were what she listened for, and they did not come.

They had begun to cease, almost like a warning, when Geebo died. For the two men, Stanley and Geebo, had made a boat for the crick and ever after they worked together in the shed out back. It was their sounds she heard moving into her head from outside that kept her in a kind of rhythm of the living around her. When Geebo died, something —Anna could not say what—something in the rhythm began to go. There was a break somewhere. . . .

From the screen she could see the shed close to her own put-up fence. And perhaps that was why she'd put the fence there—to fill the break. Or maybe it was to make it sharper so she would not think of anything there now, with a dividing line to remind her that it was all gone, cut off now. Anyway the fence was up. A good fence, nothing to be ashamed of, though it had annoyed Stanley somewhat at first, because he still used Geebo's shed. The Puerto-riqueña had only storage in it and she did not mind. It would be as if they were working there still, as if Geebo were there, for indeed he was in the land he worked. But Anna had left a cut in the fence, digging the pole in a foot from the end of the lot so Stanley could squeeze through. It gave him a break in it at least.

Anna looked round the kitchen, at the dirtied table, the cluttered oil-stove, with an intense desire in her to clean it bright, as so many times she had had the desire, standing in the doorway with eyes on the whole kitchen. But it irked her now because Stanley himself had told of the prettiness and cleanness of Mrs. Geebo's house. And Anna was tired. It was her fat, she told herself. The other woman at least was thin, she had energy. It did not wear so on a thin person, she told herself, irritated. She began clearing the table, piling dirty dishes in the sink. Again she set water to boil.

When she set the new jars of tomatoes on the long shelf, ah! what a collection of bottles was growing, she thought. And no one had asked for them back—many of them good jars, empties from the supermarket bought for preserving. The jars gleamed. She set one dirty into the sink.

The water splashed sharp-cut drizzle and she listened to the splash. . . . All the sounds came with meaning now. She had grown to love them like a kind of company around her. They were a need—that she knew. A comfort. It was true she knew other people—yes. But she did not like visiting, though she should visit. They had come, had brought everything.

Ya—even the Puerto-riqueña had come, had stood right there in that screened doorway, and said in her English that was better than Anna's own, she would like to help. Aaah! Anna remembered and she thought quick: the pride of that woman, held over her, pride to help someone before everyone else's eyes! Yet in Anna there had been a strange feeling when the woman had come to the door.

But she never came back—no. Anna felt good that she had overcome the woman's pride in her ability to help. She herself was proud to say *No, thanking you just the same,* watching her straight, proud back cross into her own yard. And that day she was grateful for the fence too. It said she could stand up by herself and that this is mine to take care of.

Now, almost as if her thoughts were real in her eyes, the figure came across the lawn. She stopped scrubbing the oilcloth cover. But it was Stanley. The bucket was empty, so Art White had taken the crabs. Good! But there should be no crabs left. He held a bundle.

"Eighty-four cents," he said, unclenching his fist empty onto the table.

"How he pays? How much each crab?"

"By pounds, not by crabs anymore," he said.

Eighty-four cents. Anna scowled.

"Why you got?" she said, eyeing the bundle. "You buy something?"

"Mrs. Hannibal asked me to go," he said, starting out the door.

Anna watched him curiously. The same look.

"What she give you?" she asked before he got out.

But when he turned around, it was his face again. Anna could not tell, she was not understanding it, she felt . . .

"Nothing."

"Nod-ding, she gives you; just a boy. Aaaah . . . she gives nod-ding."

Anna turned back to the sink. Her hands felt for dishes in the hot water.

"She got pension," Anna grumped. "Give nod-ding."

She waited for the sound of the door slammed.

"She proud woman," Anna said. "Don't want be seen in store—eh? Too proud be seen in store—eh?" And it pleased her, supposing this. She smiled. "She give nod-ding. Fine thing be selfish—to boy. Got plenty, that woman. Pension." Her eyes were on the garden. In the evening darkness black stalks swayed and patches of black flapped in the wind and quick-running sprays of silver streaked across the yard.

"Eh—Stanley! Why you don't go, eh? You go now. You—" In the water her hands were not moving. For it was strange in Stanley that he stood so—stranger that he looked at her so—and fighting too in his look and in his hands held tight around the bag—and backing away he was, slow . . . slow . . . from her. She wiped her hands on her dress, sensing.

"Stanley? You go—you come quick back, eh?" But it was not this she meant. No, it was not even the tone. And it was helpless, that look. So she felt it was no good even trying to talk to him in Polish.

"What—eh? *What!*" And now was the first time she had talked to him so.

"No!" It was shouting he made, holding the bag she reached for. "She's not a bad woman. She's good," he cried. "Better than us, Ma— better!"

She took the bag from him. She opened it and looked at the empty glass jars—two.

"I bought them at the supermarket for her, because she hasn't got no empty ones."

She held one up. Now she saw behind her, without looking. They were clear to her now.

"That woman!"

And before Anna could say the words she felt so hard inside, he took the jars, the door slammed and his footsteps sounded faster and faster away, thumps around the fence into the Hannibal yard.

She watched out the window. She held her hand up to shield the screen from reflections of the kitchen light behind. "Stanley!" she shouted. He was running across the radishes, clutching the bag to him. Anna's feeling was thick and heavy in her. She blinked into the dark. Her eyes followed him, stinging. In the blow of the wind she could hear his jerky crying blown to her. He was running into the clearing by Geebo's house. Dark shadows fluttered thick about the house, the trees bending—but away, in the clearing, the dark shadow of the Puerto-riqueña stood waiting, still, only the skirt fluttering out wildly. Stanley ran to her and in his crying she held out her long arms, and held him. Her mumbles, soft as warmth in the wind consoling him, came to Anna. . . .

Behind Anna was the kitchen, and the work. She thought quick of it—the table and the stove and the dishes in the sink. . . . But there was something—the rhythm (she did not know), and the jars. . . .

Her big hands raised again to the window. She looked out at the dark pair, hopelessly. The screen seemed to hold her in. They were still there, the two, far on the other side of the fence, and here she was. Between, she could see long silverish streaks of wire and her hand on the screen seemed to stretch over, touching. . . . And in the dark the steely barbs seemed sharp and painful.

The Man Who Made People

I DON'T SEE IT," she said.

"There." As a guide, he flung his arm out straight.

From the porch her eyes followed the two hundred yards or so over the water to the Cat Rock. It appeared through the barest fog like the back of a prehistoric monster emerging from the sea. The ebbing tide swirled about it, flicked seaweed, making it rise and fall, loosen and cling.

"I can't imagine how big it must be underwater." She had said that so many times before. "Or how old." Wisps of gray-brown hair whipped over her face in the wind that came always off the Sound.

"Since the great glacier," he said. His eyes scaled the sea and the sky —it was late, the sun almost fallen—and gazed deep into the invisible meeting at the horizon. Sun touched the fringe of the Sound gold, minute by minute receding into fog.

"Do you suppose it's ever moved at all?"

"The sea wears it down, but who can tell that?"

"How much of it do we see?"

"About an eighth of it, maybe. I've never seen more than that, and I've watched for years."

"Watched?"

He laughed, rather cryptic. The tone piqued her slightly. "I keep thinking I'll look out someday and it won't be there," he said.

"No chance of that!"

She shivered. The late September air penetrated; the wind was relentless.

"Cold?"

"It's my Southern blood." She laughed, but drew her sweater about and latched her arms. Despite years on Long Island, she never grew used to the early fall cold. Her eyes always held Carolina, her arms wrapped Southern heat about her. But he would never live down there. He had told her that years ago. Her purgatory. She would have to suffer it.

"It's so ugly," she said. Along the beach occasional boulders lay embedded in the sand cliffs. At low tide others appeared, dark, ugly, ridden with brown seaweed and slimy green tentacles and barnacles that could draw blood if you fell against them. And the number of gulls doubled. How graceful they were, flying; but tottering awkwardly over the stones, tearing at refuse, they were quite ugly. Feathers that looked white became, close to, smudged gray and withered brown. And fog laid a grim gauze over everything. It was rolling in steadily now. Gradually the entire sea turned from crimson, darkened.

"We ought to go in," she said, crawling close to him.

He looked up at her. His eyes carried a searching look. "You go—I'll come in a minute."

"No," she said. Her hand touched his chin and settled on his neck. It surprised him. She was not given to a show of affection.

"Why don't you let me into your thoughts?" she said softly.

"I did that when I married you."

"Married," she said, not bitter, but deep soundings from a place strange to him. "In a way it's all a kind of betrayal. . . ."

A long silence fell between them. She no longer threw up with staccato urgency her desire to go back home, away from these barren winters, away from the never-ending wind and the breaking of waves against the shore. She resented the unsociably few houses and the flat land, where nothing pushed upward and the dark sky came so close, so near touching.

"Why don't you answer me?" she said.

"I guess I can't."

"After all these years?" A quiet desperation came into her.

"We just have to live it out together—you know that."

"Do you think we'll know then—when it's all over?"

"Shouldn't a man be satisfied just living it, Margaret?"

"You have to do that."

"Yes, but it's how that counts, don't you think?" he said.

"You're trying to make me answer my own question?"

"Maybe."

"But how can I know you . . . completely if I don't know what you think?"

"You really want that?"

"You know I do."

Since he went silent again, she said, "In half an hour we won't be able to see a thing." There was still a narrow, lidless eye over the horizon. That too would be gone soon. The fog was thickening. They would not see the lights on the Connecticut shore tonight.

"But it will all still be there in the dark," he said.

"Who cares!"

"You wouldn't say that if you had to row out into those rocks. You've got to know they're there, always."

"Oh, Jason—you belong too much to all this. I never *will*."

"You're part of my life, Margaret."

"That's what I mean. I want to be. But am I? Sometimes you're so far away. You seem to sail off—in your mind, I mean—and leave a shell of a man here beside me. I feel so helpless then. Sometimes I think you want to go out into all that, Jason, and never come back. You see what I mean?"

"You feel that lonely?"

"At times. It's why I've always longed to be somewhere else with you—not only South, but anywhere."

"I'd just take it with me."

"This place, the sea, the whole thing?"

"All of it."

"Wouldn't the memory be enough?"

"Is North Carolina inside you enough?"

She turned, but not before he saw, in the diminishing light, a tear on the edge of her lid catch the sun and fall into darkness. The sight made him palpitate, want to reach out and make her feel his palpitation, but he did not.

"Margaret, on the second shelf get— No, never mind. I'll show you myself." He rose. The night air was cooler, and heavy over them.

Inside she said, "How wonderful the stillness is here," smiling gratefully.

"Don't put on the big light," he said. Near him the window framed a patch of night but the bit of light she turned on sent it farther off.

He took down the old Almanac, so yellowed. He had insisted—years

—on saving it. From it he took a few doubled sheets, aged too, un-
evenly torn notebook fillers.

"This is all there is of him." He emphasized the flimsiness between
his fingers. Browned chips flew off onto his trousers.

Taking down the coffee cups, she stopped. "Who?"

"Let's have coffee later, okay?" he said.

"All right." She sat then, slipping her legs up on the divan, all curious. "You haven't said who."

"A Polack from Easy Street."

"Polack! And you Yankees razz us about niggers back home."

He smiled. "His name was Badlowski—Sinic Badlowski."

"But he was a criminal!"

"Criminal?" His eyes seemed to wedge into the floorboards. "That's
a hard word."

"He *was*. They said he violated— But you knew *him?*"

"Yes, we were friends."

"But you never told me before."

"Once, we were nearer brothers, I guess. Perhaps still are."

"A common criminal and a lawyer!"

"I hadn't made up my mind to become a lawyer yet."

"Think of it—you and him!"

"Ah, you'd have reason to say 'him' that way if you'd seen him as I
did. I was practice-casting. Oh, I was no fisherman—you know that; but
I'd spent years here, my whole family had roots on the island, and sum-
mers I was driven back—it's what the sea does once you know your
blood has salt in it. Besides, I had to make money somehow; for a year
after high school I went on the skimmer boats—the *Annie B,* pretty
much of a wreck in its own way, half the time in dry dock because of
a sulky engine. Had a good skipper then—McCurdy his name was. I
was green, too green, though I did know the water—always before
that on small boats, yachts that we took fishing parties on, one summer
on the ferry between Greenport and Shelter Island, and once on the old
Catskill out of New London, and all my life—don't laugh!—rowing
in the crick for crabs, casting lobster pots in the Sound. Oh, I knew
you'd smile, but you *do* like the old seafood, don't you? Well, somebody's got to get it.

"I was casting, and I'd sent the line over the side, wrong at that,
when somebody let out a whoop, cursed like hell, and an instant later

shot up over the ladder. I rushed to; we almost collided. His voice sounded so big, a harsh heavy rumble, but the sight of him jolted me: he was small—all hair he looked like, uncombed long brown hair that hung over his eyes and ears like a small animal's, and unshaved. The way he leaped down beside me, with a spring, made me cower, and me a foot taller at least. He thrust his arm out to show where I'd hooked him and pulled. There was a stain of blood. 'You do, eh? You? Stoopid!' He tore the hook out so roughly I cringed, feeling it tear out of me. 'From now on, you keep. Unstan me?' he shouted. He looked ready to pounce. You could see the wiry little body through the drab black shirt and trousers. 'Now *look,* it was an accident,' I said weakly enough, but he shot back at me: 'On ship ev'ything exact—*see?*' And I got his point. The others—Jib and Mel and an old man I didn't know, Club Halsey —cut into him, jibing: 'Come on now, Sinic.' 'Let the kid be.' 'Drinking again, old boy?' But when Mel said, 'Come off it, Baldy,' his hackles rose, he swerved, then, catching their laughter, abruptly twisted his head back at me and laughed—howled, I should say—showing a perfect set of white teeth. Quite unexpectedly his arm flew out and slapped me on the back reassuringly. 'Okay, kid, you forget, eh?' he said, with a clutch and shake of my arm, and I would have forgotten it instantly but for this: He looked up out of that ugly face right into me, the sun struck into his eyes, they glowed a serene blue fire, a whole blue sea inside him with such deeps that I felt I'd fall into them. It was like a warning. And I was half afraid.

"That look haunted me—I didn't know why for a long time, until after he was gone, when those notes about his victims were brought to me."

Jason looked up, beyond her, into the square of night, where two nearly invisible stars pierced faint needleholes in the darkness.

"Why to *you?*" she said, edged forward, scrutinizing, so lost he was.

"Yes, why to me?

"There were eight names in the notes: two single women, one married, the manager of the five-and-dime, the two men from the lace works, a nun, and my sister."

"*Ellen? Our* Ellen?"

"Yes. It never occurred to me there was anything really to know until the end, and even then it was thrust at me. When I finally saw Sinic lying there between the rocks, still and small as a child, I remembered a story of his—and how could I reconcile that with the stories about those people when they all came out? Sinic had a story about kids— I can't say if or when it actually happened, or where—but there were four of them, beautiful little blond things between four and nine, absolutely inseparable. The next to oldest was sick—of something incurable, Sinic said. It was the first time I ever heard his deep voice tremor. It unnerved me. The mother was a sensitive young woman who tried to ease the separation in the best way she could, trying to make his death—journey, she called it—less painful for them, saying he'd be away a while and all. If they asked when, she fixed—Lord knows why; it was her great mistake—an arbitrary date, much too close. The kids were afraid they'd be taken away from each other. Somehow they knew they couldn't keep him, but they could go with him, couldn't they? Well, when the date came she was out and the oldest locked the doors and thrust rugs up against them—God knows where he'd seen that— and when she came home, she found them all trussed up together in a cozy huddle, hopelessly gassed."

"Ahh," Margaret murmured, stricken. Tears sprang to her eyes.

"It's not to upset you I told you—I'm sorry about that—but to understand him. You have to remember he'd not been in the U.S. long and he had no family. You'd think Easy Street would've beaten the feelings out of him, but he'd tell you of Tessie McClean's sixth baby—she'd no food, couldn't support one more bastard—found by the garbage man, wailing in the garbage pail. But he was used to the worst. Well, you can see what he came from before, how strong the human animal is—

"Whenever his escapades had begun, it certainly was long before I knew him. Nothing struck me as strange at first. The work on board, hard as it seemed, was all pleasure to me. He taught me a good bit on the ship and sometimes off hours: how to hold the opener, split the skimmer in one clean easy motion, turn the flesh out into the barrel whole with a lightning flick of the wrist. Oh, he was always next to me. One day it dawned on me how Club always talked a blue streak with me but never around Sinic. I watched that happen over and over. And to test it, I planked myself down close to Club one morning—it brought Sinic over, and Club was afraid, nothing very obvious, but still and watchful and not taking his eyes off Sinic or the movement of his hands.

"I couldn't get it out of my mind so I asked Club. He sloughed it off —I knew he was lying, but why should he? What'd *I* do? Maybe conscience? For they all knew they were pushing me into Sinic's reach to rid themselves of him. Now that I'd caught on, they shifted eyes. I said, 'Come on, what is this?' and then Barry White said, 'They's been stories.' I *had* heard there were stories about Sinic being rough, getting into trouble and scandal. Yet if they were afraid of him, it wasn't because they couldn't handle him, but because of something *in* him. I couldn't explain it except that I sensed it coming closer all the time. Oh, Sinic never intruded. It was simply that he began to tell me things, things I didn't want to know. He never told them *anything* and I didn't want the—responsibility of knowing, because his telling me somehow committed me as a kind of accomplice—and against them.

"At times Sinic simply did not show, missed the ship and did not explain where he'd been. He could get away with it, he was that good a worker. But when he came back, he worked with the energy of a repressed geyser, precise and clean in his movements, with a rejuvenation that made every man there envy him. We wondered what it came from, how. We grumped about him. We hid our admiration under condemnation.

"And at the end of our third trip out, we felt justified in condemning him. The police picked him up when he got off the ship. Sinic was not surprised and did not resist. The arrest left us all mystified.

"But the next morning he was free, he came striding up to my place. I was sitting with Ellen. I didn't say anything, but he said, 'She drop charge.' Ellen got up and left. 'She?' I said. 'The lady in movie. I touch leg, and after touch hand—she change mind, she's make no charge.' He was smiling. 'Christ,' I said, 'they can kill you for such things.' 'She drop charges,' he said. '*She* did, but suppose it's somebody else?' 'She's drop charges—see?' Either he did not understand or saw that I did not. 'What you tink I do?' he said. 'I don't give a damn what you did,' I said, 'but you can't go through life molesting people that way.' He frowned and looked up at me helplessly. His deceptive innocence galled me; I wanted to hit him. He started to reach out—to explain?—but I backed off. My action struck deep. He looked lost, I couldn't bear his innocent, hurt look—I couldn't reconcile it with his actions. 'Sinic,' I said, exasperated. But he turned and left.

"After that, I avoided him, beginning to sense why the men were afraid of him—perhaps they didn't want to share his exploits, they too felt a kind of commitment if they gave the nod. Yet if they could avoid him, I could not—he was always beside me, half from habit, half because I was the chosen one; and when time came to go aboard again, he was inevitably there beside me.

"Back in my good graces—the one time he dared confide so much in me—he told me about one of his eight—victims, I'd have said. When the boat was in, he haunted the beach if he was not on the dock or at Helen's bar. One late afternoon near dark, he saw this thing far off the beach, like a boulder; but it moved— He went closer and suddenly it billowed out. She, for it was a woman, grasped at her skirts. A nun! He intended to turn back, but he was curious, and she smiled when he neared. She was welcoming him, and he couldn't resist (and the note says, 'Her smile was a hungry smile, and her hand was hungry, and all of her was hungry, but she did not know'). Then suddenly she was laughing—at the water, at the sky, and the wind on her. 'The doctor told me I must get good air and walk lots, for I am sick, I am inside too much.' He could see there were tears—but of sadness, pain, joy? How could he tell? And he was affected.

"She came late everyday to avoid running into anybody on the beach. And he started passing intentionally. He knew she was waiting for him.

"Once, talking to her, he reached out and she withdrew. The gesture hurt him. He got up and left, but a long way off, when he looked back, she was still there against the rock, her hands flattened against it. She looked so alone, so he went back. Still she leaned there, stiff and eternal looking as that rock, and he looked at her fingers and said, 'Fingers got no blood, they all white,' and she said, 'I'll be glad when there is no flesh on them either and I am all bone.' 'You be dead then,' he said, and she sank to her knees and cried, and quick she was talking fast about Jesus. 'I eat Jesus every night,' she said, 'every night. I cannot wait for the ritual. You understand? I cannot wait for the ritual.' She kept crying. And he said, 'Why you do this?' And she said, 'Because if I eat Him all, He'll be inside me. If there's nothing left, I won't have to do this anymore. He'll be all alive inside me.'

"And Sinic put his hands on her shoulders, she gasped and shrank back, and he said, 'No,' and put them back on her and set her against the stone again and told her 'You rest, huh?' and close to her he rubbed her arms through the black cloth and kept touching her until she closed her eyes, still crying but softer now, and he sat closer and put his head in her lap and she clutched it with her hands touching all his hair as if her hands did not believe, and he put his own hands on her ankles and slid them up her legs and pushed back her skirts and kissed her thigh and set his head back into her lap, and they lay there still for a long time. Then they slept a little.

" 'I don't believe you!' I cried—why did I cry it out violent that way? —thinking at once that I had discovered the truth: he was becoming a master storyteller, his very broken English a source of attention because it made me listen harder.

"He stared at me, crushed. 'You tink Sinic lie, you too, Jase?'

" 'Yes, *yes,*' I said. 'What *did* you do to her?'

"He turned away, smaller, like a beaten dog struck into running. And I was ashamed. But the boys, hearing my shout, gave me the nod as if they'd said, 'Atta-go, Jason.' So I felt better for a while.

"The rest of that trip he worked silently beside me until we made our big kill and went back to Greenport some two weeks later. For a time I didn't think about him—if I did at any rate, I didn't want to. But bit by bit new stories brought up old. What perplexed me was how far back they reached. Club had turned against him first, long before I ever set foot on the *Annie B,* because Sinic had hung around Bill Potts, one of the foremen at the lace works. Sinic walked right in one morning and started to clean up the Potts garden. Nobody in town ever got into the Potts house, a showplace once when Bill's father owned the lace works. Again and again Bill threw Sinic out, but he went right back gardening for him, a beautiful job too. Somehow Sinic got in good. For Cash, Club said—loathed him for that. Then Sinic went to Fred Hampshire, the rival foreman. Nobody knew what he did or said to Fred, though people gossiped avidly. But Sinic got Fred into the Potts place. The two men would sit out there in the garden. They said Sinic had something on them, it drew them together, and they had to take Sinic in.

"I tried to keep my distance from him, and I might have if the men hadn't slurred him, edging wisecracks into him so that I have seen Sinic nearly break a metal pipe in two, bending it in suppressed anger. 'I don unstan you,' he'd say to them. 'You got no respec—for nodding.' No respect! Sinic saying that! It made for laughs, but they were grim, sardonic laughs directed at themselves.

"Sometimes in the wake of the laughter one of them would mention his daughter or his brother or his wife even. Then something akin to hatred came into their faces with the same focused intensity they demonstrated while working the dredges, but now it was still and contained and cruel. Sinic felt it too. I shall not forget that moment when, in the midst of our work, he looked up at them, he stopped working, he looked at me, those devastatingly serene blue eyes darting over me. *I* felt his fear too in that one moment when we were so understandingly, intimately close—for I looked into his eyes, I could not look away. He touched my shoulder. He said, 'What, Jason?' I saw *their* fear suddenly reversed and thrust into him. And for one instant I felt something of what he was, I was *with* him—as if he were in me—and I turned to them and cried, 'We don't understand you,' instantly realizing what I had said, *we*. Their faces registered it in smirks and cryptic smiles and Club's sudden bellow and their belched-up laughs. That very instant the gulf widened, I wasn't *of* them anymore, and they knew it.

"I was furious for a long time. Unfortunately I am not the kind who forgets easily—perhaps it has been both my undoing and the making of me. My fury pleased the crew because it turned me against Sinic, yet my outburst had alienated me from them. I was an island between Sinic and them. I couldn't blame the men for holding me suspect, but I blamed Sinic for making me side openly with him.

"I had only one more trip with them by then. I was eager to end it all, though with a certain shame, or cowardice, because nothing was resolved between us. So when I was paid off, I thought I had escaped. I did not know that leaving what is not finished is no escape. Nor did I know that I was not yet through with the crew, that it would come back into my life—not directly, but through Ellen. She was twenty-nine then, plain and quiet, unemotional, a stay-at-home whose eyes condemned the town as a shallow pace offset by the private world she had created for herself.

"For two weeks or more I had not seen any of the crew—it was September, I was getting ready to enter Columbia—but I had to confess to a hankering to see them as you do when you're goaded unconsciously by something unfinished. I'd had little company—Ellen was out every night, extremely unusual for her; my mother with her clubs; my father working late a good bit. So I finally ended up at Helen's. The usual ones were there, and in a strange way I was happy. Perhaps my very blood was conditioned to a yearning to go back to the ship, for, as it happened, they were about to go out again.

"Now that I wasn't actually one of them, the comradely way they took me in soothed me, like an indirect admission that I was not actually to blame for anything. Almost immediately I forgot myself in the juke box jumble and laughter and dirty jokes and beer and the T.V.—until Wes arrived. I didn't even understand what he meant when he came to me and whispered, 'Your sister.' 'My sister,' I said. 'Come onnn—quick,' he said. 'Ellen?' 'Who the hell else!' he said. The others caught Wes's intensity. 'Wait a *minute*,' I said. 'What the hell's going on?' 'It's your sister—and Sinic,' he said, quietly enough, but still loud, almost deliberately clear. As I got up, the others rose too. I didn't think then what that meant. I merely saw them in the pane getting up and following me out with Wes—along Front Street, a block from the waterfront, and down to the dock. 'Ellen!' I said—

"She was leaning against the piling with her hand on her stomach; she was crying. 'Honey, what is it?' I said. She cried with little chokes and looked up painfully. 'Ellen, tell me,' I said. 'He's gone,' she said, and bent over. '—sick,' she said. I took her shoulders. 'Ellen, what happened?' And she said, 'He's gone.' 'I know that—but who?' 'Sinic, that's who,' Wes said. 'Is that right, Ellen?' She shook her head yes. She was trembling violently, not like her—all her life I'd never known her to be really upset. 'You're sure?' I said. 'Yes—yes, yes,' she cried. 'Did he *hurt* you?' She fell against me then, convulsed. 'Yes—struck. Oh yes,' she said.

" 'Wes, you take her home, will you?' I said. 'Okay,' he said. And I looked at the others. We would go for him, we would not stop until we found him and— Almost by instinctive assent, we went together, six of us in Club's car.

"Finding him was not hard—in this town he'd few places to go. Despite the dark and a drizzle, he was on the beach—he'd just dragged in his rowboat and moored it—hurrying toward the sixty-seven steps that led up the bluff to the road. He must have seen us at the top, but he didn't falter, kept coming at a brisk pace in the sand.

"We went down to meet him—Jib, Club, Mel, Hulse, Bennie and I.

And seeing him come, I couldn't understand what kind of criminal he must be who had a history of attacks and accusations, who had violated Ellen, yet would come straight at us as if nothing disturbed him.

" 'Sinic, what did you do to Ellen?' I cried. The wind was hard; it smacked the words back into my mouth. He stood directly below me on the incline, near the water. He opened his mouth— The waves crashed his voice dead. 'What?' I shouted, and he shouted again: '—hit her.'

" 'Mel, don't!' I said—out of the corner of my eye I saw Mel move closer.

"And Sinic moved then, stepped up a level onto the white stones.

" 'What you tink?' he said. 'You?' And the pain on his face arrested me, and a despair in the futile slope of his shoulders, his arms hanging so limp. But I couldn't resolve that look with what he'd done. One more lie. Was he lying again, as he had before—God knows how many times? *I will not be taken in.* 'You—Sinic!' I shouted. My hostility must have pierced him. He jerked as if jabbed, and suddenly bolted—why did he do that if he were innocent!—but Mel and Hulse pounced on him almost as he leaped and held him fast. He didn't say a word, but he struggled furiously, almost breaking loose.

" 'What'll we do?' Hulse said. 'Just give him to me for ten minutes,' Mel said. 'No!' Club said, and he looked at me. 'We owe it to Jason and a lot of other people. . . . Jib, get the rope and hooks in my trunk.' He tossed him the key. As Jib scaled up the steps, Club said, 'Whatta ya say, boys—the Cat Rock?'

" 'For what he done that's too good—he ain't fit to touch nobody, damn 'm,' Hulse said.

"Jib stumbled down between us, ropes in hand, the iron hooks clanking down against the stones.

" 'We'll give 'm a good dose—when he's tied out there awhile, that'll cure 'm,' Hulse said.

"Still Sinic did not speak. I hated him for his pure defiance of us all. I wanted to hit him though he was down and held. I forced my hands against my sides.

" 'Well . . . ? You say the word,' Club said.

"And what held me back even then? I looked at them—Club, Hulse, Mel, Jib and Bennie. And I looked at Sinic. 'Goddamn you, Sinic! Why don't you say something!' And I looked at Club again, and I nodded, I nodded yes.

"And quick, Club said, 'Get him to his rowboat.'

"In a few minutes we were on the way to the rock. The tide was going out, the suction is deadly enough in the Sound, but the wind was strong, and rain, and Jib had to fight, with the oars deeper. I took one side.

"The rock was slippery. Wes had to use one of the hooks to grapple us close, then another on the opposite side to steady us. They tied Sinic. Hulse and Jib dragged him onto the rock. Seeing him lying there with the whole sea beyond him, not moving, not looking at me or anybody, simply into the dark sky, I nearly gave way. Club said, 'Think of Ellen, you fool!' Yes, *Ellen.* . . .

"They stretched his tied arms out and tied his feet together, pulled him taut. It seemed to take forever. Hulse dropped the hooks down, deep, grappling for the rock edges, hooking at the base of the rock, finally drawing the ropes in wide circles about the rock, and tight, then tied them over Sinic. How could he shake free of that?

"We shoved off—I dared not look back—and suddenly we grew giddy, Jib laughed and it set us off, a volley of nervous laughs and jokes and curses. We leaped onto the beach and hauled the boat up.

"From the bluff I looked down—it was growing rapidly dark, the water was uneasy, distorted by the wind. Sinic seemed to be lying still, only his head shifting from side to side. The waves swirled about the rock in quick white lashes, came up over his legs and arms. He was nearly underwater but the tide was receding.

" 'I said, 'Club—'

" 'Don't be a sucker! You need a drink,' he said.

"Sinic would be there all night, through the ebbing tide and the change and the rising tide, and at high water his head would barely be out of it, he would have to struggle, he would know then—

"The rest is very simple: Hulse bought a bottle and we went back to his place. Wes came later—he had taken Ellen to spend the night with Anna Lincoln to avoid my parents. Early, a little after midnight, I went home prepared to get up at five and meet them on the beach, even then feeling that the inevitable would happen—

"And in the morning I woke up stark. I had slept through the alarm. And did I *will* that? Then I heard with incredible clarity—not the rain, which *was* coming down, a stiff rain in a steady wind, but the sea. It was not unusual, just the same relentless crashing. But so clear! *'Sinic!'*

I said aloud, thinking: the others will be there, he'll be freed by now—.

"No one was there. The Sound was gray as far as my eye could see. I could hardly make out the Cat Rock just below the surface, and even then I could not be sure, but I saw nothing, no clothes, no body, no head above the water. I did not know then, I do not know now, but it bolted through me: by some agreement, had they intended to leave him there to die as he deserved? (For—could I have known it—at that moment they were getting ready to pull out in an hour on the *Annie B.*) And had I, too, instinctively agreed to that?

"I went down to the beach—

"I found him wedged between the rocks. His hands and feet were still bound. How he had dragged himself up between the rocks, only God knows. By now the waves had mounted to his waist. No telling how many times he had been sucked back and battered helplessly against the rocks. His head was torn, bruised almost unrecognizably, and bleeding. But he was alive.

"But that was not enough! After I had taken him to the Eastern Long Island Hospital, that very day I learned the truth from Ellen. 'You fool!' she cried. *'Touched* me—not that way, no sex!' She was hysterical again. I didn't believe her. Only struck her? I couldn't let myself believe her.

"'Struck me and touched me and moved me—yes—for the first time in my whole life made me feel like a woman. He woke me up. I'm not dead—you understand? *He* did it. All the time I think he intended to leave me. Do you know that?' And I thought: she's still hysterical, she's illogical, she's sick, there's no proof, we can't go to Sinic to find out—

"No, Sinic did not die. Over two months later (I was home for Thanksgiving vacation), not long out of the hospital Sinic wandered into town on a Saturday morning. I saw him on Front Street. 'Sinic!' I called. He turned around and he looked at me. 'It's me, Jason,' I said. But he stared at me with no awareness of who I was; he stared with the vacant eye of the dead. And what accusation could be worse? And what death—for him—that or the other?

"He had relatives abroad, in some small town near Warsaw. From Poland they had written that they were poor, but if he could get passage they would be overjoyed. . . . The whole town of Greenport chipped in and he was sent off to New York to be shipped back there.

"Ah, if it could have ended there— Wasn't it enough that there was

no testimony against us but each one's knowledge of the other? For we could no longer come together except by necessity or accident—in the grocery, coming round a corner, at the movies—and even then with a self-conscious amenity which in itself was a confession of another bond which we had never dared define. And now at each meeting I saw Sinic's eyes in their eyes staring at me—but with what guilt? We each could grasp, as we did, for some accidental justification: 'If Ellen were not violated, hadn't there been the others?'

"But it did not end there.

"At Christmas his old landlady came to me. 'Sinic write,' she said and handed me these scraps.

"I stared at them. *Sinic.* It was as if she held out those blue eyes and I was caught in them again.

" 'Why *me?*' I said, feeling the old fear.

" 'Your name, not?' she said. On the first page: *Jason* was all.

" 'Yes, my name,' I said, and long after she was gone: 'But why me?'

"I got Mrs. Landowski to translate them with me, and with each word I saw Sinic as he was led from the boarding house, faceless and vacant, with a permanent innocence now that would never grow, yet there the words peeled away the Sinic we had known, there on the paper he grew whole, he emerged unbelievable. Listen: 'In the night my Matilda's hand is on me, and I know it is real, the field is around us, and I smell grain and night and hair, and from her hand comes burning. I am burning. I want to burn till I die.' I would never know who Matilda was, but whatever happened or where, Sinic never forgot.

"The slips were not dated, merely numbered. I could make out eight different people, and though he did not explain all, there were patches: he had stolen glasses from Ogilvie's and dropped them into the five-and-ten manager's pocket. Henby thought twice before accusing anybody in his own store after that, but the blot never left him. And the foremen: he had tricked them into a battle over their old hobby, flowers; it had appalled them when they realized it. And there was Edith Evans, the woman in the theater; Sister Theresa; the other two women and Ellen. . . . He did not seem to care if they hated him. He made them act. And there were two lines to 'J'—to me, Jason?

" 'J—— If I am cruel, kind, good, evil to them, what does it matter? Let them live before they die. To make them do that, I would give anything.'

"And reading, I felt the old fear in me again, the crew's fear and mine, but closer now, as if it were in my own heart. No, I lied to myself, I could not admit that it was not Sinic we were afraid of, but ourselves, what was in *us* that he let out of himself so freely. And those eight victims, would they lie too—like me? And instantly my mind fixed on Sister Theresa. Surely she would not lie, I could believe her. *She* had suffered: 'Sister Theresa must suffer. I cannot live for her alone. She would hold me in one life, and this would destroy me. I must be free for who comes. If I am not, I die. Matilda showed me I was born for this.'

"At the Catholic school they told me she had left the Order the first week of September.

" 'Before the accident!'

" 'What?' the Mother Superior said curiously.

"I felt caught. 'I was thinking aloud,' I said. She smiled.

" 'A medical withdrawal,' she explained. 'Her health . . .'

" 'And there's no way to find her?'

" 'Her mailing address—there,' she said, 'in Lake Ronkonkoma.'

"On the weekend before I went back to Columbia, I found her. She was small and very pretty with intense eyes that always seemed to study you, and waiting, anticipating. I told her about Sinic.

" 'Yes,' she murmured. She was obviously moved.

" 'Sister—,' I said.

" 'Lucy. Lucy Malvina,' she said. 'Now.'

" 'Of course. You'll be perfectly honest with me, I know. It's very important. So much, so many . . . depend on it.'

" 'I didn't lose my honesty when I left the sisters.' She smiled capriciously, but her undeviating eyes measured me.

" 'You see, we didn't believe. *I* didn't believe him. We accused him. Rumor led us—'

" 'I hated him—because he gave me such pain—and oh yes, joy, such joy. I needed him. And then he was cruel to me. I told him: It is too painful being all this, but he didn't care. He said: Leave it then. It was too much to give up. The sisters would never understand. I had to—'

" 'Then I interrupted. I read her this: "Sister Theresa put her hand inside my shirt. She said: I want to feel your heart. We are beating together, she cried. Why have I missed my own blood before?"

" 'Yes—you see why I hated him? He would not satisfy me. He would make me struggle and be miserable. I told him that too, but he laughed—he was cruel.'

" 'Then you *would* go back to the sisters!'

" 'Never! What made you say that? He made me hate him. And I'm glad! It made me know so many things. I hated him—he was too pure. What would I have done, though—die, just die?'

"So Sinic was not lying— What few jottings he made were the few words which might have explained his actions, though we knew, yes *knew*, he was acting out of his deepest self, as we might have, but we were afraid.

"What drove him to paper at last? A thousand times I have asked myself: could he have suspected that sooner or later he would end in some way as he had and so written those scraps to try, once, to bare himself to someone else? But why me?

"I had only two nights and a day to see the crew, for I *had* to tell them he was unquestionably innocent. I could not go back to Columbia without doing that. So I went to each of them. At sight of me, I saw at once, the fear came back: as Bennie opened the door, at the way Mel's brother said, 'It's Jason,' in Jib's speaking without looking up. They were afraid—of me, as if I were Sinic. And I felt them: Sinic is not dead, he's in me—because he made me tell, the notes drove me to them. And I could hear him, standing on the deck beside me, for the first time telling me he knew me: *You see now.* And I heard him the second time—through those notes—daring to lay bare his final self to me, for it was not enough to know, he had to be known. I wanted to tell him *Sinic, maybe I understand, maybe I know now,* but knowing comes always too late. Yet for those few moments when I saw each of the crew and told them Sinic was innocent, I did not feel alone.

"But on the way out, it was Club who accused me.

" 'What the hell you tellin me for?' he said, 'How bout you? You think you ain't involved? Who give us the nod? You forgettin that, boy? *You*—that's who. You. Actin like the livin Jesus, are you?'

" 'I know that. I had to come to tell you Sinic is innocent, he never lied—to make sure we all know, that's all.'

" 'What good's knowin do?' he said.

" 'What good,' I said, closing the door.

"That Sunday night I took the train back to Columbia."

Jason was silent then, and for a long time he did not look up. They sat listening to the waves strike, retreat, strike, close to the pilings under the porch. When finally he did look, it was not at her, but at the window—and outside: all dark, and the fog hung thick. He could see nothing.

Margaret stirred. She said, "I didn't know you could be so . . . transported." There was a tinge of disappointment, of hurt, in her voice. "You were not yourself."

"Not myself?"

"I didn't know you."

"Then I offended you by telling it?"

"Oh, Jason—no. But that happened so long ago, you were young. Why cling to it all?"

"Perhaps never to forget what I am."

"But you've repaid him a hundred times over in the criminal cases you've taken on."

"For his life?"

"You've saved *many!*"

"It's not enough, Margaret."

"But what more could you want?"

"Maybe to throw down some last barrier around me or—"

"But now that you've told me, you're free of it!"

"You think that?"

"Of course! Why else did you tell it tonight?"

He was standing now before the window, peering out into the darkness.

"Why, indeed," he said as she went for the coffee things.

He moved onto the porch, stumbled against her chair. Outside, the night was deep. He could see nothing, neither water nor sky. Now the dark seemed to move up over him, over the house and the stars; now the beach and the rocks and the Sound itself disappeared in the depths. And for a moment it was as if there was nothing in the darkness, but soon he was aware of it, of its sound, of its relentless presence: the waves beat against the shore.

One of the Boys

Every night I waited for Millie to say it: "Will you see Red tonight?" And I would think: Don't resent it, she can't help it, maybe she's even trying to give you a little of that freedom she's heard men complain they never have, and she's Red's sister, I'm glad she cares that much about him.

But I was *not* going to Dom's place, though I might walk past, I might look in, I might even see Red . . . .

Red is one of the boys. You can see them any night at Dom's, a few standing at the end of the bar, Wag and Buff at the dartboard, the others huddled in a semicircle, their feet hooked on the stool, their voices constantly erupting as they talk, argue, laugh—and in the midst of it Dom, whose mammoth Greek head is perched on a walrus body that can barely lumber its weight along behind the counter, who would be unhappy without a world of men. Dom tends his own bar. After a long, sickly childhood he has at last found his health in the lithe athletes whose out-of-doors world comes to life as the boys recreate the games play by play. Night after night, wreathed in their own tobacco laurels, their voices louder as the night grows shorter, Dom lives his unlived youth.

That late August afternoon when I first walked in, the boys were all there. Nobody paid much attention to me—the usual flick of eyes with that casual and imperturbable condenscension which customers acquire when their long-standing business gives them proprietorship. After all, I was the interloper.

I took out my handkerchief and mopped. I felt the blowers but I was still hot. Outside, a sheer crystal sea poured up from the Atlanta pavements, and the sun blinded. So for a few seconds inside I couldn't see—the figures were simply ashen silhouettes before the darkness dissolved and they dropped one by one into my eyes and made that living tableau that I see even now. For a moment I thought I was back in the service, that it was war, a world of men, and there were no women. I can't go through that again, not that, I thought. And I would have turned and gone out, but Dom said, "Yours?"

"Bud," I said.

I am not an afternoon drinker, but I blame that beginning on the heat. Like some impersonal force which was not chance or fate, but simply itself, the heat had driven me in with a prodding insistent hand, and even inside it seemed to hold and cement us together in that room on a particular afternoon that could never be undone.

But of course, then, nothing happened.

I sat at the bar, put both my hands around the glass and closed my eyes to let the coolness of the beer run up into them, then drank it straight down.

It was that bottoms-up that made the boys turn because Dom spoke again.

"You wanted that bad, hey?"

"Yes, I wanted that bad," I said, and laughed. An old man just beyond me laughed too—and I could see him in the mirror almost head-on—and two of the gang around the end of the bar looked curiously but they didn't laugh. I knew at once it was that proprietorship again: you don't give a stranger the advantage. That would admit him. Okay, I thought, okay, I get the message.

But the shorty—five feet two maybe, with red hair in a coxcomb that added two or three inches to him—stared a minute. I heard him too: "Creep." Okay, I thought. Wait.

So I listened to them, the sweat subsiding after a while, as Atlanta burned outside, and this den cooled like an earth hole despite the smoke coils above and the beer and sweat inevitable between the cleanest walls that are crowded with drinking men and vats and nicotine. And it was two hours just sitting and watching, listening to them wind up the old plays, argue about scores:

"Hey, Dom—get the Almanac."

"Now wait a minute. Buff's right. One forty-eight runs."

"Get the *Almanac*." The oldest one. *"I* can remember. You guys are too young."

"Too *young!"*

"*Get*—the—*Almanac.*"

"Cut it down, boys. I got other customers, you know." But he brought them the Almanac. "Here."

"Okay, Dom."

"Yeah, look. *Look,* I tell ya. One forty-three. *Three,* get it? Now I'll take that beer. Hey, Dom—one draft on Tom."

Laughter.

Maybe, after the hectic irregularity of my affair with Lettie, it was the reliable reputation that made me feel at home at Dom's, the slow habit of hearing the same phrases, the same arguments from the same voices until after a while you expect them with a regularity of sound that grips you slowly and which you begin to long for so that looking at your watch at a certain hour of night you say, It is almost time, and then, It *is* time, the boys will be there, and you grab your jacket—

Lettie was sick that afternoon; she did not want me around. Besides, she had quarreled with me before her illness, so it was only kindness—no, why should I lie to myself? *duty*—that made her see me then. She kept saying she wanted to break it off; she wanted to try somebody else, for its own sake, until she was sure; she didn't trust me, herself, sex; she named her friends, how bad marriage had turned out for them; on and on. . . . It was tedious. Yes, I felt sorry for her. Yet I wanted more than sex, I wanted to touch her *inside,* just to let her hand touch me and me her in a place our sex did not touch. But she misunderstood. "I'm sick, damn it," she said, "sick." "You don't understand," I said. "I understand everything." "Everything!" I said, angry, though I didn't want to be, I didn't want to upset her more.

Our trouble was more than illness. She was edging away from me toward a precipice which she would soon fall off. I could not save her. No amount of begging did that; and pleading tenderly, kindly, and then angrily only agitated what I had thought to soothe into submission. To tell the truth, we had both been too easy with too many people and knew it; in the back of our minds there was a remote, mutual disrespect. Our break tore our habits; it left loose nerve ends. And I walked in a crooked line with no magnetism at the other end, so I reached out for habits—

"Go then. Go!" she shouted when I went back to try once more that afternoon. I did not return or call after that. We both used pride as the excuse, I know, a lie to cover up our freedom for a new enslavement.

So I went back to Dom's place. I sensed all along that it was what I would do. I felt I had found something familiar in myself that I couldn't define, but I recognized that I had to find out what it was— because it was in Buff and Dick, Tom, Eddie, and Line—and Red. Mostly in Red. And in what Dom's place was to them.

It was Red who began it. He stood next to my stool at the bar, just outside the circle of raw light that encompassed the gang, and he could not help hearing me talk to Dom about England.

"Hey, you guys—he been to England," Red said. He had sidled into the light; it spilled into his red hair, which quivered like a menace. Those faces behind him turned to glance with diffident scorn at England in the flesh. So I played it by ear. "Yeah," I said. Not *yes*. "Yeah." And his eyes froze an instant, with jarred stillness, and then made a suspicious roam over me.

"Bet you play darts too, ahn?" As accurately as your eyes do, I thought, and I felt them all penetrating me. But I didn't answer.

"Suhmatter? English too good for us, uh?"

I had thought silence would cool him off, but the others stood up in support of him, a circle of controlled alien faces. I still didn't speak, but I did get up—perhaps it was the way I did it that saved the night, I don't know—and held out my hand for the darts. It didn't shake.

Buff handed them to me.

"Okay. Who with?" I said.

There was an instant's silence before anyone moved. And then it was Eddie.

"I'll go you," he said.

"Me too," Tom said.

Line made a fourth. We paired off—or Eddie paired us off. What was strange was that Red hadn't offered to oppose. He leaned his arm on the bar, high and awkward for him, and watched us all the while. He was then just beginning to grow fat, his stomach sloppy over his belt, his chest a bit sagged, and he had that habit of tucking his thumbs into his belt, arms akimbo. His pants were too long, the cuffs creased with a crippled look at his ankles, and dragged. You expected him to turn any minute and walk pathetically, with Charlie Chaplin scuffing, down the aisle, out the front door, and into the distance.

As it turned out, Line and I won the first game and Red could not even say, "Thanks to *Line*," though his eyes glowed with hope when we lost the second. We played until closing and our team carried the day, thanks to Oxford pubs and the boys at Pemmie during my Fulbright year.

The victory was enough to make me go back the following Saturday night. Red wasn't in sight, and the boys scarcely spoke. I was still the once-a-week stranger. I sat alone a good while before anyone spoke to me.

"Hey, shark—" It was Red. He'd been in the Den. He was very drunk, which meant he must have been drinking hard because he was a veteran beer holder, and he was smiling warmly with rheumy eyes. "Shark, I want you to meet my sister. C'*mon*, shark."

She was sitting alone at one of those huge oak tables for eight or ten people, which made her look small and lonely and very much self-conscious and afraid, though she wasn't.

"I've heard about you all week," she said, taking my hand. She didn't let it go; it rather guided me to the chair next to her, and Red closed in—he dragged a chair around tight between us.

"He's the cham*peen*, Millie. Y'oughta see those throws."

She was gazing at me, her face rather wistful, and did not reply, yet her green eyes were alive with a strength that reinforced the tight clasp of her hand, as if she and I had (and both instantaneously realized it) something to cling to in the quiet storm that always goes on about us, as if we were two of the islands of this world she was to speak of, which will be swallowed up by something that crouches and waits beyond the horizon toward which we slip day by day. Between Red's praises, surprising in themselves after Saturday's silent treatment, came gradual powerless little grunts. The alcohol crept into the regions of his body so that we could watch one after another the parts of him die for the evening. Behind his wet, half-open eyes there was only the remotest recognition, which came out in ribald, smiling twists of his mouth and weak grunts, between which—or instigated by them—she tried to explain.

"Partly it's the times too. You feel that? The atom and all. The islands are still here, but they're people. People are the only things we have to reach out to. These days we depend so much on touching, but when your hands *can't* touch any longer, you can't find people, you get frantic, you flounder, you want to shout for something bigger than you to take you up and hold you, and even that's not there, it's dispersed like everything else, and you *want* to cry out, you *try*, but you don't have the strength, it dies in your throat—like Red's—and the worst thing is you begin to forget anybody's there. . . ." She at last let me go. My hand felt so empty and I wanted to cry out—she must have seen that on my face because even as she reached over and touched Red ever so tenderly so that he felt it, so that he sat up and stared with what seemed like a tremendous effort to comprehend where he was and what was happening, so that he recognized us and smiled, she did not take her eyes off my own face, and I was sure in her own way she was trying to tell me she had not let go, she was still touching me.

"What are you doing *here?*" I said—in a bar with a brother who hung with the boys and left her alone in this enormous Den, where college kids and locals whooped it up nightly so that the very noise drove your loneliness goading back into you.

"He doesn't get drunk very often. He drinks a lot, he knows how, but sometimes . . . well, I just know when the times are. You understand? I come—just to be here, I guess."

"He's got the boys."

"They can't go as far. There's a certain point they can't go beyond, even when they want to—you understand? They're . . . useless, I guess."

I got up feeling a bit like them, useless, and I said, "Yes," and stood there.

"Ohhh—I didn't mean. . . ." She too rose, both of us standing awkwardly almost against each other.

"No, I didn't take it that way," I said. "You misunderstood." I hadn't taken it personally either, but now her saying it *made* me take it personally.

"It's just the way things work, I guess," I said.

Red lolled in the chair, his small kangaroo arms hooked over the side. His head balanced awkwardly on his right shoulder, his lower lip clutched over his upper, and the scraggly thick red hair fell over his ugly face. I say ugly, but I mean that bizarre grotesquerie which makes sad clowns out of some of the homeliest of men.

"Well," she said. "We've got to go. He's in no condition to stay."

"My car—"

"No," she said, rather emphatically I thought, until I said, "Well, then, the boys—"

"No!" she said more emphatically. I did not understand. Was she putting herself between me and Red, without reason, and between the boys and Red?

"I only meant that if *I* offered, the boys might be offended. After all, he's their—" I didn't know how to say there was a code at work in these things.

"That's too primitive." She laughed and, bending over, took Red's face between her hands. "Red. *Red!*" Her voice roused him like a conditioning which spoke beyond his immediate mind, and she managed to get him up and guide him out and left me standing there like a fool, feeling—and why?—a peculiar inadequacy but—worse—a resentment that she had made me feel that way.

Even now I am not sure if it was to eradicate that resentment that I wanted to see her again, though I told myself it was. So, rather awkwardly, I began to stop by after work, about eight, to pick up Red on the way to Dom's place. I went more often, I got to know the crowd, and on the nights that Millie came along she rode with me; after closing we lingered in the Impala. And sometimes, after she was gone, I could hear her soft breathing beside me, or waking that night the same soft breathing, until I clamped my hand on my chest, like trying to hold her, make her *me,* interrupting the sound with a start at discovering that it was my own; but the breathing would creep back into my head until I could only hear the one, mine and hers, and then Red's too, and the boys', everybody's, until it flooded over me, all at the same time, from one big body. . . . After that, I would sleep.

With Millie beside me, I forgot about Lettie most of the time. I acquired something I had never had before, a link with life, I was held *in* life, saved from being out of it as an observer watching Red, the boys, Dom, life itself. And now I knew I could not stand *not* to have that. So when I touched her, when finally my hand was on her thigh and her hands tore over my back and we sucked and bit, it was not simply sex at last—it was that I had got *to* her beyond that resentment; we had fought—we were fighting then—and we both knew it but could not say that it was the struggle itself that we wanted because our conflicting wills made us live.

"What about Red?"

"Red? Why . . . I could never leave him." She was incredibly matter-of-fact.

"I know that," I said. But why thrust him onto me? I thought, yet I couldn't imagine what it would be like if she had not. "That needn't change things. We're getting married anyway."

"Yes. And Red will live with us—or maybe, if you want to, we'll stay here, and you can move in with us."

"No—" It was somehow the one condition I'd have fought for. "We'll find a bigger place, a place of our own, with a good-sized room for Red."

"You really want that? You'll do it?" She smiled, almost too pleased at that. Yet there was a perceptible antagonism in her voice.

"For you. You know that."

I was not then thinking of the boys—not that they had fully accepted me. A good shot at the dartboard and the approval of a few members of a club are not enough to make you belong. There is a trust which comes from years of anchoring in another's habits, and I knew, the moment Red came into the apartment a few days before we began to move to the new flat, that beyond the surface a tumult was at work. I did not know how subtle the workings in Dom's place were.

"I got me a place around the corner," he said finally. "McCorkell's. You know the house, Mill. Her husband's got the wheel chair, sits in the sun parlor all day."

Millie's silence was worse than the fiercest sun—for an instant I thought she would cry out, so taut was she. But she worked on until she subsided, then she said, "It's McCorkell's then?"

At the table his hands edged the cloth. "Aw, come on, Mill. What'd you expect? I mean, a guy can't let somebody else—"

"You'd be paying your own way. I always made you do that," she said calmly. "But obviously you won't be." It was his dismissal, though he didn't go at once. Abruptly he turned to me. "You! What the hell you think you're doing anyway?" And he left.

"Red!" I called, but only the stubborn sounds deep in the stair-well reverberated, then the shut door, and hollow, irregular steps down the street.

"He'll come back—he will, won't he?" she said, and for the first time in weeks I sensed a loss of that touching, because she was reaching to something beyond me, to some need I couldn't and she couldn't supply. "He will, won't he?"

"I don't know, Millie," I said.

That night she did not really have to plead with me, though I'm sure she thought that was the reason I finally went to Dom's to talk to Red. It ended with a kind of pleading on my part—for her, I said. That gave him importance and a triumph which he lorded before the boys: "See that—I told ya she'd come after me." I sensed a different rhythm among the boys as they played darts, talked, joked, fought over reputations and scores. Something of the old status quo had been reestablished. The boys retreated into the circle of light, and I was the ignored stranger again. I was angry; I felt I saw them for what they were: a self-contained bunch of peacocks, ex-athletes living on ex-games, with thick waists, drooped breasts, beer-swollen jowls, and bleary eyes blind to the world outside. There was only one thing missing: Millie, their audience of one. And she was mine now.

"You shouldn't feel as bad as I do, but you do, don't you?" she said.

Her insight startled me, for I did feel bad. Something had been torn away from me too. Red was fixed on an opposite bank from us, and as long as he was there we were broken, all three of us. Millie was disrupted; her lost routine wrenched her out of socket; naturally it was impossible to plant her years-old fixation for Red in me. She fretted. I saw the loss in her face even when she didn't say anything to me, when she turned inquiringly to me as I entered the apartment, that happy but frightened look of disappointment, the brief constriction from fear of permanent loss which separation brings.

"You seeing Red tonight? *Are* you?" she'd say, and I had to sit beside her, I had to say, "Millie, don't you understand—now you and I are the same thing to him. What's you he identifies with me. He's going to react the same way with me as with you."

"But you could *try*. He's my brother." It grew then to a new stage—she would begin to cry, taut, soundless tears. I could not get close to her. She made me feel what islands we are, how we can't stand what islands we are. And I would promise, "Tonight, Millie. Tonight I'll talk to Red."

Returning late, I knew she would speak out of the darkness: "You talked to Red?" Sometimes in my first silence she knew: "He won't come. . . ." I couldn't understand her. I wanted to say, "You're not married to Red. You're married to me, Millie, *me*." Immediately I regretted thinking it. How small I was. Never once did she reproach me for the few times I drank too much with Red, or after Red had gone, though occasionally when we were downtown, when she did say, "You don't really want a drink, do you?" I felt a probing in her understanding, and as I looked at her, reproach must have been hard in my eyes because she would say, "I'm sorry, I *am*." At such times I was aware of how she knew there are, simply, inexplicable presences which cement others together, without which what was can't exist again in the same way. But whoever stops if he does believe that?

Finally I succeeded: whether Red was actually lonely for her or whether his own resistance, even with the support of the boys, was not enough to sustain his own broken routine or his emotional dependence on her, he decided to come to dinner on Wednesday night. Cautiously, to fortify himself, he wangled an invitation for Line and Buff, perhaps to show he had the boys' sanction, perhaps to hold back her onslaught, or more typically ("primitively," she would say) to hide a man's fear of acting alone.

Millie was beautiful that night. She glowed with the strength of a hidden source of energy that compelled every move. Red's face as he came into the room registered his pleasant shock as he stared at her. She laughed.

"Red!" she cried as if she hadn't seen him in years. In her laughter the timbre of happy tears resounded so strongly that Red himself could scarcely speak. The boys felt it too. For a while they enjoyed it like a sound aimed at each of them separately. They had a brief, breathless look into a happiness they hadn't yet known, an inkling of what woman, marriage, home might mean. It kept them quiet for a time, just watching, until Red started talking and laughing spontaneously, already steeped in the apartment, not at all a stranger.

His pleasure was a threat, and in Line and Buff something happened, some animal secretion at the scent of danger threatening their species, and Buff said, "You sure got it cozy here, Millie, just like I had before I left the house. My mother, she drove me to it—ya know? That's the way they all are." He slipped comfortably down into the chair, long and, if a little too heavy, still lithe, and strummed the end table in quick rhythm—he used to play the snare drum, you never forgot that. He kept glancing at his watch and it made Millie nervous, she laughed at nothing, especially with Red joining in because he was getting a little high on the wine, which he seldom drank except on special occasions. Line said, "You put too much of that away, Red, and you know that beer at Dom's won't mix, you'll wind up pretty sick."

"Oh, *Line*—" Millie reproached. Something of the glow left her.

"Well, *you* know, Mill. You don't want him sick, do you?"

"Yeah, Mill. You don't want me sick." Red pushed back the wine. Buff looked at his watch. He smiled at Red. "You all right, Red?"

"Why shouldn't he be all right? Of course he's all right," she said.

"Aw, Mill, I didn't mean anything."

"Of course you didn't." Her lower lip loosened, down, as when she argues with me.

"Well, I didn't, Mill. You know that."

"All right, all *right!*" she said.

"Come on now, Millie. Don't get upset. Buff only meant—"

"Yeah—" Buff said.

"I *know* what Buff only meant!"

"Well, if you're gonna take it that way, Mill—" Buff rose. Like a shadow, Line rose too. Red scuffed his chair back. "Look, Mill—"

"*I* know. You don't have to tell me. These are your *friends.* Go ahead—*say* it: 'These are my friends.' "

"Well, they are!"

"Who'd ever guess?" she muttered.

"Okay. *Okay*—'f that's the way you feel. . . ."

"That's the way I feel."

Red turned at the door. "Okay, Mill . . . ," he said, but she turned away from him. She did not look at me. She stood there, keyed up but not trembling, contained as stone; she did not move until after the door below closed and a torn laugh sounded down the street. Then her hands hooked up, helpless, at the air; she trembled with anger, tears came, and a thin tight cry in her throat. "Millie . . ." I drew her close. "It's all right, Millie." She let herself flow into me, her tears hot against my chest, her pulsing like my own; and I had a queerly perverse gratitude to Red for making me feel this. But it was *not* all right. No matter what I felt, the minute she broke away I knew again that if Red had thrust us together for that moment, the separation was greater because he was gone.

"I can't give him anything, that's the trouble," she said. "You can only go so far with somebody else—*he* doesn't know that, and you don't. He's a sweet, ugly little man. If he had a wife, he'd understand, our relations would be serene, he'd know then why I can't leave him alone. He may never know. *Think* of that—he may never know. He can't go on like this always. Can he?"

And I saw the boys at Dom's with her eyes: night after night for a whole lifetime, drinking, laughing, throwing darts, arguing about baseball scores, their athletic frames gathering paunches, their faces fading with a more open desperation, their heads gray and oily with baldness—

"*Can* he?" She searched me, but her eyes went beyond me, and I thought, Jesus, Mill, what *is* it? How much do you want?

"Why not?" I said, and I have to confess that at her startled look and the way she arrowed "Paul!" at me, there was a shock in my words for me too. "What do you mean?" And I didn't know then. But her question was thrust back at me after what happened Saturday night: because I left her alone—she wanted that, actually argued it, thinking I might bring Red back or give him back some of our companionship and relieve his loneliness, which she grieved about day and night. I hadn't seen Line or Buff or Red since Wednesday, so I was not really prepared for what happened: they smiled at me, first one then the other. "Hey, Paul—" Buff said. Buff never said "Hey, Paul" to me like that—quick, spontaneous, without the reserve of a minority group that sized you up for a whole evening before it acknowledged you verbally. Silent Tom actually condescended to grunt and Eddie talked a blue streak though it wasn't aimed at me. It was Buff who finally egged me into the Couples' Den.

"Hey, Paul. Come on 'n sit. There's plenty-a room." He strolled into the Den and sat facing me. "Dom did a good thing opening this here new room," he said, scrutinizing me. And then I saw her—he *knew* I saw her—and the insidious look of pleasure on his face communicated it to the bar, because I heard their soft, undertoned laughs behind—

"You know *her?*" he said.

She was sitting at the table behind him and I could see her over his shoulder. I half rose. . . . *Lettie*—And Buff rose too, smiling that treacherous, knowing smile which coated me dirty inside with its implications.

I went over to her table and sat. "Hello, Lettie."

"Paul—" she said with a look of near pain, as if the word hurt.

In a way I was pleased to see her and I told her so.

"I knew you would be," she said, but she had misunderstood.

"I mean—"

"I know what you mean," she said. "After all is said and done, I know, and I had to satisfy my instincts—to see you in the flesh just to see if there's some change, if it's that girl—Millie?—you really want, what it's done to you."

"Wait a *minute,* Lettie. You're going too fast for me."

"I always did, didn't I? But I was right, you see—you're not changed, you're just Paul, you don't even look 'right,' you just look like . . . Paul."

"What in hell did you think I'd look like?" Certainly I did not want to become exasperated—ours had been a history of exasperation—that would only confirm whatever her feelings were.

"It's not what I thought you'd look like—different somehow, and whole, with that smug self-satisfaction a married man at least ought to have. Well, you haven't got that self-assurance."

"Who has it for long? It comes and goes in anybody's life."

"Now you're throwing barbs."

"I didn't mean it that way. *You* had to live through things to make up your mind too."

"I have," she said. Her look was wrong, too confident, filled with some pity poured out to me; and I felt if I held out my hands I'd catch it, she'd touch me. I dug them into my pockets.

"Lettie," I whispered, aware now of the shadows, the heads on the floor at my feet, beside my chair.

"I *have,*" she shrilled with the faintest hysteria in her whisper.

"It can't ever be," I said. "I'm married. I'm committed—"

Then I felt the presence of Red beside me. He laughed. I can see the beer in his hand, yellow, close to my face, the foam like slops, spraying up and over the edge, over his hand, dirtying it, making me feel dirty; and the heat of his hand touched me—

"Committed!" he said, with an excruciatingly painful edge to his own voice. "So that's what you are with my sister—"

Behind him Buff laughed, and there was a muffled echo, a guffaw, and someone stamped a foot. The darts struck unusually hard in a rapid three into the cork.

"Red, I didn't mean—" His eyes, redwebbed and tired, glared with a petty triumph I didn't want to see him descend to, and I felt sorry for him. I wanted to grab his hand and tell him, Red, Red, I didn't do anything to you, I didn't take anything away from you, I'm trying to give you something, when Line (I once thought him the kindest of the lot) stepped forward. "Aw, come on, Paul, give the lady what she came after." His voice nudged sharp as an elbow in me. There were only a few people in the Den—they were discreetly talking—but the boys all heard Line, they laughed, yet they were tense too; it was in the air, in the still, hard way they blew their cigarette smoke. I simply wanted to get out before the release. Somebody was out to destroy something, and nobody—I'm convinced of it—knew what it was. But they would go on, and I stood there.

"Yeah, what's the matter with you, Paul?" Eddie said. They all laughed again. At the other end of the bar, Dom, unaware of what was going on, smiled and waved to me.

And then Red seemed to come to—things were now going in the wrong direction. He turned on them. "Hey, fellas, *wait* a minute—" But they laughed again. Buff thumbed at him. "Millie's my sister," Red said.

"'f I had a lonely girl, wowee—" Buff said. Shamed now for Lettie, and angry, insulted, and feeling Red on my side, with a fast wild pulsing in me that struck my temples, coursed in my breathing, I said, "Then you *got* one, boy—go ahead, I dare you." I edged close and looked up at Buff, and then at the boys. "All of you," I said, grabbing Lettie's arm. "What the hell *would* you do? Well, here's your chance, you dart throwers, you goddamned strong-man clique. All talk and

no action. That's what you are—talk talk talk. For the next fifty
years that's all you'll do. No women and no life, just this cozy little
bunch of deadheads. Why the hell don't you do something *useful!*
Why?" And I shoved her forward. She knew what I was up to better
than I did, and for just a second a smile flickered over her face before
the fear set in it.

The stillness was deathly—in that brief interval before they
realized what the words meant in this unstudied vacuum I had set
them in, before Eddie's lightning fist plunged out and struck me in
the left shoulder, I saw Red in the mirror: he was staring into his own
image, dead still. His face had a raw, peeled-away look; his arms
hung, and his stomach sagged absolutely inert over his belt. *"Red—"*
I said, instantly ashamed, but he didn't move until I struck the bar
and rolled over and Buff jumped me and dragged me up again. *"Hold
it, Buff!"* Red shouted and leaped at him. The whole gang tensed,
ready for Red and me when Dom cried out, "What's the matter
with you guys!" probing his way down the aisle. He grabbed Buff's
shoulder. "Now let's cut it out! You wanta make trouble for me?"
Loosed, I sprawled against the wall. I thought it was over then, but
for Red, who gripped my jacket, his beety face thrust against my
chest. "Now you listen—" he said, realizing that I had set him against
his own crew. "You caused enough trouble. Now you get out. Leave
us alone, *alone*—you hear?"

"Red," I said. His action was the last thing I had expected, but
the boys began, at first with a sheepish softness, to back him: "You
tell him, Red."

"Alone!" Red shouted. *"Hear?"* And maybe I was the only one to
see his wet eyes and hear his hard breathing.

"Red, please—" But I knew it was futile, I could not ask what it
was that moved him—because I had exposed the boys? set the rift
deeper between him and Millie and me? told some truth about us all?

"Get out!" he cried. Not even Dom protested that.

I turned and went out, and Lettie followed. I heard her behind
me. I didn't look, I was standing on the street in front of the glass
window, between the letters c and a of the word DELICATESSEN spread
over the pane.

"I'm sorry, Lettie. That was a rotten thing for me to do."

"It was my fault. I shouldn't have come."

"No. It would have happened sooner or later. It was bound to come."

"I know that too," she said. "You had to learn it."

"Yes." And in that instant I could have taken her hand and told her I realized it now, but an interval is sometimes too late, and I heard her steps round the corner and then her car door slam and then the ignition.

After she had gone, I looked into the pane. Through my own image, a faint ghost of a man in the glass, the boys were gathering around the bar again. They took their glasses. From their midst Red looked my way. . . . For just a moment his face quivered, then froze— He stared at me and I at him as if we were caught in each other. If I reached through my own shadow I felt I might touch him. The pane was between us, but I'd got inside him and he inside me, and we couldn't get out. I was ringing with the discovery. And then he laughed, the way the defeated do under the guise of triumph, and he goaded the others—they all began to laugh, I could hear it through the fan vent. Laughs. Laughs. But the laughter didn't matter now. They were all alone. The laughter made them feel together. How multiple and subtle our treachery is. I didn't need them anymore— because I'd been one of the boys all the time. I was alone, like them, and Lettie, and Millie. *Millie*— I had to hurry back. She would be waiting. . . .

She was sitting at the kitchen table, and she asked the inevitable question: "Did you see Red?"

I gazed at her.

"Well?" The still way she looked up, I could tell she knew something had happened to me.

And I said, "Yes."

She waited, her vigilant eyes expectant.

"I stripped him," I said abruptly. "I *did*. I told them all what they were. I didn't mean to, Mill, but now . . . I'm glad." I looked out the window in the direction of Dom's—it was so far away in the darkness, but I felt closer to the boys than I ever had before.

"And I'm sorry for them, for everybody—because they're alone."

I heard her get up. And for the first time she touched me.

"I know," she said.

"You know?" I saw her beside me in the pane. She was smiling. And then I saw her night after night sitting alone in this apartment, I saw all the nights of her waiting for me, waiting for my confrontation with Red, with myself, knowing it would happen, trying to *make* it happen to free me, waiting alone while I pursued Red and myself.

And now she knew her waiting was over.

"Millie . . ."

She clutched me. I could feel her behind me, her hand against my neck, her arms slipped around my chest. There was nothing to separate us now. We were all the same, Red and Lettie and the boys and Millie. And I could feel her blood pulsing against me, and her touch, like that laughter, bridging the islands we are. Let us have this, I thought, covering her hands as I looked out into the darkness. And I could see our hands in the pane, I could see Lettie and Millie and Red and the boys, I could see them in my own eyes.

All the People I Never Had

(For Sue)

REMEMBER THIS:

In the front bedroom of that little Parisian hotel on the Rue des Capucines, Dannie Marouski took an empty whiskey bottle and broke it right there on the bidet at two o'clock in the morning and scraped the fine edge over his forearm, not even flinching from his own drunkenness or the sight of sudden blood. "There!" He held his arm out to me. Blood crawled straight down and dripped hot on my skin, scaring the living hell out of me. I was eighteen. I wondered what strange thing he could be at such an instant, what he was doing to let his blood drip on me like that, even if he *had* known me for all of six fast army months. The blood caught in the hair on my arm and dried. (I was awake half the night, touching to see if it was there, hard and crusted. Now and again a clot crumbled into dust under my fingers.)

"That's me right there—Dannie Marouski. Un'stan? I never been this close to anybody, see?" He was too drunk. He was always friendly when he was drunk, but never this friendly before. "If we get in trouble, you'll fight for me, hey?"

"You know it," I said. He didn't know that I was sick, but I couldn't keep it back. I felt gripped by a hand—white inside, then drained.

I had all I could do to drag him to bed, undress him, finally giving up with half his clothes on and rolling him onto the bed. But the spot of blood on my arm still felt so much like a burn that I had to turn the light on every once in a while to look at it, then at him, at his face all greasy in the light, dark and homely with thick nostrils, hairy at that, the same hair thick as shag on his brows and his straight animal lashes that had no fine shape to them. But the worst thing was the faint little ribbing at the corners of his mouth where the blood had dried after he'd sucked his arm, and the long stab-streaks dried on the pillow by his face that lay in the crook of his arm, in sleep.

When he woke up the next day and saw those streaks, then the broken bottle, he said he didn't remember any of last night.

But he would have extreme moments like that, though he would go for weeks with only the slightest word to anyone. "The quiet one," the men called Dannie—with respect, because they believed he was tough in every way. Sometimes I wanted to tell them the truth, but I knew only that something had happened in me, between us, and I didn't know what. Yet I sensed that when the discovery came, it would be as sudden as a flower grown right out of my chest, rooted so deep I could never get it out, and it would go on growing. Well, it did too.

For months after, whenever Marouski was lying in the upper bunk and I below, I wondered if he thought I understood or if he feared I'd tell the others about the morning in the hotel, unbidden. Anyway, Dannie was ashamed that he'd shown me something inside him, but it was the kind of shameful action you don't withdraw, even when you can, because you are perversely proud that you dared to go so far. It is a new kind of adventure.

Picture me now with Julia, lying every night in a different bunk, a floating-air mattress with no metal framework to hold onto. This bed is on wheels. Once—yes, let me tell you—once, after the war, when I was near pneumonia (I had been married only two months to Julia), I struck the wall and sent the bed sliding into the middle of the room, unmoored. And in my semi-delirium (but only semi, mind you), the bed spun very slowly, just enough so that the walls smeared in a slow circle with a kind of silent singing. All I could see was the light in the white ceiling. I went drifting far off, my arms swept up after the bulb and I could see them far ahead, they were elongated and the oversized fingers grappled for the light, but closed on themselves. Again and again I grasped, but it was futile. I was exhausted and terribly weak, and the longer I stared at the light the brighter it grew, it hurt. The whole ceiling was a white cloud. It came close, clearing, and in its center was Marouski staring out of the light, smiling, and then sad. A tear dropped out of his eye, slid down his face, and fell onto mine. I cried out, feeling it hot. Julia came running into the room.

"What *happened*, darling? What's wrong?"

I felt my face and held up the hand to show her.

"You're sweating," she said. I looked at the hand—it was damp, but not red. And when I looked up again, it was Julia's head, Marouski's was gone, and there was only a common light bulb and the same dismal crack in the plaster where the ceiling had begun to leak during the last storm. Then I slept.

It was the same kind of fitful sleep I had sometimes in England in the months following June *1944*, after the outfit had made its missions to Normandy, when you never knew whether the C-47s and then the glider pilots would make it back. If the barracks door struck to, if a siren sounded, if someone called from the latrine or the ablutions, you flicked your eyes open in complete awakeness, there would be the stark ceiling and all the beds empty as tombs waiting for the return of bodies that were roaming God-knows-where. I wasn't very often that alone in the barracks. Because there weren't enough clerks to fill a whole barracks, a few mechanics and radio operators—Anderson, Butts, Klein, Marouski, Simpkins—bunked in with us, next to the orderly room, nearest the line. So we heard all the sounds in the area before anyone else did.

That was how I knew Parks was back after the great drop over Bastogne. The last thing I could remember was the mass of gliders, the whole 436th, stark clear as a flight of doomed birds against the British sky, headed toward the Channel and the Bulge. They hovered in my head. In the stillness, with my eyes closed, the drone of the C-47s filled the silent barracks so loud that I expected the windows to break. But none of us had really had much continuous sleep since D-day months before. We knew why—it's better to go with them sometimes, better than waiting, which is more flagellating to the spirit than any physical pain is. So most of us slept little, wondering who would be first to come up the road on the return.

One by one they had begun to straggle back, however they could.

P. J. came in the middle of the night. I heard the door long before Ken Hummett had slipped from the officers' barracks into the enlisted men's to tell me Parks was back. P. J. was lying there in his bed next to Ken's, just lying in the dank British morning (the fire was out, the windows fogged), with his arms crossed under his head, and his eyes wide open staring at the ceiling. I stood for a minute beside the bed. He didn't even move his eyes, but I knew he saw me. I sat on the edge of the bed; then I saw his eyes were bloodshot—he was crying without sound. I knew that even if he saw me, he couldn't see me clear.

"Hello, P. J.," I said. For a second it registered. He loosed his hands and raised himself up on his elbows, but he looked out the window, not at me—as if the new sun had made the sound. Then his own sound crashed into the room: he cried out, jerked me close and flattened his head against my chest, his hand almost breaking my collarbone. "I killed, I killed," he cried, but when he realized what he was doing, he threw me away from him and stared incredibly at his hands as if *he* would dirty anything he touched, holding them away as if even *he* didn't want to be touched by his own hands.

"P. J.!" I said, but he didn't speak, just pulled out of his pocket a handful of white: "Here! I brought some lace—all the way from Brussels. For Julia."

"P. J.!" I cried, but I couldn't stop him: he threw it at me and ran out of the barracks. I followed to the door. He'd got on his bicycle and was riding wobbly down the path, black and small in the beginning sun. Ken started after him, but I grabbed him back angry.

"Let him be!" I said. At Ken's sudden embarrassment, I grew ashamed too. I was sorry. I was sorry I'd ever mentioned Brussels lace— *or* Julia. "He'll be all right," I added, knowing it wasn't quite true. I knew where I'd find Parks later. He would be out in the field next to the squadron Intelligence office. I'd find him lying in the haystack. Maybe he'd be asleep by then.

He knew that meadow. Often, long before D-day, I would come upon him standing in the open field, sloppy and out of uniform, a skinny man so shriveled up that he might be a shrub sapped by his own Arkansas droughts. No telling how long he would look out over the shorn fields where the shadows cut the furrows sharp as fleshless ribs. The haystacks were black against the sky, great dark dooms over the tired countryside. But P. J. didn't see it that way. I knew that, but not so well as I did one day when we went to town together. That late afternoon we walked past the field toward the gate, where we could hitch a ride, an officer and an enlisted man violating code of rank. The thing that always struck me about P. J. was that he seemed to be getting constantly thinner, skinny. There was a fire in him, and he seemed to be wasting away kindling his own flame. This day the fire glowed in him; even the dying sun raged in his eyes as he confronted me. Stand-

ing still, he said, "Look!" His arm went out like a crooked stick flung
at the field and all the land beyond and at the sun dying.

"You want to write, don't you? Well, what do *you* see? Go ahead.
Describe it."

I couldn't. P. J. stood there. He wasn't looking at me, he was looking
out over the fields into the sun. He waited. I couldn't speak. I was
humiliated. The terrible truth was I didn't even see the fields, only P. J.
as withered as my own talent dying inside me. I knew then he hadn't
expected any description. He was looking at me, and it wasn't even
P. J., it was some kind of vessel: he'd prisoned the whole scene in his
eyes and was holding it out to me, spilling it out to me to hold. There
was no word for it—didn't I see that? The sun was in his head and as
it slipped irretrievably over the brink, I wanted to walk into his head
too, to go with it, because I felt I would never see it whole again if I
didn't. But a jeep came down the road, and we hailed a ride in it.

It was Julia who first reminded me of that moment—when I finally
gave her the Brussels lace, after the war. You see, I'd never sent the lace
after all. I'd kept it sealed in an empty C-ration tin in my barracks bag.
Somehow it seemed wrong to entrust it to the mails.

Instinctively I knew when I mentioned the lace that we were going
to have an argument—on my second day home from service, too. Oh, I
hadn't been discharged, but I would be soon. V-J day had just been de-
clared, and since I was in the high-point bracket, I would be discharged
in the first group. I hadn't quite gotten over the terrible joy of V-J day
—to know war was over, to know I could have Julia and a home, settle
into a lifetime job. . . . But it was a depressing thrill too, because there
were the buddies you wouldn't see again, the change in routine, and
before Julia, the house, and a good job, would come college, studying,
struggle as usual—

The struggle started with the lace, at our first celebration in public.
The initial twenty-four hours we spent sleepless, lying on the Newport
beach nine miles away. But we had to let people "see" us, so we'd gone
to the yacht club for a drink before driving out to dinner. Rustic, almost deliberately shoddy, but with a belyingly well-kept dance floor and
a cozy bar off the club: smalltown New England yacht clubs are like
that. From the bar you see across the bay past those tiny islands to the
Point, which drives a wedge of land into the bay towards Newport. For

August the water looked raw, and because we were inside, the whitecaps seemed icy. The few boats (fuel was at a premium) looked helpless trying to make headway to the island beyond.

Julia was heady on two martinis. From the minute we'd seen each other two days before, there was a tense excitement in each of us that hadn't run off its electricity. To me it was emphasized in her legs— they are long and wild-looking and she uses them wildly, in quick movements from which you can almost hear a kind of static that drives right up through her and climaxes in her laughter.

She laughed. It filled the bar. No one minded. We had chatted all over the place. They knew what we were up to. Even in that crowd they were discreet in the usual open way—everybody taking part, but nobody dousing us with himself. The radio murmured over the bar "Long ago and far away. . . ." Julia's fingers played the rhythm at the back of my neck, keeping lazy time.

I reached back and captured her hand.

"Let's go for a drive before dinner, hmmm?"

She laughed and ran her hand inside my jacket, along my chest.

"Why? Have you got something for me, poor darling?" She crinkled her forehead, pursed her lips in a tease, mingling genuine sympathy with anxiety over all our waiting, all the time that was gone, simply unaccounted for.

"Yes," I said, and her mood changed, deepening, when she caught, as she always did, the least change of tone in me, despite her sometimes disguising the discovery.

"You . . . You *have.*" She drew back and eyed me circumspectly. "You really have, don't you?"

I'd already given her all the war souvenirs I'd collected, and for a minute she looked puzzled, pertly lip-biting, before her eyes fixed in revelational stillness on me.

"Oh. . . ," she said. "Why, it's the lace, isn't it?"

"Yes."

"Of course—the lace." She bit the words. They sounded chipped.

"Jule," I said, "let's go for that drive."

"Of course, baby. We agreed we would, didn't we? But aren't you going to give me my lace?" A kind of croon came into her voice. She touched my chin with her lips. "Hmmm?"

"Yes."

"Well?"

"Not here, Jule."

"Why not? It's not an engagement ring, you know."

"I know that, but—"

"But what?"

"I don't know, it doesn't seem right, somehow."

"Oh?"

"Well, you know what I mean."

"Do I?"

"Well, don't you?"

"I'm not a mind reader. You know better than that. Besides, it's only a little piece of lace, isn't it! What's so difficult about that?"

"It's *not* only a piece of lace. Well, it is, but it's more than that."

"Is that why you wouldn't send it through the mail—because it's so . . . so valuable?"

"Damn! It's *not* valuable."

"Then why've we got to go through a private ritual over a piece of lace?"

"It's just . . . I mean, you have no idea what P. J. went through to get this lace, that's all."

"And exactly what *did* he go through?"

"I don't know myself."

"There!"

"Well, I've got a damned good idea. I just don't know for *sure.*"

"Oh, for heaven's sake, why all the fuss then?" Her eyes stilled, pensively. "Are you sure that's the reason?"

"And what does *that* mean?"

"Maybe you didn't send it because you didn't want me to have it."

"But I do want you to have it!"

"You'd have sent it then. You must have had a reason for keeping it."

"What would *I* do with it?"

"It isn't what you'd do with it, it's that you wouldn't let it go because . . ."

"Well?"

"Because it was his, and it would be like letting *him* go."

"*Look,* Julia—"

"Don't you *dare* speak to me in that tone of voice!" She reeled up, nodding precariously. She was trembling.

"Why, it's the silliest thing I ever heard," I said. "You're jealous."

"*Yes!*—of all that out there, all those months yours and not mine," she said, unsteeled.

"Julia, everybody's watching. Come onnn, honey."

"Don't you *come onnn, honey* me!" Her hand went up to her hair, she touched out to the window and stared through her fingers toward the islands beyond.

"Baby, come on— We'll take that ride," I said.

"You. You can take it alone."

"You mean that?"

"*Yes.* I—mean—that."

"All right then—" I felt like a fool leaving the bar. I'd seen it done this way a hundred times, but I felt more like a fool than I'd have believed. My self-conscious footsteps sounded almost like myself following myself, the loneliest sound I ever heard. I got almost out of the building when the bar door opened.

"Hon . . . ? *Hon!*" she said.

I turned around. She was there, swaying a little, her arms loose, her hands without anything in them, so alone and lost and needed. Then she moved.

"Don't ever do that," she whispered. "Please don't." And we stood there against each other until I realized I was holding her off the floor, I could see her wild legs dangling and her toes wriggling to keep her shoes on.

Yet at the moment of that very closeness it was as if she had disappeared, or were dead or dying. Even when we unlocked each other and went for the drive, in a silence I could never explain to her, I could not separate her toes from the dead. I could see her toes—only they were not wriggling, they were twitching like something you know is dead, but that won't stop dying in front of you.

You see, they were Tony's toes I was staring at. I was holding him in my arms, and he was dying, and I could feel his breath in quick tongues of heat just under my chin.

I didn't even know how long I was lying there, only that I had fallen right where I was when I heard the German convoy come around the hill. My face was almost flattened into a puddle, facing away from the road. There were dead everywhere. Maybe the Germans would think I was dead too. I didn't know exactly where Tony was, I didn't even think of it. The only thing I felt was the thunder of vehicles trembling the ground under me. I thought it would never stop. Once I heard a terrible cry, but I didn't know what it was. For a while the wheels stopped, there were confused voices, the running of feet, then a dull quiet, broken by voices and laughs before the motors started again. Then there wasn't any time, just sounds going on and the pain in my throat from constricting it to slow my breathing. . . .

When I thought they were gone, I opened my one eye that was not flat in the mud. I was staring into the puddle; there was an insect there, like a fly, and for a minute I thought I was somewhere else because it was too cold for flies. With the drone of the engines gone, it was too quiet, but then I heard it again—one lone drone. Was it the end man to the convoy? It went. Then it broke again—a cry this time. I jerked my head up, I couldn't help it. The Germans *were* gone. I heard the cry again. I got up and ran. About a hundred yards away was Tony. He must have dropped right where he was when the cry to take cover had come. He was lying face down, moaning. Something had run over his body and his left arm. His right arm flailed, and his feet kept twitching, his eyes were open, they saw me without knowing me. I kept saying "Tony," but he didn't answer, just moaned, letting out that awful cry without words. Why hadn't the Germans killed him outright? I couldn't understand—unless it was a trap. But I didn't care at that moment, only that it was Tony, like all my life—all our town, our growing up, our high school days, my own self in him. And he was dying. "Tone?" I kept saying. His eyes were wild with seeking, but he couldn't find me. His hand touched, it went all over me. I turned him over—I had to— despite his crying out. "Tone, it's me—" He was trying to talk, and I didn't know how he could stand the pain. I raised his head close to me. "Tone—it's me." I said it in his ear, and his arm was on me, his hand against my chin, and then in one sudden choking whisper his breath was all over my face, he said, "Don't cry. Please don't cry, Julia." *Julia!* And his hand was on my neck, it crept behind my head, and he went on brokenly, "Julia, Ju—lia . . . ," and with his one arm he drew himself up, incredibly. "Kiss me," he said.

"Tony . . . ?" I said. Beyond, the others were coming now, out of the woods, across the gullies. "Tony, I'm here. Tony . . . It's Julia," and as fast as I spoke, his arm clutched hard on my neck, and I drew his head up, and bent over and kissed him.

In a few minutes he was dead. Two of the men were running now. Up ahead they were gathering again by the side of the road.

Someone made a marker for the medics. Then we were ready to move out.

I have never told Julia all this— Maybe she'll read it someday. Stumbling on this, perhaps she will feel the same indescribable closeness I felt for her at that moment when I learned how distant we had been from one another without my knowing it, with Tony between us, and perhaps we will have gone over that bridge which must sometimes be crossed in silence before we turn and really see each other in a final understanding closer than flesh. Then she will come close to Tony— because I am appalled that Tony is not finally dead. For, once in a while when she kisses me, I am fixed with an inner shock which must register on my face, because she looks at me strangely.

"What's wrong, darling? *Darling. . . ?*"

And her lips—I stare at them, I have to touch them with my fingers. "Your lips . . ."

"Well?" She laughs, but in her tone there is a quiet probing.

"They're so warm."

And between us there is a sudden perilous chasm. I have seen it before so clearly as if the hardwood floors had split asunder, the house divided, and I was hopelessly reaching for her across the imaginary divide. At such moments no physical intimacy can cement the distance. Time itself is suspended just as in maximum sexual closeness it is suspended—an observation to which she always replies "Moments of closeness have nothing to do with the body. You know that."

But she is simply echoing, in my head, words which she could not possibly know the source of—fortunately! I say fortunately because she always disliked Liz Walham, even in those days when she and Tony and Liz and I were in school together. "High school slut!" That's what the town did call her then. But there were Liz's words: "You're in me, but you're not even close to me." How did *I* know what Liz meant? And now I wonder how she, just a girl, could have known then what she did about life. When we were freshmen, Lyle Talbot made me do it—not of his own will, of course, but he said he'd had Liz. He talked of nothing else, but I knew it had been his first time—he wasn't fooling me. Actually I suppose he was trying to share her with me; he shared everything else with me, but I knew only that we were buddies and I had to be close to him. I was robbing myself of something, he said. How could I know what it was until I tried? So he drove me to it by goading. What's more—I wanted him to. Curiosity, desire and fear all mingled.

"She's coming down the street now," he said and went out the back door. I went to the front window, rapped with my ring, she waved, then I ran around to the front door.

"Liz!"

She stopped. My anxiety must have been all over me, because she laughed.

"Come in," I said.

She came in. I don't even remember how I managed—or maybe Liz managed it—but we were lying on the kitchen floor because we were afraid to lie on anything telling, her panties down around her ankles and her dress up and crushed between us, and she saying all at once those words: "You're not even close. You're in me, but you're not even close to me," first laughing, then serious, her arms, mouth and legs all suddenly swallowing me too fast, dragging me all down into her and me quivering and gasping with the wonder of it all over so soon.

And it was after, when I was with bragging Lyle, that he stopped talking about it, because he looked at me and he knew. That seemed to satisfy him. After that, I would forget most things about her, except that I'd had her and didn't have her at all. And one other thing: the picture of that girl, not even that girl, just a girl, running down Main Street, getting smaller and smaller, going away from me, until she disappears where the tree limbs meet the sidewalk and she is lost in the anonymous, repetitive pattern where no one thing can be discerned. And when I saw her running that way I didn't want her to go, I was afraid for her, I wanted to tell her to watch out, she might be caught somehow. But nothing came out of my mouth. I stood watching her run, and I admired her strong legs and her speed and the don't-give-a-damn run of her she went deeper and deeper into the web of trees and sky and sidewalk and disappeared.

During the war years she fared well. She had everything other girls didn't have. I sometimes see her now—drifting through a downtown store, occasionally walking through the neighborhood with her three children whom she is simply too sluggish to keep up with. Though she is still attractive (she married comfortably enough, an auditor at that), there is about her a hangdog look, as if she were skulking somehow, not before the eyes of neighbors who know she still has "friends" when the children are at school, but before something that is following her and which is useless to run from. And once—just once—I thought I recognized the lost Liz in her:

She was standing at the Rexall Drug counter. She took out her mirror and stared into it for a moment with growing surprise—like catching something familiar—and then her eyes fled to the wall with a bleak, hunting look as if all had escaped her and she would find it there. I felt like an intruder into some inviolable trust. I turned and went out the rear exit.

I had been mistaken to expect, let alone to look for, the Liz I once knew—because the truth is that the woman is a stranger to me and has no connection with the girl Liz. And I wonder if she has lost the girl somewhere in that jungle she has lived. I want to tell her that the old Liz is really still alive, but I can only hold the girl inside me and offer herself to her, hopelessly. Although I could never put my hand on her flesh as I did that afternoon on the floor, I am closer now than touching—

Yet when I actually do reach over now, it is Julia whom I touch, lying there close to me night after night, her breathing muffled in the pillow, her flesh slack under my touch (she is in her mid-thirties, but she shows the shape of her mother, it begins to come). Even touching her, I feel she is too far away from me, and I am appalled when I look at her and think "Who are you, Julia?" Besides, other people crowd in —Marouski, P. J., Liz, Tony, all the rest; they harry Julia out of the present, standing between us. And they are all alive and real, I am so close to them, I have them more intimately in my head than Julia is in my hand, and I want to break through, to pour them all into her too, to share them. And I am P. J. at that moment—I know it now—holding all that in me and wanting to pour it out. I want to turn to him too to tell him I have him here, in me. But I know now: you have to die with all the knowing. It harries like a nightmare—that is how it always is.

Listen— Last night it was dark—I don't know the hour, but you know how it is in the middle of the night, totally dark, and when you awaken the darkness is so sudden, and the light from the street comes in like a shriek. Well, I woke up in that. I was staring down at my feet. The

branches of the trees lay in a web over the bed; it quivered, like growing. Outside, the wind was raging. I could see the shoots flattened
against the trunks like hairs on great legs. The wind slapped out a
persistent, blunted message.

I got up and went to my son's bed. The web quivered over him so
that he seemed hidden under the strange design. I bent over him. In
the protective darkness of my shadow I thought he slept peacefully.
Yet I put on the bed lamp. Yes, he was sleeping evenly, his hand thrust
up under his head. Julia woke up and mumbled:

"Bennie wake you?"

"No." I pulled the window shade down, then put out the light. The
branches plunged back in a network of nerves on the shade.

I got back into bed. Julia rolled close, warm and cuddling. And she
said the words I want always to say to her:

"Darling, don't ever leave me—please."

"No, never," I always say. And I feel an overwhelming love for her, I
want to draw her close, closer than flesh, I want to hold her and Bennie
forever in me, safe, secure, and permanent. But more: Now I know what
it is to be had. All the people I never had reach out through me to
her. They are all in me now. The whole world soars through me, in the
blood of me. I want her to feel it. I hold it out, a whole ocean in my
hands. But I can't hold it long. "Julia!" I whisper. She stirs. Perhaps for
an instant I can make her see. But even as I near the gulf, I know I am
like Marouski and Tony, Liz, and P. J. forever holding out the sun, I
know I am doomed like them to stand forever here on the brink of
giving, because there are no words to tell it— And I want to escape this
doom. I must try. I must have my reprieve from isolation. "Julia," I
whisper. And as I draw her close, my own voice harries me: Remember,
it says, this escape is only a reprieve. Remember this. But I must try.
And I draw her close. "Julia . . . ?" She stirs, holding me, and I kiss
her, and her lips are soft and warm and full of life.

The Moment of Fish

(For Molly Daugherty)

IN THE WATER, just under the surface, between shreds of seaweed, he
saw the eyes. Slowly they came closer. He had an irrepressible instinct
to move forward, reach at the precise moment and clutch— He sank
his face underwater, nearing the thing. His hand rose. But even as he
moved, thinking, I'm *in* the dream, I *know* I'm inside Will's dream,
he saw it was *Tim's* face, and he reached. . . .

The sound of stones chafing deep in his ear woke him. His eyes
flicked open—painfully, for the sun overhead seared. "Loretta?" He
rolled over. The stones scalded, a smother of heat under his face. His
whole body wrenched—his bones scraped like stones. "Achhhh." Will
and two other boys were digging in the sand. But *she* was there. He
had got her to the beach at last. He must do, say, nothing to destroy
her afternoon.

"Webb—what?" she said.

"Nothing. Half-dozing," he said, feeling sweated out, dehydrated
to the bone, as if, crumbling, he would filter into the sand. He could
not seem to remember a time when he did *not* dream it.

"Will?" he called. *"Now* what? I've tried forty-eleven times to nap.
And your mother too."

"Centipede," Will said, without glancing up. All three boys kept
digging.

"Centipede!" His flesh prickled everywhere, his scalp—not, evi-
dently, dehydrated. And scarcely a breeze. The barest lap. Quickly, to
confirm where he was—on the real beach—his eyes scaled the low sand
cliffs, over the miraculously white stones, then sand, then the infinite
deep—too blue—and a sky, air, so clear you could see the Connecticut

shore as if it had drifted miles closer overnight. Such clarity of vision pleased him. Sometimes the mists and fog hanging low over the Sound were so close and impenetrable you couldn't believe there was water or land or anything out there, beyond. Turning, he watched Will and the boys. He smiled. Me. Five more years of me. Six, with the womb. The thought eased him. Someday Will would be staring across at the same shore—himself extended, another three score and ten.

"What's he *doing?*" Loretta said. She was lying under the umbrella, balled on her side, straps loose, her hair flared—like a sea thing crawled up on a dark rock. Her back was turned toward the Sound.

"Weren't you sleeping? I thought you were." For her breathing had become so regular, a good sound. The day at the beach was the right thing, the time was right. She couldn't stay away from it forever. He'd let it go long enough as it was. And she loved swimming—but that would come later, slowly.

"Sleeping?" Something incredulous came through. He did not pursue it. Rest. Let her.

"Are you watching him? You promised—" she added.

"The boys are with him. And I've half an eye out most of the time."

"Half an eye!" She sat up. So thin now, she might have been sea grass thrust up miraculously straight. Her hair fell gossamer in the sun. Her eyes avoided the water.

"Retta, there's no *need*. Darling?"

"No. You're right." She sank back down, but her voice was resigned and tense. He reached over and touched her arm. She jerked, then laughed—"Oh, you! I thought it was a bug"—but let her arm sink into his palm. For an instant he drove the dream back, gave way to the feel of her, succumbed to the warmth, the myriad sounds he almost willed himself into, not simply the hush of waves, the nearly windless brush of wind chafing grains of sand near his ear, but the whisper more faint than a sigh of some infinitesimal thing close—a spider, a flea, an earwig—and, too, sometimes up from the water, crossing the line between sea and beach, the sound of a thing striking stone. And he felt himself slip under. Far ahead, deep, he saw the thing moving toward him. He swam under, down, toward it—

"*Dad*—"

He opened his eyes, taut. "What the—!" he cried, already squirming at the centipede Will dropped on him as he cried, "I caught it!" Relieved, he laughed, but with discomfort—not so much at the centipede, but because, standing over him, Will looked so big, deep into the sky, his head thrown back as if receded—like his own balding skull—but mostly the eyes and teeth were so strange in the blue sky, the mouth talking upside down. It took his orientation away, set the world askew, the dream spilled over into the blue sky, the—

"You ready, Dad? You said we could go"—he glanced toward his mother and dropped his voice the way he did whenever he mentioned *Uncle Tim*—"back there—" Beyond, up the embankment overgrown with sea grass, wild roses and sweetpea, to the pond cut off from the Sound. . . .

"Yes, but—" He glanced at Retta. He hated to break the ritual. For all his life he had gone there. He loved traipsing the flats, where the bank was a fine, dark, slippery mud, with holes traversed by fiddler crabs, a motionless edge of scud laden with brown and green seaweed, but in spite of scud, so still was the water that, if they stared, a hundred other forms crept into the eye. There were insects everywhere, sudden darts of waterflies, the still motion of dragonflies, and occasionally even a hummingbird whisked over.

"There's bound to be lots of new things since the storm. Come onnnn, Dad."

He stood up, peering over the ridge: the pond *was* high. When the Sound crashed over in storm, it always filled. He did not *want* to say no; he knew if he did, out it would come: Uncle *Tim* would! For Will had taken to going with Tim. He yearned to go with the boy, but he said, "I'll stay with your mother. You go—with the boys. But be careful. And remember—you don't swim in that water, you know."

"Sure! Heyyyy—Andy, Ralph! Come on. I kin go." He leaped, kicking up sand, and raced over the mound.

"Webb!" Retta said, rising, a chalky scrape in her voice.

"*Hon*—" he said, with the least impatience, instantly ashamed. "Look, he's fine. It's just the pond."

"Just. . . ." But she sank down—as he did. The sea slowly drifted up into the sky, washed over. He couldn't hold it out. For a time, though, even he could not look at the water without seeing Tim and Russ struggling toward one another, just as he had seen it in her eyes when at last she could tell it—for she had lost her voice, couldn't speak, for days after—but when she did, she stared through him and poured it out in all her terror and anxiety to say it clear, get it out one time:

"I *saw* them. The boat capsized. The tide was turning, the Gut was beginning to churn, whitecaps everywhere. They'd built the boat themselves. They were trying it out, it was the *first* time! Tim called *Russ,* Russ was swimming toward shore where I was, but he turned and started back when Tim called. Then Tim went under—I could see everything—and Russ went under after Tim. He came up, but *no* Tim, and then went under again, but didn't come up—gone, both gone. I called and called—and one time I saw a head, I don't know whose. Then I ran up to the lighthouse. The old man was there, the two sailors were in New London on leave. 'Get the boat out—quick,' I said, but he said he couldn't in that tide. He *couldn't*. I shouted at him, 'Couldn't row a boat in that? I'm a woman and *I* could.' But he wouldn't. He went to call the Coast Guard and I said, *'I* will, then.' And I ran down to the shore. Russ and Tim were nowhere in sight, gone, nothing. I pushed and pushed. I finally got the boat into the water. The Coast Guard cutter came around the point when I was crawling into the boat—"

They were never found, sucked under and out to sea by the current no doubt. But a woman wants to see them through to the end, buried, finalized, in the family place. Until then, they were somewhere, going on, maybe not dead, might one day walk into the yard, enter the house. . . . And she would not, *not,* go near the water, even driving would not look up, but turn her eyes into the pines, the potato fields, deep into the towns they passed through. It hurt her when it rained—especially stormed—and the water came down heavy and lay long in pools, occasionally flooded the yard. She did not want to step out into it. It was then the sea came nearest, her eyes forlorn, themselves the ocean. And then he too feared Tim and Russ, held in her, haunting him. Then she would say a thing, implying *They might come, do you suppose?*—out of the water, out of some town, walk up and come back—*You must stop! Loretta, stop!* he wanted to say. But his heart swelled, words died. He knew: she needed time, time. He had to help, to work toward the moment when her eyes would soften, her lips relax, the scowl thin out smooth, and the tense moves of her body with its sudden wiriness ease into her old fluidity. Too long it had taken her away from him and Will.

"Hey, Will, wait up!" It was one of the boys—Andy. He stopped

at the crest on the mound. "We can't go. We have to go home. S'long."
He charged down, back. Beyond, toward Southold, the beach was nearly
empty. A car gleamed on the ramp far off.

"*Go* with him," Retta said. "Please. You want to. I know you."

He laughed. "Sure you do. Who better?" He kissed her shoulder.
"Back in a while. You—" But why say it? She knew. Perhaps alone,
little by little, she would turn and face the Sound, let it come back into
her eyes, and reckon with it. Besides, the more he went with Will, the
less the boy might think about Tim. There had been those moments—
"Ma, kin I go clamming with Uncle Tim?" "When's Uncle Tim coming,
Ma?" "Uncle Tim said he'd take me to Mill Pond"—moments when,
watching his life go off with Tim, he felt *he* was the uncle, Tim the
father. Tim was always in and out of the house, like the breeze off the
Sound, felt, vibrating everything with his kind tolerance, the broad
deep-down laughter that somehow cleaned through the house, a happy-
go-lucky sailor walk about him as if he met the very shape of earth on
its own terms. "Tim's coming, Will," she'd say. And how she warmed
to him! They'd always been so close. In her strawberry blond hair he
could see Tim's—her pride. It bound them. Not so with Russ: the quiet,
judicious sage of the family—like a father. Respect, not love, she had
for him. Still, they were her brothers. . . .

"Look, Dad!" Abruptly the pond came into view, a still blaze of
blue sky caught in the earth. It spread deep to the woods' edge, bushes
and trees coiled around, with an open end of sand. There, and in the
potato fields beyond, were moles, rats; now and then a black snake
slithered through, and birds were everywhere. Gulls never came. Groups
of them lingered on the beach, where the bait was live and picnic
throwaways lay naked to view. Will charged down, like himself almost
thirty years before.

"You don't even *see*, Dad!" He was squatted, his hands balled one
behind the other to make a telescope.

"What?" He too squatted and imitated Will's telescope.

"Way over there, near the woods, in the deep grass. . . . See them?"
Two—swans! "Well, I'll *be!*"

"*Seven* of them." Yes—there were five tiny gray ones, floating
easefully between, protected.

"So *that's* why you couldn't wait. In all my years I never saw one
swan here." He watched the serene white move with miraculous still-

ness in the reflected sky. "I suppose we should keep our distance," he said. "Let them have their private place."

"Uncle Tim said they'd come. I got to *tell* him."

"Will! Now you stop that—you know what I told you—especially in front of your mother. You know how it hurts her. She's not over it yet."

"I don't have to tell *her*. She knows. Sometimes she's there too."

"Where?" But he knew: in the dream she was standing on the edge, waiting—

"With us, at the water." He walked into the pond—into the green-brown seaweed and scud.

"Now *Will*—" But he glanced quickly (where was he?) to verify—this day, the serene untouchable blue sky, the thick darkest green trees, sea grass and wild roses and the pond laced with scud—*not* the Sound.

"Well, she *was*. And Uncle Tim too. I was with them. So there!"

"But that's gone, son." He held his voice still. Yet he saw the water, deep, and the thing floating under— It was beginning. . . .

"It's not either. I saw Uncle Tim last night. He called me. And I knew where he was. Only *she* didn't." He bent over the water, peering under, lowering his face and cupping his hands over his eyes.

"Will!" His blood seemed to still, all the sounds go, his vision close in—as if his head were under. In a minute the eyes would come up close, he would see. . . .

"And I thought it was a fish, and stuck my face under and opened my eyes, but it was Uncle Tim, and I reached—." Will moved in up to his waist. The surface broke, scud drifted.

"Will!" He was suddenly wet, prickled with perspiration. *I'm dreaming Will's dream*— "Come out of that water!"

"No. I got to find—"

"Will!"

"I *like* it—it's warm."

"You heard your mother."

"She said it was okay if *you* came."

"Well, it's *not* okay. The pond's filthy. Out!"

"I won't. I'll tell Uncle Tim."

"Stop that! You won't tell *anyone*. You can't." He stepped into the seaweed. Slippery silt drove between his toes. He tried to hold down his blood—it beat, the water pulsed with it. "Come on, now—please."

But Will dodged away. "You don't *want* me to find Uncle Tim. You *don't!*" He scurried up the sand. "I don't care. I will! I will!" he cried and disappeared over the crest.

He leaped after Will up the slope, but stopped, suddenly weary, as Will ran straight down toward his mother. The boy half-dived into the sand and slid, as she turned over.

"Will. For heaven's sake!" she said clearly.

He stood looking beyond them for a moment—at that span of familiar shore he had known all his life, as his father had, and his, and his before him. It lay in his blood, like the whole Sound beyond. Even the great monolithic boulders which dotted the shore, for so many years fixed in his vision, seemed to have been deposited there by a self older than time. But now they struck as impediments; they marred the view, obstacles breaking the perfection of that clean slim line of coast between heaven and earth. And he wanted to reach out, push the boulders back into the sea out of sight, turn his back on all that, return to the house. But he knew—it would all come back. Nights, as always, he would hear it ebb and flow in his blood, a soft never-ceasing hush in him. But now, when he closed his eyes, he still saw it, only he was not sure, never sure now, because it was always *Will, Will* on his mind. When the sea came close and he looked into it, he saw the eyes of fish staring up at him. They stared across at one another, motionless, the eyes primordially familiar. And then he moved toward the water, and he felt so close to something, felt with joyous terror an instinct to cross *into,* and when he moved— Miraculously he knew he was in Will's dream—could he get out?—and the terror and the joy doubled, that he was so close. How far into it could he go? He stood on the verge—

But Will—what would *he* do if he thought Tim was there? Where would it lead? My son, mine, he thought. Me. His heart caught, a fine net of pain.

"You go wash that muck off you—right now, young man," Retta said. Seeing him approach, Will was quick to respond—raced over the gleaming white stones toward the water.

"What'd you *do* to him?" she said.

"What'd *I* do!" He plunged down on his knees beside her. "It never occurs to you—"

"Well, you needn't shout. I asked a simple question." She was piquant, but her eyes, fragmented into a green web by the sun, half-smiled understandingly, though they were tired, the weariness of the past weeks dark under them.

"Sorry, Retta. Things—I shouldn't let them, I know—get to me lately."

"You mean *that,* don't you?" Her gaze fled with the swallows fluttering from their holes in the cliff.

"The drowning, yes."

Her head wrenched, her eyes fixed on him in quick pain, but stayed. "Yes, we ought. I need—to hear it, don't I? But must you?"

"Yes—and now, Retta."

"Now? Why now?" But she turned quickly—after Will. "Him. Yes, we must think of him. Children live in another world. They're perfectly capable of—" But she didn't know. Her hands rose and fell.

"Not only children. And it's not where they live, it's how deeply."

"I *told* you," she said. "You think I don't know, but I do—because he's yours, he's you, Webb. Do you think all these nights I don't see *you* there, no matter what he does?" Yet he could not tell her: where Will lives, thinks, feels. For an instant the air felt too heavy on his flesh, flowed like blue water down between them. He wanted to touch and fix her in it and tell her, but there were no words. There are distances you can't explain, you want to go toward them, you have to stop at the skin and wait. Is that *mind*—seeing beyond, but waiting? "But Will's only a child," he said, yet there are intuitions beyond all knowledge, deeps that defy adulthood. Still, you have to live *this* life, now; you *have* to—

"Will?" she cried, rising suddenly with a wide look, blunted by the sight of what she had refused to look upon. The Sound grew enormous in her eyes; he felt he would lose himself in it. "Will—! Webb, where *is* he?" For there was no one, nothing, not a trace— On the ramp the car was gone. Silence. Only the gulls. She started down the beach. "Will!" Running, he passed her. "Behind the rocks?" she cried. But he wasn't, nor—quickly—up the bluffs; they were too far. "Webb!" she cried, desperate, pressing her hands against her temples, worse than a scream: I can't hold it all, not that. But he was studying, scouring the water, the great Cat Rock the kids always dived from, the myriad boulders barely emerging from the water in the incoming tide.

"There!" he shouted. The little body came slowly to the surface, face down, easing up toward the sand. He was crawling underwater, drawn to the water's edge like a strange fish that had developed arms, raised its head, gasping for air, and hoisted itself up onto the sand. But there too was a skate, an enormous white phantom fluttering its great winged fins. The tail slid off the stones and deeper down; all of it slipped into the dark beyond the ledge. Instantly he was hauling Will up, and instantly she was beside him, crying out, "Will, what *happened?*"

"You said wash off the muck, didn't you?"

"Did you *have* to go under like that? You frightened us to death. I ought to—" Her lip tremored, water sprang to her eyes, she took his arm.

"Well, how could I get it all off? Besides, I *like* to!"

"Didn't you see that skate, young man?" He glanced into the water: it was clear, and all dark beyond.

"Yes!" He tore his arm free from Retta and lunged a few steps ahead.

"Do you know what the spines on a tail like that could do to you?"

"Yes. But it wouldn't. I didn't *do* anything to it. And it saw me. I looked right in its eyes. It was all white and still, and it didn't even move once. I swam all around. I know everything down there. So there!"

"Will, don't you dare talk to your father that way! Oh, *Webb.*"

And *he* wanted to shake Will, shake but embrace him too—me, mine, don't *do* that to us, son—and suddenly grateful too, suddenly still: because Retta had her feet in the water, she was standing in the Sound. . . . She raised her eyes to the shore beyond. "It's all right, Rett." He dared to smile for a moment as she looked at him, holding the ocean up to him with infinite understanding.

She tried to smile too, but said, "*I'll* come with him tomorrow."

"I'll get the things together. You go on, with him," he said to her. "Will!" he cried, but the boy was far along, headed toward the path through the woods to the house, alone, trying to walk upright in the pliant sand. He felt suddenly the weight of the boy in his arms, catching again the sight of his eyes, *mine,* knowing he had to let him go, but fearful. For a second he cast a quick last look into the water, all clear, and then dark beyond, where Will had been swimming, farther than he himself had ever known.

The Deepest Chamber

LET THIS dying summer end. The air is hot and thick with the stale smell of fallen roses, and pine and salt, and the rot of plants dead in the ground. The temperature is in the eighties. Nobody budges. There is a stillness such as death alone should hold. It is broken only by the water that pours from Mill Creek under this stone bridge, toward the bay.

An anvil rings clear as a bell, a single strike in the still air—one of the kids playing in old Timeo's shop there across the road. The shop is deep under the old oaks, an old room attached to the great house where Timeo still lives with his daughter Mona and three sons (Antone, Matt, and Filipo) and Antone's wife. But—make no mistake—there is no blacksmith shop now. That went out with the times. Timeo himself has a little trade as a barber, not much, enough to keep him in cronies and to keep his arms and legs moving, to make him feel useful.

It must be Matt's day off. He is arranging equipment—maybe going crabbing in the shallows, for the hand nets are out and the oars. The rowboat is moored by the jetty, near Mona.

"Hey!" Mona hears my yell and answers, "Hi, Eddie!" with a demonstrative dive into the water, then climbs back up onto the piling, and sits smiling. With her long, gangly limbs and her long black hair straight about her face, she has a strange other-world, almost ghoulish look. She draws her thin, bony legs up at a funny grasshopper angle and looks distantly over her knees at me.

She has come to expect me. Everyday at the same time I come up the road—for exercise, to get out of my grandfather's sickroom. I hate to leave him (my mother and I live in constant fear of his dying at any minute), but I am still weak, sometimes a little ill, but mostly it is merely rest that I need and this little daily walk outside in the sun. One day I stopped here at the bridge. Now it is my regular daily aim to come and sit, stare into the water, talk to Mona or old Timeo. Soon I shall be strong enough to go back to the university to undertake the strenuous teaching load. But now nothing is more pleasant than establishing that quiet equilibrium that comes with merging quite comfortably into the mindless nature of things.

I stand lazy on the bridge. Heat comes up visibly from the pavement, and from above, it presses like a soft muggy hand. The sound of water lulls. Below, it is one silver glide, slipping over moss-green rocks, gently tearing at pieces of fast-clutching seaweed, and flows into a wider stream, then rounds the bend into the deeps toward the sea.

"Tom!"

I raise my eyes. Someone has called—my grandfather's name. But Mona is still sitting there engrossed in the water. Beyond, on the far side of the creek, is nothing but a gossamer mist doubling the distance of the bank. Yet I am sure I heard a girl's voice. "Tom!" Yes, louder this time, and frightened. *"Tom!"* I scan. . . . Yes—in the water, near where Mona is perched, there is a girl—struggling.

"Mona!" I shout, pointing.

She waves back at me.

"No, no!" I cry. She laughs and dives into the water—but she passes the girl!

And there *is* a girl there. Her hands strike the water violently. Her head and body (she has a white dress on) bob and dip. The water sucks her away from Mona.

"Mona!" But why am I calling Mona? She doesn't hear, she swims back, she ignores my frantic gesticulations.

And Matt waves too.

"No, *no!*" I cry to him. And the girl—she is drawn down; I see her moving towards me, beseeching me, her arm half out of the water, clutching. It sinks. . . . She is drifting toward me. I can't believe I see it. But there, below! She drifts under this bridge. My God! I cross the road— She comes slowly out of the dark tunnel into the stream, just below the surface, catching the light.

"Angela!" I shout at her. Something in me wants to leap after her. But I cannot move. I stand rooted. Incredible! Even my hand refuses motion. I would swear it rises, I want it to rise, to lift me onto the ledge and help me leap—

"Angela!" Something in me cries out to her. I look back. *They* are still there: Matt and Antone and old Timeo sitting under the tree. Auto parts clink as Antone works. Their talk is very clear, but no one moves.

"Help! Matt! Antone! I need help. It's Angela!" I flag desperately. "Timeo!"

Matt rises. He carries something to the jetty, drops it into the rowboat, loosens it, jumps in, and flings the rope down into the bow. Then he waves, smiling, and his thick hands fall to the oars, drop them into the locks, and he begins to heave slow, long strokes—but in the wrong direction!

"Matt! Matt—*here!*"

But he glides into the sea grass and disappears in the flats beyond.

My throat narrows, taut, strickened. I hear nothing but the silly voice of someone distantly calling me, "Eddie! Eddie!" Nothing else. And the girl in the water is groping for me, pulling at me. Something in me cries out to break this prison of stillness. I will break it too, will it, *will* it—yes—

At last I tore my arms up, clutched at the wall, swung over, and dropped into the water.

And I swam, full-scooping, sweeping the water back.

Somewhere ahead I thought I saw white cut the surface. My arms sprang my body ahead in smooth, even thrusts until, despite the regularity, my lungs were afire and my arms pained. I felt a tautness coming into me, for there was the turn into the sea, the sound was coming closer—the waters would come on me in a sudden meeting where they would churn and suck the stream into the ocean.

But where was Angela?

I plunged forward—there was the Point, and where I swung round into the sea. It crashed— And Angela? The white grew into caps, crests of waves, all was suddenly white around my eyes. With an energetic burst, exerting all my pressure against the water, I flapped myself up seal-fashion, suspended an instant in the air, to snatch one glance over the waters, then slip back. Angela was nowhere in sight. I dived into the current and swam out a way underwater. . . . Once a slow flurry of white fanned out from behind a rock. My hands reached out toward her, but it rose quickly, up, up, and then, caught in an abrupt, invisible channel, it was drawn down, all her white dress swept off mournfully, beckoning. Instantly I followed, I went down. It was all pitch, and so soft. I seemed to lose my sight. There was only soft, dark water over me, growing around me, deep darkness and so soft— But the pulse suddenly thundered in me as if it spoke for me. "No!" I turned. I went back. I plunged up.

The agony was too great. Physically I couldn't bear it. My sides ached, my muscles were taut with strain, I couldn't stay down, and my heart seemed to swell and burst, pushing at my chest, crushing against my stomach, and my mouth parted in a terrible silent cry of anguish, and water poured into me.

Then I was rolling myself out of the water onto the dry sand, choking. The light was a great pain. I was breathing great heaves that ached me. My hands clutched the sand. I rolled over and lay exhausted, staring bitterly at the blinding sun as if my hot hate at losing Angela would drive it back. My eyes filled with salt and tears.

Someone in the distance was calling.

"Eddie!"

The girl is still calling me. I look up. Coming down the road is my cousin Ev, Aunt Luella's oldest girl. I know what she wants, but I can scarcely see her through the sudden tears. Mona is still on the jetty, old Timeo and Antone in the yard beyond. Now I am aware of how hot the sun really is. The stone wall of the bridge is scorching. I have been standing here too long, I am sweating, and under my hand I feel the heat of the sun in my shirt, and my blood is coursing, so alive—

But my grandfather is dying, I know it. He is crying out to me, a searing scrape like a torn fingernail drawn over my heart. My breath tears out at her:

"It's him?— No, don't tell me. I know it." But she already has told me in her nod, the quick lowering of her eyes as if in shame—for *me*, yes. I want to strike her for daring to feel shame for me, but I am still shaken from the water dizzying under me, and the white foam, the dress, Angela. . . . My wind pulls. And when I instantaneously try to strike at the girl, it is in my mind only. I know it is a fool's gesture, that she is right, I should never have left him, but I needed sun, escape from the oppression of that dark room. Isn't it enough that this room we live in is dark most of our lives? We yearn for the sun, its soft infusion of life, health. Ahhh!—*careful* there! My cane, as if executing a fleeting thought, gives way. Ev's arm shoots out—

"Are you all right?"

"Yes, yes."

But she holds me secure until I pry myself loose from her.

"Don't!"

"But you'll fall."

"No, no, only a touch of vertigo from the sun." The cane sends the ground away. I feel more solid now, pushing ahead on it in a kind of hump-down, *hump*-down rhythm. I concentrate on managing the cane, thinking that will drive out other thoughts, but they goad with insect persistence: my shame is too great, to let him die without being there after all the arguments, after so many years of flagellation, petty bickerings which demonstrate my, the grandson's, superiority.

"Is he dead?"

She looks back. "No, but he will be if you don't shake a leg."

She too can flagellate—and at such a time!

"Damn you! I can't move any faster." The ground is sailing under me as I move in long strides, surer with the cane now. Sweat forms and sops. My clothes cling, itchy, but I am aware only for an instant because my grandfather is back, his fingernails digging into my head as if he is trying to get into it, to fling open the top, his own vault, and get in whole to rest, and I will not let him. Why? Why? Because he can't die until I get home. He *must* know. I won't let him die until I get there. And he won't either—he will have life from me, yes.

"Hurry!" she says. She infuriates me. As if she is trying to make me feel that I am deliberately not hurrying—I who have been with him all summer, goading him into life since the very first moment of his illness. Didn't I, by making him lash out, assure him that life was there? Oh, it was misery—more for me than for him, but *he* didn't know that. He thought I meant the misery:

"At last, admit it! You're trying to put me into the grave, eh?" Yes, that's what he would cry out.

"I'm trying to keep you out. You hear me? *Keep—you—out!* Isn't that clear?" Naturally he would have none of it, so I retorted: "And if that's so, where are your children—that holy hive who say they'll come? 'Anything you need, Pa, just write, I'll be right there.' That's what they say, is it? Well, where are they? *Where?* And I, your oldest grandson—"

Even I cannot control myself. My tears drive him face to the wall. I have to leave, frantic and more exhausted than he himself. But at his first sigh I am back. Oh, no, not as myself! I have assumed such a multiple personality that I scarcely know who I am anymore. My God! When I think . . . how will I teach next semester, as myself, myself who left the university last spring? Then he moans. Always I listen. Tending the ill makes the ears hypersensitive. The least hover of breath over a pillow, the least scrape of the turning toe against a sheet—these send one scurrying to the sickroom. But when he moans, it is not for me. "Arthur!" this time. Yes, call him—the reprobate son who would scarcely speak to you—so ashamed of you with your crippled hands that he would not come near your house, who would even keep his son, *your own* grandson, away from the house. And don't forget his wife either, nodding to you in passing—like an acquaintance!—and leaving you standing there alone. So you are turned away, hapless, forlorn little man, drying, beat, as if someone has suddenly drawn the puppet strings up taut in you and told you to go now, walk. And now— O my God, dying!

—but I learned how to answer your "Arthur!"

Thank God the shades had always to be down. In the dim light he couldn't know. I could sit just outside the light, and seated just so, my body tilted right, then *I* could be Arthur. Rasp the voice a bit. "Ha . . . ha . . . !" he would anguish. Just to hear him laugh was joy, but at Arthur, *Arthur,* who deserved only his venom, though in my sanest moments, yes, I could be grateful even to Arthur for bringing him these last pleasures, those lips curled rather than downbeat in pain.

And yesterday Irene came. Her visit will give him happiness, I thought. But repelled by the powerful odor of cancerous putrefaction (there is nothing that will relieve its ponderousness), my aunt stood in the doorway and would not enter.

"Go in," I whispered angrily, almost inaudibly. But to him the least whisper is a roar. How he would weakly call out to my mother, walking on tiptoe as she was, "Don't walk so hard!" Poor woman! Oh, no professional nurse would do what she has done for him—cleaning, burning, washing heavy blankets, forever lying with one eye, one ear alert, rising on the least windblow over the floor, the brush of a curtain, the cat's yawn. . . . No, no professional nurse. Such a labor is a true test of love. And what had the other six children against him? Whatever it was, couldn't they hold a reprieve and let him die with illusion instead of standing there in the doorway like his own daughter, Irene, while I hissed, "Go in"?

He cried out, "Don't talk so loud, it hurts," but smiled, his hand touching where he thought she was.

"Irene. . . ." His false teeth out, his mouth was sucked up in a fish slit so close to his nose that his chin all but disappeared; and with the eyes half opened and his hair shocked back, still hard with life, a lot of blond in it yet, his face looked all lids and eyes.

When Irene left after only a minute's suspension on the sill, he squinted as if he had lost her.

"Irene," he said. I had to explain she'd got herself out of a sick bed to come, and with no nurse for the children, things were difficult. But my explanation did not relieve him. I had blundered. "Irene sick?" He wanted to get up, but he slumped deeper into the bed. I had created a pain worse for him than his own.

"But she's well enough now to come, isn't that fine?"

My remark gave him a glimmer of relief, but it did not wholly satisfy. I picked up the newspaper and read to him in a voice so soft that the restraint made me hoarse. Now he motioned me away. At least, there was some serenity in him, for he wanted me to read only when he was in great physical pain, as if, in a battle between hearing and feeling, listening distracted him from the pain. Anyway, when the physical pain was minimized, he liked to lie calm, though I cannot speak for the nature of the mental pain caused by Irene or the others at such a time. Or maybe it was a consummation, the final happiness that at last his family were gathered around him one by one, his issue made visible. "And there will be sons of sons of sons." His words. When he lay there staring, was that in his mind?—because he would smile, his eyes fixed . . . there beyond me, beyond my mother, as if to him we were not even standing there, but through us something was clear.

But to see his children come to him, even for an instant, with their wretched word-of-mouth tribute was a complete reversal. Now they came from social duty. They had stopped coming years ago. Yes, it can be traced almost to the instant when they forsook him: that explosion at sea.

I have seen a hundred times in the smoke of his cigarette, as he told it, the burning flames of the ship he was on, and heard the screaming cook that was my grandfather caught in the galley, cracked flesh, raw-red and bleeding from fire. He was a human statue of bandages for months after. I remembered him that way sometimes (the sight my grandmother used to tell): only his eyes emerging from the bandages, then his body, and then last the crippled-for-life hands that in dark whispers his seven children spoke about—because it was his hands always that lay in my grandmother's vision, hands that reached over and touched shivers into her lying in bed with him when there was no excuse, no sick children, no company, to take her from his bed, her mouth drawn up tight, sleepless nights beside hands that her flesh could not warm to, mother of his ten, cringing at the loving crippled hands tightened into claws now that must run over her body. "I can't, Tom. I can't—" But no word from him. The quiet peace of wise and wretched acceptance was his.

The children left him, as she had left him first.

But when they buried her body years later, he stood beside her second husband, only it was he who had to be held up by his sons, kept from falling in his weakness. "Mother of my children, wife—" His knees buckled. It was all they could do to hold him up; they supported him to the car. You could hear his quiet whimpers all the way back from the cemetery.

The cemetery is on my right. I don't look. I know its each aisle, the sound of the caretaker's mower, the familiar clink of shovel against dirt. I know I must come back to it too soon.

"Is the doctor there? and the minister?" I ask Ev. "Is my mother alone?"

"Well, who else could come for you? And how could I do that without leaving her alone?" Her answer—quick snarls for everything. The well-trained daughter of her mother. I can hear Luella now—"protecting" her daughter from this "reprobate father," against whom she herself has prejudiced this child. On the day he fell ill, Ev asked her, "Who is sick, Mama?"

"No one you know, dear. Only my father," Luella answered. Only *my* father! Not *your* grandfather, but *my* father! I ask you: How is a poor child to know that a part of her own self is going? But enough of this. It drives me to such a frenzy that I will fall if I am not careful. I press down sharply on my cane.

I must hurry before he goes. I must tell him that I have seen his

Angela, I knew who she was. For a moment she was my Angela. He cannot die without my telling him that at last I do know what he meant, what he has always tried to tell me. In actuality, whenever he said, "I am a thousand, twenty-five thousand years old," I thought: Such a joke! He would laugh. And he would joke about being in the arena with the Christian martyrs: "Don't you remember? Well, you will. Someday you'll know what it's like to have a lion sink its teeth into you. Your mind is already as old as mine—older, yes." And from these words I derived that expression I use, "Tell it to your grandfather, he's younger than I am."

"You're exaggerating," I'd say.

"Perhaps, but how else can you get people to see anything these days, eh?"

Even I, with my hatred of ignorance, with a mind trained in the most truly scientific manner to accept nothing as final but only as a stepping stone to infinite possibilities—even I dared to laugh in the vulgarity of my learned ignorance, while he with his sixth-grade education dared not scoff. Always he probed, though (make no mistake) he had a faith beyond science, yet he did not let that hedge falsely and hinder practically. God's is God's, and his his. Witness—in the hurricane of 1938—how, when the tree fell over the kitchen and his twin brother threw his sixty-odd years down on his knees and cried out, "O God, forgive me. Never, never will I sin again—" old Tom cried out, "Get up off your knees, you damned fool. You should have prayed years ago. Let's get this tree the hell out of here."

At last our tree is in sight, a great green umbrella over the house. I can just see it from here, doming high, and then the house, the small second story, then the bedroom el—his sickroom.

"Hurry!" I cry to her. She has fallen against a tree, resting.

"I can't, I'm dead," she cries.

Don't use that word, I want to cry out, but what's the use? She's still a child, she doesn't really know him, and I can't stop to look at her again, I'm almost there. Ah, that house—what have we come to—that the house once built as a stable by the richest mason on Long Island should someday be the birthplace of his great grandchildren.

I am sweating, my heart about to burst in me, but everywhere things are so still—no breeze—and the sun burns. The grass is scorched brown, pine scent is thick, even my breath is dry. Only the trees are green; I want to throw my arms out, hold their coolness, hold life. Yes, everything, everything is so still that I hear it—I hear his breath, it scrapes like a dry leaf over my flesh. Gramp! The cry is in my head. It echoes cavernously through my summer-dry body. "Gramp—"

Hurry!

Since my own illness, I have changed. I am even closer to him than I was before. I hear, I see—well, I can only say there is *more* of me when I am ill. Oh, my illness is a slight thing now, overwork at the university, agitated by this illness of my grandfather, a slight break-down. What a miracle that my mother still holds up! We have been expecting her to collapse any day, but she washes, cooks, carries, a regular workhorse. Unbelievable! Work that would kill a regular nurse.

She is standing in the doorway, her hands caught together, little wrenches twisting in quiet agony. Her life, like his, has been a wretched series of disasters, a pattern traceable through generations, handed down in silent reluctance, waiting for the right will to break it. Is that it? Is that life?

She withdraws after a hasty beckoning, indicating that she is a little relieved. The Reverend Endwater's car is out front, and the sleek black car of Doctor Simpson. —and the ground wavers, suddenly I do feel my heart, it is thundering in my head, but my face is cold, damp, my hands are wet as I open the door. . . .

Gramp?

My cane strikes the door accidentally. The doctor glares at me in condescending patience. The Reverend Endwater drops his eyes. I hand the cane to my mother.

"Can he talk?"

"He hasn't said anything for the last half hour. Once he called you, then he called someone else. He's been mumbling, but nothing clear."

"Angela," I whisper, but my mother couldn't know.

I go into the bedroom. I have to tell him: Gramp, I understand now how we are, you and I, all of us.

How small he looks lying there! His toes are the most prominent, but the rest of him is sunk under the blanket (he is constantly cold), his chicken breast strangely small now. The largest part is his head, so fleshless that it seems almost solid bone, the skin drawn over the skull, the eyes hollow parchment-flutters of flesh, and that jaw bereft of the false teeth is pressed together under the nose, a final taper of the high cheek bones. I lean close, touching his cheek with my lips. So close, I can see the hairs that have grown since yesterday and feel them chafe my lips. He is so dry, but there is a little silver streak of saliva between his lips that finds its way down into the corner nearest me, and the slightest dry warmth on my face from his nose. There are long hairs in its hollows.

"Gramp?" I set my hand on his forehead lightly, pushing the thick growth of hair back. A sigh so soft, but no movement, and then his lips move, barely perceptible twitches, more perceptible, more— Is he trying to smile? The lips part. The saliva glistens in the light.

"Gramp, it is me—Eddie."

His lips remain as they were. But—yes, there is the least change in his breath, as if he were trying—but no, I must be imagining it. I take his hand. It is hard, as always, always immovable, with its tendons once burnt tight and the bones inflexible; and all he did with those hands crowds into my mind—built a house, cooked for himself, made toys for the kids.

"Gramp, listen to me—" I touch his hand and his feet both, whisper in his ear. "Can you hear me? It's Eddie, *Eddie,* Gramp." His mouth twitches, a least flutter of his lids. They draw up, sink—so effortful!— draw up again . . . finally held back, and his eyes blue and glistening in that dry flesh—so young, though at once they grow rheumy, there is a little spill of water over the lower rims. But he is staring up straight, not at me. His hands begin to rise, ever so slightly, and fall. His lips move; sibilant, whistling sounds almost inaudible come forth. He tries, tries, tries, but I can only make out ". . . cold . . . snow . . ." And then it comes over me that the light slatting through the blinds, striking the cream blanket, must appear to be snow to him, he is cold. . . . Cold! My God, dying! I set my hand to his face. "Gramp, I must tell you. I was at the bridge. I saw Angela. She called me. 'Tom, Tom!' she cried (he smiles!), and I went in—yes—*without* moving, I went in. You understand? I was you, Gramp. I felt you. I know now." And he is *still* smiling, the faintest curve, and the eyes seem to rise, to be lifted a little out of his head. I crowd in close, set my face before his eyes. "You hear me, Gramp? *Do* you?"

"Eddie!" my mother says.

Ignoring her, I say it again: "Do you hear me? I saw Angela." And his eyes stare up, but not at me—through me, yet without any relaxation of vision. I sink back into the chair. What is there? Is what he is seeing close? Is it Angela again? Will he believe that I was with her, the Angela he had lost, drowned, so many years ago? But more: Does he know that I understand? At that moment on the bridge I was the grandfather inside me, I was becoming more of *him* as he lay there depleting? I want to *tell* him that I know his first love, inside me, that's been with him all his life, to make up for the discouragement he might have had from me and give him a final joy in knowing that at last he has succeeded in communicating—not merely in handing down unconsciously whatever he was, but that at last someone was aware of himself *in* us for all time.

But no! The smile goes, the flesh grows taut, the eyes flutter, close. Only his hands try to move up, up— They fall, and then sounds come, hollow air breaks through his lips, puckering them with weak sounds. Behind me, my mother says, "Oh, no—" The doctor moves me, he takes Gramp's hand. The minister, who has already prayed with him now begins to mumble quietly. The sounds grow faintly louder, my mother touches me, we are all waiting, waiting, not even knowing the true sound of the end of this object of waiting until it comes, the deep distant sound of water sucked faintly into its last pipe, and then a sigh.

And at the same time the Reverend stops, his eyes upraised. The doctor rises, nods to us, and I feel a heavy weight, for an instant staring at Gramp, still. I have failed, I have failed you, I didn't tell you— Or did I? At this moment it is not the dying, but not knowing if he has heard that is so terrible. But as I stare at him, I know his grief now —mine is the same grief *he* had to bear, we all bear—that we are never to know until it is too late to tell, that we are never to know but the anguish of wanting to tell what we feel lies behind our permanence. I see my own children to come, in my head, and when I tell them, they will not believe *me* either, as I have not believed him until— For one moment this afternoon was I not Gramp? not myself at all? but in another time, here and now, *in* me?

My grandfather clouds. I cannot see the doctor or the minister either, only this room spreading unrecognizably in my tears. And then I clasp my mother; at last she gives way—all the months of agony in caught, choked little cries. I bury her head in my shoulder. "It's all right," I say, and I hold her tight, close, as she cries. Gradually she subsides, and I can feel the blood strong in us—no, stronger now—and warm; I can feel the beating of her heart, as if something has passed into it from him, through her, into me. I want to tell him that, but it is too late. We are cursed with unbelief until it is too late, and then we are cursed with never telling. But we can feel it, yes—for I hold her and I feel the beating of her heart, and I can feel his blood in her, beating, echoing in me, in the deepest chamber of my heart.

IN THE MORNING the snow was low on the mountains, and a cold breeze came down, cold but refreshing; and Agnes liked to sit on the terrace because the cool air made her feel her own heat vibrant and real in her. She reached around herself and let her hands clasp her arms tight. She let her palms rest on her thighs until she felt the heat penetrate her flesh, two hot spots in all that coolness. Sometimes the fresh air settled over her, incredibly still and weighty, in a vice that almost assured her she could not move if she wanted to; but even then she would laugh within because she felt her heat accelerate, her personal acetylene torch that could burn its way through the cold vice. It was her mental triumph: thinking her way through the penetrating cold, without moving.

None of the guests had come down yet. Through the glass wall which lined the terrace (giving, from within the dining room, the most breath-taking view of the mountains), she could scarcely see anything, the snow casting so bright a wall of white against the panes that it blinded her a bit. But she persisted.

Usually she was the first to arrive. And it was the neatest game to try to figure out in which order the others would come down every morning. Now she saw white on white, the white jacket of one of the waiters, then another, and still another beyond, through the reflected snow. So she must have been sitting longer than she knew. It irked her. She must have missed the first ones. She rose, sending herself into her reflection, a bright red sweater more startling than a stanchion in that white purity around her. She wore it so they would certainly see her, though they never missed anything. No one here would miss the red, it being so rare. She caught her own smile etched in the pane. The color supported her, making her feel a courage appropriate to red. And buttressed by the cold which had so awakened her own blood, she was braced for the day. She slid the glass door vigorously aside, stepped in, drew it to, and turned, rather brightly, blazing red with sun so that immediately the eyes at the first table caught the red sweater in their own bloody network of capillaries, filled with abrupt rheum, and glanced down in such rapid flight that they seemed to burrow into the cereal.

"Morning," she said.

The eyes were room 21, Philadelphia, seven months.

Her pride increased as she thought it out: rather *saw* it out, remembered from the door of his room, where she should not have been, sure too that once she had seen the eyes sitting on the balcony (though at that she was so far away she felt her own vision might belie her), looking out over the tennis lawn, where shorts and rackets zipped up and down, from side to side, after a ball she herself never once managed to hit properly.

Her repertoire grew every day—she could now identify some forty guests. Her memory, she assured, was indeed in good shape. Impeccable. She laughed throatily, stepped confidently across the dining room, but 4, his two shoes implanted as precisely as always—separated, one firmly against either front leg of his chair, tapped with his foot, rather faintly this morning. His signal caught her ear—the fact excited her: how sharply he touched, how quickly she reacted—and she rapped his table as she passed. In acknowledgment, he clicked both heels weakly against his chair, and she went on to her table, sat, preening for a moment, letting her hand rest diaphanously on her hair, where it was still warm from the flood of sun. In fact, her scalp prickled a bit, hot, slightly sweating, with a life of its own which sent pins of joy down into her very heart.

One of the white jackets immediately sailed over, sailed so silently —the carpet such a plush silence itself—that he quite startled her with his similarity to the snow beyond.

"Ah, there you are," she said. He had placed himself between the snow and her, cutting off the sun, and with his shadowy presence she felt oriented again. "The usual breakfast, I think," she said. "Bacon, coffee, toast and marmalade. And two eggs."

Almost too quickly he returned and sailed off again with that liquid

water-motion, shades of Southern girls in crinolines who always seemed
so legless.

But—one egg! There was only one egg!

Her scalp prickled again. She drummed her fingers on the table,
forgetting but only for an instant—and then only because 51 had
come through the inner French doors—that she must not object, must
accept, resign herself, make a special strength to relax, avoid errors,
take deep breaths whenever she was so excited or felt that there was
nothing outside herself.

She watched 51 move, with some difficulty but admirably intact,
toward the sun—which he loved—and pull all his fine network together and sit next to the window, gathering his nerves around him
to give the white jacket free access to the aisle. His nerves made a
beautiful black web against the glass, an incredible amount of surface
absorbing sun, a multitudinous little tree, a quivering ganglion.

She nodded. From the top down he tremored a wave in acknowledgment. She turned sideways to look into the mirror, her hand gently
rising to preen at her hair—she dropped the hand almost in the act.
She felt incredibly stupid. There was no mirror, though a fine line
showed where the whole wall had once been lined with them. "The sun
is so bright off the snow," the manager had told her. "Mirrors offend
the guests, double the light, and occasionally—so glaring is the sun—
we've had a guest, rather tragically, walk smack into one—yes. Quite
a bad accident."

"And in the rooms too?" She had surveyed the bedroom, her living
room, and then the bath. There were none.

"We return to the purest kind of nature," he said. "No cosmetic
disguises."

She laughed. They had warned her she would be right at home with
him. And she was. Instinctively he understood all her impulses, so
there was almost no need at all for words. But she had not seen him
much. Once, when she wanted to talk about the maid, who kept her
rooms impeccable but whom she never saw, she said, "It was only to
tell her how well she worked, and tip her. . . ." Now the manager
did the laughing: "But they're incredibly well paid. Besides, we pay
them to keep out of your way."

"It was simply to give her. . . ." She dangled a glass neckpiece, a
slithering line of green beads that shimmered into a hundred colors.

"You won't be needing it anymore then?" he said. The green chameleoned his eyes, made him a stone statue for a moment. She drew the necklace in so taut she felt the beads cut into her breast through the thin white blouse.

"It is not a question of needing it. I wanted to give it to her, to thank. . . ."

"Ah," he said. "No. It is not allowed. You see, they would work perhaps with the expectation of gifts, and as people are constantly leaving. . . . Our order would vanish. Control. Discipline. You understand." A certain disappointment had crept into his voice. He was staring at her neck. "But you can use it, surely?"

"Oh, yes." She swerved around so rapidly that the chairs in the lobby topsy-turvied in her kaleidoscoping vision. Abrupt vertigo spun the lobby in a white whirlpool and she clutched her sides, the green beads fell, she heard the sound, and then the manager was standing there holding them out. . . .

"You're all right?"

She said, "Yes, yes," but he stood, a black post in the white lobby, cutting directly into her vision of 39, his left face tilted up at the ceiling. 39 was the first she had met, the only one really who talked to her any length, though sometimes his acoustics were bad and she had to strain, leaning forward to hear, somewhat disconcertingly because from a distance it must look as if she were bending over to whisper some secret or, worse, to kiss him. Beyond, two or three shirts had their arms propped up on chairs; in a corner two hands held a newspaper, and several crossed legs indicated a composure which at the moment she was determined to reproduce.

Collecting herself, she poised her arm, signaled to 39, whose left face nodded, and she said, "Excuse me, please," to the manager, who was scrutinizing her with some care. As he did not move decorously, she skirted him and said, "39, I didn't think I'd see you this morning."

Now, looking across the dining room, almost in a repeat performance, there came 39—his usual rapid face whisking past the others, almost directly to her, and she nearly cried out, "I didn't think I'd see you this morning," suddenly downcrest as she realized that he had his left face again. She had *so* hoped this morning, at last, he would satisfy her and come down with the right face. She so longed to see it. Once, at night, she lay long imagining how the two faces—

provided the one was nearly like the other—would be together, but she couldn't piece them to, largely because she realized two halves of one head were never the same size, exactly that is, so all she could envision was a distortion, gross.

"Didn't expect to see me this morning?" His mouth was dry, down-bent, curiously dissatisfied and almost oversatiate. Somehow she had said an error. She didn't understand.

"I meant—" She pawned a laugh. "I meant I wanted to be surprised. I expected. . . ."

"Expected?" His eye held her, full sun, red sweater, all. For one moment she felt wholesomely lost in him, part of his eye, and she closed her own eyes a second.

"Are you faint?" he said.

"Oh no no no," she said. "I had a moment of joy, tremendous joy."

He frowned. "Because you got your surprise, what you expected?"

"No no no, though it *was* a surprise. What I expected was . . ." But she could not say it.

"What?" he said.

"I can't tell you, of course. What makes a surprise is its precisely not being expected, and if I told you— You see?"

"Ah, yes, I didn't think," he said. Furrows engrained his forehead like visible pain. "Didn't think." His head tilted as if it rested on fingers she could not see. Rodin? Could it possibly—? She laughed.

She wanted him to sit, an old impulse—against the rules of course— But he now crossed the aisle (a gray, rigid bar down the plush brown carpet) and sat at his own table, rather a disadvantage in some ways but at least his left face confronted her and his eye encompassed her well. It kept him from seeing the long pellucid blonde hair at the table beyond him, hair which tossed and tremored in the most flirty way, occasionally emitting an intense electrical crackling.

Down the aisle came red hands to deliver his order—the jackets were hovering in the far corner, only one moving down toward another guest.

Hands set down the tray, moved with a certain lightning efficiency. They came too for her dishes. They were less red this morning. Drying. Brown here and there, though the skin was gone, and the nerves pulsed beneath the blue. Her hand—she could not help it—went up, touched out (discreetly the hands fled a few inches), and fell onto the tablecloth. She smoothed away a few crumbs, peered into her fruit. . . .

She was nearly ready to leave when there was a slight commotion. Over by the window wall, jackets fluttered, hovered in a mass, streaked quickly out into the foyer; the manager streamed with hastened dignity toward the table; here and there legs uncrossed, flicking against the tablecloth, shoes tapped, a chair creaked, 39's face turned, nearly disappearing at that angle—

I'm going to faint, she thought at first sight, something's happening to me, my eyes are going, or I've got vertigo, I'm so dizzy. . . . For she saw eyes, a pair of eyes, moving vertically, and then she realized it was 21, one eye over the other, something had happened. . . .

21?

She rose, she flagged. The moving eye did not respond. Something of a glaze seemed to stand between her and them.

But I see *you,* she said to herself.

Abruptly, between her and the vertical eyes, stood the manager. "Is the egg bad?" he said. "Fresh this morning."

Egg. One.

"Oh no, but . . ." She looked down where the one mangled eye had been, where her breakfast plate had been. She pictured the egg—so like . . . eye. She said, "I was confused. I thought . . ."

"Mustn't," he said. "Depletes."

"Ah," she said, smiling, "of course," and watched him as he bowed and made off rapidly to other guests.

She looked across for 39 but he was gone. She saw—over the hedge beyond the window—a thin slit walk into the distance.

On the terrace appeared the manager. The sight of him there made her aware that the corridor was quite free, and the double realization impelled her to move rapidly into the blazing white hall toward the staircase to the second story. As she passed them, she gratefully acknowledged a slight swelling of stomachs and lungs and the flapping of one admirable pair of kidneys. Now, they must be . . . but no she hadn't seen them before. . . .

Except for the far end, the second story had no windows in the long corridor, though it was less dark than the third, much less dark than the fourth—beyond that she wasn't sure—and she could not see the numbers very well, coming as she did from such blazingly alive light below. Ah—she traced with her fingers, dropped them to the knob—21. But she forgot—no knobs. She pressed, the door gave slightly, caught then in the lock. Frenzied, she pressed again. Nothing gave. But it must!

How? How?

"21!" she said. "21!"

What happened she didn't know, but she was groping in her purse, groped, wanting pencil and paper. Some message for 21. But she didn't have any purse, of course. "Listen, 21—," she said. She might scrape a message with her fingernails on the door so the eyes could see it when they came out. She began to etch in a frenzy, rapidly, before some came, because she heard footsteps. With all ten fingernails she scraped, the wood splintered, she cried out, plunged her fingernails deep into the wood, as deep as she felt they would go. "21, listen—," she said. "I'm writing." And in an instant, she was banging on the door —someone had hold of her, two hands, redder than her own, and suddenly—she felt them. She tore more vigorously at the door, feeling the hands on her own wrists—felt so strong—and she cried, "Yes, yes. You see, 21?" And it was as if the hands realized what she meant, for they dropped her own, she jerked up. "Don't!" she cried, reaching for the hands to come back, but the manager was standing behind them, smiling.

"3?" he said.

"Agnes," she said, watching the blood on her fingers, on her arm.

"Yes—3?"

"I wanted to write a note to 21," she said, "to tell him I'm here."

"But he knows that," the manager said.

"He didn't see me when he left," she said.

"Ah," the manager said, "it is to be expected."

"When will he come down?" she said.

"The door is locked," he said.

"He will go—?"

"Yes—higher," he said.

"I wanted to give him—"

"Save it," he said.

Below, she saw several. The new kidneys were basking in her chair. It made her heart beat quickly. My chair. A momentary resurgence of strength came into her. She smiled.

"Tell 21 I wanted to enter," she said.

"21 knows you are too comfortable on floor one. He would not believe."

"Not believe?"

"No one would sacrifice the comforts of one to someone on two," he said.

"But if he knew, he might be able to come down," she said.

"That is something you cannot know, something between me and 21."

"Yes," she said, having forgotten for an instant.

"Of course you must reserve your sympathy," he said.

The two hands were still there. She wanted them. Indeed, she felt them on her and the memory gave her a quick impulse to movement. She ached with joy, and she said, "But just now I—" No, she would not tell the manager.

Besides, she was staring at the hands, and they were quite small now, and they hung limp. She gave a rapid glance down onto the lawn.

"I'll go down now," she said. "I won't come back."

She saw the manager's smile, a painting loomed in her head, that beribboned lip of Mona Lisa, and she flung herself forward. . . .

"Don't hurry," he said. His advice was good, she felt awfully weak, tumbled against the wall, and when she reached out no hands touched the plaster, she struck with a shoulder, shouted, and fell to her knees— or what she thought they were, on the carpet, though she dared not look down; then straightened herself out. She did not look at her body. She stared straight ahead, measuring the steps slowly. Weak. And for a moment stopped and looked back. The manager was glaring at her. But she did not give way with another shout. She said, "I'm sorry. . . ."

He smiled. "You are doing admirably," he said. The smile was rigid. She knew she was in some error. She must watch her errors. Once moving, down down she went past the cool, into the warm sun, and then outside—such glory!—white white with a sun glaring that made her whole body swell slightly with pleasure in the felt, slow movement of blood through her.

She surveyed the lawn. There they were, so many, and from the distance, still and unmoving, scattered like so many stones over the grass. From the edge of the lawn her vision could encompass them all—and as if she herself pulled them all together, placed them there, for a moment she sensed what it was to be able to see them all in a glance: here 4, his shoes uptilted; 51 spread gloriously, multiple octopi quivering with joy in the sun; and 31; 17; 42— How pleased she was racing over her repertoire, learning it, rehearsing—blunted abruptly because she realized that four—four whole numbers—had changed today. She would have to learn them anew. Such a challenge every day! This game . . .

And then there was 21. Her eyes sailed up to the balcony. . . . Nothing. She tore her eyes back down, embraced the lawn, embraced each isolated part, all scattered so far apart; and her voice, unspeaking, reached out. She wanted to say: 21 is up there. He's moving. Her hand went out, it sailed up with her thoughts as if she had cast both out and let them go, when someone said, "Don't you want to go and lie down for a while? I wouldn't recommend, for you, the strong sun. It debilitates. The shade—and with the healthy air to breathe—is simply marvelous beneath those lindens—there." A veritable cascade of shade, as blunting as Niagara or Iguazú, seemed to pour over the whole left end of the lawn, almost solid, down from the trees at the foot of the mountains. And the sun, just beginning to go, threw the whole mountain down over that end of the lawn. "Oh yes!" she said, for an instant ecstatic in the beauty of it, and moved toward it, a canvas chair already set out there for her. Prepared, she thought, with a sudden disappointment that the spontaneity had gone from it. . . .

When she awoke, it was dark. At first she felt a cool breeze, just a breeze, then sat bolt up: startled, because she was in her room, and the breeze was simply the hygienic ventilator. That is, her body seemed to shoot up, but her head somehow felt as if it were still lying on the pillow and she could not feel her legs or, for that matter, could not feel with her arms toward her legs. Her body seemed to be quite inert, but how deliciously her heart was beating; *thump-thump* she could hear, it gave her a tremendous joy in that sudden surprise to hear it *thump-thump,* and her ears sounded, they pounded, *that* she could feel so strongly, *thump-thump,* and she laughed and when she did even that came out *thump-thump,* so that she did not move so caught in that motion was she, and as she listened it grew *thump-thump* THUMP-THUMP, and she exulted as it filled the room, splashed over the walls and reverberated against itself THUMP-THUMP THUMP-THUMP THUMP-T H U M P THUMP-T H U M P T H U M P, growing like a vast river around her, making her smaller smaller, infinitesimal, so that she was caught up in it, carried, and she wondered for the first time where it came from, where it *was* coming from, for it felt from somewhere beyond the walls, beyond the green lawn outside, beyond the mountains, beyond sunrise and sunset—oh how her mind reached out, reached out, until it pained, and when she could not imagine the end of the river she was caught up in, she made up her mind to get up and go out, down the stairs, onto the lawn, into the mountains and follow the road at the bottom of the river of her blood, all that blood had inundated her, and swim beyond until she could see where it came from. Even forgetting that she could not remember coming up from the lawn, eating supper, returning to her room; and even forgetting that she could not remember what she wondered, she rose, feeling nothing else now, only her heart getting up, the lightest feeling it had ever known, and pushed open the door and floated down the stairway—

It was dark, and the heart did not know what was happening, but the whole darkness was vibrating with heat and movement. Life, she said. Everything's beating. I feel it. It is in me, around me.

Miraculously there was no one downstairs.

She sailed out the front door, down the steps, onto the lawn, glanced back, the whole building loomed up behind her, white even in that vibrant red feeling of night, and she wanted to flee, but first: I will wake them all, they must feel it too, I want them to *know*.

And she turned around.

And she wanted to throw up her hands, but she couldn't.

And she opened her mouth and she couldn't speak.

But her heart beat more violently. And she could feel the grass under it beating too, and the earth, and the air against it.

And she tried to shout: Wake up! Wake up! And she directed her arms and her voice and her eyes and all her energies at the one single light she saw in the building on the second floor—

It's 21! she said, beating harder and harder. And with one nearly ferocious effort, jerked, trying to summon up voice, but nothing came.

The light went out. No! her heart beat, and she felt it diminish a bit, not so violent. No! it beat again. But the light was gone—sud-

denly, as if her eyes were gone. She could not see! I can't see, I can't
see! The building went, and the night, and the lawn. She could feel
the grass and dew and earth and air, and she felt her heart expand
as if it would break. 21! she screamed in silence. At that instant she
felt the net around her, something with a hundred little cord-like
fingers caught her up, scooped her high into the air, and someone
said, "Now now, it's not morning yet, you know that," like a hand
on her, but no hand. No hand touched. Please, her heart said, thinking of the other hand—how long ago was it? years? centuries—yes?

And she was in her bed, so quiet here now that the voice of the
manager was gone, down the hall, saying, "Ah, how calm you are,
how lucky you have all that energy. Relax, save. . . ." But in her
energy she could only think of the hands, of 21. How? How save? It
is so difficult. *How?* whispered her heart as she drifted into sleep.
How?

In the morning she woke weak, yet with a strange start. The room
was the same. She felt that. And then: no. Everything *in* the room
was the same, but—

She was higher. She felt it. Her heart wanted to go *down.* It leaped
up, but had to rest for a minute. Taxed. I want to go down, the heart
said. Out of touch it was. Too rarefied here. Too far. Remembering
earth and grass and dew and air from some time—when?—it flopped
off the bed, sidled across the floor and against the white wall, panting for a moment, and pushed at the door. Out. . . .

It was all so difficult. Exhausted, at the edge of the stairs, it slid,
let itself roll down and regain some strength, then hurled itself down
the second flight and forced itself quietly behind a chair in the foyer,
where it lay for a while pulling force into itself.

When it felt a flagging beat, it said, *No!* And the words of the
manager echoed repugnantly in the heart: Save yourself. And it cried
silently, Yes, save yourself. And pushed out across the hall incon-
spicuously, though the others saw it—and that was precisely what
it wanted—and when they saw the heart it felt energy come into itself, the blood swelled, the heart grew, and stronger, and it pumped
signs to them: Come, follow me, come.

39 came, and 74, and 28, 17, though not close—out onto the
lawn, so green, beating with chlorophyl, fused; the blood felt the
lawn now, pounding, thump-thump YES-YES THUMP-THUMP

THUMP, ecstatic with beating now—and the trees and the air rich with motion it was sharing. The others were in front of the heart now and all around it as it took its place in the middle of the lawn, but it had to be seen—yes, up onto the empty birdbath, red in that stark white. The heart began to beat, it cried out a message to them: Don't stay there. Come here. Close. Come around me.

And something—yes!—a tide began to come, the shining kidney rose, the shoes moved, that half-face it had known, 31, and even— oh, great blood!—white jackets dared to come down the lawn. But why? The movement frightened them. It tried to beat out faster, faster—Come to me. Ignore them. The sides expanded almost to bursting with the thump of blood, pressing the walls—that was it! what it wanted! to break out of itself, pour out over all of them and inundate them, make them feel the stream. Don't stay there, it said. Don't sit in islands. Come here.

And the blood tried to break out of its walls, tried to spill— And a heat came, it filled with pleasure, filling too with energy and source and time. This! This! it cried. It's not for me. It's for *you*. Break my wall, let me out. Pierce it. Destroy—

And even the thought filled the heart to overflowing. Don't you see? it cried. Touch me! Touch me! It's the only way.

And they came closer. They looked at it. They examined. They smiled.

Touch! it cried to them, swelling, heaving.

Their organs expanded. Something went out to them, over them, into them.

Not enough, the heart cried, struck suddenly by a pang of weakness—for the manager was hurrying down the steps, white jackets were running now, the others began to separate, moving away from the heart—

And it shrieked in its motion: Stop! Don't go! making an effort, making—yes, it *was* worth it—the last great effort:

For it began to cry. It was the only way—it shed tears, it shed tears faster and faster, forcing itself out of its pericardium, squeezing itself with all its muscles, contracting and expanding, contracting tighter and tighter until almost nothing remained, contracting until the tears spurt out red— For you! it cried, diminishing almost to nothing. Drink! Drink! it cried in joy, watching them come closer. It is the only way.

And they watched. The white jackets watched. The manager watched, seething.

Someone came closer, infinitely close. It was 39! The heart felt a rewarding spasm.

Drink! Drink! it cried. The others gathered around. It heaved, waiting to be taken into them at last.

39's left face bent close. It peered into the birdbath.

Drink! Drink!

"But there's nothing there," he said.

"Nothing?" A hand reached up and splashed into the tears. "Nothing!"

And someone laughed—"Nothing!" and splashed into the water. And then another splashed. And another. They all crowded closer, laughing and splashing now, laughing and splashing the water—

And the tears leaped up, shot into the air, and fell deep into the darkness.

All the Carnivals in the World

(For Kay Boyle)

HUEY WAS HUNTING bottles, carefully moving into the wind so he could breathe the salt water and pine and wild rose and keep the smell of the dump, always stronger in the July heat, and the smoke of burning refuse behind him. It cost him to dig, hunch, pry with his hoe, spread trash and then set fire to the remains. Yet it was worth it—sometimes he made fifty or a hundred dollars a month on rags and metal, occasionally more on bottles alone. He was very late, it was going on dark, but this week he could sure use the money, what with the carnival again tonight and the Fourth of July weekend staring him in the face.

With a sudden jerk, gasping triumphantly, he hauled up a dark bottle. Wine. Imported. He could just see the words but he couldn't read them. Foreign. At such times, when he looked at the letters and they said nothing, he felt a sensation of quiet pain, of a slowly drawn scraping over some place deep inside him he did not know existed.

He held the bottle up and peered through it. The last sunlight bloomed in a sudden green paradise with white fires like a Disney world before life squirmed into it. He caught only a glimpse of the Sound, a small corner still streaked by a slim finger of light that slipped over the edge of the horizon. When he lowered the bottle the dusk seemed unexpectedly light, but only until his eyes adjusted. Then he went back to searching for other bottles. He had only a little while before total darkness and every minute counted.

Long after quitting time and only seventeen bottles—a bad day. With the sun gone, the far edge of the dump fusing into sea and sky in fast blackness, the near world of the dump—his—rose out of the ground. The fires held the night up in a low arc, making a near sky, too low for Huey. Night made him feel foreign here and too small and the sky too close to handle. Besides, he never dug around much after dark because the rats came out more then. Often—they were that bold—he came upon a mound and reached down and met their eyes red with the dump fires blazing in them, like moving worlds inside things that he didn't know anything about.

He dropped the bottle into one of the wooden cases piled by his shed, thinking for the hundredth time the Hinkels might like their chicken coop back now that he'd bolted and repaired it. He circled it, surveying to see that it set okay on the two-by-fours. No more resting directly on the ground. Everything and its brother hid under it then. He appreciated the change. The Case boys were always good about moving things with him.

"*Hey*, Pa! Pa!"

"Paulie!" The boy charged down the slope and leaped up at him. "Ma says how come you're not home yet? It's awful late."

"And how come you to walk all this way?" He caught Paulie, swung him in a circle, and plopped him down so abruptly the boy staggered.

"Ho—can't stand on your own pins, eh?"

"*Again*," Paulie shouted. "Again, Pa—like the chairplanes!"

"Just one time." He saw the boy whirling, twirling above him against the sky over the fair grounds. "Your Ma'll be upset if I don't get there after she sent you."

Yet he wasn't exactly willing to go. The idea of food galled him. He had put off going home, though his body long since had told him, as it always did, how many more steps his legs ought to take. And despite the unusually long and sweltering day, he was irritated at breaking his routine now.

"What'd you do exciting today, Paulie?"

"Most nearly got drownded at the beach."

"Drowned!" He clutched the boy close a brief instant, pained at the hot breath against his cheek, and then swung him up high again.

"What's the matter with you, doing a dumb thing like that? You be careful!"

"I couldn't help it. Mitzie threw a horseshoe crab at me and I ran and hit a rock and fell down."

"Don't she know you can get a nasty bite from those claws?"

"Oh it wasn't alive, but I didn't know it. We goin, Pa? I'm hungry."

"Right away." He set Paulie down. He did not really want to stay; he was resisting, resisting almost to the point of anger, irritated because he knew he had to eat but did not want to. The food would make him at first sleepy, then vigorous and full of life. He felt it inside him. But he didn't want to be full of life.

He went back round the shack—he had to do that—to make sure. Flat over a heap of hard ashes, the board was still there. Nothing was changed. He fully expected the Case boys to be standing there too, watching him. He could see their shoes and the dirty cuffs. When the three of them had shifted the house onto the two-by-fours, a giant rat had scurried out and whisked at his leg. "Near got you," Al said. Huey laughed. "They know me, the buggers. They threaten me, but don't touch." But the rat had whacked hard at his leg. He still felt the spot. And leaning over to examine it, he had seen the tiny cluster of faded balls quivering. And then the others had seen it: a nest of rats. "Look what Santa brought you," Will said. "Ba-*by,*" Al said. Something in their voices—terribly familiar, as if remembered from a long way off inside himself—agitated him. Yet at once he knew what to do. "I'll drown them. There's enough in this place now, God knows."

"Oh come on, Huey—half the things don't die in the water, you know that. They'll float off, or something'll knock them onto the bank."

That wasn't true either. But they would have their way. Still, there was something . . .

"Here." Al handed him a stick.

Why doesn't *he* do it?

But Huey took the stick.

"Or those boulders," Will said. "Better hurry or that bitch rat'll be back."

"No danger from her."

But he did not use the stick or the stones either. He picked up the nest.

"Je--*sus*. I'dn't touch them for nothin," Al said.

There was a kind of straw under them, they squirmed, a faint warmth touched Huey's hand.

He dropped them down onto the hard ash, raised a heavy board, dropped it over them and then stepped on it, gradually pressing his weight until he felt that sensation of breaking gelatin—a give and slight shift of the board, as on grease, and the quiet crunch of chafing ashes.

"Good *job,*" Will said.

Huey said, "You better go or you'll be late for your noon stop. I sure appreciate you guys' help." Their feet shifted for a second, he saw the dirty work cuffs quiver, then Al said, "Huey's right. My old lady'll be griping if I don't bring a loaf of bread," and they went off, kicking up dust. Huey looked at his own shoes and at the board and at the ashes, then out across the dump to the sea, where he could see the glitter and shift of waves under the morning sun, forever moving. He could always count on the sea.

"You comin, Pa?" It was clearly a whine now. The boy was really hungry.

"We'll be there in a jiffy," he said, setting Paulie on his shoulders, astraddle.

At the house Lily sulked. "You could let me know. Janice has a 4-H meeting. I don't like her coming and going alone, and you know I don't like to drive that—" Though it was only a jalopy, it got there. Still, he knew it was embarrassing for her whenever it broke down, she had to walk or send somebody, since they had no phone—

"I'll send you my helicopter next time."

"You!" she muttered. She never stayed peeved very long. He was lucky in her—and in Paulie and Janice too, both keen on everything, and smart, their curious noses always stuck in something new. This was the dangerous age for him because they hounded him with questions, and he too snooped more and more, but it was hard: they had so much, these kids, while he . . . His parents had been simple people, workers day and night, in a house with a wood-fire stove which his mother spent half her time polishing black, his father always in the grocery store. The seven kids had practically brought themselves up, put out early to earn what they could and supplement the grocery income. There was never time to talk, never money to relieve them, maybe never answers because of that. And he could never forget her pained face when he did ask questions—her hands hard and stiff in a desperate pressing against her legs, and nervous gray eyes—so beautiful!—that sometimes quivered in a chronic family defect.

"Why do you ask that?"

"Cause I wanna know, Ma."

"Ah. . . ." Sullen, with a quiet drag, she moved in silence back to the ironing or rummaged in the pantry. Worst—even at the end when, of the seven kids, only he was there to see the life go out of her, they could not help each other. His father was out of town, just a few miles away, trying to raise money because she was so sick and they were down and out, and so many people owed his father accounts from the grocery.

For him dying was always her raucous sound in a room bare of all but her bed and her dresser. But something more too. . . . She was lying there sweating, liver yellow all over. He would take towels and pat her skin from the head down, gently, discreetly, for she would not let him see anything personal for the life of her. Her breathing scraped through his head, harsh and torn like fingernails chafed over flesh, and scraped in his mouth and down his throat until with each painful drag he himself feared to breathe. "Mama." She looked up, and her eyes were so bright they seemed to have their own life, apart from her body. He could see deep into them, he bent over— "What you see, son?" Being caught like that shook him. "Nothing," he said. "Son, what you seeing?" She near rose, her hand clutched his—so dry, it chafed like dead milkweed—and his heart turned. She bent her head close, rolled her eyes desperately to focus them on him. "What, son?" And he *felt* he should tell her what he saw, he *wanted* to tell her what he felt as he stared at her, into her, even through her, but nothing came—no thought, no sight; only a vague feeling half pain, half joy besieged him, and he wanted to tell her— Her eyes flickered up like oil lamps burning out. "Ma?" Her head turned, her mouth sagged. He said, "I love you, Ma"—and why did he say that, twenty-three, a man?—and the words pulled her back. Her eyes focused in abrupt stillness and awareness. "Love?" He nodded yes. A divided look of confusion and wonder came over her face, she dug her nails until he wanted to shout. "There's always something more," she said. "Mama," he said. But she didn't hear. She tried to draw her arm back, her hand crawled painfully, her eyes pressed toward it—there was a streak of blood on her finger. Her stare was so hard, so intense, that it frightened him. Blood. Her eyes clung to it. Her head pushed closer. Then the eyes drifted up, out— and he looked too, but there was nothing beyond, only the open window, the parted curtains swaying, and the hard blue sky so far away.

"Dad—?" It was Janice. Not Pa, Pop, but Dad—her newest (so-phisticated, Lily called it) word. "Where does infinity end?"

Infinity?

He looked across at Lily tugging at her rag rug, and for a moment he was sure she would not look up, abandon him.

"*You* know, Dad—what doesn't end, what's forever." Her book was opened to a vast deep blue and sets of hard cold stars. She was studying astronomy. "These are the stars, the planets, the universe, and after the universe there's another and another. Teacher says it all goes into infinity. Where's that?"

He bent low, sinking his eyes into the unending blue behind the brilliant little spots. "Beyond them," he said.

"Oh. . . ." She was plainly unsatisfied. "But where? I mean where does it stop?"

"In the wild blue yonder," he said rapidly—a hundred times that phrase had come over radio and TV all those years.

Janice was quiet for a moment, he'd let the round settle, some-what vexed because he knew it was not really settled, almost per-versely pleased when she said, "But what's beyond *beyond?*"

Bleakly he stared through the window into the dark night. He could see nothing but the reflection of himself in the blackness be-hind his image, and he tried to visualize layers of himself and then layers of dark, one after the other, his mind trying to reach out to touch what might be the last, but he couldn't. He saw hard space and then space holding it and space holding that, but no wall, no cup, just—what was Janice's word?—infinity. He felt as if he were falling, he wanted to reach out, but he could only reach out to his own image in the pane.

"Maybe it's a question we shouldn't ask."

"But *any* question you don't know the answer to you've got to ask, Dad! Don't be silly!"

"Janice!" Lily said.

"I mean—oh *you* know what I mean, Dad."

"Sure I do." Beyond beyond beyond. . . . He rose. Now, close, he could see the street, a light on the corner, pinpoints between trees, and there were, he knew, lights he couldn't see—beyond—but they were there. And he could faintly hear the sea keeping the rhythm that hushed into his head and hushed out. Beyond beyond *beyond* . . . ? Where the sea comes from and goes to, and the sky —it suddenly seemed to him a bright answer, he wanted to say it, but looking down at Janice etched in the corner of the window, he thought he had better not. She would go into the next phase. She— *he* had learned enough for today: that he didn't know, that's what. He didn't know. It was that simple. Who knew? That teacher, Mrs. Cranford? He'd like to know that—*who?*

During the night it poured almost without interruption, and in the morning, on the uneven cement walk, there were puddles in which he could see the sky at his feet. And when he looked close, the puddles were laden with dead earthworms driven out of the ground and drowned wriggling over the cement. Near fleshcolored, they were stretched out, elongated and still. The water rippling faintly gave them a false life for an instant.

"Lily, sweep off the sidewalk, will you?" he called.

"I always *do* after the rain," she called back, not scolding, simply informative. "You coming home early?"

"After a quick trip to Riverhead this afternoon."

Before going to the dump, he went as usual to Al's Diner, precisely on time for the regulars: Zac the Jew from the clothing store, Bill, Abel, Mannie the wop, Alf, Olson, the guys from the skimmer boats.

" 'F-it ain't Smelly hisself." Johnnie slapped him on the back.

"To make me out from the Polacks," he said. The others laughed.

"My turn," Mannie said and bought him a cup of coffee.

The diner was air-conditioned and too comfortable an escape from the worst July heat, sultry, clinging, his shirt already matted in a second skin over him.

"Come on, Huey—it's almost the last." Donnie nudged him, thrust a yellow ticket under his eyes. "Take a gander at that, boy—one thousand, one little thousand smackeroos for the winner."

He pushed it off where he could see it—near he could not see and often his eyes quivered like his mother's. He didn't like to think of his vision, with all the things the kids and Lily needed. . . .

"Just a restricted number. It's almost a private pool, Huey. Listen, Huey, ten bucks, no more—"

Huey whistled.

"But lookit the odds, man. You almost can't go wrong—and the drawing's at *noon*."

Ten. One thousand. More than he'd ever received, imagined receiving, in a lump in his life. Even when the bank had given him the deposit on his house years ago—five hundred dollars—he felt bigger than his skin, such a sum it seemed.

"If I do that . . ." There were so many things. And Lily's anger, though that wouldn't last long. But ten—ten bucks from his week's pay! Two hundred bottles, he thought, imagining himself at the dump, digging, bending, going at it. The thought made him rise.

"Got to get," he said.

"But it's the day before the Fourth," Mannie said.

"You got something waiting out there?" Olson said. His usual joke. Huey had never said yes, though he always had it in mind, for a second wanting to mention how the dump was crawling with things and the pond bordering the sea edge too, thick with life in the scud, the fish, plenty of fiddler crabs, occasionally even a softshell, now and again a black snake moving like a twig adrift on the surface, and insects everywhere. . . .

The thought of all that out where nobody but Huey Mann really knew about it sent a joyful spurt through him. He had that old feeling he should *be* there, something was happening without him, if he didn't hurry he'd miss it, he felt the familiar nearness to something he seemed always to be waiting for the sight of—like climbing for years up a hill to see—sudden—the whole ocean—

"Yes," he said, boosted now, "I'll take one. Ten. Pay you in the morning. On second thought—no, here." It was tonight's money. He'd have to cut into the pay when he got home; double up next week.

"Great! I *knew* you wouldn't pass up the golden opportunity, Huey. Only a sucker'd do that."

Or not do it, he thought. "So long." He moved lithely now, in a bound, his steps long, his body sailing easy. Something—he laughed —was carrying him along.

When he crossed under the viaduct past the last road and descended the slope to the dump, he stopped to look: his. That was just how he felt, no matter what anybody thought about working in a dump. A kind of peace settled over him when he downed that slope into his world, for it *was,* no one else ever came for long, they never had, maybe because they had never seen . . . what? He could never explain—that was the bad part—he could never explain to anyone what else was there because . . . Because? He could get no farther. You had to feel it, that's all—the quiet, the peace, and—he stood still, listening—all that sound that no one who did not sit for hours, days, even years—a whole life, he thought—would not hear. And something more . . . yes . . .

He went over to his shed and sat. And there it was, there it came: shivers of sound, scrapes and chafes and nudges, whispers and interminable comings and goings, risings and fallings, digs and ripples and sighs, all running into one another, all making a big rhythm that grew and grew and caught him up in the beating of his own heart (and the motion of two bluebottles, the glisten and streak, the nearly invisible wings and nearly still sound), and over it all a whispering, the mysterious sigh and tremble that the earth made as if he were sitting on one spot of flesh on a gigantic body too big to see the end of that which was breathing under his feet.

Yes, for this he had come. At such times it was—he could never have told Lily or the kids this, or anyone else—as though he almost heard something the earth, the dump was trying to *say,* and he had to be there at the right time to hear it. *Then* he could tell Lily and the kids and everyone else, yes— Often he felt his whole life had spent here waiting (he knew the dump like the back of his hand, every mound, every burnt-out hole, every new deposit or leveled area), and once in a while when he was digging or reaching down into the earth, he had a fast sensation he was getting to the heart of something, he dug faster with a passion that was near exploding. But when he stopped and there was only a mound of ash, rusted tins, his own exhaustion, and a feeling of emptiness, he wondered what had happened, why he was sweating, what had got hold of him to make him forget himself that way, for there was a dead space in his thinking he couldn't describe, he just felt . . . felt . . . and his eyes went out like two hands grappling at the sky, tried to cup and hold it fixed and draw it in and understand. But his eyes watered, the clouds shifted, the sky toppled. It was all so far away.

And it had never been any different. His Uncle Dan used to say, "Stop daydreaming or you never *will* get a crab."

He liked Uncle Dan and he liked going at the crabs with his net, but he couldn't take his eyes off the clouds in the sky sailing on the surface under him.

"How's the sky get in the water, Uncle Dan?"

"The sky's not *in* the water," Uncle Dan said. "It's up there. That's only the reflection."

He heard that—he knew the words, he understood—but he could never separate the sky from water or from himself and Uncle Dan, the boat, the crabs, the net— What was under and over and in-between seemed just one single picture moving, moving; and to prove it was more than just a reflection, he plunged his hand down into the sky and water through his own self deep as he could, and struck bottom. A cloud black as ink spread. His hand came up all muddy and it smelled strong.

He stared into the water. It closed over, the boat moved, the sky came back. Mud. He had a handful of mud he wouldn't let go. He glanced at his uncle, his uncle was laughing. There was a tiny crab clawing in the mud, and he had chiggers for days after. . . .

At the dump he spent the morning leveling off a small area, piling up junk which he carted off to bury in a deep channel he dug part of every day. "Each thing in its place," he said emptying the last load. His stomach made a quake deep inside him so he went to the shed for his sandwich pack and thermos. How can you eat down there? Lily always asked. Bad enough you spend your life with trash, bringing it home, smelling up— Now, Lily. . . . He never did smell. After, when her little tirade was over, she'd admit that he was clean, always had been, always changed clothes before going home.

He sat at the edge of the pond. There were no trees—the town had bulldozed the place; the one lone elm had died long ago— merely a thicket of brush, some huckleberry bushes, a few wild roses spreading and lots of dead twigs from the year before to be cleaned out. He took off his shoes and set his feet deep into the salt water.

Though still and warm above, under it was cool with a faint current. Over the surface islands of scud moved almost imperceptibly. It all looked so dead—that was the deception. But when one of the tiny islands drifted close, his eyes, so used to scouring the surface, detected the difference: all these thousands of green and brown and black specks, living in a mass, joining and separating. How many in a mass? (Impulsively he tried to count. Useless.) And how many masses before this? And how many years? The thought staggered him. Below, his own face met him, peculiarly black except for the faint glitter of eyes and a thin rift where his teeth were. His shadow. . . . The more he stared, the more it seemed somebody else's—his brother Tommie's, his mother's, Uncle Dan's, faces he couldn't recognize. The water rippled a bit and made him a dozen people all at once. Deep deep under, were there layers and layers of him too, and centuries of him from the first people of all? Were they still here? Where did they go? What for?

He felt strange—he could see through his own head. He could see the sand bottom, and he heard Janice questioning, and he reached down through his face and touched the bottom and thought: if you reach far enough . . .

But his face moved aside and doubled in size. Out of it came another—

"Hey, Huey—*Huey!*" it said. He turned around:

"Mannie! Jesus, you scared me. How come I didn't hear you?"

"How come you didn't? *You* tell *me.*"

"Guess I musta been thinkin."

Mannie laughed. "I don't know how much thinkin you been doin, Huey, but somethin sure brought you luck." Mannie's hand whipped out a packet and flailed it at the air. In the sun it was green green— "One thousand! All yours, Huey. What a Fourth you'll have with that!" He hurled it at Huey abruptly in one of those off-guard throws they always made when kids, shouting *Huey, catch!*

Huey caught it. "One—mine—you mean—" And Mannie and the dump rose into the sky, his own hands with the money drifted off in waves— He blinked. It all came back. "If I knew what to say . . ."

"You earned it, Huey," Mannie said. "Congrats. The boys are all real glad. Couldn't have been—"

The rest of the words he didn't hear. Won. *Won!* He had never

won anything in his whole life. He would bust, he could not hold
it, he swelled upward closer to the sky. And Mannie said *earned*.
Earned. What did he mean? How? It made a peculiar sadness he
couldn't explain. If he had collected that many bottles, sold that
much metal, piled up rags . . . You earn something. Maybe Mannie
meant— He didn't know what Mannie meant.

Mannie slapped him on the back. He heard him say, "Don't spend
it all in one place" and laugh, then saw him grow smaller as he
crossed the dump to his car.

Huey felt so self-conscious standing here in the middle of so much
waste with that packet a little too big for his hand—if they'd only
given him a check— But his thoughts leaped more each minute, the
impact had just struck home, his head was a heap of half-thoughts
and desires: perhaps a little, just a little, for the carnival tonight,
though Lily'd planned for that from the regular pay: the rides, bet-
ting, hot dogs, cotton candy and apples and the big Bingo game she
always won wine at. No, no—there were bills, needs, new fridge, down
payment on a car, bedroom plastered— But maybe a nice dress for
Lily. Even—he squinted—glasses for him (sometimes working on the
jalopy late afternoons his vision lied; only his fingers told the truth).
And the kids—but Lily'd have the answers, all—

Anyway he must go home—right now—and surprise them all. But
maybe Mannie'd been there, surely somebody'd tell them if he didn't
hurry, he'd cancel his run up to Riverhead. Instead they would all go
for a swim at the town beach, snack at the Drive-in, or cook-out in
the yard, then off to the carnival. He had promised the kids—not
every night, but opening night, the third, and the Fourth. Thus far
he had kept his word. But after Monday night, he too felt a goading
to return. People said all carnivals were alike. Maybe they were, but
inside you a carnival always felt new and new thoughts came into
your head. Opening night was like the first carnival he'd ever seen:
you come around the bend of Benton Lane and there's a cup of
light upside down in the sky and for a second your eyes almost
can't hold the shooting dazzle of colors, the merry-go-round and Ferris
wheel and chairplanes, and all that light holding the night up.

"Oh Daddy, *look*—" Janice said. Paulie was silent, but all eyes.
Lily glanced at Huey and smiled. The old feeling—his and Lily's—
wasn't gone. It was in the kids, they had never seen—really seen—

the carnival, and they would not yet, with untouched eyes. And when they were all on the grounds, in the midst of half the town bumping about them in the excitement of the first night, everybody laughing so gaily and shouting, everybody so happy—even old Lydie Bailey loud-talking and slapping her own leg—he scooped up Paulie, he said, "How about a ride on the dobbies?" swaying to the music, to the horses bobbing, but Paulie had his eyes elsewhere. His arm lashed straight out, his face rapt with the distance up. "Ferris wheel!" And Huey saw the whole thing in the boy's eyes, he crushed him close, feeling he was holding himself in his arms. He hesitated the briefest interval and said, "Yessir, son," in a jiffy whisked the boy along, Paulie taut with excitement, his little hands were like a vice on Huey's neck.

"Two," Huey said. "One half-fare."

"*One* half-fare! Who you kiddin?" The man winked.

It set Huey in highest spirits. The attendant secured the bar and as the Ferris wheel unloaded and loaded, they rose higher and higher until finally it rotated freely. Paulie laughed, a nervous excited laugh, and his fascinated eyes soared too, the whole carnival caught clean and brilliant in his eyes. He had the whole thing inside him forever and ever—Huey knew that—he would never forget, not just the lights, the height, the sweep and pull sending them into the stars and sucking them down to earth again, but a certain sensation. . . .

Once they stopped directly on top, could see the whole carnival below, the town beyond, then the sea and the deep dark sky. And it was suddenly terribly familiar, terribly intimate, like— But for the life of him, strain as he might, Huey could not say—like—? Below, the carnival looked so small, the people like ants, the wriggling lights alive, the flashing bulbs crawling in circles and squares . . . but set inside the big space beyond, the sea and the night going on and on, it grew smaller, like a heart beating in the dark. And on Sunday it would be gone—to another town, and another; and for how many lives had that gone on, how many carnivals in the world with other people in other places and other times, and how long would it go on? And suddenly he felt such a pity for everything that was going, all the people and all the carnivals in the world, that he wanted to reach out his hand and touch it all. He wanted to be *in* it, he wanted to tell them how he felt. But it was all so far away. At once he wanted to go down. But the Ferris wheel unloaded one chair at a time. And when he finally stepped off onto the trampled grass and looked around, he was confused. What he saw must have been all in his eyes. There was a vague memory of some excitement that roused him looking down over the carnival as if he were about to fall into somewhere that he was suddenly seeing for the first time— But when he went to say, to touch it, it was gone. And now it was like a great open wound—the lights were naked bright and hurt his eyes, the decorations cheap and torn and dirty, used and used, the boards warped and the ground trampled to a fine dust kicked up everywhere. . . .

But Paulie was laughing, he'd got his teeth stuck to a candy apple and Janice could not loosen it because she was laughing harder than he was.

"Just look at them!" Lily sighed and took his hand. The touch felt good. It anchored him back.

"It's them," he said. "They put the life into it."

"Yes," she said.

Yet he was thinking: I'm glad they won't see the grounds on Sunday morning.

But it wasn't Sunday, it was the third, and staring out over the dump—under the noon sun as bleak as abandoned carnival grounds—his head was light and confused and giddy with plans and desires. But Lily would straighten him out, she always did. He locked the shack—always a joke that, with *his* gold mine in it—and as he put the key in his pocket, he saw a shadow fall neatly over his shoe, and looked up.

"Aggg . . . ," he said, startled because he had neither heard nor seen him—he didn't know the man's name, but recognized one of the skimmer crew. Strange too, since the man had rounded the shed on the wrong side—the side opposite the entrance to the dump. How long had he been behind the shed? The sun was very high, and the man's face at that angle looked like stone—maybe because he did not move it to say a word.

"Yeah?" Huey said, still now.

"Yeah—"

He swung around at the other voice. Mannie back! Mannie of all people! But he couldn't speak—more startled, afraid even, standing between the two men; and his hand touched the locked door. The metal was hot, his hand tingled. Without time to think, to listen, even to wait, Huey knew why they had come, and the shock of it—why did Mannie dare to speak?—came so violently that he felt a panic and his hand shot out at Mannie, the other with the money fled automatically back, and at the same instant his eyes twitched, insisting on nearly closing, Mannie blurred, he saw his own arm leap uncontrollably into the air, the money fling high, and then a streak of blue and green and ashes. But he felt nothing. . . .

He must have lain there still for a long time because when he opened his eyes, he was very stiff, his head felt burned to the skull, and he felt sweat crawling over his face. Worst of all, he could scarcely see because his head was slightly tilted and the sun directly in his eyes nearly blinded him. He could hardly move his head but his eyes rotated easily. He made out that he was lying on the side of a low mound—he knew exactly where. Mannie and the man must have dragged him here so nobody could see his body from the gate. What had hit him? How far up had he leaped? The man must have struck from behind, but where? He felt nothing. Only the heat on his head. It drove, it penetrated him. It was almost impossible to breathe. The heat stuffed like hard cotton into his nose, pressed a heavy blanket suffocating over his face. And he wanted his hand to go out to push it back, but the hand did not obey, it would not move. At that realization his blood soared, choked up painfully into his chest, and his breathing throttled. He tried to force the hand, then the other, then one leg, then the other. Nothing moved. And his head? I'll make it, I will— But it did not budge.

For a while he lay there thinking about how—why—it had happened. He did not understand. Mannie and a sailor from the skimmer boats, yes. He would never have suspected. Who else but somebody you didn't suspect? And in plain day. But Mannie. . . . You never knew anybody or anything. You began to—

Lily. She would think he was on the Riverhead trip.

Nobody will come today, he said. Or tomorrow. After the holiday, the fifth, yes. But not today or tomorrow. Unless they search. Of course they will.

What surprised him was that despite his thoughts, he did not feel much of anything—anxiety or pain or sorrow or bitterness. He waited.

There was a whisper over the ground, he could hear it so keenly, and abruptly a bird—robin—sounded on the huckleberry bush, once, and flapped off. And suddenly he was assaulted by familiar sounds.

Nearby, papers rustled in the wind, a tail dragged over the ashes, a tin rolled down against a stone. . . .

And the sun beat down, scorching and searing, pressing the sweat out of him. The sweat seeped into the corners of his eyes and smarted with a vigorous sting, and his eyes went on burning, all his head alive with the burning sensation.

His eyes rolled over the sky. A few fragments of white clouds were edging into his pupils, a fly on his cheek dark against them. But the sun penetrated so strongly that he had to blink to keep the clouds from floating off.

His lids were so heavy, they closed over, and he listened. Close, a fly buzzed constantly. He heard the sounds of everything beating and moving around him. He forced his eyes open only when he heard something come very close, rapidly move off, rummage, and then come back. He heard it keenly. It was then that he most wanted to move—he wanted to see. He knew it was a rat. He heard it brush against his leg, and after, he felt it touch under his chin, and felt a faint breath. A white cloud came wholly into his eyes, making the sky so painfully blue it stung like a wound in his head. The pain made a rapid bolting in his blood. Blood careened to his head and beat with tremendous force—

He could feel the earth in his head whispering and beating, and see the alien cloud and sky; it was all beating and he seemed to rise, his whole head elevated.

Ma?

He was thundering with movements, and it frightened him. And the terror of not knowing what it was spread through him. Maybe everybody felt that way when— His blood leaped. He wanted just to move, to go on moving forever. Forever? Janice . . . infinity . . . inside you. Janice! Lily! He wanted to shout— And he opened his mouth, but he could not speak.

He knew then he was dying.

But he had never felt so alive before! He heard the fly at the edge of his ear. He listened with all his concentration. He did not want the buzzing ever to end. And he wanted to feel the sun as long as he could, he wanted it to burn his skin and smart his eyes and rot away the flesh. He opened his eyes wide and the sun burned, water filled them, the sky toppled, and, filled with the intensity of it all, he tried to laugh. He felt his own sound, a vibration inside him.

It was when the rat touched his neck that he knew the moment was coming, and he wanted to feel himself pulsing in something, he was afraid he would fall into the empty sky before it happened. And when he felt the claws against his cheek, the body mount his chin, sniffing, and saw the eye stare into his, he did not want it to stop. He felt every movement of it. He could feel the motion of its belly, its pulsing against him. It came up over his eye—he saw its snout, its teeth come down—and covered it. He opened his eyes wider. He could see the cloud and the sky and the rat above him, pulsing with his blood.

And he waited.

Don't Stay Away Too Long

I CAME ABOUT Lettie," I said when old Chapman let me in, though I didn't want to tell him.

He looked very tired. He cupped his tea with both hands—from a bowl, as he always drank it—and sucked at the rim, a pleasant sound from long ago, homey and comforting. The little Japanese men, badly painted on the cheap china, peered through his fingers. The place smelled of cats—two of them lay in a cardboard carton near the kitchen stove on a dirty red cushion clawed half to bits, cotton stuffing everywhere; the third, its tail coiled around his leg, kept pawing at his shoelace.

"They told me don't come," he said. "She's a little sick and couldn't come home for Christmas. I wanted her here." His eyes went up—through the window—into the dark; the elm in the near fall of light was leafless and still, a web against the sky. A little ice had gathered at the base of the pane. "A man should have more than one daughter," he said.

"That's asking for it," I said. "It costs."

"The pleasure's worth it, though—honest—she never cost me anything, Lettie didn't. In money, I mean." He reached down to rub Peekie. The air was stifling, the way old Chapman liked it. He was a thin thing sitting there, so little flesh, his clothes a loose heap against his bones.

"Who told you not to come?" I said.

"Somebody named Laughlin, the people she boards with in Chicago. Said the long trip, snow and all, was too much for—an old man." He laughed and left off rubbing Peekie. "Last year it was our Conklin cousin in Philly. She was in Jersey awhile—didn't care about it, but likes Chicago, says so all the time. Why she went that far . . . Course, she gets along anywhere, Lettie does. Only—she loved Long Island so. Last time she was here—" His eyes groped somewhere past the elm for the time-when.

"I remember," I said. Five years in March, his birthday, though she had been back once, quickly, a phantom trip, since then: three years ago. She had come to our door. My mother (she's dead now) was in. That night at supper she said, "Lettie was here today."

"Who?" I said, but my heart turned. The name, from no mention, wrenched with that familiar strangeness which twists a chord deep inside, not to untwist it again.

"Lettie *Chap*man. I forget her married name. That boy from upstate. *Oh*—Winthrop, is it?"

"Yes, from Binghamton." Hiram Jackson Winthrop. How could I ever forget that?

"Looked so peaked. She was always so quick and alive—takes after her father in that. We had a long chat, but she sat on the edge of the chair, perched—she always did—ready to flit. A couple of times she laughed, right out of the blue. She wasn't laughing at what *I* said; it startled me a little. And she kept touching her throat—so beautiful, hers so pretty white, we women always envy those things." *I* laughed —tried, but her eyes slid over me at the hollowness, though she'd never say.

"How did she seem?"

"*Thin* I told you."

"She always was."

"Not *that* thin. And anxious. She never said so, though we talked about you, but she was waiting to see you."

"Me?"

"Why else watch the clock? *I* couldn't hold her interest. She would go off, *you* know, not listen. There was something almost vagrant about her. Besides, she wouldn't come to see me, for *me,* and stay that long. We had tea."

"Perhaps it's important. I'd better go to her father's place."

"No—she's not there. She waited here until the last minute for the afternoon train. We called a taxi—she had to stop at her father's for a handbag. She'd only come last night."

Gone.

"But where *to?*"

"St. Louis, she said."

"Said? Why so cynical?"

"Well, she hadn't any luggage to speak of. And . . . she's not with her husband."

"Where's he?"

"In Binghamton. She's left him, Andy—months ago."

"Left—? Hiram? But what's she *doing?* She loved Hiram, I know she loved him. What'd she say?"

"In all the talk sometimes you don't mention the big things."

I was putting on my coat when she said, "Anderson—" I turned. I always remember her that way—tall and slim herself, her gray close hair neatly waved, her skin still a lovely pink; standing, alone there, she seemed to be free of it all. She said, "Don't stay single too long, Anderson—please."

As always, I ended up walking on the beach—the whitecaps like ice, the sand crunched hard, winter like needles in the wind, numbing. Then I headed for Chapman's. It was always warm there.

This time it was the same—very warm, the smell of cats, the air stale and sour with cigarette smoke and brewing tea. There was a constancy in it all you could count on. Was that what had always brought Lettie back before? Even now I felt something of her in the room. And there was the blue and green afghan she had knitted him—"for your winter legs because you're so good to me, Poppa"—for which birthday?

"Git, Shasta!" He shooed the tiger cat away from his tea. "Never do get enough when somebody else's eating." He looked up, direct blue eyes, clean blue. "Don't see much of you, Andy. I miss you too. Well, if you came about Lettie—"

"Yes, I did." Now, tell him now, I thought. Why was I prolonging it?

"The last letter's not too far back." His eyes quivered a bit.

"*No,* Mr. Chapman—"

"Oh, it's all right. Lettie'd be glad you read it." He reached for the change purse he carried for groceries instead of a wallet; he always kept Lettie's latest letter in it, should anyone ask. He got up to find his glasses, spiderfine gold rims, then sat to unfold it. "Yes—this's it. May it was." He mulled, his head aslant toward the light and read into the letter, but soon stopped. "It's long. *You* read it." He closed his eyes, his right hand twitched a little. "Oh, it's not her writing; least this is good and clear. Hers always gave me a hard time." It was on that cheap Woolworth tablet paper. The hand was meticulous and large.

"Why didn't *she* write?"

"Hurt her arm. She called one night—the only reason I keep the phone now, it costs. She took a spill so this friend wrote. Must be a nice guy, the way she talks."

" 'Dear Poppa—' "

He smiled. "She never could say Dad. Too stiff for you, Poppa, she'd say."

" 'About this time I'd be coming home. It's the green time and I can smell the Sound. The iris are out, aren't they? Just like a purple fence around the whole house, I can see them now. It's hard to explain after so long how the island has such a hold on me. Isn't that silly? Hi always said if I found out, I wouldn't go back—the mind works that way. But he was wrong. Hi was wrong about so many things, but I loved him.' "

"Don't stop now," Chapman said. "It gets good there."

" 'I have to laugh when I think he said if we entertained anybody I spent all the time on the flowers and none on the food.' "

Mr. Chapman laughed. "That's Lettie," he said and pulled Shasta up into his lap and puffed quick.

" 'He'd say it as a joke, but it never was, *I* knew it—especially when he said I slept too much lately or I'd go away from him right there sitting beside him, times when I didn't go back to the island anymore. I did try not to talk about it, but I had to mention the island sometime, didn't I, Poppa? He took it like I meant to hurt him for saying I shouldn't go back or leave him for long stretches the way I used to when I belonged to *him*. I did too, I knew that, I was with him even when I was on the island without him enjoying every minute of it, but I *felt* close to him, it wasn't to hurt him, but he'd say, Getting even again, and I'd say, I was born there, Hi, that's all, you come, you'd love it too, I have to talk, Hi, don't the psychiatrists say it makes you sick to think things and never tell them, storing them up inside so they rot and make you that way too? And who wants to rot? You've got to exercise some control, he'd say, but never tell me why—isn't that why we got married, I'd say, so it would be the one person in the world you could tell some things to?—I thought it was that—not even things you'd say to Poppa. Honest, I don't know why I'm thinking this now, Poppa, but I feel like writing just what I'm feeling. Mannie says I should write what I feel too. He's so good, Poppa. Three whole years, and why is it all in my mind now?' "

"A funny end, ain't it?" Mr. Chapman said. "She must've been pretty tired—or maybe Mannie, or couldn't think of anything else to say."

Tired! The girl's exhausted, she's at the brink. But I didn't know more than that. She's in New York, Mr. Chapman, she's in a hospital in New York, and I want to know why, she's so young, she's not even twenty-nine yet. . . .

And I could see her standing out there in the yard—under the willow tree, the wind blowing at her long hair, her head bent, fascinated, calling with abrupt and tense curiosity, "Andy—come quick. Look! The branch is black with them." And the underside of many branches. "They're aphids," I said. "A-what?" "Aphids. We've got to get rid of them. They'll kill it, eat it up." "Pops! Pops!" she cried, running back to the house. "They're eating the willow. The willow's dying."

But it was dark now. There was nothing here. I closed my eyes for a second.

"Tired?" Mr. Chapman said.

"A little."

"You work too much, Andy. You know, you ought to get yourself a woman. Every man ought—"

I didn't want to talk about me, not me, I couldn't, so I finally said it, "Hiram just called me."

He seemed not to have heard, but I heard his thin wheeze, he puffed quick and he stopped petting. Shasta opened her eyes and cocked her head up curiously.

"Lettie's Hiram?" his voice tested heavily, and air wheezed out of him. "She's not in Chicago, is she?"

"She's in New York, Mr. Chapman," I said. His eyes bolted up in sudden, contained desperation. He waited, his eyes fixed on me. In them I saw the naked kitchen bulb, making him look blind, and I saw me in them. I got up quickly. Shasta leaped to the door. The other two followed miaowing to get out. "She's in the hospital. We'll have to go in. Now I don't know anything else—I wish I did."

"Why didn't she want me to know? I'd've—" Already he was on his feet too, headed for his bedroom, but the cats' miaowing stopped him; instinctively he let them out.

"I'll be by in half an hour. We'll drive in. There's no train till morning."

He looked up, still but distracted. What was he seeing?

"Yes, Hi, I'll be ready," he said.

So I was doing it again, making that journey that would never really end for me. The endless night slipped over us, the streetlights like stars too close to believe, the darkness in a deep sea against the lights that made a narrow tunnel around us.

"Why should she lie to *me?*"

"I don't know. Why would she?"

His head jerked. I felt his stare, something of a reverse accusation. And I was ashamed. I heard Lettie in one of those phone calls that would come sometimes in the middle of the night: "You'll look in on him, won't you? He tried to do the right thing, he's always tried, and I wanted my marriage to work—for Poppa too. You understand, Andy? But promise you'll see he's always okay."

"Why didn't she ever ask me to go where she was?"

"She didn't want to hurt you, Mr. Chapman."

"Lettie could never hurt me. Doesn't she know that?" For a minute he lay back, breathing like a hurt dog. Then abruptly, all in a rush, he said, "What'd she do all that time? How'd she live? What'd all those calls and letters mean then? Why'd Hiram keep so quiet? What's this Mannie?" He slumped wearily. "You're walking along in the dark and thinking everything's all right, then you're falling right in the daylight. How come?" he murmured.

"Hiram said we should be prepared, she wasn't the same as when we'd seen her last, because she's been sick, lost weight, she's very tired—"

"You been knowing this all along?"

"Not all." Not the beginning, not *why*.

"How much? You *seen* her?" He leaned forward. Was he accusing me of not telling him?

"Once in Binghamton I stopped by. There was nobody home. I called Hiram at work. He said Lettie'd gone to New York for a day or two to see Miriam Walsh—you remember, her bridesmaid. At the time I didn't think anything of that, but I remember Miriam came out to the beach that summer and she never came by, never saw you either. My mother was struck, a little offended by it. I went to see Miriam later, in the city. It was then—she told me—I found out Lettie'd been drifting away from Hiram."

"What you mean, drifting?"

"That's what I asked Miriam. She couldn't say, she didn't know, and *I* don't."

At first her visits to Miriam were quick flights, feigned shopping trips, but they grew longer, extending finally to weekends. "You had to see her to realize," Miriam said. "She was gone, her eyes . . . Lettie wasn't *there* anymore, just still flesh sitting beside me. I began to dread her visits because I couldn't get to her. Until she started taking nips, *I'd* never seen Lettie drink—oh, one, two at a party, though Hi drank a good bit, for business more than anything, though I think that she started him in too. But with a drink Lettie'd look so consoled. There were times when she'd simply look at me and say, Miriam, what's happening? Or she'd arrive quite drunk afternoons, not vulgar, never vulgar, but a quiet, tender, lost drunk. She sat in the corner of the sofa—and disappeared. I said, If you don't tell me I can't do anything. She looked into her hands, like a mirror, as if she'd find it there. You think I'm lying, Miriam, she whispered to me, but I don't know, I really don't know, and there's nobody to tell me either. We had an argument finally, and that day somehow I knew would be the last. I remember it—July 18 —because she ran out on Hi the next day."

"But she loved Hiram," Mr. Chapman said.

"I know. But something was eating at her, and she knew it—so she started to run."

"Lettie liked to stay *put* when she got to a place."

"You can be in one place and drift, but she'd been all over—New York, parts of Jersey, Philly, once three months in Atlanta, a few in Chicago, Providence—" She had moved like a migrant bird which had lost its instinct.

"How do you know so much?"

"I've been following her for years, Mr. Chapman."

"You never said. Andy, you mean—"

"I don't mean *anything,* Mr. Chapman. We grew up together is all."

But I still heard her calling. She sank onto the sand, huddled over. "What?" I yelled. "I'm not just a girl anymore," she said, her hands covering her thighs. "Help me, Andy. Get my clothes." I could see blood ooze between her fingers. I ran for the clothes. When I went back, she was in the Sound, nude, washing herself. "The water burns." She was crying, and laughing.

"I thought I saw her once—in Providence, but I wrote it off as imagination" was all I told him. But my mother said I had had a long distance call from Providence—it was Lettie, but she had left no message. Yet I knew where she'd be. She had slipped up this time, I thought. She had spent just one semester at Pembroke, all she could afford; her friends had lived on Benefit Street in a shabby, nineteenth-century crate turned boardinghouse, dark, with weary steps. Some Mrs. Willis had it now. She gave me the once-over and said, You wait in her room. It was just turning that early winter dark but there was nothing to see in the room: a bed, chair, night table, bureau. And the African violet. Of course, a flower . . . The bed was not made up. The blanket was thrown back and I could see where her body had lain half-coiled, her knees up, the sink in the pillow and another where her arm must have been flung out. I touched it where she'd lain. I kept saying her name, silly, thinking it would make her come. The dark was coming down and I sat there two hours, but in my blood I knew she wouldn't come. I got up to go but I couldn't—yet. I was so close, it was as near as I'd been in years. I opened the closet. I couldn't see but I felt in—just two dresses. The empty racks jangled. I've no right, I thought, but I opened a bureau drawer too. Let me in, just for a little while, Lettie— Everything was laid out, so neat. You still have that, order, I felt, with quick joy and a sense of reprieve. Then the scent came—it made me nearly dizzy, rose petal sachet, the kind my mother used, the scent she'd given Lettie the first time. I slammed the drawer shut. I didn't want to breathe—I wanted to hold her in me. I went down into the night air—fast, and outside I suddenly wanted to breathe deep, to let her out into the grass and trees and night, into the whole air so she would be everywhere around me. Tomorrow I'll be back, I thought, and laughed out loud.

But the next day when I went back, though her door was open, she was not there. It was the African violet told me she was really gone. The window was empty. I've imagined it, she never *was* there, I said. I shouted for Mrs. Willis, but she was standing behind me. She went early this morning, she told me last night, Mrs. Willis said. She was embarrassed for me. I told her thanks.

So it began again, each empty room a beginning to the circuit I followed. Oh, I could have persisted, but each move came as a warning, a message from her that I was getting too close: Stay away, but don't stay away too long. She knew I was hovering somewhere behind her; at times I even felt that if *I* turned, I'd see myself hovering behind. She was still bound—not to me, but to something, through me. I had to know what it was.

You can't evade me this time, Lettie, I thought, I know where you are now.

"Nobody ever told me anything," Mr. Chapman said. He was smoking one after the other. You live on cigarettes—and tea, Lettie would chide. In his lap his free hand twitched. His knees made two pointed little islands in his trousers.

"Sometimes you don't know it's happening."

"Maybe she couldn't say it, but she'd feel it—I know my girl."

"Not being able to say is hell enough."

"What're you holding back?" The streetlights tore over his eyes. In the half-light his face looked eroded.

"I only know what they said."

"They. *They!* Who the hell's *they?* Might's well be air you're talking of."

Or sand or sea or stars. Or maybe we are only the wind captured in the flesh for a little while and then let go.

In the distance the city glowed, a ball of light swelling into the sky. I hated New York, all the cities, then. Around us it made the night darker. A gull cried. Mr. Chapman's head jerked. Abruptly he laughed. "She kept gulls. Knew all their calls. She'd stand for hours on the beach —no telling when she'd come home. When the spirit moved."

"I've tied a few splints on with her."

She made a ceremony of releasing the gulls that were well: you held the wings loose and gentle but taut, stroking head and gullet, while she untied the splint, carefully exercised the leg, then launched it in a smooth upward trajectory so it suddenly flapped away and soared. How she'd laugh! For a few days after the gull would come near but it soon stayed with the flock.

"She couldn't live without the ocean—she had to come back here. All those cities were just prison. But a woman's got to go where her man goes. Marriage is that."

Marriage . . . I had to tell him that too.

"Mr. Chapman, there'll be other people there."

"Who?" His voice hung.

"Chip Ladkin."

"She never mentioned no Chip to me."

"Lettie got married again, Mr. Chapman."

"She can't, she's still married to Hi."

"No. She had to make her separation clean or not at all." Maybe for her it was impossible to have part only, maybe it was the one way for her to hold and keep what was still good and unviolated inside her.

"Why'd she do that?" His voice was too weak to hold breath, but I had to go on: "One of those rich Atlanta boys with a big house on Paces Ferry Road, and time, plenty of time, and—"

The air was suddenly too hot, uncomfortable. I slit the window a bit. You could almost feel snow in the sudden air.

"She didn't, did she?" It was as if he had said, *Why* did she? It was a cry now: "Drink?"

For a long time he sat so still he seemed to retreat into the loose clothes, only now and then a faint flick of breath from him.

"Married again—and then not. How come things go bad so quick? That girl'd make any man happy. You know that better than anyone, Andy."

I said nothing. I saw his knees were quivering.

"Andy," he murmured, "I'll know it's her, won't I?"

It summoned up her face, I could not hold it in, I saw it straight ahead, growing, spreading into the night.

"There's the hospital," I said, too loud.

Inside, his eyes were bloodshot and watered in that full light. His hand reached into the long corridor. "It's all so white."

Lettie was in 609 east.

In the elevator he held onto the sidebar; his head trembled. "I never did like the smells," he said.

Outside 609 a man was sitting on a bench. I knew the long bend of him, the hair hanging thick over his forehead, recognized the stolid high-boned face as he looked up and rose with a certain dignity: and it all came back, the wedding I never went to, the long painful summer. But for an instant I loved him because he had been hers, near her all that time.

He was too thin. He stared at Mr. Chapman like trying to dredge up a thing too familiar to name. Squinting, he took the old man's hand, then mine.

"Hello, Hiram," I said, but he was staring at Mr. Chapman, who was staring at the door. "She in there?"

"Yes," Hiram said. Mr. Chapman started for the door, but it opened and a nurse came out.

"I'm her father," he muttered.

She smiled. "One at a time, please. When he comes out."

"He?" He turned to Hiram.

"Mannie," Hiram said.

"That Mannie—the friend? My letter?" he asked me. "What's he—"

"You better sit down," I said. This time he let me help him, next to Hiram. He sat quiet, his hands cupped loose on his thighs. Then suddenly he said, nearly shouting, "What's Lettie doing here anyway? What's happened? What?" And as abruptly he was still, his eyes fixed on the opposite wall as if he would read it there. Down the corridor the nurse turned curiously.

"How'd *you* know?" Hiram asked Mr. Chapman. I saw how old Hiram looked then, his eyes deep, his forehead all scowled, how gray his hair was getting—and him young.

"The Laughlins called *me*," I answered for him.

"Those bastards. They wanted their money, that was all. She'd be dead if it were up to them. They called every number they could find in her pocketbook. A dinky little hole smelling of—"

"Okay," I said.

"*Not* okay. I'm sorry, but some things feed you up to here."

Mr. Chapman said, "You knew too? Everybody knew and nobody *did* anything. Why didn't somebody do something?"

"We tried. She wouldn't let us. Maybe *she* didn't know what to do."

But her father wasn't listening. "I'm an old man but I know you got to find out what's wrong before you can do anything. If you wanted to, and loved her—no, that's wrong—you all did. But she's only . . . a girl, Hiram."

"I almost killed the Laughlins. When I got there—you've no idea —the dirty stairs and walls and in her room just a dingy bed all sunk and a torn spread—nothing—just a mirror. She'd cleaned it, it was so bright it was awful, it made it all look like two crummy rooms. Everything was stained, and plaster holes, but at least the room smelled of *her,* I could see she tried, with the whole house outside the room stinking of rancid and bedroom and piss. I don't know how she could—" He dropped his head, his hand stripped over his eyes. "Well, she wasn't there. I almost killed them—I said that—yes, gone, they didn't know how long. I yelled—I scared that woman good, that's when she called the police, or went to, but her husband was afraid, they knew what kind of joint it was, a flophouse, to look once quick. I didn't know where to look for Lettie. Why, how should *I* know? I just walked—the park's on the other side, blocks away, and there's all those people, well, twenty maybe, and a cop. I crossed the street. Someone said Let her go and the cop said Wise guy and a woman said Have a heart to him, but he ignored them and I suddenly saw Lettie—it made me sick, she was so skinny, and I knew no food, and drink all the time, and that running, and all rot inside—" I heard her father choke back a sound and I raised my hand, but Hiram said, "She was with the little girl about four, less, yes—she could hardly stand up—why'd those bastards let her get out like that? Laughlin bastards should be strung up—and I heard her say Please I want to get her home, she's lost, she was playing in the park and the officer said I'll see she gets there and Lettie said I know but I want to *see* she gets there and the cop said You don't trust me and Lettie started to cry, I was calling her, and her hands went up in the air and fell like wings all broke and I was calling Lettie, I shouted Lettie, but she was down on the ground, I could just see her shoulders shaking, crying, and kneeling to tell the little girl He'll get you home, when she fell over and rolled and landed on her side, she was out and the cop called an ambulance quick from the corner, and I had her then, nobody could touch her . . . Mannie—he heard it over the radio—we've been here. She doesn't come to. I mean she only smiles and doesn't say anything. I've been here all the time, the second day, I've been waiting for her to say something, one word, just one word for me, one word for Hiram, Lettie."

"One word for Hiram?" her father said, and something almost sadly ironic in his tone made Hiram stare at him as if he were attacked, and shamed. The old man stood up; he looked down at Hiram. "You didn't say why, Hiram. You ought to know, you're her husband."

"Was."

"No. She never changed. Whatever changed, Lettie didn't." He leaned against the wall.

"I couldn't help her, Dad. Maybe I wasn't enough. Whenever she had a whim, she went back to the island to stay with you. I went to a doctor—psychiatrist. She laughed at me— There's nothing wrong with you or me, our life's so natural, she said. But she'd go away again—two weeks, three. What'll people think, I'd say. We're people, we have to live our way, she'd tell me. I did everything, I gave her what I could, there were no other women, I didn't go out much, I drank some . . . But she'd leave me. Once—for a while it was over, she'd done with going, she said—surprised me—but then came the drinking, she'd begin to go to the city on binges—like some instinct to go moving her away from me for a little while. . . ."

"And you wouldn't tell *me?*"

"How would that have helped? Besides, to be honest—I can be now —I didn't want to admit I'd failed."

"Not you. All of us," I said. Hiram, startled, gazed at me as if to say, You too?

How could so many of us fail and not know why? It all seemed so inscrutable—even this white hospital where day and night men probed, warding off, creating and sometimes destroying, yet at illuminating moments as helpless and primitive as one man with his lone fire warding off night until the slow inevitable morning.

The door opened. Her father bolted up. We all looked up. Midway, he halted. A compact little man with an electric tautness about him, dark and Italian looking, came out. He stopped short too, as if struck when he saw us.

Hiram whispered, "That's Mannie."

"Him?"

"He's not so bad," he said. "Poor guy's been here every minute."

For one long instant he stood there with a hard look—disgust? anguish?—then turned away from us and went down the corridor. Her father crossed to the door and pushed it open—

We fell then into a long empty void, waiting. A hospital is a timeless place, you do not know how long you sit, you stare at the door, that slow timeless white closes over you and you sink deep deep into it, the quicksand of your own flesh seems to bury you, so taut with life as you listen, feeling, yearning for the faintest merging with what is behind the door, you want to reach out with your hands and tear into the stillness and make breath, give breath and hear the air, hear it cry out—

"Something wrong?" a voice broke in. I looked up.

"I'm Chip Ladkin," he said, "her husband." He was so young, almost too young for me to believe, not handsome but with a kind of beauty that startled me in a boy, and he did startle me. Maybe it was what drew her—cheeks flushed, and a healthy clear skin and eyes with a terrible naked innocence and clean blond hair. But where had he come from?

"You looked as if you were about to—"

"I felt sick," I said with a half-smile. "I guess I *was* about to."

"I'm Hiram," Hiram said.

"I know that—I knew it from the beginning," the boy said. "I was sure I could make her forget you." Hiram raised a hand—the boy was too tactless, but so unpretentious Hiram could hardly protest. "Well, I didn't. I'm not very bright—sounds funny, doesn't it?—and I live in pretty much of a party world where you get used to doing something. *Some* people do, but she couldn't. Why should I want to work?—I didn't have to—she couldn't understand that, though she went along with it. We knocked around all over the place. Only *I* could stop the party. I was trained, Ladkin's second-nature-to-me-now. But it caught her. She was sailing, oh boy sailing, enough to keep her way up there all the time where they say you don't have to see or know or feel anything. That's just a lie—because she *was* feeling it, all the time feeling, she felt too much. I got so I hated that, and ohjesusGod how I wanted to make her stop and come down and play it serious, my way, and us the winners every time. But she couldn't do it, my Lettie—"

"*Please* don't say my Lettie," Hiram wrenched out.

"Well she was—for a little while. I guess that's what it's all about—a little while that everything's got. You have to live it. You think that? Am I the only crazy one?"

"You're not such a boy," I said. For he did not look young now—innocent, yes, with an old man's innocence—without the face and the stillness.

"Everybody loses," he said.

"Shut *up!*" Hiram said.

"I always talk too much," the boy said.

"But she left you—why?" I said. I had to press it. "I'm sorry, Hi," I said, but he too stared at the boy, waiting.

"Someone else," the boy said.

Hiram. Chip. Mannie. Who else, Lettie?

"I don't believe it," Hi said.

"What else? We had everything together."

"Not love," Hi said.

"Yes—love—plenty," he said, hard, pressing.

"We're not talking about the same thing," Hi said.

The boy's face blurred now, a quick visible tarnish. "She was happy with me, she *was,* she was happy." He dropped his head then, lost. I think it was then he began to cry.

"What in hell *you* crying for?" The other voice—so strong—Mannie was back. "That won't do *her* any good."

The boy threw his head up. "What right've you got to tell *me?*"

"As much as anybody, Chip," Hiram said softly.

"Listen here," Mannie said, "you don't talk to me about rights—if it was rights, that girl wouldn't be here now, see? She'd be out living her way, not your kind of living, kid, oh no. For real—with what she got inside her, all heart and burning for things—air. *Air*—and colors, flowers—nobody ever loved flowers like her, I seen it. And when she talks about salt water, the whole ocean's in her, her goddamned heart turns blue, and her blood, and she got that rhythm of waves. If none of you seen it, you're blind. So don't talk about rights—never."

I stood up. Something was happening. He was looking too directly at us, as if he had a hard diamond in him, and I was afraid of that, I wanted to go away from him, but some insidious impersonal part of me sought him, drawn to him. I was trapped, the way you are when you want to run but follow irresistibly to see where it will lead you—

"But *you've* got those rights because *you* saw it in her?" I said. I laid bare my claim then—to the gulls and the willow, the beach and all my young life held in her. "I'm—"

"I know you—the boy back home." He laughed, too cryptic. "Dead on the vine. Oh, it's okay, Anderson, I get the picture—something always in reserve for both of you, huh?"

"Nothing like that. There couldn't have been," I said.

"Don't get all hot and bothered. That's right, there couldn't have been. You're smart to know it." He was so sure, cutting in his certainty. I wanted to cry, Don't! I came for this, but don't. Instead I said, "You know all the answers."

"You're wrong." His voice was violent, but contained, and his small frame trembled, the deep brown eyes glistening. "But I want to know everything about her, inside-out, just cause it's her. Just to understand all of her. First minute I seen her I wanted that—in Willy's Tavern, all alone. She didn't belong, you had to be stupid not to see it, and what's a girl like her doing in a place she don't belong? Not even for sex, not yet, just I had to know about her—the guys said let her alone, that kind kills you, but I got in it, I got started."

"Drop it, will you—please?" Hiram said, but his eyes fastened, he could not let go.

"Drop it—that's all you guys ever did."

"It's all we could," I said.

"*Try*—you ever hear of that?"

"I—we went after her—"

"Mister, you don't know what's going after—all the time, every minute watching, yeah—because I wanted her—"

"This is a hell of a time—"

"It's the only chance I got—for her. You can bet she'd never let me, she's too good. I wanted to watch her grow, all that in one girl—and with nobody in the world. No, *don't* say it. She didn't have you or him or a husband or anybody—because somebody cut her off. You got any idea what that means—to be *cut off?* Who knew it better than me? sleeping with her, yes sex too, hoping every time maybe at last it'd be me, Mannie, she's having it with. But she wasn't even *with me*—If only I could *make* her, I wanted her to be Lettie with Mannie, and me with her. That's what I was waiting for—just Lettie to say: I'm back now, Mannie, You made me be Lettie and I won't go away anymore. Then I'd know I was what a man was for. I sat and watched everything she did. She let me. All her habits, and voice, like water in her throat, soft, and the touch, and ribs and thighs, and her small feet. And watched her when she didn't know it too. Me, I couldn't help her. And I wanted to. But I was against her nature, I know it—me what wrote her letters and her breath on my face and telling me It's to my father, write it word for word careful. At least her words went through me, to him, and you too—me—"

Then I saw her father. I did not know how long he had been stand-ing there beside the closed door, fogged now, gazing as if he could not penetrate the white vault of the corridor. I flagged Mannie to stop. He looked back at her father, but he did not stop. Her father was mum-bling. His face looked too stunned to have heard anything. He seemed to hang on the wall, staring at Mannie, into him. He came forward, looking through us. "Where's she gone?" he said. "She's so little. I al-most didn't know her. Lettie?" He looked so small, hanging from his bones, and his clothes sagged as if caught in an underwater current. He stopped, suspended precariously, like an enormous question to us.

"Where you sent her," Mannie said.

"Shut your mouth!" I said. "He's the last one who'd hurt her."

"And you—" He turned on me. "What good's all your education if you can't see what's under your nose. You should've used a little com-mon sense."

"Some people defy common sense."

"She's not *people*, she's *Lettie*. Nobody else. Look—I'm just a cab driver, I got nothing, but I love that girl. You don't know how long I waited to see her be just Lettie. I don't know about women, but I know about her, and you ruined her, you told her she couldn't go back, and took part of her away, and that island and that house. She looked for it everywhere—you know that?—and couldn't find it. She even tried me, and I'd of been it if I could. I'd marry her now, yes, this minute, if she could just say one word to me before she died, I'd make it legal, we'd have that. But I'm not the one. She had to have two men—that was how she was, don't you see? and it was natural and healthy and real. It was so simple even she didn't see it. But they wouldn't let her live."

"Two men?" her father said, mystified. His eyes opened wide, he leaned close to Mannie, listening, nearly touching him.

"Him," Mannie said, flagging at Hiram. "And you. Nobody else in this world. She couldn't live without both of you. She needed you like air, *air*. And you sent her away."

Mr. Chapman let out a wild, wounded cry then. I thought he would fall. I caught him. "Not Hiram. Me. I sent her back to him—Is that what you mean? I sent her, I sent her, I sent—"

"You mean you made her go back to me—for good?" Hiram said, awed with the revelation of it. "That lull—then—"

"To save the marriage," old Chapman murmured.

"How saved does she *look,* Mr. Chapman?" Mannie said. "Saved for all those rented rooms people can be free in? She didn't want to be free. She already was. Why couldn't you leave her alone?" He looked back at the door hard, and when he turned to me he seemed struck, blunt, his face had lost all its violence, his chin quivered, his eyes darted. He swung around and disappeared down the corridor.

But old Chapman had my arm. "That boy's talking about me, Andy. I sent her back. I said Don't come back without Hiram. I didn't know." His bony hands clutched my arms, holding himself up. "I killed her, Andy. I killed my girl, didn't I?"

I could not answer him. The question was too deep in us all. I caught his elbows to steady him. I sat him down beside Hiram and Chip Ladkin—to wait. "None of us could have saved her, Mr. Chapman," I said finally and left him there.

I went to the door then. For an instant I stood there, staring at it: 609. I pressed my hands flat against the door and leaned my head against it. She was on the other side, this time I was sure. You have come all this way, Lettie . . . all those rooms you have traveled through. . . . My hand slid over the door. Could she hear that? Did she see the shadows of my feet under the door and wonder who it was and why I didn't go in? Still, I could not touch the knob. I looked back—at Hiram and Chip and Mr. Chapman sitting so quietly on the bench, waiting. And suddenly I did not want to see what it was they carried in their eyes. I wanted to keep that other Lettie. How did I know that, unless you see it, the dead do not stop, they go on in you, they have their life? I backed away. I turned then. I went down the corridor. I went down the stairs. I did not want to know what was there in her name and in her flesh behind the door.

The Rate of Decomposition
In a Cold Climate

I DO NOT GO BACK to the island much anymore. I could go. It is only a short drive, I am not so impossibly busy, I still have some relatives in town, and a few acquaintances, and my roots are there. But I do not go back. And I know the reason: I am afraid—oh, not with open fear, not the kind that startles the face visibly before the world at the unexpected sight of something familiar, but the kind that startles where most men fear it, in the heart, where no one can see or share the chafings memory makes, like unseen slivers of glass scraping constantly over the bleeding tissue.

My apartment in the city is on the eighth floor, comfortable, complete, and secure. Within these walls I have brought close to me the best of my world—the books, the music, the friends I prefer, those who live in the city in apartments not too unlike this or those who drift through in brief interludes away from home that become journeys into the past or reachings out for experiences that give the illusion of freeing them from the world in which they are daily entrenched. One comes, or another—Sid, Matt (twice), Sam Levine from the old 82nd, Vickie Bratton from the London office, Ev or Jay from the deeps of Atlanta, and sometimes one from the town on eastern Long Island—

And there are certain nights when—say in early October—with the windows open, the city quiet, the air is deceptively spring; when, with just a certain lift of the curtain and a freshness alien to asphalt and concrete, with a drift of perfume in the air (could it be pine and wild rose and sand?), the island comes in, my insides quiver, I think: Tonight Rennie will come; and I almost wait, listen for the elevator and the step on the carpet. His would be firm, quick, never hurried—

On such nights no one comes. That would be too kind—an actual presence would make me forget. No, of course nobody comes.

Yet it does happen. Memory tricks you—it fabricates its own arrivals. Say at Mirta's—Rod is telling his ambassador story, Mirta fiddling with her hand-touched Persian prints, Leah's soft black hair shifts under my hand, Bartok is playing, Nardeen belligerently strikes the Japanese chimes and laughs, I am on my sociable third martini—yes, it is that, the martini, not the crystal or the perfume but the olive, the green of the olive— It is the color of the old World War II cap somebody gave Rennie. So he is at the door again, knocking, I go down the stairs, I can see him across the hallway, the cap pushed back, that last time on the island—

"Paul!"

Cap, door, house, island—everything goes. It is Leah. With some difficulty it is Leah. She wants a drink. "I am *em*pty, darling." She turns the glass up, suspends it under my nose, and then kisses me. "One kiss —one drink. Fair enough?"

"Bargain," I say as she scowls curiously.

"You still here, sweetie?"

"What?" I think she has suddenly come into me, but no—she is already lost in Mirta's chatter, the Persian designs, red her favorite color. . . .

I go into the kitchen. It is quiet, nearly insulated, but beyond, their voices make an unceasing drone. We stay all evening, but the party is over for me, and I am not sure until I am back in the apartment and in bed that the thought is gone, that someone is not out there, standing at my door—

For that was always Rennie's habit even as a boy—to come and quite simply stand at the door of the summer house and wait. My mother would find him there when she went out to feed her Manx cats. "Why, Rennie, why don't you knock so we'll know you're there—or just walk in?" she'd say. He'd look up, his hair flopped in a loose gold ring under his cap—he lived in a cap—and stand with both hands on the handle of the bucket (we were eleven or so then) and the crab net over his shoulder. She'd laugh. "You don't want to let them go, do you?" He'd shake his head no, and she'd call me, though I was already behind her, waiting. "Paul, Rennie's waiting for you to go crabbing. *Careful* with the rowboat, don't lose the oarlocks or your dad'll have a fit, and keep in the shallows—*no* farther out than the crick. You listening?"

"Yes," I'd say. "Take *my* net too, Rennie." I'd take an oar in each hand with the locks slid on already. On the way the bucket and the locks would clank, a sweet sound in the early morning air, and the earth was pungent and the air good with the salt coming over, sometimes a thick perfume of pine when the wind was right.

These excursions together were rare. His father—Big Renkowski—was an old-timer, a Polack right out of Poland. I say big—he was not very tall, but massive with the bestiality of the Poles to this day in the town. He made Rennie follow him around and work day and night, as if they were making up for a thing he'd lost, but at times Mr. Renkowski had to make special hauls of potatoes or cauliflower to the city market; he would leave at five A.M., and then Rennie's mother would give him a holiday without telling his father. It was on those special days that my mother would find him standing at our door—no telling how long he'd been waiting—until someone stirred in the kitchen.

He was quick. Already he had the shape of the athlete, which would spring up almost overnight, in his early teens, lengthening him into a slim, lithe body, narrow-hipped and broad-shouldered, the kind men envy and women desire. His speed—his lunge with the net—was almost unfailing when he spotted a crab: he'd poise, his eye measuring with a perfect timing that later made him the most valuable player on the varsity, and with a quick lunge, scoop, and draw, he'd have a crab dripping in the air. I didn't know what gave me more pleasure, the sight of the trapped crab's claws dangling through the net prison or the sight of Rennie, cap askew, his face grave with the challenge, and then the abrupt bellow as he laughed full, showing all his teeth and then two whole suns glittering in his deep brown eyes.

When we finally went to divvy up the catch, he always ended by giving me all—you could bet he'd catch three-quarters of them—but justified it by telling me "I had the most fun, you betcha," sounding just like his father with that "you betcha." Once I tried to make *him* take them all. But his face seemed to withdraw into the quiet, set, with the eyes dark and brown and brooding, not really with me anymore as he gazed across the flats toward his father's farm.

From my bedroom window upstairs I could look out over the flats and sometimes catch sight of Rennie or his father far off on the tractor or hoeing or rotating irrigation. In later years, if I got to the island for planting, when his father wasn't home he'd let me ride with him and drop the young plants into the ground. If his father found out, he insisted if I was going to hang around and do chores like that, he'd pay me. What he meant was: don't waste Rennie's time. I think Mr. Renkowski knew my parents had the provincial native's aloofness to the Polacks, though they liked Rennie.

Once in a while I'd arrive in the midst of spraying—he'd be going up and down the furrows, the white spray jetting out on both sides in lethal streamers. He especially liked company then. The air would be filled with that pungent odor of sterility. "Look at it—" The field was a white dry desert; and acres of vast barren whiteness blended into the white afternoon sky.

"You oughta be glad. It saves the plants," I said.

"Yeah, but insects get through. You can't kill'm all." And when time came, here and there would be dead plants, a stem, whole leaves eaten away. "Some of them live through anything." He almost admired them—you could tell the way he marveled at how much a little thing could live through and how much damage it could do.

When I was with him in the fields, I realized he belonged to the land in a way I never could, though deep in me I longed to be part (or was it a kid's secret wish to be not me?) when I breathed the deep air and the burning scent of new-plowed earth and especially after, when I saw the new tender shoots we set out catch hold and straighten to the sun.

On one of those spraying days—the summer after I'd entered N.Y.U.—I got back from a day in the city to find him waiting on the back stoop as he used to. He had not been home from the fields to change and his overalls, his shirt, even his hair—as if defiantly, he did not have his cap on that day—half white with dust, and the odor strong about him.

"I came to talk to you," he said. There was something almost too formal about how he said it, though I realized he was trying to let me know he'd not have gone to anyone else. For the first time a self-conscious definition came into our relationship; in that moment we walked out of the shallows of childhood into the sudden deeps.

"I'm tired of killing insects," he said, so somber that I said, "I thought you bred them just to kill," and after a moment, catching my jibe, he laughed, a quick eruption which did not remove the darkness from him, it was too deep. "I want to get out," he said.

"Away from here? But everyone wants to go sometimes—" Everyone listens nostalgically to train whistles and watches the clouds drift and longs after the boat steaming out to sea—

"Him," he said, his arm flung back—his father. "His life is sweat. We always—my father and his and his, and sometimes the girls and all the mothers and grandmothers—never did anything else, just work land. And me now. That's why we come here, and he works day and night, and every day and every night. You know what it is to see just dirt? black dirt going under you? and you look down it's like black water, it even makes you dizzy so much looking, you think you're drowning—"

"I never thought of it that way," I said. I was looking at his hands, balled, almost impressed in his thighs, and when I spoke to him, his head was tilted back off to the right as if he expected something to come down—like a carnie performer with a bit chomped in his mouth waiting to be hooked up and swept off by an oncoming plane. I could see him a tiny thing dangling in the deep sky.

"Because you don't have to do it," he said—but not accusing, with no resentment for me. He was just talking out. Later, that was perhaps the worst part of it all—there was never any resentment for me in anything.

"But, Rennie, you love the land, you always have. You live—"

"You mean I can't do anything else."

"I didn't say that."

"Land!" he said, like a man who has had an argument with the woman he loves before he knows it is the woman he loves.

"I mean are you sure you want to?" I said. His father had taken him out of school when he was sixteen, and after all, with only a year out of school, you expected lapses like these.

For a second he looked at me incredulous, as if he'd said, You think it didn't cost me to come here like this? Then he said, with a passion that even that great frame seemed hardly able to contain, "Yes, *yes,* I want. I got to know, I got to see more than dirt and potatoes and insects and be—this—" He whacked his sleeve, fertilizer dust balled up, making a pungent burn in my nose. And a look of sadness came into his eyes, then a quick joy as his eyes soared up over everything, all his energy thrust into them in a run over the sky. "You 'stan me? I want to know and see—and not just the black dirt. I want, I want—" He looked at me—the words, where were they?

"I know, Rennie," I said.

"I know you do," he said. "That's why I come to you. I knew *you* would." It was as if all our childhood, all my admiration for his control, his tenaciousness in crabbing, in sports, on the land, he gave back to me in that one instant—and the weight of it shocked me. It came with dizzying speed. On me. What was I in his eyes? And that instant changed me too. How easily, how subtly we beguile ourselves, with what innocence we let it happen.

"Yes," I said, not thinking yet what he had put into my hands.

"I want to go to school—to the university where you go."

"But—you—"

"I know—I've got to finish high school first. But not here in front of the whole town, everybody knowing. I want to—can I do it where you are, in the city? Nobody'd know, I'd feel—you *know* how I'd feel."

"Yes, I know," I said again.

And there was no containing him then. He did not leap for joy, no, but his eyes leaped, his face transformed, they darted over things as if he could not wait to begin. He took the cap out of his back pocket and squeezed it in both hands, twisting it. Abruptly he laughed. "Then I'll come tomorrow—we'll talk then, hey? We'll go to the city, I'll live near you, you can help me maybe. No no—*after*. I'll talk to you after. Okay?" He started to run for the truck.

"Rennie!" I said. I wanted to say, I don't know anything; but he turned back with that smile of confidence, radiant, and—yes—in a way I have seldom seen since, beautiful—a chunk of walking sun. So I couldn't say it. I smiled. At my silence he laughed, moving his head from side to side with a look of wonder. "Tomorrow, hey?" he said.

I nodded. Yes, tomorrow.

If the Renkowskis could have seen Rennie— But perhaps that would have widened the gap sooner, for even then I felt the quiet severing which goes on unseen, unspoken, between parents and the son who has outgrown their language, a chasm that is never mentioned. Day after day for two years I saw that head bent over a desk in a 72nd Street room—not the best mind, but receptive as wool which every burr catches to. Then—a freshman—he moved in with the boys. For the university had discovered his body—two machines now, an almost obsessive concentration in that too, which made him Number One in training and pure varsity gold on the basketball floor.

By then I was a graduating senior spending three-quarters of my time with Willa Gaines, half-serious about her, *half* because Willa was chaotically unpredictable, you never knew her final secret desire, she fed all her lesser ones into a vast secret self she would never let you into, that last mystery only final love allows. She had seen Rennie on the basketball floor—with the pleasure and curiosity and normal desire that move any woman who is susceptible to glamor in performance. But she had seen him in a place deeper and more challenging than any athletic ground that has ever moved a woman—she saw him in another's admiration. Willa saw him in my eyes, through me, as I spoke of crabbing, farming, studying, the fierce driving electricity of his body in action. She was collecting his life through me. And I did not know how deeply, sitting there, still, her eyes lazing over the wallpaper, her tongue tracing the rim of the glass suspended between her hands, she was roused in the deepest place.

And more menacing: how she waited, how she never sought and pressed toward him, how she waited with me day after day—until long after basketball season, perhaps until the cheers died down even in most of our immediate memories and the activity was gone and there was routine and nothing to take its place, and the quiet yearning which devastates some part of us all began to grow in Rennie. . . .

It was all too unbelievably simple. One afternoon she went to the boarding house.

"I was looking for Paul," she said. "I thought he'd be with you. I want to see him badly. You don't mind if I wait down here a while? Please go back to work."

But he wouldn't allow her to wait in the hall alone, with the other boys circulating. He was clumsy, somewhat embarrassed, a little stunned by her look of purity.

"You got to come up. What'd Paul think if I left his— He wouldn't like it. We'll have to leave the door open—" he said.

I didn't know the meeting had meant anything to her, to him, to me—until after a year in Europe, after my B.A.

Just before graduation I told Willa, "You know we're calling it quits." We had talked of it too many times to grieve, and she was more blasé about it than even I expected. "When it's over, it's over for good," both of us had repeated a hundred times, preparing. Somewhere in the back of our minds, we were comfortable island stops, brief trips out from the mainland of our lives. More and more Rennie had become a casual presence, the loose third who would slip in and out of supper, a movie, coffee break, like a brother. I thought nothing of it.

"Keep in touch with him. He'll need some remote control while I'm gone, though he's sure on his way now," I said. She laughed. "He'll get by," she said. She was lovelier than ever that last semester —there was a quiet shifting in her, a new growth, toward the end. She wore simple frocks, pastel cottons, and I remember she developed a habit of abruptly raising her head to gaze in startled and contained innocence. She came that day to the boat, with her hair down, loose, long, and black, in a simple white dress. She was like a flower; I could not help watching her. "I want to touch you," Rennie said, laughing, but any feeling I had at the moment didn't seem to be important to me then. Rennie was doing well, she was about to graduate, I was leaving; besides it was spring—

"What'll we do without you?" Rennie said to me seriously at the boat.

"What we all do without each other," I answered, concealing my emotion.

By mail from Greece I committed myself, through a friend of my father's, to the editorial rat race in New York. I got back too late to get out to the island before Labor Day, my parents were back in Rhode Island by then, and the house was closed until next summer. There was little point to going—Rennie would not be there; Willa had mentioned in the last letter, months ago, that he might transfer from N.Y.U.—casually, the way Willa always mentioned things, and she had answered none of my letters since. I should have been disturbed then, but I burrowed into my job, trying to forget that in the traffic milling about me I was an island alone, shifting positions subtly without knowing it, Rennie or Willa becoming strong presences only when suddenly I realized I was in a place we had often been, then I was catapulted back, left staggering in time for a moment.

Even then, I might have let writing him go longer, but it was Rennie's silence that spoke loudest.

I went to the registrar to find out where he had transferred, but there was no record of any college asking for transcripts, "Though we might have made some mistake, not noting it," the clerk told me. But that was unlikely. I followed up with a letter to Rennie in Greenport, another, then another. Though there was no reply, the letters did not come back.

I finally wrote to a neighbor that I'd be out next weekend, but on Friday morning—it was a cold January day—Willa came back. I mean, she came out of the crowd, she was simply there of a sudden, admiring something in a window, not aware of me, a red knit cap on, she looked like a girl, a terribly young girl, and I had that feeling again of being lost in time. Was I putting her there? I had to call quick before she was gone, before the years were gone too. "Willa!" She swung around and against me clutching her as if I'd found someone lost long long ago, nearly crying at the sudden spring that poured in—those years and Rennie and my island all rushing back in a thaw. I said, "Why didn't you write? where've you been? I've been back months now, you didn't even tell me where Rennie's gone, I've written, he won't answer, I was going there tomorrow to find out—"

I would like to say, now, that her mouth twitched, that she was moved, upset, a little afraid even. But no. "Paul!" She shouted it. An ineffable joy sprang into the word, her face lit, startlingly small with the tight cap, her long hair loose over her mackinaw; and she clung with her eyes, then they raced over me, taking toll.

"Of *course* not," she said, "he's not there, he hasn't been, he didn't write before—didn't want to, you know how he is, he's not been home, they—" She flooded me, I couldn't breathe in the speed of it, the casualness of her breakneck assumptions.

"Yes I *do* know how he is. I *did*. I mean, I thought I did. I don't now." I didn't know. Cyclonically I knew I didn't know anything at all about anybody, least of all her. "But he *did* want to write."

"But he doesn't now. He doesn't want to."

"You seem to know all about it. How? You grad—" Abruptly it rose, a sudden sea, and broke—came down. She must have seen the effect—she smiled.

"From the moment we put you on the boat—"

"But when? Where? You said he'd transferred."

"He did transfer."

"But where? I checked. No—"

"To life," she said. "He's not in school, he never went back."

"Not in school?"

"And he's not going to," she said. Where I expected shame, guilt, some trace of regret, remorse, there was only pride, her triumph, a power that swelled in her—she seemed to rise, challenging with it, to grow. The thing—whatever it was, she had touched something of what she'd searched for—she was strong with the thing. I felt hopeless before the picture of Rennie shunted onto another track, irretrievable.

"Transferred to you then?" She caught my intonation. Her smile held my defeat up to me before even I recognized it.

"Yes, to me."

I was trying to understand. She would explain nothing. Her strength was in that—she needed no justification. Facts. "You never liked facts." How many times had she said that to me? But that natural imperviousness cast like a cloud around her would deceive me and her and finally Rennie, though at that moment she could be invincible.

"But why? Couldn't you have lived if he'd gone on?"

"Gone on? Ruined himself? Become—" She wanted to say *you*, it was already formed on her lips, but it broke. "We saved each other— because we found each other in time." She said it so serenely, with such a quiet glow in her beauty, that I almost believed—wanted to believe—they had.

"Saved for later destruction. Doesn't it always happen that way?" I said.

"If people thought that way, nobody'd ever do anything, would they?"

"You have to think of the consequences, Willa. My God, what'll become of him?"

"Consequences! You twentieth-century men—yes, that's what you are, Paul. How right your name is after all—and all the rest of you, all theory and no life. You *want* to live, my God *how* you want to! Even I felt that—don't be embarrassed—in bed with you. It begins there, you know it does, but *just* begins, everything else has to be like it, as good, but it comes from that, you know it—or why'd you go off to Europe, and me *let* you? There aren't many men left, Paul, a real woman knows it, and a woman's got to find one. When she does, she's got to hang onto the man in him, not *him* but the *man* in him, and make him know he's got it, that he'll die if he loses that, he'll walk around for the old three-score-and-ten dead, *dead.*" The first lament came into her voice then, into her eyes—for others, all the others. I watched her eyes touch them walking past us and then touch, finally, me. And her hand. "Don't you see? That's why. If *they* die, what do we poor women do? And in your world it gets harder everyday to tell the difference, the man's dying in you, and I don't want a world of phantoms. Oh sometimes I don't care *who,* which, man it is, if he's brute and tender and I bring him to life so we can go on from there, just it's two of us, two, we can bear anything if we have us—"

I think I loved her then more than at any other time, as sometimes you do the very thing that comes close to destroying part of you, her face held up to me like her own heart bared and endangered in that cold vast winter around us. I wanted to hold it in my hands and feel what must have been going on deep in her under those words. But I was too hurt, she had stirred up a blinding silt deep in me that I wanted settled, and it took all my clarity away.

"How do you know all that?" And I knew the instant I said it I had admitted what we are, how we are dying, how the yearning and the will to struggle are weak in us.

"I'm a woman. Is that so hard to understand?"

"Is he working?"

"You don't want to talk about you?"

"It's pointless—you've made that clear enough."

"Yes, he's working in a—" She smiled to herself. "Yes, he's working. It's hard work, the kind you wouldn't do—expect *him* to do either, now, though he once lived by hard work on the farm."

"It keeps him whole?" I smiled.

"You needn't be cynical, because you get near the truth. It does. The work's part of us."

"You think it won't take more to satisfy your womanhood?"

"When the need comes, we'll both know it."

"And you won't be too late?"

"Once you've been alive, you know how far you'd go to stay that way. I have every confidence." She mocked our old grossly used student phrase. We'd been standing too long, she was cold, she wanted to go now.

"I can take you home?" I said.

She stared up at me—genuinely regretful, I thought.

"You know you can't," she said.

"You don't want me to see him."

"I don't want him to see you."

"Is the world that much of a threat?"

"Yes." She was terribly honest. "Frankly, I don't mean I don't trust what he is—I do. But until there's the confidence beyond sex— beyond the easier things, your world's full of illusions that destroy too easily for too little. We've got to have our own balance first, Paul, or we can't survive it. You know that yourself. How would *you* begin—away from it all?" She watched me a second. "Hard to imagine, isn't it? Well, it's cost, it's been hard. See my point?"

I had to confess I'd seen it before I asked.

"You'd be the worm on the leaf. We couldn't have that." She laughed.

"No, you couldn't."

"You'll never believe how glad I am to see you." Suddenly her arms were about me, her cheek to mine, a quick kiss. "Perhaps—" But she didn't finish. "Goodbye, Paul." Quickly she was gone.

I stared after her, fathoming— That phrase. Without knowing it, she had let me in. I had heard Rennie talking through her. The worm on the leaf. And I saw what would defeat her—it would come so quietly that she would not know what it was because she had never shared, perhaps could not share it. It was in him, slow and steady and forever, the sea lapping at the land, the pine and the wild rose, and the plowed earth, and the struggle against insects, yes. His island would defeat her. But at the thought I felt petty and ashamed. I wanted her to hold her own, to win, but I didn't believe she could. And I could hear the sea, I could see that island that I could not get out of me either.

That summer I spent a few weekends and then the two-week vacation there. I tried not to go near the Renkowski place, though the years came back in the scent of earth and new plants, fertilizer and salt and fish, even in the sound of crickets and the waves breaking on the shore. Putting off the visit was only warding off a temptation I had set consciously before myself. I knew I couldn't leave town without going there.

His mother was in the kitchen, a bleak square with long curtainless windows, impeccable with the strong smell of wax and bleach, with shining pots and greaseless stove.

I was not prepared for her clutch or the pained scrape of her voice that vibrated in me long after. "Like son to me," she said, but her eyes went beyond me.

"When did Rennie come last?" I said.

"Don't come. Never come back now. Not write. *Why* not write?" she said. Mr. Renkowski could read English if she couldn't. I was helpless to tell her. She had aged considerably, as if the earth in her flesh began to erode and leave only the bedrock. She looked—and was —years older than Renkowski. Rennie had been born on the change, which nearly cost her life, taking all her humor, and left her grim. Renkowski, for all his seriousness, had a pleasant humor, though he hid it from her; his ribaldry escaped in the fields, on the street with women. You could tell he wanted to let it out at home sometimes.

He came, this day, across the fields, striding fast. He had thinned some, and at the stride, the upright frame, I stood up spontaneously. "God, it's—" I couldn't believe it.

"Me too. Sometimes almost not know . . . ," she said. Her eyes set on the floor, her arms hung down.

"Mrs. Renkowski?"

Her eyes lazed up to me, and hung, and slowly she came back. She had several lapses like that.

"Like eat? Got coffee. Got beer." At last she smiled. "Beer—not?" It was what Rennie loved.

"Beer then."

"Like before. Papa— Is Paul. Paul come." He nodded. He looked at me almost with resentment. Hardy, big but not fat—not youthful, but younger now. He said, "Looks wonderful, my farm. You t'ink so, hey? No—no speak. I see the eyes. Great farm, this. Better now than all time before." His arm swept out with pride, encompassing it—too much pride.

"It's a beauty. It always was, Mr. Renkowski."

"More now. Better," he insisted.

"Yes. I'd forgotten how beautiful it all was."

The remark pleased him. "Beautiful. That is. Good life—that." Dot, he said.

"Yes, I envy you. I'm no farmer, but I've always loved the farm here. When you don't have one, you want one."

"Trut'," he said, but he did not look at me, he did not look at me anymore.

"Beer." She opened mine and said, "You?" to him.

"Nodding."

"Sunday Paul go to city," she said.

He got up brusquely. "Each got life," he said. "I go set pipes. After, got roof. Them wasps up there. Got ev'yting here. You not drink too much," he joked feebly, but not looking.

"Okay, Mr. Renkowski," I said.

"Okay." I watched him out the kitchen window, vigorous and intent as he lugged and slid pipes onto the pickup.

Lying in my old summer room after, listening to the crickets and the occasional locust on the hot night air, he came back to me as Rennie entering the kitchen. I felt something in nature was trying to reverse itself, buck and hold back the tide and then turn it.

Shortly after, the company sent me to the London office. I was away nearly three years, traveling Europe and the Near East during vacations so that for a while America seemed to have too literally slipped over the horizon. Nobody told me anything about Rennie— except with that casualness letter writers have in giving you a snatch, forgetting you cannot supply the world around the moment. My mother's were crowded with numerous petty mysteries ("Bigg finally got the Republican nomination." "They never thought Wilkes would rush off that way." "Linda received the award." Finally? Rush off that way? Award?), so when she wrote that "it was too bad about Mr. Renkowski," I had a momentary pang, he was dead, I had the impulse to write to Rennie—but where?—and then to Mrs. Renkowski. But I went off to Greece instead. Yet under that cerulean sky the Long Island sky haunted me and came alive with them— I finally did write a note to her; I do not know what saved me, but I did not use the word dead, though perhaps to them he was worse than dead, as a presence labels everything his by its absence.

In retrospect there are moments we recognize as warnings, when the warning hovers in a living presence so palpable you do not wish to go near the harbinger. Mrs. Renkowski was such a harbinger. For —I was back in New York—my bell rang, and when I opened the door, she was standing there. Anyone else and I might have understood, but Mrs. Renkowski!

"You modder, *she* tell me new address," she said. She was so thin, she moved with dignity, but fragile, her hands clutched her own arms awkwardly as if something would break. She sat down, I offered her lunch, but I was trying to ward off anxiety—

She did not wait. It was all laid out in her mind earlier—without prelude, with the simplest direct logic, she began at the beginning: how happy! Rennie had come home, now two years March, a visit at last, the girl too, to introduce, to get married after, come spring . . . Maybe Rennie would come home, maybe work the farm. Papa— each month after—visited the city, had to sell, always saw Rennie and that girl—

I can hear her now. "Dot girl—"

"Willa?" I said.

"Dot girl. Papa gone—gone wid dot girl."

"*Papa*—"

"Mr. Renkowski—he run way. Go wid Willa."

I stared at her, too shocked to comprehend for an instant—then seeing Mr. Renkowski, Willa's Renkowski: the young man in him, the latent spry bestial spring, and I could see, hear Willa—there aren't any men anymore, wanting her fulfilment, wanting force and earth and simple directness and energy not broken down and channeled by us yet, going back farther than untouched Rennie to that land man, that contained laughter and energy unreleased and all the tenderness, yes, with which he could touch a young plant. I looked at Mrs. Renkowski. She was squeezed and dried, near emptied.

"And Rennie? Rennie!" I said.

"Rennie's die."

"Die!"

"S'die inside. Never talk. All time work in field. Look down. Never look up." Her hand settled over her breast, her eyes were far away though she looked at me. I knew *I* was not there for her, I was some agent, some weak wisp of hope she was clinging to, yet the only one she could move toward. "I come now—for Rennie. For me, make no difference now. I want you come. You come?"

"Yes—you know I'll come."

"You tell Rennie—got to leave."

"Leave Greenport?"

"Find something. Somebody. *Got* to go—live," she murmured. "Not stay for me."

"Yes," I said.

"You come—not today, not tomorrow." She didn't want him to know she had come to me. "One, two week maybe?"

"Yes," I said.

But I did not go then or for a long time after. For Rennie's letter came a few days later, the only letter I had ever received from him —and what a flood the handwriting brought back—that 72nd Street room, Rennie at his desk, Broadway, crazy nights in the subway, basketball practice, the drugstore we ate in, and Willa, and Rennie's face—knotted, twisted, happy, forlorn, the deep brown eyes always dark and heavy with some intuitive knowledge that seemed to make him lash out quickly for his happiness.

Dear Paul,

How are you? Fine, I hope. You know it has been years now since I saw you, and us living pretty near each other, but I know you haven't changed, some people never do. My mother is very nervous these days. I know she was in the city to see you. She won't tell me, but it's all over her. She is waiting—that's how I can tell. Don't come, you will be disappointed, and nothing seems to do any good. I want to see you but not that way. Sometime I'll see you, I hope, the old way.

RENNIE

The letter wrenched me, I wanted to go at once—I should have. Rennie seemed to be beside me, talking. I could not let go of his presence. Perhaps I had driven the real presence off long since. Perhaps I had just begun to know that you drive away the image, but the part of it which is yourself comes back more real than what's gone. Had it stopped there, had life simply gone on mundanely, letting Rennie slip over the rim into the slowly absorbing area of near oblivion—if that had happened, then I might feel clean, a slate wiped, left waiting for whatever might begin again; but I did not know that yet.

I thought it would be Willa who made me clean again because Willa made me go back to the island, some weeks after Mrs. Renkowski's visit. She phoned the office one afternoon. "I'm coming over tonight, you must see me. What time?"

Muddled, I said, "Eight. Nine. . . ."

"All right." She hung up as abruptly.

"You don't have to ask me anything, he's dead, that's all, one morning in the bed beside me—in Ohio—cold, you can't know what it is, knowing him, what he was, all that man, to reach over—" She worked herself up to near hysteria, her eyes did not see me as they stared, though she was sensitive to every movement I made. And there was a fierce calm in her body. Her raving was all in her eyes, her lips, quivered and drawn out, and in one tic-like gesture of pressing one length of her hair to her head as if it were too short and out of place. But her body *looked* quiet—it sat, so still, so poised, you'd not have believed the tumult—

"When?" I said.

"Nearly six weeks now. January 24th, in the morning, at seven, I turned over, I said—"

"Willa . . . ," I said. Her eyes were swollen now, her lips grossly uncontrolled. At the spectacle of her grief, I knew I had never known her—not this Willa, and at my word her hands reached out at last, she clutched mine, and held them and stared, simply stared at them. "Six weeks," she said, gripping painfully.

"He left me everything," she said finally. "I took everything away from him—most—legally—except the nominal—" It was Rennie she was talking of now. "—and her, oh yes, I know it, I meant to take him, I wanted him, you can't know what want is—to feel desire for your own life burning so deep in you, never to burn out, no, never, never—even now the memory, I owe it to him, he made me live, I will live, be alive always—" She was crying, choking as if the words too were fires in her throat. "Willa," I said. "Willa." And she leaned back and stared at me, like those days gone, but another girl, a woman now, but the child too—that's what it was, the child came to *me*. "But I didn't want to take even what he could arrange from his—from *her*."

"We—you—can do something about that," I said.

"Yes," she said. "You too."

"Me too." I knew what she meant—nobody is ever in anything alone. All the traps are not ours alone. Whatever it is encompasses each of us, little by little, so easily, so slowly and tenaciously that we sometimes think we are immune. I knew I must do whatever she asked, no matter how impossible it was, because I could never be separated from what happened to her because of Rennie, not simply because I knew him, but because he became part of me the day he said "Can I do it where you are, in the city?"—I could hear it now—"Tomorrow, hey?" and I not saying anything, my commitment that I would never again be free of.

"We can go to him," I said.

"No. We can give it to him," she said. "All I have—everything that's his. Give him back what's his. It's right—just. Oh, to think of *me* talking about justice! I know what you must think."

She still had not recognized that I was not doing her a favor, but trying to understand and accept my part in what we had become.

"Yes," I said, seizing it instantly.

"Tomorrow." Her head back, she closed her eyes. The momentary relief on her face was beautiful, she looked for one brief instant so serene—as if that premeditation completed the act and she was purged, purified of it all, balanced between two inevitable falls, enjoying the abrupt ecstasy of a moment's harmony.

"Tomorrow!" The rapidity staggered me. Yet I knew it had to be swift, before change, before consequences could be dwelt on, pure action.

"We'll go together." She was up, nervous and too rapid. At the door she said, "I'll be at the Long Island Railroad fifteen minutes early. We can only take the afternoon train—it gets to Greenport about eight. I'll leave work early. Okay?" Her life hung on it, her whole frame seemed suspended, waiting.

"I'll be there," I said.

And she was gone with such rapidity that I felt I had imagined it all.

From the Greenport station, we could see the town was closed down for the night, a few lights on the piers and an occasional car, one police car cruising. We took a taxi direct to my parents' place. The gas pilot is always on and in a short time the house was warm, we opened the upstairs rooms.

"I'm going to take a bath, may I?" She was so natural—as if she belonged, a glimpse of the old Willa. I could understand Rennie and his father never tiring of her.

It was already after ten, so quiet, except for the wind. I had pulled out a terrycloth robe, was taking down bedding when I heard the noise. I thought it was the tree—there is a willow that taps on the downstairs ell when the wind blows strong, like a heavy knocking. I had warned Willa. So when it came, I made the mistake of thinking it was that—but it was too regular, so I went down. The porch light was still on, and from the back stairs looking across the hallway, I could see Rennie at the front door. He must have seen the lights from his farm. I stopped there by the foot of the stairs. Willa was talking, shouting above the shower. I shook my head no. I simply stood, not knowing what to do or how to move. What would Rennie believe? I remained there, I remained almost till it pained me to stand so motionless, it must have been a couple of minutes. He knocked again. She went on talking. I could see his head in the door window, the green army cap, part of his face. I thought he heard— his head turned and his mouth opened as if to utter some word. I wondered if he could see me standing there. Rennie! I felt it shouted inside me. Why had he come *now?* But I was unable to move, unable to make up my mind to move. "Can I have a towel?" Willa said and stepped out. When I looked back, the head was gone, but the terror went on in me and I still did not move. "Well, don't just stand there," she said and looked at me curiously when I said, "Nothing at all," and went for the towel.

I did not tell her until the following morning when our neighbor, Judson Buechner, came by. The Buechners always kept an eye on the house for my parents.

"I was afraid you'd get out visiting before I saw you." He was apprehensive, quiet, and kind. "I just heard over the radio—"

"Yes?" I said.

"Last night the Renkowski boy killed himself—in the barn. They found him early this morning."

"Rennie!" I said—not to him, but to me, *me. I* had let him go. I had stood there—and *let* him go, not knowing why he had come. He needed me. I could not have moved, yet I knew—I was sure—that he had heard or seen me, her, both of us. And he must have felt it— we had betrayed him again: first Willa, then his father, then his friend. What was left? Perhaps he was afraid it would even be his mother next. Maybe he went—maybe he didn't even want to breathe the same air anymore—

Mr. Buechner stood there for a moment, helpless. Then he said, "I'm sorry. I know how much a part of you he was," so that I looked up after him as he turned and went home and I said to myself, "No you don't."

From upstairs Willa was saying, "What is it? Who was that, Paul?"

Willa. Poor Willa . . . I went up to tell her.

Once you begin not to answer doors, it gets easier. But it does not shut them out. The mind has too many entrances, and it rules its own subtle arrivals. Suddenly, whoever it is is standing there with you. Willa is in Florida now—she married not long after the Long Island trip and moved South then. Sometimes (for old time's sake, she says) she calls me, but I know it is something else, some desire to touch a deep corner of herself—as if it were not enough to have given up her part for the care of Mrs. Renkowski in that Long Island rest home.

When Willa hangs up, Rennie is back. He has never gone very far, perhaps he is inside me—at least, once, I dreamed I was Rennie and had his dream: my island was a great body. I was an insect crawling over a vast still body that smelled of flesh and sweat and urine and rotting. It did not even seem to be lying on anything. I had to eat into it, on and on, eating a groove, eating and eating it until it was all inside me, until it was all me. And I wondered how long it went on? what would be eating me?

I try to think when it was I first really let him get hold. If I could remember exactly the moment— But who knows at exactly what innocent moment anything begins or how it grows little by little, carrying you with it. If it goes on, it will consume you, there won't be anything left and it will be done with.

I have gone—twice—out to the island to see his mother in the rest home, not an old woman, but disintegrating. She did not know who I was. I suppose, had I been Rennie, she would not have known him either. Once she did say something about his dying. "One year. No—two month. Two week maybe." She could not remember. Another strange betrayal. Perhaps it was my self-castigation—the least thing I could do for him—that made me want to be him and feel what he'd have felt at that moment.

Back in my apartment in the city I envy Mrs. Renkowski her oblivion. I sometimes think I have walled myself in too. But when spring comes and the soft wind carries the inevitable sounds and the scent of breaking earth, the scent of Willa returns . . . I think of Rennie. And I wonder if Mrs. Renkowski, sitting in her window staring into the endless sky with a certain madness, sees into it. Or does she too hoard these dark things—because they are all we have—against a time when there may be no more of us on the earth?

The Game

THE POPULATION of the town is old. You would not think so at first, seeing the cottages row after row like a development of newly-weds starting out the same in life. And there are flowers, evidence of a great love, an ineradicable, growing desire to be close to the bounties of earth, a growth which the almost perpetual sun encourages with an inevitability akin only to the most inescapable disease. Each avenue has an air of newness, a Johnny-come-lateliness. Frequently moving vans, bringing in new inhabitants, encourage this air. Up and down the streets there is a good bit of laughter, of friendly greeting, of chatting among good neighbors who have already established relationships common to a lifetime's sharing of pleasures and sorrows. Early mornings the park is filled, and people line the walks, play at bowls, picnic long into afternoon and evening. In the windows the night lights are seen longer than in most towns—over bridge or pinochle, canasta or duet, through the long chat over tea or coffee or an occasional drink. The light gives an aura of lengthened gayety to the town, for the people here need less sleep than the population of many towns.

But the truth is evident if you sit for a while on a bench anywhere and watch the inhabitants at leisure (since few work here). Some are spry and quick, with that energy of defiance which causes you to say, "I don't know how she does it," "She sure can keep up with the rest of them," etc., a defiance which seems to ward off the inevitable. Others move like happy snails consciously absorbing the benevolent sun. It is difficult for some to raise their feet—their canes help—as if at last they can no longer deny their relation to the earth, and each step is only temporary in its faltering departure. And their faces too show the relationship: in the age-old movements they have become worn— wrinkled and puckered, scarred, sunken, loose on the skeleton, rheumy-eyed and staring, with a bleak November coloring.

This is a town to which people retire—to banish the sickness of the flesh with the sun's help and the sickness of loneliness with their own kind, away from the warning which the hoping, displacing young carry implicit in their every move and contact. Oh, there are young people here: a few, stranded, who need jobs; a few, money-minded, who establish business with a future; and a few, unwilling to leave their families, who choose to live here. On weekends the children and the grandchildren arrive for short stays, bringing with them the breath of that world left behind, newsy days when the past looms for a short time, like morning glories that are ready to close at noon.

West, between the town and the sea beyond, is the hospital. Seen from a distance, it seems to hold the town in, to keep it from spilling whole into the sunset, and forms a kind of channel through which—like the neat nurses and orderlies in impeccable white, who are responsible for the efficient workings of the hospital—one must pass to the other side. It sits, white stucco with rich foliage as colorful as life, a huge mother over the town, with the serenity which comes from certainty.

Nathan Stockwell didn't wish to stretch his luck. Bowling on the green at Wade Park, as was his daily custom—with Alexander Sergeant, Will Ruggins, and Dan McFall, all bachelors—he had his sudden cough. Agitated, he coughed until he had to sit to rest.

"A bit of catarrh, it feels like," he said, trying to wash away the irritation with a cup of water Dan handed him.

"You all right now?" Dan said.

"I think so."

"We'd better stop then," Will said. "We've had enough for today."

"Oh no, it'll spoil the game midway," Nathan muttered, conscious that he had already lost the battle, they would never agree with him, it was as good as over.

"Enough said," Alexander said, eyeing him with the silent experienced eye of a medical man.

"Well . . . ," Nathan said, irritated, rising, ignoring with angry restraint the arm Dan offered. "I'm fine," he said. "Think I'll take a turn around the concert stand, then back to the house."

"You do that," Alexander said, not without a touch of consolation in his voice.

"I said I would, didn't I?" Nathan murmured almost inaudibly. He sauntered off, rather nonchalantly, toward the bandstand. There he sat a minute, not actually resting, merely contemplating the direction of his movement. A glance at his watch—11:00. Much too early to stop bowls, but then they had insisted, they had understood. It agitated him that they were not more belligerent, insisting on at least finishing the scoring. It would spoil their running match, the four of them, make them revise their whole system, make them reorient to a new routine of three if he stayed away at all. And it wasn't always easy to attain such rapport; they had, after all, a camaraderie quite uncommon to many of the others in the park. Perhaps because they had never married, and the others without wives had other connections, other unshaken habits and attitudes, slight measures of friction. . . .

He looked back. They were still looking his way. Watching . . . ?

He rose. The heat striking his back consoled; it seemed to penetrate through to his very shadow below him. An instant he stopped, soaking it up, then moved on. The brightness of the sun on the pavement, on the white flowers and the bright buildings beyond, brought water to his eyes; and the pungent scent of sweet alyssum and verbena made him draw a deep appreciative breath. But it caught in his throat and set him coughing so violently that he had to sit at the first bench.

When he felt rested, he ambled on, stopping as usual to buy his paper from Old Ned, but there was a different fellow there this morning, a stranger, a short, little man with a face so chubby that it had a baby look to it, and eyes with a young anticipation to them, though he was bald, clean over.

"What'll it be, sir?" he said with offensive resonance.

"The *Times,*" he said, recovering from his blunt surprise. Old Ned merely handed it to him, the *Times.* Well . . . change.

He set down the pennies.

"Thank you, sir."

"*Sir,*" he said to himself, crossing the street. The house was a block away and he didn't stay long. He had wanted a shower, but fearing its effects on his system, he decided against it. He called a taxi and took his little bag of necessaries and went outside to wait.

"To the hospital," he told the driver.

At the hospital they put him in a semiprivate room with an old man named Banister. Ed or Ned. Well, it didn't matter. The man had great difficulty talking. Under Ed's sheets he could see certain shapes, not like a body at all. Tubes? Contraptions perhaps. He lay there all day before Ed—or Ned—Banister woke, relieving him of the sound of Ed's rasp, and they talked a bit.

When the boys came—Dan and Will and Alexander—the following morning, foregoing their game, they talked with Ed too. In fact, they talked more, he thought, to Ed than they did to him, or at least they kept their eyes on Ned when they spoke.

"You look fine," Dan said.

"Just a bit of acute catarrh," he said. "Nothing really to worry about, but I thought I'd better catch it before it got too bad. You know—" He was waiting for Alexander to say something confirming, but Alexander smiled, then shifted his gaze to Ed.

"How are you?" he said to Ned.

"Poorly," Ed said, "but I'm lucky." He smiled. "They thought I'd be dead two weeks ago. I might even be walking around in a few days."

They all turned.

"Remarkable!" Will said. And it was—splendid. They all agreed. They even laughed.

"Well—" It was Will who terminated the visit. They rose simultaneously as if by signal. "Goodbye." "So long." ". . . tomorrow." "And you behave, Ed." Laughing. Down the corridor. Gone.

Their visit perturbed him. He had wanted them to come, was pleased that they had called the house, had come without invitation. Yet he was discomforted. "Ed?" he said. But Ed had gone off again, asleep. Periodically he wanted to waken Ed, rid the air of the rasp that struck him like a herald in the room. But after a while, he slept. . . .

He slept quite often the next few days, sometimes seeing the discomforting eyes of his friends. On the fifth night, in the midst of a dream, where he saw the eyes of his friends so discomforting, he woke. Someone was in the room. A white figure. It came toward him directly, near and near, distant. It's you, he thought, you're coming . . . !

"Don't touch me!" he gasped, but the figure went past again, toward Ed, and he woke full then, realizing where he was.

It was the nurse. Behind her, they wheeled Ed out. He had a sheet over him, and the soft steps were dreadful in the silence.

They let Nathan out that afternoon.

"You take it easy. You know you haven't been walking lately."

"Oh, I'll be all right. The solid floor feels good." Of course, it *was* a little tipsy. But the cane . . .

The next morning, at the park, the men were sitting as usual. They flagged him and at bowls they crowded around him. Home. Well, they *were* a familiar foursome, now weren't they? The others, accustomed to seeing him with them, waved too, pleasant surprise on their faces—tinged with that strange look of disappointed pleasure.

"Your turn," Dan said, tapping his shoulder.

He set the cane down carefully, and rolled. . . .

"That's good form," Will said.

He sat down beside Alexander.

"You look fine, Nat," Alexander said.

He laughed. "A wonderful game, bowls." And thinking of Ed, he said, "Too bad—" But *they* didn't know. "Ed died this morning," he said. They all looked at him, questioning. "Quiet. I didn't even know until after." They nodded.

And he could not help saying it. "But I'm here," he said. And he laughed self-consciously at the faintest trace of disappointment in them. Then they caught his words. And Dan laughed. "Yes," he said. And Will and Alexander laughed, triumphant little rattles in their throats that echoed like warnings to each other.

Going West

THE SUN WAS so deep, the air filled with it, a deep golden sea flowing off the October leaves. And the old Dodge, "How it sails along!" she cried buoyantly. "Oiled and greased yesterday," Win said. "It ought to make it." "Who said anything about *not* making it? Of course it will." She laughed. "And the road's so clear. After Labor Day you can count the tourists on one hand." Win hated to drive on crowded highways or through the city, and today was such a concession. All year long she had said, without arguing, but with longing, with nostalgia, "If we could only go west . . . ," "When we go west . . ." This end of the island, from Riverhead east, was such a dearth, the end of things, the leftovers, she sometimes thought, lovely in summer, a real paradise, but for *life*—well, there was no place like Jamaica or New York. The cities loomed—130 miles as the crow flies, she'd remind him—yes, loomed, so near, yet a whole year away. . . . But at last—oh, the quick of it in her! something expanded, her skin felt too confining, if she breathed deep she'd spill out into the golden air. "Free! Do you know what it *means?*" But of course he did, lying there in that front room nearly a year. . . . She watched his eyes absorb the island, crawl over pines and wild rose, potato fields, patches of sparkling sea— In Jamaica they have those new model kitchens, our north wall could go, there's an inset ultraviolet oven, small and perfect for— Win usually said, There you go, dreaming again. And she'd say, What else is there if you can't? He'd not reply to that, but retreat farther into TV. You always take me down, she'd say. But this morning he was all smiles, visibly relieved or resigned—she could never tell which, he was always so quiet—to be out of his chair, away from living room and TV *and* her noise-making, he'd call it, though somebody had to make it; *he* could go on, *had*, for days, weeks, without giving her the time of day.

For a while her going on strike, giving him the silent treatment, brought him round, though he never could understand why she wanted to talk so. You don't talk and you don't *do,* she said. You just sit and I want— But it was so hard to say what it was she wanted. Sometimes she thought her undefined wanting was in *him,* was why she had married a man years younger than herself—to lift her up, out of this island death of silence. The wind—Win was really speeding—battered. She wanted to *feel,* turned down the window, air flooded in, her breath caught in joy, her whole flesh quivered, yet she felt the faintest warning pincers of winter in the blow. "Won't Addie be surprised?" "She'll probably keel over," he said, "stopping at breakfast time!" "Why, she's glad to see us *any*time. She's my own brother's wife—" Win kept silent, his eye fixed over the pines on a gull that soared up, then buckled, still for an instant as the gold of the sun pierced its breast, and sank easefully over the Sound. "Anyway," she said, laughing, "it's too late now. We're on our way."

On the beach, where the tide had begun to ebb, the sand was already drying. Here and there fiddler crabs came preying out of their holes, leaving fine trails behind. A dragonfly hovering over the water arrowed back toward the tall sea grass, near the fine black mud, where a blacksnake lay like a fallen branch, still. Over the sand myriad insects moved, surfacing and burrowing to reappear in treks farther on. The sun quickened everything, pushing back shadows and sparkling over the shallows. Around scattered seaweed and small rocks the fish seemed to be swimming in a crystal air. Near the shore, rockstill, rested a horseshoe crab, its tail protectively erect. Lowering it, the crab began to move inshore. High above, a gull, trying to break a clam, dropped it toward the stones above the sand line, but the wind veered it and the clam struck the water near the crab. Immediately the crab halted, the tail poised, then slowly eased into the shallow. It stopped practically at the meeting point between sea and sand. A wave fell back and exposed it to the air, then lapped high over it again. For fifteen, perhaps twenty, minutes, it lay motionless. By then the tide had gone down just enough to leave the crab isolated on the sand. A gull cried. Far off sounded the motor of a car approaching the beach.

"*There* she is!" Win said, flinging his arm out over the garden. Lily turned—why, it took your breath away!—acres of mums blazing under the sun, the wind stirring them in rolling waves, and there, just emerging head and shoulders like a swimmer, rising from a bed of amber, was Addie. "Heyyyy!" Addie flagged as she moved down the furrows, occasionally stopping to flick a bug off a leaf. Addie was a virtual workhorse, moving from morn till bedtime. "Oh, Addie!" Lily said, clasping her. Tears came to her eyes at the thought of her dead brother, who—somehow—she touched through Addie. "They're so beautiful," she said, "gorgeous." In her watery vision the garden flowed up into the sky, toppled . . . cleared. And there, on the rim of the lawn, stood a little boy. "That's Vince, my right-hand man," Addie said. "Come on, Vince, meet Uncle Win and Aunt Lily." "Any more neighbor boys like you hidden out there?" Lily said. The boy shied back, though smiling. "He's always with me," Addie said. "He has a whole world under the flowers, people and all too—don't you, Vince?" The boy nodded. "That's no way to—" Win began, but Lily said, "Now, Win— let him be. Why, he can do anything, can't you, Vince—change the whole ocean if you want to?" "Lily!" Win said. "Well, Win—he *could.*" "Come on, we'll have breakfast in a minute." "Oh, we can't stay— we're going west, just for the day." "To Babylon?" "No no, we're going all the way this time." "Then you'll need at least a quick cup of coffee." The boy followed only to the back porch but his face pressed flat against the pane, watching them. "It's remarkable what you do with the land, and *how,*" Lily said. "That's all I have left of Rich," Addie said. "Les—he's out on his own now. All I know is he's out there somewhere, playing in a band. Sides, the work's good for me and some-times I feel he's in them, he loved—not the flowers so much, but the doing." "Get much for them, Addie?" "Win!" "It's all right, Lily. Enough. I cut and pack and box them for the night train, for sale in the city mornings." "Oh, I don't think I *could* cut them, they're so gorgeous where they are," Lily said. "I thought so too but when I think of the sudden sight of them in the markets in all that dingy city and the hands that will touch them and the places they'll go—" "We'll be late getting in," Win said, rising. The boy's eyes traced them. As they came out he said to Lily, "How do you change the ocean?" They all laughed. "You been thinking all this time about that?" she said. He nodded, and she said, "Sometimes you put the littlest thing in it, that'll change it, not much but a little." "What kinda thing?" "Oh that's the mystery. When the time comes, you'll know." "Or you won't," Win said, but Lily ignored him, the boy's eyes wide on her. "And you can imagine, can't you?" He nodded. "Like under there," she said, "just imagine it different." "Will that really change it, will it?" "Now answer *that!*" Win said. "You won't know until you do it," she said. "Try." The boy laughed, he hopped off toward the mums as they got into the car.

The horseshoe crab crawled until it came up on dry hot sand, then retreated downslope toward the ebbing tide. A horsefly buzzed loudly over it and a hot wind close to the surface spat sand against the damp shell, where it clung. A car door slammed and the delighted shouts of two boys cut the quiet. "Here you are, boys," the father said. He set down a basket, opened the beach umbrella, a brilliant red against the sky, and dug the pole deep and unswerving into the sand. The boys raced to the breakwater and back. As they passed, kicking up sand in their running, the crab halted, then went on, but on the return Ben caught sight of it. "Hey, Paul—look!" "Gee, the size of him!" Paul said. "Hey, Dad, a horseshoe crab." "Well, you be careful of it." *"Don't* let it get away!" Paul cried, for it had entered the water and its motion quickened. Precisely at that point Ben lashed out at its tail. "Careful— they're real sharp, they cut." Ben jerked the crab up; its claws, losing touch with the sand, flailed helplessly. Ben dragged it onto high ground. The boys kneeled and watched it pull itself down the beach, slowly, then more slowly, not ceasing until it neared the water. "Get it, Paul." And Paul dragged it backwards by the tail, farther from the water this time. Now its descent was slower. "What's the matter, tired?" Ben said. The crab waited a long time before it tested again and moved. Ben shoved it forward with his foot, the tail angled up, but the thing did not move. Ben toed it forward again, and the sand ridged before it, impeding its advance. Now so much sand clung to it that shell and sand were indistinguishable except for a vague outline. The boys were growing tired of waiting. Paul seized it, ran to the water and dunked it. "Don't let it get away," Ben said. The crab came out bereft of sand. "Okay," Paul said and circled round and round like a discus thrower winding up, then flung the thing high up into the air for later. Far off, it landed with a thud.

"Do you hear a noise?" Lily said, for she felt her sound palpitating, spreading itself into the sand, the grass, the blue—oh, she wanted to tell him how she felt it: echoes in the sky, in the wind, everywhere.

"Yes," he said. "It's me," she said, laughing, "me," throwing her arms out. "It's the tubeless plop-plop on the asphalt," he said. For an instant she felt deflated. You always take me down, she nearly said again. But no, she wouldn't. Today—yes—she'd be patient, he'd been sick so long, it was their first trip in—oh, she'd really forgotten—eternity! and there would be no agitation. The Dodge skimmed over the road, the green drifted past, great gobs of white clouds fluffy as dumplings floated over them. "Talk to me, Win," she said. Her hand fell onto his leg. "What do you want me to say?" "Oh, anything." "When something comes to me." You never talk—she bit it back—and you never *do* either. Up loomed the porch with its leaking roof, the beams needing buttressing in the cellar, the sink piping and linen closet—years of untouched promises. And her new kitchen that she always dreamed about. It drifted into her vision, suspended high over the green elms— "It'll have to come down," he said. Come down? The kitchen dissolved into the green foliage. "What?" "The swamp willow. Loaded with mites. They'll kill it and everything around it. Besides, it's growing against the house. Taps against the bedroom corner, and the roots'll be into the cesspool." "Oh. . . ." Always wanting to destroy—but never to build. Without the tree, in winter there would be no protection from the hard wind, there would be only the sight of the barren Mallard lot, of their bald gray house. Win was smoking again, his fifth since they'd left, but no, she'd not say— "It's going to be hot in the city," he said. It was already—you could see it in his face, he sweated so easily. "We won't stay too long—not long at all. Is that all right?" she tested. The traffic was thickening and he never liked that. His eyes blinked constantly. She could hear the whack whack of cars passing against the wind. She knew the city was not far off when the vista of houses broke off abruptly and the fields of cemetery stones loomed, row after crammed row of stone monuments thicker than crowds, elbowed one into the other so that the land looked like a garden of pure rock growing, gray after gray after gray plant of it. "Now I know where we are," she said. Theirs, in town, was small and green. Her whole family was there, father and mother, the baby, her one chance, the miscarriage, the hysterectomy, and then past the age. . . . The sun glared over the monuments. She moved closer to him, pressed her head against his shoulder. "In the morning I'll make you the *big*gest blueberry pie." She sighed. "You will?" She felt the rumble of his lungs in his flesh as he laughed, and her eyes darted anxiously ahead, anticipating the sight of the golden city to come rising out of the sea.

The crab landed on its back. Its claws lashed out and, striking nothing, continued flicking and scraping soundlessly, at first with all its claws, then in twos and threes, then only a lone claw flailed. It pressed its tail deep into the sand, raising the shell slightly, rocked as if to turn on its side and fall righted. At the peak of its effort, all the claws moved again in a desperate clutching and when the shell fell to the sand again they went on making sporadic involuntary quivers. Time after time it prodded, pushed and wielded its tail until the forward end was jammed into a ridge which poured sand backwards into the basin of its shell, burying the base of the claws, filling their sockets, absorbing the salt water so it could scarcely move. The slightest motion made a scraping sound against sand. For increasingly longer intervals the crab lay still, the sun high now, burning down into it, and, as if in sporadic fury, all the claws would suddenly lash out for but an instant, then still. Three gulls, not far off, moved closer. One flew up, soared low and, as if in signal to the others, landed nearby. The two joined it. The first made its way directly to the crab, but the two boys came running, barefoot now, and frightened them so all three flapped up over the bay. The sight of the gulls so close to the crab called their attention to it. Ben said, "Come on, let's give it a swim," scooping it up before Paul could answer and plopping it right side up in the water.

"How long?" he said to her, slipping the parking ticket into his pocket. "Give me two hours. I think I can manage everything. On the way back we'll go off the road a bit and relax. How's that?" But she was already off, the asphalt and the close buildings sending up a warm sunglow, and she in a hurry, but each window hooked her back, and when, standing for an instant still on the corner, she looked into all the passing faces, she laughed aloud—she wanted to tell them all how it was, what joy to be here. In Greenport they said the city was always there, you could go in anytime, but something, life, always held you back. She pushed her way into the crowd—the *feel* of it! all that energy. Suppose—all this motion in the world added up! The vision was staggering, a great unimaginable white light of energy burning forever and ever. Into the department store she swung with a silent inner laugh, wafted, yes, wafted in on a sudden cloud of scents, and the lights—*how* she'd forgotten!—brighter than stars, everywhere. How different from her little kitchen, and the one great light the sun rising and the sun setting every day. But here there was no end to this firmament of light burning perpetual joy down over the myriad counters—islands of beauty, so many objects that for a moment in her desire simply to look, to glide past, glimpse everything, absolutely everything, she seemed to have forgotten her list. Oh, drift a bit, she thought, who knows when it will happen again? Her eyes scaled the rainbow of colors, her fingers touched out to brush lightly over pure white wedding satin as she took the escalator up to Ladies Wear, and looking down, being lifted up that way, moving along like a goddess on a ranging cloud, she saw the floor take on a sudden order, trim and neat as her own kitchen. From above, the people, small as insects on the beach, seemed to be moving about lost and for an instant she felt a quick pang but the heads of—*"Angels!"* she said aloud, dimly embarrassed when a woman several steps below turned to her curiously— came into view. They hung in a choir, golden hair ablaze under the lights, diaphanous wings, so ethereal. "And Christmas over two months off yet." Directly before her spread the costume jewelry—mounds and drifts of it. Her great weakness. She had to buy a piece, one—it would *make* her day. After, she lay the packet of amber earrings tenderly into the bottom of her purse. From floor to floor she went, as quickly as she could, higher and higher up—might's well, just this once. She was about to turn down when her eyes fell on the Steuben glass, drawn on, dazzled by the serenely pure vision—so delicate was it, she was sure she was imagining it. And then she saw the sign: FURS. The temptation of it! She vacillated, but only for an instant. She had hoped, dreamed . . . and now she was so close (she had had three, the beaver, the sable-dyed muskrat, and that flimsy fox-pelt collar). . . . It was the last level. People were scarce here, the heads of several women in the distance and a very well-dressed man speaking in a whisper. And the rug! She sank deep, soft as a cloud. But the *furs*—one piece more exquisite than the other. She had all she could do to hold her hand back, for instinctively it wanted to flow out and touch, caress each one, ever so lightly. And when she came to mink, to chinchilla, then to ermine—looking up, her eyes filled with tears at the sheer down that would, surely, dissolve, vanish softer than air before her very eyes. "How do you do, Madame. . . ." The voice rode over her. She didn't reply. "Something wrong?" "Oh, no," she said. She turned away. Whatever had come over her? "I was just . . . I—really I was looking—" She didn't know what to say. "For hardware, pots and pans," she said. His brows rose, his eyes glided off. "The basement," he said crisply.

Freed, the horseshoe crab crawled off instantly. Ben waded in. "Wow! It's cold. I can't see it." He froze, waiting for the agitated water to still. Under the crab moved serenely, midway between them, toward the deeps. Vigilant, they watched silently. The crab moved into an area of fine stones, flimsy seaweed. As if in accord, the boys simultaneously shifted a few steps sideways with it. Where the crab was headed, the bottom darkened, seaweed fused with stones, and sand moulded with a deposit of silt. The crab seemed to quicken. "*Get* it!" Ben cried. Paul lunged. "Missed!" Ben lunged. "Watch the tail!" But Ben had it, difficult to manage under the water, the tail was slippery, the water gave the crab mobility and the claws latched onto seaweed. "The bugger's putting up a fight." But Ben held, pulling steadily, not jerking for fear the tail might cut and he'd lose hold. When the crab did give way, Ben nearly lost balance, but he swooped it up and held it dripping in the air while the claws expanded and contracted as if at some invisible prey. "Not getting away this time, mister," Ben said, hurling it close to shore, where it lulled upside down on the waves for a moment, but it was heavy and slowly it filled like a cup and sank. Going down, it turned over, then lumbered back toward deep water. "Now come on— we're waiting," Ben said. "Let *me* this time," Paul said, blocking its path with his feet and forcing it inshore again. Again and again they took turns at it. "Let it go," Paul said, tired now, "We won't see another one till next year 'f-we're goin' tomorrow. *I* know what—let's hide it in the deep grass."

Down in the hardware section, there was such a crowd! And the *time* —poor Win, two hours she'd told him. She tracked down the pressure cooker advertised at the enormous saving in *Newsday,* she had the clipping in case there was some doubt. After, taking up her pocketbook and heading for Men's Wear, simultaneously she felt the violent clutch of two hands on her right thigh and she heard someone crying. A little boy! Three, five . . . ? "Why what's happened?" she said, kneeling. The boy sputtered half-words and half-sounds, burying his face against her leg, now wet and hot from his tears. "Are you lost?" Her eyes ranged for searching parents or an information desk. First level, of course! "Come on," she said. The boy dragged behind, his crying ceased, and his head wrenched around exploratively. Scarcely off the escalator, they were confronted by a woman and two men. *"Ed*—die!" the woman cried. "Why can't you stay *put!* We're *so* sorry—we *are.* You!" She jerked him, submissive, after her. Lily watched a second, relieved, then went on for the men's shirts, but recalling her list, clutching tight at the cooker, she groped— "No!" she said aloud. Her purse was gone.

Alone in the deep grass, the creature pushed its way along, at first at its normal pace, but gradually plowing free of the grass, it dragged sand, its underside filled, it pushed up ridges, yet it drove constantly, at a diagonal, but always toward the water, slowed until it could scarcely move, barely inching along, stopping, then struggling again, then still.

"They used that child!" she said. "Then they were gone, the manager did all he could, he had all the detectives in the store on the move. I—" Beside Win in the front seat, she was making it happen all over again but she couldn't stop. "And the money and everything. Waiting a whole year to get into the city and not a thing to show for it. If only I had—" The watery road spread, telephone wires undulated, the poles shimmered like giant stems and the great dead bulbs floated over her. "Well, *say* something! You never *say* anything." "Why don't you put the package in the back seat," he said gently. Her hands still gripped taut around the pressure cooker. She had forgotten it was there. She twisted to set it behind. "Did the manager take your name and address in case—" "Of *course.* What do you think I am—stupid?" "I just thought—" "You just *thought!*" she said. She turned her head away. Outside, the sun lay in a still sheath over everything, early afternoon shadows just beginning to emerge. The shadows of the wires crossing overhead lay a fine net down over the highway. She closed her eyes. Win turned on the radio. Instantly the transistor spoke. "You can't wait to get home to TV, can you?" she said. "You don't want to hear anything about it." "We can't do anything about it now, Lil," he said. "We have to accept it as a fact." "You *never* want to. Always leave it to *her.* I know things don't bother you. Let *her* worry." He sighed deeply and turned the radio off. "Is that better?" he said. *"Yes,* that's better." She lazed over, facing him, more aware of the odor now. "You went into a bar, I can smell it." "Yes. I had a drink and talked for a while." "Whiskey," she said. "You *know* you're not supposed to." "One, the doctor said." "The doctor said Scotch—Scotch, not whiskey." "The doctor doesn't know what it's like." His hands flicked over the wheel and tightened. Though the sun was behind, he kept blinking, widening his eyes and arching his brows periodically. "You tired?" she said. He nodded. "Win . . . ?" she said. It was quiet, the traffic was lighter, the sun glinting off the passing cars made momentary blind spots in her eyes and sometimes a quick, fine pierce. "Do you mind if we go straight home and not stop anywhere?" "No," he said. "Could we go a different way? Could we take the back road in, please?" "Sure, honey," he said. His lips thinned, pressed close, and several times his brows twitched involuntarily.

When the boys finally set out to look for the crab in the sea grass, it seemed to have disappeared, but Ben followed its traces until he found it nearly buried in the sand. "It must be dead." He turned it over. Its claws quivered. "Wait up!" Ben shouted. He found a rock and brought it down on the back of the crab with a loud whack. The shell cracked. Ben turned it over. A whitish liquid oozed up between the claws. "There!" he said and ran after Paul to the station wagon.

About an hour from town, they took the back road past the potato and cauliflower fields that sloped up to the ridges overlooking the Sound. Shadows were lengthening over the road, and the blacktop made a straight arrow out—into forever, it looked. With all that wide space and the sky so far from touching, she shrank down into the seat, feeling so small. Little ermine clouds drifted almost imperceptibly behind the distant trees. *Them,* she thought, seeing the two men and the woman and the boy there. On the horizon the faintest veil of fog seemed to be forming. "Something coming up over there," she said. "Did the papers say—?" But the car careened ever so slightly sideways. "Win?" she said, looking at him, and then "Win!" for his face was wet with sweat, his skin drained of color, his lips taut to whiteness. His left hand was still holding the wheel, but the other pressed flat against his chest. "Lil?" he said. "Your pills. You didn't bring your pills, *did* you?" Unable to speak, he grunted and shook *no.* "Pull over. Stop!" she cried. The car jerked off the road, bucked and dragged over the loose field dirt, a cloud of dust burying them for an instant. "Trying to prove you don't *need* them!" she said. Both hands grasped his chest, his shirt was soaked. She knew he was in agony, but she said, "Does it pain terribly?" loosening his tie quickly, opening his collar. "Lay back, don't move." She wiped her forehead with her hankie, thinking, Someone will pass, they have to— Then abruptly she said, "I'm going." But she didn't know where town lay—must be at least two or three miles across the fields to the right; left were the fields to the Sound, but—there—ahead about half a mile she saw a white patch in a clump of trees—a house, it *must* be. "Win, I'm going. I'll be *right* back. They'll have a phone. Call a doctor—" She headed across the field, striding, then running, kicking up dust, the wind driving it along after her, she coughed it up, running faster, long weeds and dying vines and twigs at her legs and ankles, the dirt so soft her heels sank and caught. "Take your shoes off!" she muttered, sweating now, a fine dust clinging all over her by the time she came to the clearing, to a hedge, which she skirted, which ran into raspberry bushes. "Against vandals," she said, but *where* to get in? "You!" she shouted. "Hey!" and pushed finally through the hedge and saw clear to the driveway and then the house—every window boarded up against the enemy. She stood panting for a second, her vision blurred, thinking how the other time it had happened in town, she'd got to a drugstore, but Win didn't have his prescription, there was the futile long-distance call, the pharmacist's resistance, she had to argue for Win's life with him—one pill, to hold him. But it's against the law, he'd said. "Against the law to save a man's life?" she cried aloud now and ran back across the field. When she got to Win, he was dead. She knew it when she opened the door: his neck and face were swollen, bloated, like one of those porgies that swell when you touch the belly, the lids puffed about his eyes, slits but still open, motionless and staring down the road. "Win, Win," she murmured, leaning against the door, and stared in the direction of the city. It was 3:50. She waited fifty-two minutes before a car came by. "Send us the police," she said.

The changing tide washed in, at first in steady low waves, then gradually grew stronger, thrusting deep at the sand. Far out, at the mouth of the bay, a fine haze was gathering. A gull soared down—Ha! Ha! it called—and lighted by the crab. Unhesitating, it went close, its hooked beak jabbed between the claws and pulled, the claws made the faintest response. Almost quietly, several other gulls alighted. They crowded in, with rapid hooks at the crab's belly. Sharp click-click-click cut the air. Coming out of the pines, an old man carrying a bucket and a clam rake crossed through the sea grass, curious about the gathering gulls. When he was still comfortably distant, one of them gave the warning cry and promptly flapped up, and in response the gulls all flew off and descended far down by the breakwater, waiting. "So they did you in, old boy," he said, eyeing the net of myriad tracks around the crab. "Well, I guess the chickens'll have a big feed tonight," he said, seizing the crab by the tail and dropping it headlong into the bucket.

In the kitchen, for a long while she sat in the gray dark, by the window. In no time news would be all over town, and of course they would come; but for now she did not yet want to see anyone, for this brief instant between, this small reprieve. . . . Out the window was the neighborhood, the lights in kitchen windows, the blue-lit TV screen in Addison's, the crown of trees losing their leaves, and old Mr. Welsh crawling to the corner grocery for his late paper. I have looked upon it all my life, she thought, looking left, down the long expanse of land, dim to the horizon, a thin knife edge that separated, and night coming down fast over it. A moment later she rose and switched on the light. The kitchen sprang up close around her, the white so sharp it seared her eyes a second, nearly bringing tears: the dishes from Washington, D.C., the hurricane lamp found on Plum Island, Gram's old buffet taken down to its original grain. She did not move, but her eyes touched them. The family was all there, all of them—their faces flashed into her mind, sharp and clear. Everything was sharp and clear. "What is it?" she whispered, startled to hear herself, to feel herself so *loud* in the house. Others had gone from her, and there was that emptiness following their loss, but at this moment the house was too full, there were too many things, they caught at her eyes. I have looked upon it all my life, she thought again. But now they seemed too heavy, permanent. My kitchen, she said, seeing it as it was; my house, holding it in her eyes as it was. And suddenly the house rose up, it filled her vision, overwhelming her—abruptly the kitchen *was,* and all the objects *were,* hard and cold and clear—and she saw bills and calculations and plans and details of money, the burden, and she knew it would not stop, it would weigh on, creep always into her mind, eat at her time, little by little push out her dreams. All those years of dreams. . . . *Oh, Win!* she cried for the first time, silently. "Win!" she cried aloud. She wanted to *tell* him, she wanted to thank him, thank him for all those years he gave her time and a place to dream in. "Win!" She fled to the window, the night was a near-solid wall now, the few lights beyond were vague, and the pane threw up herself standing there, and the kitchen clear and full behind her, filling the pane, leaving no room, not an edge, not a whit— "Win," she said, and she sat at her sewing machine, she pulled out the half-made pot holder she'd left yesterday, and she bent her head down, she stepped on the pedal and let the whirring fill the room.

In the chicken coop, at first the hens flocked to the horseshoe crab, pecking at its underside, pulling at its innards, one by one veering off and now and again returning for an isolated peck. After a while the crab lay neglected, the shell, the hairs along the claws dry and stiff. The liquid began to thicken, to coagulate and dry and smell. And the smell attracted flies and insects. And there was a heavy buzzing over it. In a little while the darkness covered it, and under the darkness the dead crab lay swarming with life.

The Transfusion Man

I T CLOTS FAST. That's why my blood's so good for operations," he said. The nurse was one of the good ones. She relaxed him with her soft voice, and she was efficient in an easy fluid way, chatting into his eyes, with only one quick glance down when she penetrated his arm. She adjusted the bottle and straightened the tube for free flow. Slowly his blood rose in the bottle, himself flowing out of himself.

Whatever hospital he went to, the rest was always the same—a peculiar cartilage resilience, a dreamy weakening came into him; then with an imperceptible glide the nurse withdrew the needle, pressed cotton over the puncture, and he doubled his arm to prevent bleeding.

This time, when he finally sat up, a sudden perspiration came, a cool wave, and the slightest singing in his ears.

"You feel weak?"

"Wobbly. Woozy."

"Better stretch out a minute."

"I'll be all right—in a sec." And he was. The sensation ebbed away and his body set back into motion. At first his heart pounded, blood resounded in his ears, but gradually it coursed smoothly. All through him he felt the flesh awaken, gathering. It was this afterflow he loved—the feeling, through his weakness, of resurgence, of burgeoning.

Down in the lobby, he pushed through the revolving door, but—*Uuuuuuuh*—too fast. The cement steps wriggled, people rolled up in waves, his legs nearly buckled. He leaned against the wall. This time he really *was* weak, but he tried breathing deep—innnn, out, innnn, out. . . . His eyes cleared, the world came back, the quick cold passed, a pleasant warmth flowed through him with each deep respiration.

He was thinking of the woman, the Mrs. Wallace Aito who

needed blood, type AB, at St. Joseph's. He would never see her, of course, but an image of her rose, though the image kept shifting (it was the advantage of not knowing her)—now she was young, a wisp of life under the hospital sheet, blonde and delicate against the pillow. And that baby. The image brought back Clara.

"Clara?" Moving down the steps, he said it aloud. Her bleached-blue eyes stared down from the sky. They seemed to speak to him again: "Are you surprised? You could never make anything." For their own baby had been born dead. He had seen it—insisted on that—a shriveled-up little huddle hardly the proper size for burial. It made him feel very impotent. For days after, everywhere he looked—at his friends, his fellow employees, people passing by, into the trees or the sky, he saw it superimposed, they became *it,* or it *they,* as if all the world were shrinking. From what?

"We can try again, Clara. Some things weren't meant to be."

"Some people weren't!" She muttered something about his paintings, the book he had tried to write, the monotonous clerk's job he had, all his little—abortions.

"Forgive me, Clara," he said now. For he had forgiven *her* those words long since. She had been, after all, in the throes of loss; she had counted on the baby so; but in days after, she did not let up. He would go home and she would be sitting there with the stereo or the TV going, sometimes the vac or the electric beater in the kitchen, she sitting suspended, lost, having run down. It was then he learned his patience. "Clara?" he'd whisper, and she would emerge from it, slowly, smiling in the distant half-transported way she'd had when he was first her boyfriend, then her lover, before they were married. Then, as if he had been unmasked before her, she would recognize him. That insulting glare returned, she withdrew abruptly, in dread of his touch, whispering, "Don't. Don't." Yet she was quivering with desire. He knew her: one touch—even with that violent resentment, or because of it—and she would succumb. She had yielded once, but only once, since the baby, but immediately after thrust him away, perhaps because of some remorse or terror that she had conceived twice, killed twice. And he had not seen her again until the next morning at breakfast. He had given her no pleasure. That was the terror: he could give her no pleasure, nothing gave her pleasure, unknowingly he had taken her pleasure from her.

"Clara," he muttered, going down the hospital steps. I want to give you everything, all the pleasure in the world, my Clara. It was the thought of all his life, what he married her for. She was tiny, and she coiled into him, clutching at his fingers—loved kissing his right hand when it rested on her shoulder. The soft, tender brushes roused him. But after the baby, nights, whenever he opened the front door and saw her sitting there in the living room, he remembered the girl inside her, the Clara she would no longer let out. Guilt came into him, he felt terribly helpless. He had tried everything, hadn't he? One evening he dared to broach adoption.

"*Adopt!* That would be fine, wouldn't it? Showing all the world what we couldn't do. And what makes you think that wouldn't be just another abortion?" And she added their lives all up again, and he said to himself, *Patience, patience;* but he couldn't hold it in much longer when she sang out her favorite phrases, "Your whole life, one big abortion."

My whole life . . .

For a moment, in the street, he saw his whole life suspended in the sky over St. Joseph's and watched it—himself falling through blue blue space. And he wanted to laugh at the sight of that little thing, an incongruous puppet, falling. . . .

And he did laugh—because he was *not* falling, it was so warm, he felt nimble with sun, his mind (That Aito woman!) leaped with a queer joy, there was the park. But his legs did not respond, he lifted them with effort, the flesh was a drag on his bones. So he was glad for the park; a quick tide of green came up over the crest, and twisted oaks, thick shade elms; and forsythia sprayed up in still fountains of yellow fire he could hardly hold in his eyes. Thank God Trumbull had given him the day off.

He eased onto the bench in plain sight of the World War I soldier, a hard corroded bronze against the blue sky. A squirrel twitching its tail nervously stared at him. Under the shrubs a robin hopped. Beside him, a centipede shining brilliantly sped over the dirt. And in the wind the leaves made a curious rush; there were tremors everywhere, creaks, crackings, pushing. The earth palpitated into his legs. Dark violets pulsed in the grass.

"Pa-*pi!*" The little girl darted, flung her arms up, circled, and threw her ball blindly, and chased it down. The white dress opened and rode like a blossom downwind. "Pa-*pi!*" she cried, thrusting the ball again, and doubled up in laughter as it struck Papi's head. "Beatriz!" he said and went on in—some foreign language it was. The words cut him off. It distressed him. He rose. "Clara," he said.

He was still a little dizzy—all the other transfusions must be catching up with him. Taking their toll. Eat foods with iron, the doctor said. Around him the green undulated up the tree trunks, merged with the canopies of leaves, and made the sky glow the richest emerald green. His head floated up with it—so light!—eased onto the waves, lulled in that current. Pure emerald joy. If only he could tell Clara how it felt. You're too locked up in yourself, Clara.

But he couldn't say that. She would glare at him so! She *had*. "Transfusion! Why'd you *do* such a thing?" And his explanation, put into words, did sound strange: "I was sitting beside this man in the drugstore—you know the one, across from Mercy Clinic. He was talking to himself. He said, 'I don't know what I'm going to do, I just don't know,' so I said, 'What,' and he said it was his son, dying maybe, he wasn't even sure the doctors were telling *him* everything, and the son needed blood bad, the blood bank was near empty of the right type— AB. It sounded like my dog tags—remember the army I.D.? 'That's me,' I said. 'I'm AB.' You should've seen his *face*, Clara—all bright eyes eating me up. 'Jesus, you don't mean it,' he said. I thought he was going to cry on the spot, just from knowing there *was* some AB. 'I don't have any money, but course we'll pay, we'll borrow,' he said. And I said, 'Let's go to the radio station,' and we did—WDED—and they announced it. By six, we'd enough. Mine—direct transfusion it was— was right near him, that boy, just lying there, scarce breathing, and me with a peculiar weaklike drain, but I could hear the breathing, that boy's breathing getting louder, and after a while that's all I heard—air going in and out, in and out, in and out—I couldn't tell his sound from mine, mine was his; and when they finally pulled the needle out and I saw the tube free, I knew—my blood was in him and my air too. I looked over—he was lying so still, but his chest was moving, up and down, and I couldn't wait to get home, I wanted to tell you, Clara. But the nurse said, 'You just take this shot of whiskey first and be sure and eat a good rich steak.'"

"Alf! Cut it out. Stop," she said.

"Clara, listen—"

But it was over—until the morning after the boy's transfusion, when she opened the mail.

"At least you were paid for your—services," she said.

"Paid?"

"Twenty-five dollars." She flagged the check at him.

"For what?"

"Your blood," she said, "blood."

"It's a mistake. The nurse knew I donated my blood. Send it back. Give me that!" He wanted to tear it up. He *gave* his blood. He wouldn't let her take that from him.

"Oh, *no* you don't. We're not so well off you can toss away twenty-five dollars."

"That man couldn't afford it. I won't accept it."

"Well, *I* will. Don't you know what money means?"

"That's not the point," he said.

"Well, exactly what *is* the point then?"

And what was it? He couldn't say it, but he knew. . . . The memory of that moment when he felt himself flowing out of his body, felt himself breathing on that other bed in the boy's lungs. Perhaps that was why he went back—to experience that sensation again. (One day the boy came to the house, but he was out. Then the boy phoned, and Alf told her, "Clara, that voice—it's our voice, Clara.") The wonder of it struck him, how his blood would generate corpuscles in that boy's body and make breath and voice and motion, and in all those bodies, for all those generations, in so many places—and in the air, everywhere. He wanted to tell her.

"Clara, listen—" he said abruptly, with urgency. He wanted to touch into her—not her flesh, no, but somewhere deeper and softer than flesh where she was vulnerable. His urgency—his voice must have compelled her—made her eyes settle apprehensively still on him. "Let's try once more, let's have a baby. Please, Clara?" At the sudden shapeless fall of her face, the down motion of her mouth, the sagged eyes, he felt such pity for her that he said, "Clara," soft, and did reach out to touch softly on her neck. At that, for only a brief second her eyes darted, her lips quivered, her hand shot up and clamped over his own. Then she bolted up, shook free and stood—so rigid it pained him. "No," she said, "no no *no*." Then it was over, she went to the sink, turned on the tap. She braced her hands against the sill and stared outside. In the yard the apple tree was blooming.

Moseying along the street now, he dreaded going back to the house. Whenever he had a day off like this, he took to wandering—through the park, along Wilmot Avenue into the crowded shops, to the zoo, amused by children dragging weary parents along behind them. Besides—with Clara gone—the house, small as it was, had grown so big, too much space to roam in. Fine coats of dust lay over everything despite Mattie's coming now and then. But his sister had cut down on her visits since his brother-in-law put his foot down. "You can't go charging to Alf's for nothing. Let him pay regular maid's wages." He had overheard Will—didn't mean to—and went back down the stairs, then called Mattie next day. "I got a girl to come in," he said. He knew by the long silence that Mattie understood, maybe even guessed what had happened, but what could you say at a time like that? "Sure, Alf," she said.

And on such days as this, the heat pouring down in a clean, golden waterfall over him, the house was too dark. Three great office buildings rose in eternally dark glooms about it, the sun always too far above the dark pit. Only at high noon did light eddy into the front room, though the porch cut some of that. One day he'd have it taken off.

Yet he headed home now. He needed a deep deep sleep. Tomorrow was the semiannual inventory, he must be ready. More—he had to recuperate, he had given blood too frequently. The doctor said four months between transfusions, but he *would* go on, there were so many who needed, so few type ABs. And lying in the hospital bed, wide awake and seeing, there was that joyful discovery—first his own diminishing, then growing, extending, becoming—

The traffic was halted, the light turned green, and he crossed between the yellow bars to the traffic circle, where the new Kennedy statue pierced the blue, announcing its brotherhood to the world.

He was hungry. Meat was the important thing. Build up the blood. He always had meat in the refrigerator. Still, no cook like Clara. He smiled, thinking of one of her meals. When *she* went— A fast nausea swept over him, dimmed his watering eyes—Kennedy rose taller, thin as a needle. "I don't blame you, Clara," he muttered aloud, "no." And he didn't. She had her vision of things, though he did not know what it was, she would never say, grimming her lips. Even when he came home with new fervor after the first trips to the different blood banks, she merely said, "Again?" with quiet resentment. But when she found it was beginning to drain him, making him tired, despite his enthusiasm, she became all direct attack. "What right?" she cried. "You talk like I'd taken something that belonged to you," he said. "After all, if you'd—" "Well, it affects your job, *our* living, doesn't it? If you're tired, you're not putting out the work properly, are you?" "But if you, if we could have—" "Don't say it again!" she cried.

For whenever he mentioned the two of them, she seemed to sail off —first her eyes, then all her senses—to somewhere, something else. She'd go into another room, most of the time even sleep there. And he lay down in a private flood which he yearned to share with her. Giving blood at one hospital or another became an action she refused even to recognize he did, though she knew the very day, the hour—it hung on her when he walked in. Different then, she would move differently —strike things, shove furniture while cleaning, burn pots, stay up late working noisily.

One morning—five in the morning it was—he went into the spare room, knowing she was shifting about, awake. He sat on the edge of the bed. "Clara, please. We could avoid all this," he said. He reached over—in one of those now rare and terrible moments when he was aching with desire—and her eyes made mad hummingbird races, her hands clawed the sheets up over her, the desire wild in her too, she leaped back as his hands probed toward her. "Go. Go back to your hospitals. Go—to that!" She did not know she was shouting. And he— he was aching, aching, and his hands insisted, they touched her. She moaned. "Clara," he whispered, his hand sank into her thigh. And her arm lashed out, *struck, struck*—twice. And he froze there, violently still. "You're"—it was incredible to him—"jealous," he said. She lashed again, but this time he was too far away and she fell forward on her face in the blanket, convulsed—hard, dry coughs that hurt his own throat with their sound. He rose and went back to his room, dressed, and went out to the diner. When he came back at six-thirty, she was not there. Her clothes were gone.

"Mac?" Something touched his shoulder. He roused—he'd been leaning against the Kennedy pedestal, the granite was cold. As his eyes focussed, he turned to answer. "I'm not Mac. I'm—" It was a policeman.

"Stand up, Mac."

He stood straight, blinking. The sunstruck cars passing pricked at his eyes. But the park beyond righted, the road spread clean again, the buildings came down.

"Been drinking, eh?"

"No. I mean—one."

"Sure," the policeman said.

"It's not drink—not pleasure. It was just—" It sounded absurd, even to himself, he couldn't say it.

"I know. You better come with me," the cop said. The light was red. Behind it, cars lined up. The squad car stood at the curb.

"You couldn't know," he muttered.

"That's right. Come on."

"I don't drink," he said.

"Sure you don't."

Beside him the cop loomed. He hadn't realized how tall he really was—the Kennedy statue dwarfed him so. "Get in."

He wanted to cry out, Something's wrong. He thought: Clara, hospital, blood, sun, house, inventory. Yet he obeyed, he hunched, crawled in and sank back, his head held up with difficulty. Gradually his equilibrium came back. Everything went by soundlessly now, but the rolled-up windows trapped the metallic voice on the intercom.

At the district station he sat with three others—an ugly little man in a torn navy sweat shirt, his arm in a sling, and an elderly spinsterish woman in purple clutching the hand of an old man who resembled her. When the lieutenant called, "You," he stood up, so hungry his stomach was pulsing.

"I'm Alfred Singleton," he said.

"Let's see your driver's license."

"I don't have one. There's no need for a car in the city, the subways—"

"Any other identity?"

"Yes." He reached for the wallet. "Social security, credit cards—" His hand groped. "I—" Nothing. "I had it—this morning—right here." Gone. Without her, he was—was he slipping?

"Sure," the policeman said.

"Don't keep saying that!"

"Calm down, Mac."

"Not Mac. Alfred. Singleton," he said. "Singleton."

"Sure."

"I did have it. It must have fallen out when—" But there was no need.

"You employed?"

"Yes."

The officer waited, but he offered him no further information. Suppose his boss—

"Where?"

"In an accounting office. I'm assistant. It's my day off."

"Where?"

Sinking, he said, "Peabody and Ebb. But don't call. There's nothing wrong. I'm not feeling well, a little nauseated is all."

"We'll just check—it's routine—on your identity. Sergeant—"

He could hear the dialing. "No— Look. The truth is I just gave a pint of blood. I'm weak—all in. I just need to sleep some."

Indifferently, the lieutenant said, "Well, which *is* it?"

He was watching the sergeant's fingers. "Sergeant—" he said, but it was hopeless and he sat again, not wanting to hear. But words fell over him, hot pricks at him: "Alfred Singleton. Yes. District four police. Yes, he's here now. Can someone come identify him? I see." He shuddered.

"Said an Alfred Singleton's off today. Said they never heard of such a thing. Course they won't come."

He slumped. "Clara," he whispered.

"Who's Clara?"

"My—she's my wife. Ex," he murmured.

"Call her," the lieutenant told the sergeant. "What's her number?"

"No. Call St. Joseph's—please."

The lieutenant stared at him, measuring. "We got plenty to do here. You don't look so good. Somebody ought to come after you. Call his wife. Lady—" He turned to the woman in purple now.

"My wife lives with her sister. Emma Webb. 317 Willis," he told the sergeant. Clara. He saw her face, dreading the scowl, yet he wanted, *wanted* to see her, wanted her to see him. He could not explain. But Clara would not come—never.

"What?" he said. The sergeant was beside him. "She'll be down soon's she can," he said.

"She—? Clara's coming here?"

"You'll be gone in no time, sir."

Sir. He wanted to reach out and shake the boy's—he *was* only a boy—hand, but he slid back, slumped into the chair, so tired. He was very nervous, and hungry, so exhausted he was nearly asleep when he heard her voice. "I'm Clara Webb. Singleton," she said. "You called me."

"Clara!" he said with that shock which expectancy brings. She had not seen him against the wall, behind her, as she entered. The sight stunned her. She doesn't know me, he thought madly. Have I changed that much in a few months? But he *had,* he knew it—thinner, tired, even a little grayer, and shabby—not neat, like when she did his clothes. He stood up. "Clara?" Staring across at him, so far away, gulfs away from him in that little space, she did not speak. He made a step forward—and smiled. "Hello, Clara." For the shadow of an instant her face went soft, it trembled, her eyes took him in, seemed to swallow him, something quicker than memory made her look lost, so vulnerable that he thought quickly, *My* Clara, and unconsciously his hand went out to her. But that gesture called her back.

She turned to the lieutenant. "Yes, it's him," she said.

"You're free to go," the lieutenant said courteously. "Better be sure you carry your papers from now on."

"Clara, wait—" He followed her down the steps.

"Now what? Isn't it humiliation enough—" Her face was racked with the sight of him.

"I want to—thank you." He made no attempt this time to go near, to touch her. Maybe it was something familiar in his voice—he didn't know—but something arrested her, she looked long at him. "Was it so terribly painful, Clara? Now it wasn't, was it?" he said softly, letting his voice touch out. And she said, "Yes. Yes it *was*—so terribly painful, Alf." *Alf.* She said his name that way, Alf, soft and tender. And he thought, I can get to her, I *can*. He stepped close. "You'll have a bite with me, Clara?" Whether it was the step or the hand, she shook off her nostalgia, whatever it was. "Don't be a fool. What's done is done. I've done my duty." "Duty!" "Yes, what else? And *you,* drunk. You've sunk to that, have you? Look at you!" "No. Not. Not." He struggled to push his jacket sleeve up. "I've been to the hospital—see," he said. "Blood." But she drew back. "Now *you* look! Leave me out of it. I'm divorced—understand? Divorced. Go back to your hospital. Maybe that's where you belong." Her voice was filled with scorn, but her eyes were wet. She ran down the steps. He called after her but his own sound was weak, a whisper dying on his lips.

He walked past the neighborhood orphanage, beside West Park, along the river bank. At the boat house he stopped to listen to the shouts of the children and watch the couples young and old going on the river excursion. Farther on, where the river widened, he started across the bridge to West End. He stopped and looked down into the water. Clara? What happened? What did I do? He stared deep, deep into the water. What did I do? And the longer he stared the closer the water seemed, almost no distance between him and the water, and the thought of Clara, of his job—his boss would not understand, he would consider the external circumstances only, the company's reputation, public opinion, they would say . . . The baby. Clara. The job. The days would stretch out endlessly, all the days, into months, into years, into his whole life. . . . He gazed deep deep into the water below, watching it go endlessly down . . . and he could go with it, he could let go, be sucked down, let himself drift, drift, forever and ever. Ahh . . . .

But he felt the sun still warm on his back—that sun!—and he wanted that, and the fresh deep air, and the gleams of light everywhere. It sent his blood pulsing, and he felt that puncture on his arm to remind him—blood. Clara, he thought, but no—he blotted it out. She did not understand how he yearned for it—he wanted life, there was that, and his blood everywhere, yes—in the air, the rain, in flesh. It was all in him, in his blood, and in them. He would watch and wait. And when the time came, he would answer the call again, he would give. And as if the thought impelled him, he hurried over the bridge, under the cables webbed dark against the afternoon sky, hurried down into the declining sun, toward the house.

The Itinerary of Beggars

B Y THE TIME night comes the authorities of the Hospital Emilio Civit—nurses, doctors, administration—are sure the baby is stolen. The mother is nearly out of her mind. The basket at the foot of her bed is empty—all the others are filled. When she sees the babies or the vacant basket, she cries, screams, faints. Her husband, their parents, friends hover about her. Everybody is talking at once. The other women in the ward keep asking for their babies; they want to hold them, to feel secure, even be certain the babies are their own, yet they don't know how— Mine, they say; but the room is filled with doubts, fear lingers with the creatures in their arms. Still, they have one. They sink back. Even pitying the despairing woman, they feel a certain complacency.

So he is put on the case—who else?—a matter of routine, wander the streets, you know the routine, where to go, a Mendozan all your life, you know these people inside out, you're one of them: while the Jefe sits, fatter by the day, drinking coffee, chomping medialunas, dribbling crumbs all over the papers Manuelito is called every five minutes to clean up. So be it. At least he'll be outside on the street, in the Mendoza sun. Who can complain of that, even if the people look away from him more now, sheepish under the new government. He knows: bureaucracy, the military, too many policía, not enough ayyyy not enough *any*thing but policía. Go ahead, you bastards, say it. You're right too. He hears the Jefe telephoning: "How is it possible? Such things don't happen here in Mendoza. Such things—" And then to the two on guard, "How could you let it happen, eh?" Ayyyy, Jefe, where have you lived all your life under that dead skull? What did you say last time they hauled a kid off? So it's me again?

How can you be wherever a thing happens, I ask, 300,000 minds to anticipate, eh? Babies they have every day and every night, dead babies, in baths, washrooms, latrines, in the lavabos, flushed down the drain, spilled onto sheets. Sacred. Who says? Shit!

LA CLARA (Clara Rita Montecasero/27/b. SAN RAFAEL, MENDOZA/single/residence VILLA MISERIA): Twenty times he been this morning, like watching me—and what I'm doing wrong?—me what comes here every week of my life and sits and does to nobody nothing, not a thing, sitting here like this; and you don't think, mi hijito, this stone's not cold on my ass, you try it sometime eight o'clock in the morning and stick out your hand all day and feel it's going to break off and hold the kid in the other till you can't feel it and the cold till you think *dying*. He's smart, that cop—not like that reporter from *Los Andes*. They both come all the time, they know babies, like measuring the size, even if I cover the kid up, sometimes big, sometimes little, but who's going to bother us?—not even the policía, they'd have to feed us then, or the Nación, but not a chance of that, Perón's gone. They don't care you're pregnant, some man screwed you one night—which?—and it's his and don't care; and this one in my belly—*I* know: them going by always saying, She's pregnant again, poor thing. Shit, why they think I do it if it ain't a living carrying these goddamn things around? When this one comes I won't have to rent the García's or Antonini's or whatever one TERESITA don't get to first, that bitch! Jesus, that García machito cries all the time. Who wants that trouble on the street? This one, she's good and you don't got to run every minute for something to shove in the mouth so's it's not crying. Pregnant's the best time, the men love it then, a little blood and if you say it hurts they get hotter than hell; you put yourself on the street for that, anything for a good fuck; that Antonio, son-of-a-bitch, he's in the bed now and don't give a shit just I come back with some money and he'll give it to me good then, he's got it too.

Everybody knows the reporter. He won a prize. Which? Who remembers? But he won a prize. His picture was on the front page and he was given an honorary membership too by the Yankees from

Life magazine for how he covered the avalanche at Las Cuevas, years now. Nobody knows the city like the reporter. He knows everything, more than the policía. He never looks like a man working. He's always on the spot, but everywhere too, never hurrying, but moving every minute. He goes down LAS HERAS Street: she's there—LA CLARA by the BANCO DE LONDRES. Of course, it's Tuesday. MONDAY she's at the MERCADO CORDOBA, TUESDAY at the BANCO DE LONDRES, WEDNESDAY at the GALERIA TONSA, Catamarca entrance, THURSDAY by the bus station TAC, FRIDAY at the CORREO CENTRAL, SATURDAY at the ALAMEDA. They think you don't know, the reporter thinks, but it's a round, fixed. Sometimes beggars coincide, but always you find them the same day at the same place. Today the old man's there too at the rear end of the BANCO DE LONDRES: SQUINTY, all wet-eyed like he's crying, but not.

Over the city at 8:00 A.M.—you can set your watch by them, the sun rises by them—it is like a magical moment, open sesame, the great clock strikes, they are there: LA CLARA, SQUINTY, PETISA, ITO, JUAN CARLOS, LA POLACA, MIA, TURI, MANOLO, ROQUE, NINA, BIZCO, MAURA, LA TURCA. . . . They are a map of the city from one barrio to the next—LAS HERAS? DORREGO, EJERCITO DE LOS ANDES, VILLA MISERIA, SAN JOSE DE GUAYMALLEN, BARRIO DEL GAS DEL ESTADO—a miniature invasion, a quiet infiltration that goes unobserved. At 12:30 when the negocios close, they disappear. At 3:30 they are there again until the negocios close at 7:30.

PETISA (María del Carmen Huerto/50/b. province of SAN JUAN/birth unrecorded/single/spastic/residence DORREGO), corner ENTRE RIOS and SAN JUAN: Snooping. Policía all time snooping, but they get me afraid. I never been in jail, I ain't going neither, I done nothing. Ayyy, mi madre, if she knew how they drug me from SAN JUAN to TUCUMAN when she died, and me nothing—making me a slave and kicking and beating me all the time. How could I help it spilling water, knocking things— and the people sometimes, yes I hear: she puts the shakes on, her head don't go like that, you watch when she leaves and takes the micro, she don't do it no more. I'd like to see *them* do it—even one hour, they'd know then. "Gracias, señor. Dios le va a ayudar." 20 pesos. Ah, sí—good: chickens' feet, patas, they sell me for ten; Don Fernando'll give them for eight, a little rice—nice soup that. Antonio—my mother's own brother—beating me to make me go to TUCUMAN, a shack by the cañas, all that sugar growing, kilometers, the only beautiful thing all my time there—that sun and the field all moving. Making me watch chickens, those sick *aves,* and tying me down once, yes, pulling my arms out like to kill me and my head too to make me not move, like *you never going to shake any more if I tie you this way.* Mentiroso! A lie to crawl on top of me, ayyyy bastardo, *I'm going to make you a woman.* But Dios, He helped me—yes. Somebody—who knows?—got Antonio one night and gave him whatfor; I don't know, he didn't come back, but I saw him dead. Ay, Dios mío, when I saw him cut up like that I said *Jesus, gracias, gracias.* Ayyyyy, forgive me, God, saying it, I'm ashamed now, but ayyyyy I ran ran ran, no more TUCUMAN—you know how far? Hooooo, I can't tell, days, days, walking. They gave me to eat on the road, and cualquier finca, any old farm . . . and I slept, ayyy, in what fields, by the road, always with my trapos, but such good rags I had . . . but like an angel slept, knowing *no more Antonio, no, no más, never.*

The policía is a little tired talking to so many, feels his way, like It's a good day, what sun, eh?—casual—it was cold at your place this morning? And the others in the house, they felt it? Ah-ha, the brother's got catarro? And the little girl, how's she? And so on—to ALEJO, LA FLACA, GIANNO, MALASUERTE—down LAS HERAS, along SAN MARTIN, down BUENOS AIRES to SAN JUAN and up RIVADAVIA to the PLAZA DE ESPANA. . . . But tired too because *my people.* I know them so well, mine, all my life. . . . So he is feeling betrayal. I am undermining something, destroying to protect—and with what sense?—accusing them because—they're what they are? Like asking in my own family—and them not guilty either. Like a spy, but spying on everybody. And what proof? There are no lonely women *not* beggars? men *not* beggars who steal to sell? Margarita says But it's your duty, Miguel. My duty! And yours? I ask her. Mine—? What's wrong with you? I'm your wife. She doesn't

see it's the same. And what's between us? I ask her. *Es otra cosa,*
not the same, she says. What's the same, then? I say. "Hola, JUAN
CARLOS, how goes everything? Look at you, all rigged out in a new
jacket. The tourists flooding you with cash, eh? And—the other—
what's her name?—ah, sí, MARIANELA, she's doing fine? She's
never on the street. Must be her time, eh? She was big, you ever see
such a big thing? Like triplets, no es cierto? Ah . . . sí? A boy. Big?
How old now? In the hospital—which? Ah, not the hospital, but a
partera. But a good midwife, for sure? Sí? Where . . . ? Ah, well,
if she's gone to another province, my wife—if the time ever comes
—won't need her, eh? Right? Bueno, JUAN CARLOS, good luck.
Chau. Hasta luego."

8:30 BICHO, 9:01 EL GATO, 9:20 MIRAFLORES, GUILLERMO
in front of the CAFE COLON, where the policía stops for his morning café expreso and then steps outside, 10:53 CARLITOS, 11:20,
LA CAMARADA, 11:44 BUITRE. So? Back to the office, face the
Jefe. What've you got? Well: the beggar MARIANELA had her
baby, the midwife's gone; besides, the baby—JUAN CARLOS says—
was born long before, it'd be too big to be the stolen one. And when
you get there, who's to say it's the same baby, not exchanged, carried
off? The midwife's gone—no name, or so they say—one of those
women, sí, roams from one provincia to the other. JUAN CARLOS
has a new jacket, but I don't know—a woman?—where from yet.
LA CLARA's carrying a kid, six months maybe, and's big as a boat
herself. EL GATO's getting fat on something, living with a chick,
maybe. LA VIEJA ESA's beat black and blue; that means she's been
days in the acequias shacking with some stranger—she goes off like
that, a week, a month, then comes back: she loves to show her bruises;
they get her more cash. My sons beat me, she tells. Wouldn't know
her sons if they dropped a paper bill in her hand. The way BUITRE's
clothes are sewn together for a change, he must be holing up with
women somewhere.

Down COLON comes NOAH'S ARK, muttering, "Paper? Diario?
Los Andes?" scuffing along, too fast—with short mechanical legs, impelled ahead as if by his own words, "Paper? Diario? *Los Andes?*" At
the corner of SAN MARTIN he stops, stands still, closes his eyes,

sways, two minutes, three, five, inclining forward, then back, miraculously upright, napping, then moves on, moves, as if forever moving with these interludes of sleep, "Paper? Diario? *Los Andes?*" He turns onto SAN JUAN.

SILVINA (Silvina Derecho/70/b. mountains of LA RIOJA/ domicile SAN JOSE, tin shack by the zanjón/four sons, all on the street): Oooof, RICARDO thinks Silvina don't know cause she's old, can't hear good now, but I'm knowing he's bringing putas into the place when I'm not there and to get me out, boot me, yes, cause I'm old—and what I'm to do then, eh? And ROQUE and GUILLERMITO and ISIDRO ain't going to let him do that to their vieja, oh no—not JUAN either. But he got something in his head, that hideputa RICARDO, and all my life on the street for him. "Señor—" Ach, they don't give up, the policía and the newspaper in one day. "*Gra*cias, señora. Que Dios le bendiga, señora. . . ." By now, sí, 200—210—224—230—239—262 pesos. Bueno. "Hola, m'ijito—so you're around here again, uh-huh, and Silvina she knows when you reporters got something up the sleeve, eh? *Ba*by! Hombre, a woman of seventy! You young ones, always thinking of making the babies. . . . In *my* place? With four boys in the house, when's time, I'm asking you? No, no, no, m'ijito, I got my own problems—no babies. That's for the young ones. How'm *I* knowing what young ones? I just stick out my hand, I take what comes—what more, eh? Adiós, muchacho. Que le vaya lindo."

"Paper? Diario? *Los Andes?*" Along SAN JUAN, up ENTRE RIOS, along SAN MARTIN to GODOY CRUZ—NOAH'S ARK stops, still, closes his eyes, sways—then turns onto 9 DE JULIO, up LAS HERAS to PATRICIAS MENDOCINAS. . . .

In the MERCADO CENTRAL, LA CLARA rests the kid on her pregnant belly while the woman holds up one potato. "Sí, that one. And the onion. You got a little parsley to throw in, no? And ayyy, por favor, those two carrots—look at them, they're half rotten, eh—you can't sell those, eh?" The woman gives her a quick hard look, but chucks them in and thrusts the bag into her hand.

"La Santísima Virgen," LA CLARA says, but the verdulera has heard all that before, turns to the next customer. LA CLARA mutters *La mierda* to herself, *shit*, weary from carrying. She climbs into micro 15, which passes the VILLA MISERIA, sits. *Jesus*. Ached to the bone. She clutches the rented kid. Jesus, I'll be glad to put him down and drop this goddamn thing I'm carrying inside me too— when? Antonio'll be hungry. She clutches the bag. Anything for a good fuck.

The MERCADO CENTRAL closes at 12:30. The city is arace, micros jammed, cars all activated, taxis busy, the streets floods of horns and motors, nafta fumes fill the air, black spurts from the rears of droves of busses. PETISA takes number 47, GUILLERMITO 17, MANOLO 4, BIZCO 8, LA TURCA 72. . . . BUITRE crosses the railroad tracks to the RANCHO CHILENO restaurant, ITO goes to the PARK, NINA to her corner of the PLAZA DE CHILE. Streams . . . The city streets seem to die still. Only the kiosks are open. Magazines flutter. The policía descends at PARANA, he sees his wife passing the mop over the tiles before the door, she smiles.

The reporter enters AMIGORENA 85, obsessed—there are babies everywhere in his vision, his mind is churning. The food is lousy in AMIGORENA 85, but there's plenty of it, why every kind of character low on cash jams in, it's busy all day long. The tables are full; the place sounds like a terminal, waiters shouting orders, everyone letting the morning out, talking laughing gesticulating. But it is the place to come. The waiters nod, the barmen, the owner—everybody knows him. He comes here all the time; it's his mine, always loaded, plenty of info, talk about anything, and sooner or later somebody says something, nobody keeps secrets but the dead, he knows that; let us be weak, it's better, we know each other. He spots URALDO the pimp with one of his putas, GISELDA, and sits down. They are glad to see him; they know he'll pay for the empanadas. Good to have a friend on the paper. Tit for tat. "How's business?" URALDO asks, taking the words out of his mouth. GISELDA passes a leg. She'd like the reporter one time, he knows it—she'd give it free, a matter of pride, class, woman. But she knows all the girls everywhere, the midwives, abortionists as far as CHACRAS DE

CORIA, POTRERILLOS, CACHEUTA, SAN RAFAEL, USPAL-
LATA, no deceiving her: spots a rounding belly anytime, and knows,
without knowing where they are, the ones who've left for some safe
reason for CHILE, URUGUAY, COLOMBIA. . . . "Hooo," she says,
"they work so fast, who's telling where's a baby one minute or the
next." She gives him the list—in her way: taking it out on each,
"GRACIELA, the bitch, stole my cotton dress. . . . That one—you
know her—LILIA, she's traveling with the scum of the earth, RO-
DOLFO the chantajista from DORREGO that bribes his own mother
when he gets the chance. . . ." And so on. He gets her point. They're
the pregnant ones. She orders three more empanadas, a bottle of vino
de mesa. The reporter circulates, a word here, a word there. By the
time the meal is over, the city going into siesta, the sun thirty de-
grees warmer, ablaze over the Andes, downtown a cup of heat, he
is both groggy and stimulated: babies, babies everywhere. He is going to the *Los Andes* office, then to the public library on SAN MAR-
TIN, then to the BIBLIOTECA CENTRAL on BUENOS AIRES,
then the CIUDAD UNIVERSITARIA library . . . how many babies
stolen, murdered, kidnapped. Babies. It is extending in his mind:
how many stolen in MENDOZA, and in SAN JUAN, LA RIOJA,
SAN LUIS, SALTA, JUJUY and toward the Brazilian jungle, LA
RESISTENCIA, EL CHACO, FORMOSA, ROSARIO and south to
the cold regions, BARILOCHE, NEUQUEN, EL CHUBUT . . . and
across the border to PARAGUAY, URUGUAY, BRAZIL, BOLIVIA,
CHILE . . . and north to CENTRAL AMERICA . . . ? His head
is teeming with it. He follows the street without seeing it.

They sleep the siesta till 3:00—on dirt, rags, bare mattresses, blankets,
burlap, plaza tiles, benches, under pines and palms, in the dry culverts, the basin of the río Mendoza, against mud huts, on the street,
against trees, in the terminals, backs of pensions, patios, doorways,
buildings under construction, ruins, the hippodrome, all over the
park. . . .

By 3:15 he is on the way back to report in to the Jefe. He feels fine,
for the moment purged—he has eaten little, but has had his afternoon sex—always he is tired getting off late at night—and today
with vengeance as if he has tried to create the missing baby, and his

wife hot and violent. Since the change of government, people pay less attention to him, drop their eyes more—which means they are more aware of him, and there really are more policía stationed more carefully, and in civil dress. Still, some things you can't avoid. . . . He thinks of the baby—of no consequence, except for them, the family. Too many babies anyway. Poor, dying, wasted. He tries to imagine them. No face comes to mind. No voice. On the street he sees a woman with a baby, tries to imagine her without it—he sees a blank and he feels nothing; she looks the same. He greets the Jefe, but he has his afternoon already planned. He registers in, then starts the round of beggars: VICENTE, LOBO, GLADYS, CONQUISTA, DOLORES. . . . At the corner of SALTA, NOAH'S ARK is scratching his back frenetically. Not for nothing he's called NOAH'S ARK —with two bichos of every kind crawling over his body. He stops scratching, still a moment, then walks on. "Paper? Diario? *Los Andes?*" But at least he makes his own living, and so do the blind— not one blind beggar in this city; but look at the beggars: all over the place. Ahead, he sees VICENTE. He braces himself. He feels like a spy.

VICENTE (Vicente Esteban Cabrera/42/b. ROSARIO/residence GODOY CRUZ/jailed, multiple counts, total 10 years/missing left eye/sex deviant).

ANAMARIA (Anamaría Matilde Bianchi/33/b. SAN LUIS/8 children/residence mud choza, LAS HERAS/three times jailed, stealing).

VAGO (Lancelote Amado/42/b. CALABRIA, ITALY/residence none).

ANTONIA, DOLFO, RUFFO, BERTA, LAFCADIO. . . .

VIEJO (Lucio Fanini/64/b. Mendoza/residence with 8 men, patio of Doña Alfreda Mirón, one shed/4 sons, illegitimate, whereabouts unknown): sits on the tile sidewalk, legs outstretched, his hand out, his eyes staring into the treetops, knowing it's *her* territory on TUESDAYS too, LA CLARA's. If he turns around, she is there, glaring. Coming down the street, people get to him first; that must kill her, him robbing her like that. He knows his wet eyes trickle like sick, like crying; it stops women mostly; and the sores below his neck—he opens his collar wide—so they can see them too. He lets his beard go a few days, white now, and his hair is mostly gone. He never says a thing when they drop monedas in his hand, keeps his mouth wide open like paralyzed; but he moves the hand forward, curves it round as they go by and when something is dropped into it, he crushes the hand to his face to see how much. He drops the bigger coins into his pocket. Always he keeps two centavos in the hand. This day is not good. This morning: *140* pesos—nothing. He fingers his neck, the sores, tears at them a little with his dirty nails, opening them. He spreads his shirt open. A little blood always helps.

The reporter leaves the library. He is back downtown at *3:30*. They are back, each in his place. He is struck by their order. You can count on the beggars—all over the city. VIEJO, LA CLARA, TURCO, SQUINTY, they are all as if fixed, destined for the spot—if he went away, months, years, he feels that when he returned they would be there in the same place, on the same days, in the same positions. The thought is like a seed in him. He feels excited by the discovery —a certain inevitability, a pattern is revealed. He wonders why he is on the search for a missing baby, why always when a similar thing comes, he chooses it. Because I am an hijo natural, a bastard, though nobody knows that? Because I completed only sixth? Because I made myself what I am? And there creeps in a suspicion: he is looking for something else. He feels he is going backward in time, getting younger, swimming against the current of the past, deep. He is studying the faces, beggars, men and women alike. He is filled with the question: suppose I am staring into the eyes of my own mother . . . ?

On LAS HERAS, ROQUE (Roque Alfonso Lluch/58/b. BUENOS AIRES/residence none/4 sons, whereabouts unknown/separated, whereabouts of wife unknown/one-time contrabandist) has to pee. He ignores the hundreds of people passing down the main street. He turns to a tree and pees.

"Café, coffee, café?" His cylinders on his chest, ARMANDO wanders up and down, in and out the streets. Mostly it is the shoeshine men of the union who buy his coffee—the four thermos bottles strapped to him get lighter as the day goes on.

"Paper? Diario? *Los Andes?*"/stick out your hand all day and feel it's going to break off/a little rice, and nice soup that/a little blood always helps/"Que Dios le bendiga, señora"/faces, like roads, like rivers, like tracks/"Café, coffee, café?"/anything for a good fuck/maybe we are all ants/a perpetual roamer, wandering through the city, its bowels, intestines/Such things don't happen in Mendoza/"Paper? Diario? *Los Andes?*"

Miguel knows they know—not just somebody, but everybody must know where the baby disappeared. He even thinks at times that the mother may be an accomplice. Babies are sold every day. She's putting on an act? Who knows? He tries to track down more news of the midwife who "went away." VICENTE, MAURA, DOLFO, ANA-MARIA, they give hints but no betrayal—or they're not even hints? Already he's learned of twenty new babies in the city—not born at the hospital, not in the Registro Civil. How many more before the day's over? He must get to VAGO. He's the one—knows more about the traffic. Should, at any rate. He's always arranging rentings —call VAGO and he'll get you a kid for the day easy. VAGO's in front of the IGLESIA DE LA VIRGEN INMACULADA, his hand on his groin as usual, eyes hooking at people. Miguel stops beside him, gets his shoes shined. "Qué tal, VAGO? And how goes it?" "Y . . . ?" He is smiling. What can he do? He must take the cash as they drop it. Rattles his jacket. "You know the economía," he says, "bad—all over the Nación." But his eyes don't look up at him; they trace the girls' tits, the legs, the men's baskets. Miguel drops a 25-peso moneda in his hand. "You know my wife's pregnant," he says. He gets VAGO on the track. He knows what the bastard is thinking: I can get you plenty if you let your wife out by the night. We split—what say?

TURI (Bonaventuri Carbone/71/b. MILAN, ITALY/residence none/no family/tubercular/always accompanied by dog) is too tired to move and his skin is wet and then too dry and he hears his air loud. The dog looks at him, his ears go up. TURI wants to

cross the PLAZA DE CHILE. If he can make the block to the
railroad station, there's BIZCO who'll give him a sip of something. He's so tired, sometimes he cannot hold his hand out, it
falls under his burlap, nobody drops a thing in it. He can't talk
now to ask, he can't raise his hand, his breath is tearing, even short
breathing hurts, his eyes water. He hears breathing. He thinks it
is somebody else. But hears the hurt. He can't raise his hand to
where he hears it hurt. He thinks it is chest, but cannot raise hand
to chest. The dog comes close, licks his face, but he can't raise
hand to dog. He drops his head on the dog. The dog licks. He
feels hot. What is it? tongue? sun? rags? He closes his eyes. If he
could get to BIZCO . . . But he . . . BIZCO? He feels dog, dog,
dog, always lapping, but hears his chest hard. He rolls over. If he
can crawl, drag . . . BIZCO. One sip. Almost nothing in days
. . . not vino. Water from the acequias would be good—yes—
but even the gutter is far, but he hears water. He tries to drag, but
his eyes close, his hands clutch at the tiles, his breath stops. The
dog noses into his neck, moaning.

How do I know *I* was not stolen when I was born? the reporter
thinks. Maybe I'm a beggar and for that reason I'm looking for
something. He feels very close to them. He wonders why sometimes
watching them he is perverse, he should be nothing more than lice
in the hair of a beggar, a worm in his wounds. What is it makes him
wish that? Like the attraction we have for sewage—dogs rolling in
shit, babies love muck, decent men marry respectable women but
want whores in bed, and the filth, the self-debasement of priests,
saints, sinners, fools. Sometimes he feels them crawling all over him
like bichos, ants, coming from invisible distances underground. Maybe
we are all ants, he thinks, crawling over somebody's scalp. Maybe I
was stolen, sold, even by a beggar—and so somehow avoided my
fate that I am looking for. He feels a perpetual roamer, wandering
through the city, its bowels, intestines—the acequias: *they* live in the
acequias, the viaducts, under bridges, in any hole of dry dust. But
they are so fixed. There is LA VIEJA ESA, then SQUINTY, MARI-
ANITA, each in his place, as if they know like fact, as if they must
be there, it is destiny to be in front of the BANCO DE LONDRES
on TUESDAY, or the MERCADO or the CASA DE CORREO. And

he goes from one to the other, searching, certain only of their certainty, as if he were trying, saying beads, like one of those simple women muttering down the Stations of the Cross.

At 7:30 PACO (Federico José Jiménez/48/b. BARCELONA, SPAIN/residence LAS HERAS/separated/Civil War veteran, immigrant/blind one eye) stops at the GALERIA SPILIMBERGO. A new exhibition is opening—the paintings of DUCMELIC. There are many people. There is wine on a tray. PACO wears his only shirt around his head in a turban. Paintings always attract him. It has always been so. He has never missed an exhibition in Mendoza. He goes along the wall. He has to. There is something in the paintings. He hears them. He pays no attention to anybody. He hears the people's words; they don't make sense to him. *They* don't know. He looks at the first painting. He understands the strange lines, the broken things, lines like people. Something makes him want to cry. He is touching something. He doesn't know what it is, but he knows the country of the painting. He goes into it. It comes around him. He feels he is inside somebody's streets, and the sky opens.

The husband of the woman whose baby is stolen is violent. The Jefe squirms. The office is in quiet turmoil. The clerks work furiously to appear not to be listening. The man has broken down several times; he is near tears, firm nevertheless: "If I must go to the Nación, the Policía Federal—" he cries. The Jefe explains that he has one of his best men making the rounds; he has sent what is tantamount to a squadron of men into various parts of the city, and if he doesn't get results . . . He knows, however, that he will not. But he thinks of Miguel Allende, the pressure. Something he must do to satisfy this man, the higher-ups, the community, the ones who may complain; and a dismissal alway seems to bring satisfaction finally. This time it has to be somebody like Miguel, not an ordinary cop. "Sí. Sí, señor," he says, "I assure you we will do everything possible, within human possibility. . . ." The husband finally leaves. The clerk stops typing. The Jefe turns, furious. "And you—!" he cries. The clerk fumbles at the keys.

LUZ (María Luz de Borello/30/b. MENDOZA/residence VILLA MISERIA/widow/three girls): He thinks I don't know nothing, that reporter. Luz don't say, she looks—and grabs, sí, grabs, what else? "Sí," she says to him, "I know the hospital—how not? Don't I go when somebody's sick, eh?" He thinks Luz don't know what he wants; he's crazy if he thinks that: could be I know, but not *who*. They's plenty I know'd take that kid. Why not? They's plenty more, you can't stop them coming. "No," she says, "I don't know nobody sick now. Hace mucho. A long time now I don't go there. . . . Nobody. No, how'm I knowing what all those others do—me, what never sees nobody, eh—how?" "And if you had to get rid of one stolen, where'd you take it?" he says. "Ooooof," she says, "and why not use it—to rent, make some money! Why get rid of it? Who knows one red thing from another anyway?" "Then you'd keep it? But suppose somebody else—where would they send it, you think?" "How I'm going to know what's in their heads, eh? Why you playing games, eh, with la pobre Luz?" "And if you were a midwife, partera, then—and I went looking for you—? Where'd you go, then, Luz?" "Mas allá," she says, "beyond." She raises her hand, points north. She is sure. It is natural. She knows. And tomorrow, if he asks, she points south or east or west. But they're there. She knows. Like faith. "Where?" he says. "Mas allá. Beyond." She points.

The policía Miguel sits for a minute at the PLAZA DE ITALIA. The stone bench is still warm from the afternoon sun. He is tired—from walking, inventing questions, nosing around, watching like a hawk their faces—SQUINTY, TURI, BIZCO, ITO, NINA, LA POLACA, ROQUE, LA CLARA. . . . And he has clomped all day, his feet are tired, he has never felt the pavements so futile. Streets, roads, alleys—no end to them. He gets up. One more stop before he goes back to the Jefe: MIMI by the BAR LOS TRIBUNALES. Another illegitimate, he thinks. It's a fact—almost all the beggars are illegitimate. A whole world, he thinks, a nation of bastards, hijos naturales.

The reporter goes back to his little apartment, washes, makes coffee. He must be at his desk at 8:00 P.M. The map of the city covers one wall of his bedroom-study. Pins mark every beggar he knows—not so many as people think. Ordered, on the map the pins make fine lines, thick in the downtown section, a web that thins out toward the edges of the city, like thin connections off the map, running into other countries. They seem to lead somewhere beyond—like roads, like rivers, like tracks . . . a network. The roads must lead somewhere. He has a yearning to follow them beyond the edge. And he has statistics—babies born, died, starved, stolen in each province, such statistics as he can gather, but what of the unrecorded . . . the unknown . . . the unmentioned? He multiplies the figures in his head, figments. The mechanism, channels, roads . . . somewhere, the baby moving from hand to hand, place to place. He sees it go from MENDOZA to SAN JUAN, LA RIOJA, JUJUY, cross the border to BOLIVIA, ECUADOR, and how much farther? One baby. And he sees others, a swarm, a web of motion, a confusion, but not to the beggars: they seem as quiet and ordered as if they are sure of the destined roads, where they lead, what more? He stares at the network, wondering, if he could trace it, where it begins, where goes—which path, he thinks, for that kid stolen yesterday, what destiny? By now—almost thirty-six hours—it could be in BRAZIL, URUGUAY, PARAGUAY, COLOMBIA, CHILE, ECUADOR, or south in NEUQUEN, PUNTA ARENAS; and he thinks of the past six months, of the recorded stealings, ROSARIO *10,* BUENOS AIRES *70,* JUJUY *8,* LA RIOJA *14,* SALTA *3,* LA RESISTENCIA *14,* and of CENTRAL AMERICA and of NORTH AMERICA, and thinks of all the others absconded, given at birth, voluntarily rendered for sale, thrown onto heaps, abandoned, murdered. Well . . . it is near eight. He must get to work, go to *Los Andes.* Fifteen minutes exactly. He goes down in the elevator, goes down Emilio Civit. He always goes the same way.

"Café? Coffee? Café?"/if the son of a bitch is in bed with somebody else?/they's plenty I know'd take that kid, yes/too many policía, not enough *any*thing but policía/best thing ever happened Antonio died, God forgive me/"Gracias, señor"/"Paper? Diario? *Los Andes?*/*my people:* I know them so well, mine, all my life/the midwife's gone/in La Rioja 11 babies dead this week, starved/mas allá, beyond/roads—

there's no end to them/has a new jacket, but I don't know where from/"Que Dios le bendiga"/on dirt, rags, bare mattresses, plaza tiles, benches, in dry culverts, the río Mendoza/"Café? Café? Café?"

The policía Miguel wonders what she will make for supper, he is particularly hungry. At the kiosk he reads in *Los Andes* that a baby is missing in BOGOTA, COLOMBIA—ach!— He wants to go back to the house, but first he must report in, see the Jefe, then sleep, sleep. Good thing he took his sex during the siesta. He is too tired. Wants only sleep. And then the morning. Dios mío! Ah, well, if I can't count on Him always, I know in the morning at eight, when the negocios open all over the city, the beggars will be there.

Where Was My Life Before I Died?

H E HAD TO find Rinaldi. A week now and Rinaldi had not come. There must be a good reason, yet no message came. Surely he would come this morning. He would be there—sitting in the restaurant GOM, watching the people go down Las Heras. Yes, Rinaldi would be there—his cigar, gold chain, the bulge of his watch, richly black shoes shined by the little Turk on the corner. He would explain *I couldn't come last night, Victor, because . . .* He would be grieved, but Victor did not want Rinaldi to be grieved, no. After all, he *couldn't* come. Always life intervened, a little thing of wife, friends, house—who could help it? Victor understood. Wasn't theirs a real friendship? Hadn't Rinaldi pledged that together, with Victor's knowledge of books, Rinaldi's awareness of what the public wanted (he could hear Rinaldi's resonant voice), they'd have a nice little bookstore, glass front, in a fashionable new gallery or, better, an old established one? The times were right, Victor's regular clients missed his kiosk, and since the municipality had enforced the ordinance and removed it, there was nothing like his kiosk in all Mendoza.

He must hurry. . . . There was so little time. *Why* always so little time? He flung the warehouse door open. Light burst in, fresh air made the windowless room piquant with smell of sleep and warm wool, musty paper, gasoline, stale wine, and his own body steeped in its own odor. Days he had not shaved. He stared out at the clear morning. The patio was crisp with spring, the tile gleamed red, the cream walls bit his eyes with naked light. His blood leaped at the sight, his eyes gripped the sky, his blood sang. Words—his own poem—leaped from his heart: *Never shall I betray you, life. . . .*

He felt so light, but his clothes were heavy on him, sagged—this black jacket, the brown pants larger now (he'd lost so much weight) and too long over his shoes, and his shirt (how many days not off now?) buttoned at the neck and tieless, and even his sweater drooped long now.

Without his kiosk, the warehouse was doubly crammed—books floor to ceiling, shelf after shelf, twelve feet high; books sideways on top of other layers; table and desk laden with indeterminate piles; everywhere pamphlets, manuscripts, and rare, unknown, hard-to-get magazines piled on the floor around his bed—how at home he was among them!—and somewhere in valises, in packets and notebooks were his own works, and on slips stuffed into jackets, pant pockets, the old overcoat, poems like threads hanging loose everywhere.

Now the mattress on the floor would not be so cold. Clothes would be enough, no need for anything more, with the cold fled back to the cordillera until next winter. And he didn't cough so much now. Besides, there was a green tendril growing through the crack under the door. The delicate sight made his fingers twitch.

He clutched the bottle of wine, crossed the patio past the glowing pink geraniums, and pushed open the great front doors. Across the street the Plaza Independencia flowered a giant oasis, its great luxuriant palms probing the blue sky. Later he would cross, sit in the sun, and rest—there, under his special tree. He glanced down Espejo toward the corner café. He dared not look long—no money, not a peso, days now. Rinaldi . . . And what stillness—but how intense he felt!—he almost *heard,* yes, he strained, listening . . . a sound, distant music, a language beyond hearing. It was coming, it *would* come. He sipped the stale wine, sipped. . . . How keen and alive it scalded down. *Rinaldi.* On him, at last, depended his upward movement—perhaps today.

He wanted to run. He had so little time. Was it always that way? Where had he been in his life? He wanted to make a longer journey leisurely, from the beginning. He left the warehouse door open, the air to pour in freely. Always he locked, alas, but this morning—open. He lunged down the street toward the GOM. . . .

But when he got there, the sun, a gold eye on the pane, blinded. He crossed the street, pressed his palms about his face, and gazed in —over faces, faces— No Rinaldi. It *couldn't* be. He went in—to confirm: yes, to the waiter. "Rinaldi?" he asked. "Who?" "Ri*nal*di." But it was plain the *mozo* was a blank.

Outside, two doors below, the kiosk had been, now like a gap in the very air. He stared through it to the *mercado central* across the street. Now water trickled through the *acequia* under the very spot between curb and sidewalk which the kiosk had spanned. Here the upper walls had opened, displaying the colorful magazines he loved to touch, paper between his fingers, knowledge running over his flesh. Each book was a life held in his hands. Ah, to hold a man's worth. . . .

Always ideas stopped in this or that professor from the university up the street, and he loved to watch the students go by, the beautiful *chicas*, voluptuous with life and curiosity. Prowling his shelves, they left their fragrance in the kiosk. After, he stood inside, breathing deep their sweet perfume. Always Ponti the photographer stopped—such a friend!—and like so many other clients, he'd sit outside the American Bar or the GOM and talk Vallejo with him, or Mauriac or Marx, Martínez Estrada, Lukács, *peronismo, sindicatos*. Now the wood itself—rotting even then—was gone.

Gone. Where? And he—where was *he* going? To find Rinaldi, yes. But there was water—he heard it—and the crowd rushed through the great iron gates of the market, the cafés were filling down the street, and overhead the trees passed in great canopies over the road, already beginning to make a lush yellow corridor. And he could not stop following the water—why was he doing it? such a fierce impulse!—to the market far off at the corner of Córdoba, where the city had let him open a second kiosk, where an *alameda* of flowers filled his eyes while he worked. There, vandals had broken in.

He halted. Abruptly he thought, Suppose Rinaldi went to the warehouse while he was out?

He wanted to run back, but he was torn—he wanted to sit down, rest, watch water flow through the canal. Besides, if he went back, Señora Martínez would come onto the patio. He didn't want to see her yet, not until Rinaldi. She was asking for rent now. Ah, how kind she'd been through his bad times. She'd let him have the warehouse free, and when he'd moved from the pension paid by the night, without telling her, to sleep on the warehouse floor among his books, she didn't say a word. Only last week she reminded, "You know,

Victor, the rental laws haven't kept up with inflation. People are paying the same rents, frozen since Perón. What's a woman to do?"

"Sí, señora. Don't worry. I sold—some time back—many books to the university, but you know red tape. And a few professors owe me, but sometimes they have problems too, they— I'll go this very day, señora."

"I'm sorry, Victor. . . ."

"Ay, señora, don't apologize. I know your generosity—the big family, cousins, and hospital bills for the bad leg—"

"And your house?"

"Right now construction's stopped, but when I've got another payment accumulated, they'll go on. . . ."

"Ah, sí? I'm glad." She smiled genuinely.

The four walls and inner divisions loomed. How he liked to go out to the edge of the city under the empty blue sky and look at it: *mine*. It awaited the roof, the window frames and windows, the plumbing, electricity, yet four walls demarked that piece of earth— his. Together, his friends had virtually given *for the poet* the initial payment. Oh, they'd opened accounts to justify the loan, but they had taken no books.

Now Rinaldi had all his papers, savings book, credit *abonos,* the investments of Randolph—ay, that Yankee friend who had left him a bit toward a shop *absolutely not to be touched except for a kiosk, Victor.* Now, yes—it was no betrayal, Randolph, no—the purpose was close at last. "Give me your power of attorney," Rinaldi had said. "With my own resources I'll triple yours. I'll make a complete evaluation, books, insurance, everything. Two or three, four million pesos' worth of books, you think?"

"More or less four—"

Rinaldi's little moustache twitched, a gesture Victor enjoyed, the intensity of the man; and his eye penetrated the soul, gave you— what?—a feeling he comprehended you instantaneously, almost intuitively. No articulation was necessary between them. Rinaldi would solve the problem. Think! Their contact came from literature—yes, they had that in common. "I'm a *licenciado* in letters, from the National University." Rinaldi had said it with such warmth, such nostalgia, that Victor succumbed completely. How could he help it? He too had lived those same books—Gorki, Dos Passo, Rousseau; and, ay, one night, discovering they were devotees of Jack London, Rinaldi howled right on the street, clapped his hands, embraced him, *"Martin Eden*—you too?" and for an hour without moving off the corner, with wild gesticulations, they relived London's struggle to learn and write, holed up in that boardinghouse in San Francisco. In that moment he came to love Rinaldi. "Rinaldi, my brother." He laughed. Arm in arm, they went to Los Tribunales for wine.

"Los Andes?" The face of a little boy vending morning papers stared up, eager. Los Tribunales, Rinaldi, *Martin Eden* fled. The water was trickling below again. He had time to read SEVEN CHILDREN DEAD OF HUNGER IN LA RIOJA, LACK OF MILK before the boy, so small he could scarcely carry the papers, registered his refusal and ran on. His father's in bed with some slut, Victor thought, and they'll beat him if he doesn't come home with a handful of pesos for wine and *empanadas.*

At two one near-freezing morning, he'd found a child near the GOM, asleep in the doorway of the Jesuit school, and tried to wake him. He lifted the boy up. "You're hungry? Cold, eh? Come—we'll get something hot. Then we'll put you on your *micro,* eh?" At that the child squirmed, a worm in his arms. "No no no!" He slipped down Victor's leg. "What's the matter? You don't want to eat?" *"Sí."* "Or go home?" *"Sí, pero deme la plata, por favor."* "Money?" *"Plata, sí."* "And if you don't bring money home, eh?" The boy looked up at him, but his eyes saw through him. "Beat you, eh?" The boy didn't reply. "And if I give you something and put you on the *micro?"* *"Nooooo,* just give me the money, not the *micro.* I'll walk." "Ayyyyy," he said, but gave it, though watching the boy race down the street, he knew—the kid would sit in another doorway begging. And as he watched, they rose out of the sidewalks—boys, boys, hundreds of boys like him—and others pushed through them, grew through them, out of the tile, out of the water; they turned their eyes to him, their heads tilted tired, and their hands went out; and others pushed up through them, grew out of the asphalt, and others— *I must stop this. It must stop.* He had turned and fled to Espejo, closed the door and bolted it, put on the light, shocked by the familiarity of all his books around him and by his own breath tearing at the air.

But now the air poured down gold morning, sun leaped like laughter off the canal, jonquils seemed to grow out of the cement

and walls, and for a minute he felt he would fall into it all, flow. . . .
He was so *hungry*. The swallows of wine had soared to his head.
Trees palpitated, they shimmered gold over everything.

Go to Professor Lancilote, *he* would pay. So many people owed
for books. They would pay one day, yes, but *now* he needed. . . .
Surely the professor had money. They had reinstated him at the university, there was no more overt talk of politics and religion since
Onganía, and all real dangers to the government had been downed.
He could remember when once they were all brothers working together, no vast rift between, none.

He had written Lancilote a letter, written hundreds of letters. It
had begun when he read Debs: "While there is a lower class, I am in
it; while there is a criminal element, I am of it; while there is a soul
in prison, I am not free." Truly the divine was everywhere among
men when he heard words like those. He wrote: *Eugene V. Debs, I
have heard you, I am here.* He piled up letters to them all, the living
and dead and unborn. Now he was writing letters to his own unborn children. They were the beginning of a vast poem, a motion
toward the language he must find, the perfect expression of his life.

"Vic—tor! Eyyyyy, Victor!"

"Ah—" There across the esplanade Ponti came flagging that tattered
brief case always jammed so full of sample baby photos—Ponti, a
streak of energy and graying hair, and graying dreams of being a
poet too. But the man's poetry was his talk; he couldn't exist without an ear to pour out to. Alone, he sank into the introspective
melancholy of a *porteño*. "Victor!" His eyes gleamed brown in his
dark face, his teeth shone. "I was just thinking about you, and like a
miracle there you are. What does *that* prove, eh?"

Victor laughed. He heard his own voice in jagged, high pitch.

"And you—what doing here?"

"Here?" The second kiosk had been here—three whole months.
That was all. Vandals kept breaking in—robbed it. The city out-
lawed that one too, size, lot. . . . But why *come* here? "I . . . Nothing. No reason." He laughed again. His own sound clipped. "Toma-
mos café?" he said, but without thinking—he hadn't one peso, no,
for a cup of coffee. So he stopped short, confused. His hands fluttered.

"*Va*mos, hombre." Ponti's arm around him pressed him up the street. "I just collected from the widow—with the six children. The group—remember?" Six heads—yes—young eyes staring out of child-flesh.

"Ah, I remember," he said. But that money: there was Ponti's wife—and the two children, the bare rooms with no heat and little light, but such a beautiful grapevine hanging over the patio, ahhhh. But they had to eat.

He wobbled a bit, he was so tired. *Why* tired so early? The sun dazzled in the *acequia;* flicks of gold flashed from the water. The trees streaked yellow reflections, and his blood flamed up. *Stop.* He had to stop. It would carry him off. Ponti's arm felt good.

At the 1515 Pizzería, the dwarf Antonio, finished sliding his mop over the tiles, disappeared inside. Mario, ready for the day, stood in the doorway, a clean white towel over his arm. "Buen día, caballeros." His jacket, so white at a distance, was soiled and frayed and here and there unseamed.

"*Hola,* Mario. Two wines—red. And, Victor, you can eat an *empanada,* eh?"

"*Bueno. . . .*" Saliva leaped warm around his tongue—like in Tucumán when there'd been only the sweet sugarcane hacked from the field and pressed to his mouth to suck. Always on warm nights that taste was on his lips. He saw his mother's proud Indian head bent over, oily black hair parted a perfect line, her dress covered with dust, canvas slippers worn to holes, and always he smelled the soft dank warmth of her flesh. And bamboo and thatch he saw, the dirt where his father, exhausted after the day in the canebrake, lay out-stretched, his face pressed against the ground, saying, "We come from this, *hijo.*" *And where do we go, papá?* he thought. But why hadn't he asked it? "This day I found a book, my son. What's from a book, eh?" It lay beside his father. He dared not touch it. His mother was pounding corn with now and then a grunt. His eyes loved the book. But he waited till they both fell asleep. In the dark he walked far—to the city, where he sat outside in the light of a *bodega.* He went deep into the book.

Ahead was a world of books, all life calling. Buenos Aires burst in the air over the pampas, a golden promise ablaze in the heavens. *I am coming. I will be.* And he had run away from Tucumán, cane-brakes, thatch, mud; days he ran, months, years—always it seemed,

running. . . . From benches, shacks, dirty rooms, lying there, he saw
it all. In Buenos Aires, he worked in a bookstore. And he wrote
poems. *My own store someday I'll have, selling my own books too,
written out of this experience—how I was made alive, awakened: a
poem. All flesh in my poem.* His book was out of print now, not a
copy even in his warehouse—*The Birth of a Citizen,* five hundred
copies, numbered, his claim sent out from his flesh. *Let my poem
go into you.*

And his mother and father? *Years* he had not seen them! Were
they still alive? Were they dead? He wanted to run—run—run. He
would seize them before that happened—hold them in his heart,
never to die there.

Run run *run!*

Suddenly they were there in the trees over Salgado's Stationery.
His eyes sought them madly among the shifting leaves. He bent
forward, rising. His hands shook on the table, spilled the wine. "Ach!"
Red smudged his fingers.

"*Está bien,* Victor. It's okay. Who—?" Ponti turned around. "Don't
stare into the sun like that," he said. "Your eyes are watering, Victor."

"I thought—" Thought *what?* He sat down. "Ah, *sí,* now—yes—I
thought I saw Rinaldi coming—"

"Who?"

"Rinaldi. *You* know."

"*Toma.* Eat, Victor." The *empanadas* were hot. Broken, they steamed
from within, burnt the mouth. The taste made him giddy, his stomach
jerked convulsively. Quickly the wine eased it.

"R*ina*ldi." Why didn't Ponti see the enormity of it?

"Ah—from Buenos Aires?"

"*Sí, sí, sí,* the *porteño,*" he cried giddily. "You remember now? He
came at just the right moment. How do people know timing, eh?
And such a brain the man has. Success pours from him—ay, I don't
mean clothes and the diamond and—such elegant fingernails! No. But
the humanity—*sabés?*—he understands the heart of things, *al fondo,
sí.* How he knows Dreiser and Vallejo and Neruda, so much more.
And just to listen to a voice with such magic—rhetoric even a *político*
would envy. And his eye! He came . . ." As his friends had come
in his long feverish hours in the TB sanatorium in Buenos Aires, as

if they had crossed the hundreds of kilometers of the pampas on foot to save him. "You re*mem*ber?"

"No."

"But, *hombre,* he ate at the Galileo with me time after time these past weeks."

"No, I never saw him."

"You *must* have. You—" He couldn't believe Ponti, almost his only close friend, did not know Rinaldi, his *way* at last. You give me such confidence, Rinaldi. I'll work, I'll redeem your faith in me, Rinaldi. You'll see. You'll see. No more betrayals. Such faith can't be empty.

"I haven't eaten at the Galileo with you for maybe three weeks now, Victor." Ah, ah, for shame—Ponti looked hurt. It was not that Victor had veered in his allegiance, not betrayed . . . How could he neglect the man who took him in, fed him, gave him a rug by the stove when their own room and the children's had no heat? But Rinaldi . . .

"And Martirio asks all the time, When's Victor coming, eh? Think of these *pastas* he's missing. And the *chicos* too—"

The words pierced him. Isn't it enough you feed me? What can *I* give? Some days no man comes, not a book's sold. Since the kiosk was closed, I peddle books in my valise, always the wrong ones. And in this province how many read? Ah, if people could *know* books. But more and more they don't buy from me—and why? I've got books, or I'll find them, and I'm no *político,* no military, no—

But there was always Rinaldi. Victor saw already their new locale. *With your lifetime of reading, you're the only one in Mendoza, Victor, can tell them what's in these books we'll sell.* His head reeled with titles. They clung to the leaves. He gulped the last of the wine, red flared momentarily over the sun, the heat passed down his throat. *Must go. Professor Lancilote.* He rose.

"Look, Ponti . . ." He wanted to tell him *now* about Rinaldi, but no, he would surprise Ponti the very first one—lead him to the *galería,* make him stand casually before the shop until he looked up and saw RINALDI-CASTELNUOVO, LIBROS; then he'd laugh, embrace him, and they would drink to the future. "Look—you come tomorrow. Promise? You *promise,* eh? I'll—no, no, I won't tell you. At Espejo, tomorrow, eh?"

"You're excited, Victor."

Victor tried to hold his eyes still, and his hands. He laughed, laying his head a minute cheek down against the cool tabletop to calm himself. "Ah, Ponti, Ponti," he said, laughing, hearing his sound resonant against the metal. Soon, soon he would show Ponti, show all his friends what they meant to this citizen. In Ponti's *comedor,* his friends had gathered to read his poems aloud, Martirio grave but affected behind the stove.

"Something you're hiding, Victor?"

"No, no. . . ." My poor Ponti, with the little he has, wants only this bond of friendship. And ah, the children. In the *acequia* below, the water ran swiftly, eyes glittered there. *No.* He rose. "I go," he said. "I must collect. Tomorrow—*seguro,* eh?"

"*Sí.* I'll come after the siesta."

Tomorrow. By then, he'd have seen Rinaldi, the thing would be settled. He was seething with it.

"Adiós, Ponti." He veered up the street, the sidewalk shimmered with the growing heat. But he felt so airy. The wine lifted him out of himself. The day drifted past. He would like to close his eyes, float. . . .

But *collect.* Go to Lancilote's first—a short walk, no bus, save tickets.

At the Plaza Chile the fountain looked so cool that he stepped quickly through marigolds, *chinitas,* masses of red orange yellow and with two hands scooped water and flooded his mouth cool, then stumbled back across the tiles to the shade of the plantains. The Lancilotes' was a bright white stucco finished in dark wood. Creeping geranium hung from the balcony in a warm glow; the sight sank like wine into him. He brought the bronze knocker down. Almost at once the door opened slightly, the maid's eyes dropped over him. "We're not buying—"

"Ah, no no." He laughed. "I come to see the señora."

"You—" He saw himself a dark ragged thing in her eyes, but checked her arm in the act of pushing the door to. *No no no!* "Señorita!" The sudden force of his own voice startled even himself, but it arrested her motion. "Tell the señora the bookseller wishes to see her—urgently."

"*Pues . . .*" She shut the door. In a few minutes the señora ap-

peared. "Oh, Castelnuovo—you! The girl said bookseller—imagine!"
The door drifted open. In the dark interior flicks of light glittered—
from the chandelier, pieces of silver, the edge of a gold frame. From
far within came the sound of plates. Like a drawn thread, a tan-
talizing scent of meat cut into him.

"I come, señora, to—"

"*Sí, sí, sí,* Señor Castelnuovo. But—you can see—we're having a
celebration. Yes, my son is to be married. Imagine! Señor Lancilote is
at the airport. Ah, I *know* you understand. It's not as if—but then
you *can* come tomorrow, no? I'll tell him. He'll expect you. Gracias,
gracias, Señor Castelnuovo." She closed the door softly, leaving him
embraced in a subtle scent of flower. For the merest instant he saw
Mercedes' white breasts and her wondrous dark eyes. How long
since he'd had a woman? How many months since Mercedes . . . ?
So she preferred that bum from the *villa miserial* Well . . . Thank
God for Rinaldi. Without him . . .

Suppose Rinaldi *had* gone to the warehouse? Ah—perhaps for
that he had left his warehouse door open today. Yes, yes. His blood
surged, impelled him down the street to the Plaza Independencia—
green and quiet against the insane traffic of the *centro* below. "Rinaldi?" He lunged into the patio, halted abruptly, swaying a second
before the warehouse—empty as a tomb. Rinaldi?

Something *must* have happened. Rinaldi wouldn't delay so long.
Sick? Hurt? Poor Rinaldi. Well, then, go *to Rinaldi*—he had not
once thought that before, for always he associated him with far-off
Buenos Aires. Buenos Aires . . . Benches, those rooms, the port
leaped into his head, and ayyyy those Julys—cold to the bone he felt
suddenly—and TB, and the river Plate below his sanatorium window, flowing into his eyes all those months. He slapped his jacket
for the wallet. Rinaldi had never given him an address, but he had
one—maybe not even his—torn from a book, a slip of paper with
Baudelaire's poem "Le Voyage." He'd meant to return it. Ah, he
found it. Yes—from Las Heras he could take number 13 bus. . . .

But first, try the *barcito* where they sometimes met, the one last
possibility. He went up the street, following the shade. Day was
getting hot. But at Belgrano, the shade disappeared and he shielded
his eyes, fearful always for his vision. Across, the railroad tracks
glistened—to Buenos Aires, to Chile. Once—he'd been near death—

his friends had flown medicine in on Aerolíneas. How long ago it seemed! At the curb he looked both ways—hated autos, feared their coming on him suddenly. Death, pain he hated, even the least bruise, twist, tear of skin, the sight of dog's teeth—though he hated the kids' treatment of strays—and, ayyyy, in Tucumán, those giant spiders, *araña pollitos,* his father'd warn him about: "Not *quite* so big as chickens"—he'd laugh—"but listen, Victor, you always hear them coming, the hairs on their legs scrape loud. . . ."

On the run he crossed the street.

An old man lay turned to the yellow wall outside the bar. The empty green bottle lay beside him. Through the beaded curtain Victor blinked into the momentary dark. No one. . . .

Beyond the bar the Estación Belgrano made a dark iron web against the sky. Rinaldi, he thought, but could not help turning into the soft darkness of the station and walking along the platform, surprised to find he did not have his valise, though he felt the weight of it, and felt—yes—young, so young! to be in Mendoza for the first time, to step down from the train after escaping the fury and pace and lostness in Buenos Aires and coming here to begin. *I will make my way.* Only here in the provinces could a poet breathe the air of the people, close to the earth, the true Argentina. He was giddy with it—to find a cheap pension, a locale for a kiosk, to collect books, spread the word that a poet had come to this Mendoza, *tierra del sol y vino.* His kiosk would prosper and between times he would compose, compose, compose—words more beautiful than Venus flowering, more fertile than love, to penetrate all flesh. Here, he would evolve the great language of this modern Argentina.

"Ha! Ha!" His laugh echoed in the great hollow above. The office and ticket windows stared flat blank eyes at him. He laughed again, staring at the tracks that went off into infinity. *I'm going to Rinaldi,* he thought, surprised—no valise, no train, no people. And the kiosk? How long had he *been* in Mendoza? And he laughed again. *You fool, Victor.* But it pained: where *was* it all? Gone, quick as breath.

"Back—to Rinaldi," he murmured.

He got as far as the kiosk below, where he'd bought his first copy of *Los Andes* years before and had asked the *kioskero* where a cheap pension was. The man had sent him across the street—there—to the Hotel Italia.

"Hola, poeta!" It was that Manzoni kid—and three, five, six of the gang who used to hang around his own kiosk. Such headaches!

"Ah-ha, Manzoni, still wearing out the sidewalk, eh?" He laughed. Manzoni hated to be kidded about idling.

"Y tú?" Manzoni slurred—not *vos*, not *Vd*, but *tú*. Pain ran through him at Manzoni's scorn. Well, no matter. . . . But before he stepped across the *acequia*, someone shoved him from behind, laughs broke out, Manzoni's hands clutched him and he sailed back, his head tilted, trees soared in a green blaze overhead, his eyes watered. The boys shoved, hauled, threw him from side to side. All the while voices —Vázquez's, Uriburu's—cried out: "Poet! Hey, poet!" "A free ride!" "How you feeling, poet?" until, in a suspended moment above their heads, he closed his eyes, thought *Rinaldi*, and in a thrust of rage he shot his legs out, swung wide, shoved Manzoni against the kiosk so that the vendor cried out, "Jesus, take it easy! Look at my magazines!" With authority Victor shouted, *"Sinvergüenzas!* Get off the street and *make*—make something, you understand? You poor fools, don't you see? Don't *call* yourselves *argentinos. Be!"*

His head ached, and his legs. He was afraid if he stopped, he could not start again. His head reeled. *Rinaldi.* He pushed his way onto the bus, to the rear. Packed in, the bodies held him up. The smell of *nafta* was thick in the air. The bus stopped and started with such abruptness that his head sailed. When the crowd thinned, he sank onto a seat, his head rocking against the pane.

At the stops, he stared down into the raised eyes, but closed his own quickly. Even when the bus trundled on, he felt them coming, a flood of eyes, eyes, following. If he turned— How could he hold it all? The flood came like music, surging him upward. Someday he would *hear* and from the highest wave of sound turn to face them whole and utter at last the word of his naked soul. He would dare. If he could only find the language . . .

"Señor," he called, "you'll tell me when we reach San José Street, *por favor?"*

The driver nodded. *"Cómo no?"*

Years he had not been out this way. It had been mere plain then, flats farther than God. Now the bus rumbled past whole new barrios, public squares with trees, fountains, flowers—all burgeoning. Then came space, a few *chozas*, and beyond—nothing.

"But . . . *here?*" he said to the driver.

"You said San José Street? This is it."

"Esta?" This—unpaved dust, crude ditches of water alongside the road, five adobe *chozas,* huts with window holes cut into dried blocks. A green cloth hung over the nearest opening.

"No mistake?"

"No hay error, señor," the driver said.

He stepped down, the bus went on, spinning out a great cocoon of dust; it balled around him, sifted over his clothes and into his eyes and mouth. He blew, blinked. From the first house came a little girl in a green dress the color of the curtain, a little girl barefoot and dirty, with hair thick and black as his own. She smiled candidly, her teeth and brown eyes sparkled. "Hola!" she said. She laughed, doubling over, and peered from the corner of her eye coquettishly, then raced into the house but thrust her head between the burlap over the doorway.

"Your father's home?" he said.

"Ma*má!*" she cried, disappearing again.

"Sí, nena?" The curtain was swept aside. "Señor?" Her deep, hoarse voice came with enormous force; he felt it vibrate over him. One thick hand covered her breasts—her black dress was pinned clumsily—and she smiled broadly, unmistakably the girl's mother. Suddenly he wanted to laugh, wanted to lay his head on her breasts, sink forever into that flesh . . . ahhhhh. But Rinaldi—"I'm looking for Rinaldi," he said.

"Who? Ah, *sí*—you too?"

His heart leaped. "Then you know him? *Here* he lives?" But where the gardens, the twin patios, palms, the glass-topped tables, the library . . . ?

"No. . . ."

"Not? He *doesn't* live here?" Again his heart leaped.

"If it's Rinaldi, he comes—goes." Her eyes fled—down the road, over the mountains—he didn't know. "For two weeks now—more—he doesn't come. . . ."

"But where'll I find him?"

"You have to have a miracle for that. Who knows where he—you say *Rinaldi?*—lives?"

"But where's he come from? He must have a family somewhere."

"That one? Ha! Who'd have him?"

You, he wanted to say. *Me.* "But Rinaldi—"

"Rinaldi! You're sure?" She laughed again now, but the sound cracked, sun went out of her, a gaze sad and hurt came. *"Rinaldi!* That's the name he gave *you?* He calls himself first one thing, then another— or Guevara, Castelnuovo— Ach, what *difference?"*

"Castelnuovo?" Me. *My* name, he wanted to tell her.

"Sí, Castelnuovo."

"And *not* Rinaldi? Not dark, husky, clean—"

"I never heard it," she said. "And you—you have something important with him?"

"A— Yes, a little business, nothing more."

"No está. He's not here. He may never come—who knows?"

"Never?"

"With him who can tell?"

"Ah, I see. *Sí,"* he said, his eyes groping far. The whole sky fell into them—he couldn't hold it. The little girl wrapped one arm around her mother's leg and smiled—dark eyes.

"I'm sorry, señor. Others . . ." The woman smiled with deep compassion. He wanted to touch her.

She dropped the curtain down. He stood there an instant. Which way to go? Where? His eyes fled over the barren dust, across the flats, where flowers sang golden from the sand. He turned away. The soft dust gave under his feet. He would go back to the city. The heat came up soft in waves: he wanted to drift on it, close his eyes and be carried. . . .

"Rinaldi?" he whispered, startled at the sound of his own voice in that infinite space. But no answer came. All the plain beyond was empty. The mountains stood hard and impenetrable behind, against the west.

He crossed the street to the wood stake, 13, to wait for the bus. The wind fell away. In the stillness he could hear his blood, a quiet *pum*-pum *pum*-pum, now in his head, now deeper down in a far-off echo. And slowly he could hear the earth breathing and the air beating *pum*-pum *pum*-pum. He heard roots pushing through the ground, flowers pressing red blue yellow heads through the soil—and deep deep the trickle of water in caverns below, deep in him too. In a moment flowers would burst through his breast and arms and legs, his face. The cry of children playing some game echoed down the street. He glanced—the green girl and brown boy and white white gleamed in the sun. But the cries echoed in the cavern inside him. He closed his eyes but deep in

his hollow they echoed Eyyyyyyy, Whoooooeeeeeeeee, and their eyes rose
—*no, no*— He opened his eyes.

Abruptly, from far off, he felt the rumble of the bus over the ground
and saw it preying down through fans of dust, bumping like a clumsy
beetle over the road.

It stopped. He mounted. Rinaldi was not driving. It was a pale face
with green eyes, not Rinaldi. He turned to gaze at the faces. Rinaldi?
No. Rinaldi? No—a woman, but eyes, *sí,* like his. "Rinaldi?" he said.
She smiled—some mistake?—and turned her face to the passing street.

He sat in the rear, his eyes fierce on the earth, probing the houses
the trees the streets that passed, and all the sky. And he heard the softness following, following, softer than air over his flesh, growing in a
hush and then a flow, coming down from far off—the mountains maybe,
yes—coming faster. He could hear waves and feel the rush close behind, filled with eyes. He need only turn and let them come down over
him—blue and green and brown and gray, small, large, wide, narrow,
slitted, euphoric, violent, timid—eyes, a soft flow of eyes rising in
waves behind, yes. . . . But how could any man hold them all with
love, *how?* Rinaldi, *Rinaldi,* I must learn the language. . . .

He looked up. There imbedded deep in the blue sky the sun burned
down. He heard its heat reaching down to him, and he dropped his
head humbly before that pure golden eye. He wanted to stop the bus
and throw himself down on his knees there in the dust and cry out *O
show me the way.* And he *did* see himself out there—Victor on his
knees: *O what have I given my people?* And he prayed, Rinaldi, teach
me the language of madness, I must learn the world's language, I must
speak . . . *O teach me.*

Streets and faces and fronts people gardens green went by, and he
stepped down, giddy, so light—lifted, yes, walking on air, for the heat
came up so hot now it seemed to suspend him over the pavement. He
smelled heat, heard it shimmering. Eyes were coming down behind in
a flood. In a *minute*—

He raced down the street, swept along on waves of heat, the eyes behind. Heat drove to his core, his blood fountained up. He was afraid
even to blink because he *saw*—clearly—yes, it *was* the way: no words,
never again words, but to let the eyes see. *Rinaldi, no matter where you
are, I will speak to you.* And he felt it coming, what he had never before heard in all his life. *I forgive you, Rinaldi. Without you, I'd never*

know. O madre, padre, friends—forgive me all my betrayals.

Listen!

He must hurry—to the warehouse: behind the paper cutter, under the carton, yes there—the gallon of gasoline. *Don't turn, Victor, not yet.* He heard the eyes flowing—all the children's eyes, all his people's, all the peoples' of the earth flowing down behind, about to break and inundate him.

He went through the patio and into the warehouse to get the can. He smelled the *nafta*, felt his pocket for matches. He whispered silently, *Eyes, stay back, wait,* not daring, not yet, to turn and look up and hold out his arms and let them all pour into him RinaldiBurnichónCastillo WelkerPereyraDaughertyMoyanoDiBenedettoMcKeeOrtizOrozcoCastillaGuevaraONealHernándezFrancisCúneomenwomenchildrendogsallall
—all—

He clutched the can and headed toward the Plaza Independencia.

He saw everything sharp and clear and deep—everything.

Fiercely he crossed the street.

Fiercely he sat beneath the palm tree.

He bowed his head. He saw nothing. He listened:

Yes! The silence came singing into his flesh. *O my people!*

He poured the gasoline quickly over his head, down his clothes, legs, feet.

He raised his head, listening fiercely, and struck fire—

Flames leaped to his flesh.

He raised his eyes, burning . . . .

Contemplations of Ecstasy
On the Day of My Suicide

1. *I visit the local insane asylum and am baptized into everlasting life:*

We would every day go past there. It was halfway to the next town, on the right side, a long building with a face stiller and deader than theirs, windows that in the morning you could see straight through to Mount Hope far off and that afternoons gleamed like wet, but just as dead. "Just like a chicken coop," I said. "Never saw chickens like the ones inside *that* place," Lyle said. "A lot *you* know!" I said. "Well, my *mother* oughta know—she spends enough time collecting things for the looneys." "So's my aunt and you better watch the way you talk. I get soap in my mouth if I call people that." "Well, who's gonna hear us out here?" It was September grass, tall and flicky, and it'd get in your eyes when the wind blew. The wind blew other things too: "Smells like a coop too," Lyle said. "Old folks smell like that," I said, " 'f-you get close enough, specially their mouths. 'N they feel worse'n this grass, all dry too and the teeth clicking." "Some of them *got* no teeth. My mother says it's a disgrace they can't chew things and nobody giving them teeth. Boy, I'm glad I got teeth, ain't you?" You could smell the salt water, it was getting cold, school was almost to open, and we wouldn't have many nights till she said, "It gets dark early now and school's on so you just get into that bed." I wouldn't have many more chances to climb Mount Hope and spend the day coming down back of town past the brooks and over the fields to the crazy house and by the harbor. The boats'd be all tied and swimming and fishing stopped and then cold would come, it'd be so dark we couldn't even go to the Common to play ball or anything. We'd have to play in my cellar or Lyle's attic; we'd never see the buildings way out here, just eyes in the dark we'd long to get closer to, and them half the time covered with snow so they looked like dead animals buried, still as our snowmen. "Well?" Lyle said. The sun was near gone, the house was black in it, and we couldn't see far into the grass now. "Okay," I said, and we crawled through the grass the way we did on Mount Hope, pretending to be Wampanoags fighting King Philip's War. It was Lyle's idea. He said, "You think the circus's something— well, you just wait. . . ." He told how they were, everyone he could remember: it took a long time; there were a lot of crazy people in my town, and not all old either. It was scary all right. "I thought they were just people," I said. "Well, they *are*, silly—only they're crazy. Get it?" I said yes, but I didn't. He was people and I was, and I couldn't see what made them so different they all had to have a house to themselves together. They never came out: I guess that's what made them different. "Are you sure we can't look in the windows?" I said. "We got to go *in*—there's nothing to climb on and they're too high anyway. Shhhhh," he said. We were close. I could see the cellar door, not bolted. "See—? What'd I tell you—it's not locked." "Maybe it's hooked inside." But it wasn't. He'd scooted across the clear dirt by the clothesline and jerked up the door and held it. I ran and ducked under, then he did, and we let it down easy. A cold feel came, a kind of strong apple smell came. He took my sleeve; I pulled a little. "Don't be so scared," he said. "I been before. Just come on." I grabbed ahold in the dark. The dirt was soft under my feet and the smell so strong I was afraid to breathe it. We touched the wood steps. I saw the light clear under the door now, and said, "Lyle, are you sure?" "Sure I'm sure," he said, and I already heard the knob moving. "Just in this little hall and there's a window slides back and forth to hand things in. We can see from there good." "Suppose somebody comes? Then what?" My father and mother and the minister and the principal and Miss Chancellor and the cops all leaped up. "Nobody comes. My aunt says it's quiet hour, whatever that is, and nothing happens till supper— then, woweee, you oughta see that!" He had the door open, the floor was wood and a little creaky. "Come onnnn." He pulled me. "Look, but don't say a word—" In a second we were in front of that window: it went into a big room, and I could see the whole place. Just a bunch of people, I said to myself. Lyle was pointing. Nothing but two sofas and some big chairs. Mostly they were old men and women and skinny, but some not so old, women *and* men. I was disappointed—nothing happened. Only thing was it smelled like a zoo, and I wanted to turn my head away but Lyle would get smart if I did, so I watched: how they walked around, and stopped and stared sometimes, and sometimes touched each other and shook a little bit, and talked. The more I looked I could see their mouths moving with no words, like fish, no teeth either—so Lyle was right—and their necks looked long and chickeny and everything seemed to hang, their arms and loose clothes and even their skin was long on their faces. We watched—it was forever—but nobody did anything and I thought Lyle lied, and I was wanting to go before somebody caught us. I could see enough old folks just as quiet and still like that, only smelling better and with good clothes, every Sunday at church. Only one of them spotted me—an old man. He was standing smack across from me, and looking. My heart stopped—then banged so I couldn't even breathe. "Lyle, look!" I said, but I couldn't move. I was watching him walking across like trying to creep up on something to catch it. He kept coming, and Lyle said, "Let's git," but I couldn't. He kept coming, and stopped—and stood right there: he looked at me hard, and I looked back, but he didn't do anything— looked and squinted a little bit—and then I thought Maybe he's not looking at me, scared, and turned around to see what he was looking at right through me, but there wasn't a thing. And when I turned around his hand came up slow and reached for the window—I ducked down low but his hand came through: only it didn't reach for me; it didn't touch me, or even try; it just reached through that window and stayed wide open with all the fingers out and twisted and turned a long time and then went back in. After a while I stuck my head back up, and the old man was standing there looking at that spot again—looked like he didn't even see me moving; and then he backed up, slow, backed up all across the room, and sat down on the sofa. Well, I'll be! I thought, and Lyle was whispering, *"Okay?"* So I whispered back, "Yes," and him, "We better git." I was game and I took a last look just when that old man was opening his mouth— He opened it up like a hungry bird, only he kept it open, wide open, like waiting for something—I thought, *He's crazy*—and a sound came out. His throat screamed. *Ahhnnnnnnnnnnnnnnnnnnnnnnnnnnnnnnn.* "Jesus Christ!" I said, scared to death, thinking if my mother heard me say that or Jesus Christ himself I'd be struck down dead on the spot, the way she said. His

throat stung me—worse than a wasp—inside. He did it again—
Ahhnnnnnnnnnnnnnnnnnnnn—only louder. I was scared. I was going to pee. I couldn't hold it. He was still looking at the same spot.
Ahhnnnnnnnnnnnnnnnnnnnnnnnnnnnnn. It went right in me. I couldn't
move. Lyle said, "Hurry up. They'll catch us!" I watched the man's
mouth. I opened mine too. I had to. It got louder—because some of the
others started too. They stood right there where they were and opened
their mouths and started crying *Ahhnnnnnnnnnnnnnnnnnnnnnnnn* like
they wanted to make it louder and help him so somebody'd hear. It
got louder and I could feel it. I was shaking. My mouth was open. I
watched his eyes. He wouldn't let it go. I wanted to see it too. Maybe
if I screamed it would come too. I wanted to know what he was crying
to. They all wanted it. It must be something big. And I wanted to know.
I'd find out too. I'd look forever till I found out. They were all screaming together *Ahhnnnnnnnnnnnnnnnnnnnnnnnnnn*. The voice filled the
place, everywhere. I felt it in me. I opened my mouth wide, waiting
for the sound to come out. Lyle grabbed me.

2. *We get into St. Agnes' and I am taken in by drinking from the
    font:*
Saturday, after ice skating, when the sun was near dead and it was
near dark by the church, I said, "Come with me, Jessie."

"What's with you?" he said. He wasn't used to me ordering him.

"Come onnnn." It was easy to slip into the Catholic church before
the priest locked it for the night.

We went through the vestry. It was cold and dark as the day I fell
from the column we were climbing—the same spot up there ahead.
"I fell right here," I said.

"I know it, stupid."

"You know what this is?" I was at the font. He looked down the
aisle into the deep black, night in there.

"Yeah. My grandfather's always telling me once."

"They baptize'm here."

"Anybody can do that."

"No, anybody can't. You got to mean it. It's got to be ritual," I said.

"You mean formal. The old man said that too."

"What old man?" He never talked so much about any old man.

"My grandfather."

"Was he a preacher then?"

"The old bastard thought he was. Only Protes'ant."

"Then you're baptized."

"I got me a name, ain't I?"

"There's more than a name. It makes you clean. You got no sin then." I stood behind the font, him on the other side.

"Who's got sin anyhow?"

"The Blood of the Lamb makes you pure and part of everything, my father says."

"You got to shit too! How's that so special? One part of me's good as the other. Blood! Ain't it all holy? I got me my church."

We were close. Our voices were like vibrations in my ear. In the dark the sound was loud. I felt him breathing on my neck. "Let *me* join it. Listen, Jessie," I said. "I'm your brother. We even got the same names almost—Jessie and Jess."

"You're shit too."

"I *am*, Jessie."

"You think cuz your mother wants to give me your name now I'm alone, you're my brother? You simp!"

"I know that. Why do you think I brought you here?"

"Now what game you playin'?"

"It's no game, Jessie. It's for real. We're gonna make a sacrifice. I'll show you who's a brother and who's not."

"I suppose you gonna give me a transfusion?" He put his hand in the red light of the big window high up.

"What's that?"

"You need blood, don't you?" He said. "Confirmed in the church—"

"Something that *means* something. Like my father puts juice in a jar and it makes something else. Catholics got white clothes—"

"It's got to be real or I ain't game."

"But it's the same. My father—"

"You and your father! Crazy as my grandfather was, that's what!" he said.

"Well, if you *believe* it, it's the *same*."

"Then it could be hair or eyes or a chunk of your arm—and who's giving that away?"

"We got to *imagine* it, Jessie. Can't you? *Can't* you? My father says you got to believe you're inside everything and then you're a church —see?"

"*You* think I can't imagine things?"

"I didn't say that."

"I practiced all that stuff with my grandfather." He was itching to leave. I could tell.

"Will you, Jessie?"

"Okay, but it's got to be real—or I ain't Jesus. You think Jessie's Jessie, don't you? That old bastard called me Jesus, and with His reputation what fun's it for a guy having a shitty name like that?"

"F you're really Jesus, prove it and make like he did and give what you got to everybody—and me too. F-you can't, you're lying, you're no Jesus, and you—"

"*Okay.* But you got to take it inside you—promise? I'm me—see. And you're crazy—I ain't you and nobody else till you show you can take it. *I'll* make you sacrifice, if that's what you want—only for real. You back down, and we'll *never* be brothers."

I didn't think he'd do it. The whole place was beating. The dark filled with blood. The church beat, the floor and the air, and I touched his skin and it was hot beating.

"We got nothin' to use," I said.

"*I got it,*" he said. I heard his breath in the dark; then he held it. I heard it pour. "You ready?" he said.

"Yeah." My own voice was just whispers. *You got to believe,* my father said. And I whispered to me, *Brother. My brother Jessie.*

"Put your hands in the font, damn it," he said.

"That's not for confirmation," I said.

"Don't matter *where* or what," he said.

I felt for the edge of the font. "I got it."

"Put your hands in it," he said.

I sank my hands down and cupped them. "It's warm. It's—"

"Take some in your hands," he said.

"But it smells—"

"Take it," he said. "You believe. You said so. You want to sacrifice. You want it inside. Take it. Drink it. *Drink* it, goddam it!"

"All *right!*"

"It's me—part of me, ain't it?" he said.

I held it in my hands, warm, and bent my head into them and drank, not breathing, swallowing.

"It's pure," he said.

You. Brother.

I choked for air. "It's piss," I said. But, quick, I said, "But you can't ever change it now, and not me either—"

"I ain't the one to change anything," he said.

3. *I eat Jesus every night:*

My mother looked at the streak of blood on Jessie's mouth and the small knife and the red chunk in his hand. *"What,"* she said, looking sick, "are you eating?" In the dark of the tree his face looked foreign, Syrian she always said.

"Kidney," Jessie said.

"And heart," I said. She shot at me a dirty mad look.

"Raw?" she said.

Jessie was cutting a slice on his old brick.

"Stop that!" she cried. "Stop!"

I sank deep against the wall and hid my eyes.

Jessie said, "What?"

"Stop. Don't—eat—that—"

"Why?" He looked wide at her, his hand clutched his meat and drew it closer, blood smeared over his blue shirt, clean this morning too.

"Now look what you've done!"

"It's only blood," he said.

She was very pale, she backed off a little. *"Why* do you eat that? I've cooked—" But she couldn't say more.

"It's good for me."

"But raw!"

"I like it," he said.

"We like lots of things," she said, "but they're—impossible."

"This ain't," he said.

"People don't do such things!" she cried.

"I do."

"But why, Jessie? I never—"

"I do what I have to."

"Then *if* you must, you don't need supper, you can go without, both of you, you can go without all your meals until you think better."

"But *I* didn't," I said, quick ashamed to look at Jessie the minute I said it, and then clamped my mouth shut; but Jessie kept eating, not looking up at her when she walked away—hard, so I knew how mad she was.

"She's sure mad," I said.

"Don't know what for," he said. "She don't have to eat it."

"No, she's got a good meal. We don't."

"What's this f-it's not? You can go," he said.

"I can't eat, can I? *I'm* punished—so I'm staying with you."

"Nobody asked you to take it."

"I got to share."

"You got to do no such thing."

"I want to."

"Come on," Jessie jerked my arm. I bolted up, ready. We went around the shed, and then Jessie shut it to, quiet. We were in dark, with only a hole of light like a tube all alive with motes, and a thin rim of light around the door. Jessie scooted into the corner. "There's a spider here. His name's Ringo. You wait. Sayyyy, what you shiverin' for? Come over here 'f-you wanta see it."

"Spider?"

"What the hell—"

Jessie moved a second; then his hand came down in the light—the spider was in the palm. "See—he knows me." It was small and with thick hairs and a big ant body. "What you pullin' down for. Look—" The spider came close under my eyes. My breath raked hard. "Stop that breathin'—you'll blow him off. You scared of him?"

"No." I shut my eyes. When I opened them, the spider was edged onto Jessie's hand and looked like peeping down over it into my eyes. "How can he see in the dark?" I said.

"It's easy—"

"You mean, you kin?"

"We're here, ain't we? This is where I hide—*she* never comes in here."

"Momma?"

"Yes, your momma."

"She's ours now."

"Not mine."

"She *is*—we're brothers."

"You got to be born brothers—like me and him." The spider was busy crossing its legs. "See?"

"He's mine too. I'll show you." My hand went up into the light, the motes jumped like mad.

"You're scared. You're shakin'."

"Who's shakin'? Looky here—" I straightened out my hand stiff. It trembled a little. Jessie began to laugh.

"Stop that, you," I said.

"Aw, shut up," Jessie said.

"Gimme it." My hand joined Jessie's, thumbs together, and the spider moved; it crawled onto the thumb and down to my wrist and stopped. My breath stopped too. The shed was dead quiet. Then Jessie's breath made thunder. I had my eyes closed. My back scraped the wall.

"Don't be movin' so much. And listen—" Jessie said. The dark was deep and it felt heavy. A hard sound came close. "Shhhhh," Jessie said. "Now gimme the spider." I held my hand out, near invisible. I felt Jessie's hand touch it and then move away. On my hand the crawling was gone. "Now get back there," Jessie said to the spider. Then we waited a long time.

"What's goin' on?" I said.

"F-you can't keep your mouth shut, you can't stay. What you tryin' to do—spoil everything?"

"Spoil what?"

"Shhhh—" The sound came. "He's hungry," Jessie said. "He always knows."

"That spider?"

"No, dope. Him."

"Who's him?"

"*He* lives here too. It's time to eat—and he knows what I got in my hand. His hole's under the burlap."

"You mean a *rat?*" I shot up, pushed myself straight up with my feet. My back scraped the wall loud.

"God damn it! What you tryin' to do—scare him away?"

"Jessie, it's a *rat.*"

"Jesus, I know a rat when I see one. Come on, boy," he said. He was almost hissing, so low and with no breath; and the sound stopped— then it moved closer, and stopped again.

My breathing got loud. It made a noise in the air.

"Stop—" Jessie whispered even softer this time. "Clamp your damn mouth. Scare that rat and I'll kill you."

I held my air in. The dark felt so heavy. "I'm hungry," I said, quiet.

"Then whyn't you eat? There's plenty gizzards left."

"Gizzards . . . ?"

"*We* eat'm."

Jessie had the knife out and the gizzard in one hand. "Well, you want some?"

I didn't answer.

"Well?"

"I never had it—raw, I mean."

"You're missin' the best part."

"Blood . . . ?"

"In the dark you can't see the blood. Satisfied?"

I didn't answer.

He began to whisper again, not words, only a soft hiss, and the thing moved. He plopped a piece of gizzard against the boards. "Atta boy. We're waitin'." A quick sound came, and a drag, then it was quiet. "See? We eat it. You want some?"

"I think so. Gimme," I said. Jessie cut it off. I took it and slow put it in my mouth. For a while the two of us just sat there and ate.

"I'm leavin' this chunk for him. He expects it. Don't chew so *hard* —you got to chomp it slow and let it slide down and go right into you," Jessie said.

But I shot up, I streaked straight through that tube of light. Before I even touched the door, I heaved up the meat—it struck the wall. I gagged three or four times and shot out air hard, and then groaned. He got up. "I'll do it, Jessie," I cried. "I'll practice every night." But he got up and opened the shed door.

"Brothers—shit," he said. He went out across the yard without looking back.

4. *I attend a wedding of horseshoe crabs and get ideas about my future:*

It really was my rock. I staked it out. At high tide it was underwater and at low tide it was on the beach with the rest of them—boulders so big nobody could move them, from the glacier. All those years I was used to them—they were like friends; I could come over the sand cliffs and look down and know they would be there, like the Sound, forever and the same: everything else too—moles and rats and black snakes and the swan, eight of them, on the cut-off pond over the sand ridge; and in the bay too porgies and crabs and minnows and sometimes a sand shark in the shallows by mistake, and in the Sound the skates and lobsters deep under. I spent time knowing the cliff swallows, how to catch them without hurting and hold them in my hand, beating; and I fed the gulls till they'd come pretty close before they flapped up. And one day I started in by my rock—I'd have dived in but it's dangerout at low tide, hundreds of small rocks under, and so close to seaweed tangles to give you the willies—and when I went under I saw the thing coming along the floor, over the rocks, and up the ledge (the Sound goes down steep there). I stood up—and watched: it was a horseshoe crab; it was clamped onto another horseshoe crab bigger than it, and it was pushing, pushing and shoving and guiding. The front one didn't seem to do a thing, but the smaller one did all the work—not letting up, gliding over the bottom, over rocks and seaweed and sand right up to the edge of the beach; then for a while still, floating easy just under the soft waves, up and down, up and down, still (its long sharp tail was flat out behind, a rudder), and then it moved on—in a circle, around that rock, under the shadow of it for a while, and then it drifted, and pushed. I couldn't see its claws under, but I could imagine those rows of claws scudding over the stones and sand and how it gripped and sucked onto the shell under it, that female. I'd find every summer in the long line of seaweed and debris dozens and dozens of tiny horseshoe crabs dried out and bleached, shells only. I'd seen grown crabs—all kinds—clamped together but never to follow, until I went back the next day to my rock, and they were there. I thought *Dead, Floated up;* but they were under, and instantly sensing me near, he shoved, one whole body, smoothly followed the floor and disappeared behind the rock. It came out later. He pushed, guiding and pressing, and clung taut over her. Then they went off—into deeper water—and I knew I wouldn't see them again. I'd swim. But in a little while there they came again, close to shore. He's trying hard, I thought, thinking too *With the whole ocean behind him, and all the things in it, bucking like that.* And with every push and prod I admired him more—against that

obstacle—his persistence. And the third day when he paddled right
up under me, indifferent, not knowing I was sitting on the rock, I
couldn't believe it: three days in the same place! He came so in-
sistently to it, I wondered: Did he choose the place? Did he recognize
it? Or was he doomed to it? The more I thought, the more it made
me happy and sad—because I knew I wouldn't see them again, they
wouldn't be here tomorrow. Gone. And later on in the summer I'd find
the little crabs tangled in seaweed, drying, here and there, dead—and
they would finally be hundreds and thousands and millions somewhere,
like the fine white moths of summer that came like snow once a year,
and wasps and mosquitoes, the August bass, and the October bay scal-
lops. I got up. The crab was going deep. *I hope you get through,* I
said. But I had a terrible feeling. I wanted to get home. My mother and
father, I wanted to see them, their place, mine. And on the way down
the road in the thick perfume, with starlings and swallows and crows
and robins making noise and twitterings, and green shifting trees, and
fields of yellow and blue weeds, past the flowering potato fields, with
the clouds floating on the high air, I thought *I* have to find the one
too. And I had that sorry, terrible feeling again: I wanted to touch
them, my mother and father; and I thought of *me* and pitied them
hoping for me. I thought of what I had to do someday soon, and quick
I had a warm feeling for that handsome Jimmie Watson down the
block, who had a wife and four kids of his own but who laid half the
women in town and bragged about it all over town when he got
drunk down at Helen's Place.

5. *I take a long trip up to the aorta with all the others:*
    That night she touched me (not like all the other girls' nights, but
her night) with her mouth, from the rear, on my neck, during the
dance at the Pi Kappa Alpha house. My neck burned and then my
mouth and my hands where I held her, and I turned turned turned
all night tossed. I could hear her saying *You'll have to burn for me,*
laughing, *and quench it by plunging into me and going right into my
heart, if you love me.* I was already burning red fire; and in my dream
dreaming I opened my eyes and saw the river, burning as I was, but
had to quench myself—I was dying of thirst for her, she was con-
suming me—and threw myself into the river, my mouth wide open,
and the river poured in; but it was hot too, burning, and I thought

Get out, but I couldn't: the river pulled and sucked, thrust me. I was in a tunnel. In spurts the river heaved me. Up ahead I could hear Marylin calling *Jess! Jess!* So I went with the current then, not fighting, plowing with my arms, thrusting myself ahead with it. But everywhere strange long things writhing came at me, reared suddenly out of the red, ugly dragon things that made me yearn for weapons, swords and armor and dreams of glory; but I swung, struck, lashed out with my arms—near drowning, but saying so I could hear myself *Smite, Kill, Save*—for she was at the end and in all that she was the only white thing, I saw her white, that skin, those soft cool hands to soothe my body, take the red hot flow out of me and cool me. She called again. Dragons leaped down from the walls, slashed tails, fire came from their red mouths. The river stank, hotter, pumping such a tide that I struck walls, fell, hit dragons, creatures, Godknowswhat, clawing lashing scraping me: they came in multitudes, an army of what I'd never seen, forms never before seen but recognized. I flagged. *I can't,* I said, *I can't,* but her voice was in my head calling. *I must,* I told myself. And her voice came again, a song: a song so heavenly from the heart of things that it echoed in me. I opened my mouth and the song came out, went back, up: and all the forms never before seen stopped, they lifted up their heads, they listened too. My heart stopped, it seemed, for an instant: they looked like me—stopped waiting listening, all with my face. Then my arms went out to them, we all turned, I rode with them, up, up, up. *Marylin!* I cried, we're coming—we went, in servitude, in service—and we all went together—in orders for her, made one sweeping surge, a trail, a host, a whole dragon moving in the tide, rising; and she cried *Jess!* She was sitting there high up on a mound, pulsing with joy, and extended her arms and we rose up, all one, and poured up to her: she opened up and we poured in against her, burned into her, one. I woke up, wet, sweating, sticky, drained— she was the only one, the only one I would ever want, have.

6. *For 700,000 and one I am heartily sorry:*
    On that day the newspapers said 700,000 were wiped out—destroyed, starved, diseased—in the Pakistan earthquake. And Marylin, one, alone, was sitting in a bedroom on Tenth Street in Atlanta and calling me, all day trying—me furious because she'd run off and left me in another fit of anger and jealousy: of my books this time, Law, the last final

exam in Law coming up. Left me, her husband, and only six months! How could you, Marylin? Don't you see what I'm doing is for both of us? We're going the route together. But she said Are you sure of the route? Suppose we're going down another? Suppose we only *think* we're going down one but all the time being sucked down another? Her eyes would get wild. What's happening to you, Marylin? *You* should see, she'd say, you *must* see—everything, or how can we be together? And when I bounded up the steps, there was her call, her words wild, intense; I felt her hand reach right through the receiver, in her voice, go inside me, squeeze my heart, my blood burned and pulsed, *Marylin;* and she saying I want to see we're going somewhere, both of us, you and I, and all them . . . but I keep thinking 700,000, and dead—I can't see—can *you?*—or even imagine that many heads, faces, bodies. . . . How much space do you imagine? How much time? the smell and feel? Do you suppose they're crying out, calling, screaming? *I* hear them, Jess—yes, and I see our calm placid indifferent empty maybe even selfpreoccupying worried concerned faces behind which maybe like me me me going mad they are, are they? Maybe they too see the 700,000, maybe *are* the 700,000—do you suppose that?— we in this country the 700,000, that we are all going—*Marylin,* listen to me, I said, where are you? She laughed: I'm in Atlanta, right here where you are, about seven miles to downtown, I'm high on something, maybe just on thought, drunk out of my mind with thinking, but I *want* you, I don't know how to get you—I mean not the Lawyer, the future Law man, but the one wants to know where we are going, you and I, all. I've got to find it through Law, I said, it's my way, a man has to have a way, Marylin. And she wailed Yessssssssss—you used to say through *me;* and she screamed I'm your way, darling, don't you realize? I'm your way. And I knew she was right, she was the only way. And my heart swelled with her, but before I said Yes, it's you I want, the only thing, the only way I'll ever be happy, I promise you, no matter what, we'll find it together, we'll try, she had hung up: the cold click, the cut-off, The sky cracked, I felt sick empty, I couldn't hear. Marylin! *Me*—I let her go, I sent her, I was blind. Me. Now all I was was only *me* to me; and she was down there on the strip, no telling what might happen, where she'd go, what do—not from desire, but from despair —my wife, *mine* that I didn't know the meaning of but just *me.* So I went, dropped the exam, left, walked the streets, house to house; asked;

went into restaurants, bars, theaters; and yes found that room; those walls she stared at, I stared at; I would not move; I sat, I waited, did not eat, stared. She must come back here, there are some dresses, there's makeup, but more, there's a picture—me. I hoped, but I sat and scarcely moved, shamed. I did not eat. I prayed to love, charity, what was in her heart, to come—or I would die, shamed. Forgive me, Marylin; forgive me my selfishness, my love; forgive me my blindness, my 700,000, my Marylin; I understand, I am ashamed— I wanted to beat myself but no worse punishment than to want her and not have, to yearn to be filled with her, fill her, and not. . . . On the third day, wandering, vagrant, dark, sick, dirty, she came. She stood in the doorway, she clutched her hands, she looked up, and she screamed, she screamed, she screamed. I'd heard the scream long, long, long before. It came into my blood: It shamed me before all of them. Oh, my Marylin, I am heartily sorry. . . .

7. *I find a way to give Extreme Unction and slip past suicide into heaven:*

"You'll never have anything," my mother said, and my father silent beside her, mulling over his banking, the town, the world he'd looked upon all his life. "You're my son," he said, "and I had hoped for a law future for you here—a town not too mobile yet with some solidity for you, not so bad in a life where most things are unstable."

My Long Island village. . . .

Solidity. Unstable. Marylin is dying, I thought. Without even dying, she's dying. They really think, everyone thinks, she's out of her mind. And that *I* am—because I know she's not. If she's done things, taken everything into her body, tried everything, it's to live, not to die. I tried to tell them that. *She* tried to tell them. And I tried to tell them, everyone, that once long ago I was in a place, I heard an old man, I was lifted up on a wave that I knew could carry me, with eyes at the end, to see. But then they looked at me the way they looked at her: apart, separate, maybe even dead. Pity—cold. "Where is she?" my mother said. "In a room downtown," I said. "I only came to say goodbye." "Goodbye!" My mother stood up. The first instant of hysteria came into her, she was too still standing there. My father was alerted—I felt in a moment he'd grab me, hold me, and like all the others with Marylin when she screamed, in one way or another straightjacket me.

"Is she—?" "She's all right, fine—she always was. There's nothing wrong with her. There never has been. She's alive, open, so alive she's spilling out and nobody to catch and hold it, nobody to want to, nobody—" I said. My mother looked at me in terror. And I knew what was happening: I was Marylin for her, I was spilling, and she couldn't reach or contain— "She'll destroy you," she said. "People like that—" And I shouted, *"Don't* say that!" She backed away, she began to cry, she said, afraid, "Don't come near—" And my father said, "Don't shout at your mother that way!" Poor man, he didn't know what else to say. But I knew I had to go to stay with Marylin forever. I had to go down to her, cross over, get inside her, be her—no matter what happened to us, I wouldn't let the Marylin in her die, but play it out if I had to follow her to the end of the world. I'd let myself in that opening, probe it with her, and see what would happen, what we'd discover in us, or beyond. I said to them, "Someday when you're close enough to dying, you'll know." And I quickly conjured up what they'd say and what I'd answer.

They'd say:	And I'd answer:
But you'll starve.	We've more food than a lifetime can consume.
But you'll die bums.	We'll always be together.
And when they take you away from one another?	We'll be together in a deeper place.
No, you'll have *no* place, no respect, no recognition in the world's eyes.	We'll have feeling and love. Maybe we'll even breed a little charity.
It's insanity, Jess!	We invite the world to it.
You'll move constantly away from us, from everybody.	We'll be moving closer to you all the time and you'll know it someday.
You'll end up nothing.	We'll find everything.

But they didn't say anything. They looked at me as if it were madness. I said Goodbye to them in my madness. Their looks said Death: because I chose Marylin against them, everyone, Marylin sick and, to them, dying, by her own choice never to be reclaimed, free from psychiatry (How clever she is! they'd said). She doesn't need one, I said, nor I. They think we're mad. We realize our insanity. We can smile, laugh, together. We know, we begin to know . . . each other.

We begin to think like one, be one, move like one; and so we die—but, little by little, happily, we die into each other. I said Goodbye to my parents. I went for Marylin. Nothing's ahead for sure, she said, it may be just hell, you know. Hell with you's all the heaven I know right now. She laughed. That's everything, she said. If just *you* understand, I'm free, she said. I'll take it, I said. Where from here? she said. Up that road to the city, I said. Okay, she said, let's go. I made a happy bow. I asked for confession. I threw a wreath. There, I said, lies Jess. I made the sign of the cross, I sprinkled. I do hereby confess and bury this my suicidal victim—*him,* I said. And you? she said, seizing my arm. I touched her hand. Who are you? she said. You, yours, I said. I'll have to baptize you then, she said. She touched me. We turned down the road, under the green elms, and began to walk toward the city. A robin sang.

Running

Momma and Poppa

because there wasn't a thing in that house, not a *thing*—a man and a woman and me Dorothy, three of us all moving, *moving around* and not touching —not one time. You'd think we were sailboats out on the bay making sure we never got in the same wind for a collision: *wham* and it'd be done because we'd hit smack on and had to grab ahold. It was like that and now I'm wondering what they're seeing; maybe all the time they were seeing the same thing I was but couldn't do a thing, didn't know how. I thought Go back; but I know how it is—you do the same thing, sit and think you want to do something and maybe they'd sit and think the same, but nobody'd move, nobody. Why? What gets inside you so it grows like a pole right out of the ground so you can't move it's that firm? And all the time the wind is blowing warm, you can feel that in you, and the flowers and trees, silver maples, and Blackburn's dog on the lawn and the sun in the leaves and making diamonds on the grass: you can feel all *them*. Maybe if I went back I'd feel them wanting to feel and that would be a beginning. Maybe if I just took their hands I could break it and break into them.

and Manny

I kept calling *Manny? Man?* When I thought of him it was a cry of everything inside me to him because they tore the nearest thing to a heart out of me as if one side of it went and the other half's trying to hold on till it comes back: because Manny

said They don't want me me neither, I been to jail,
they don't trust me, they never trusted me, they
won't give me a job, they never will, a decent one:
cause they don't know me, they don't even want to.
I do, I said, I want to know everybody—you know
that? He said I know. How come you know? I said.
But he *did,* he knew and you see how *I* was sure he
did? He told me I'd be sick if I changed, he'd never
met anybody who talked as clear as I did. Well,
that's a joke, I don't, but I saw *him:* he was like me.
I told him If you're looking for something, I'm all
there is, all of me right here, but nobody wants just
all of you I guess. Why? Isn't that enough? And he
said It's too much, that's why. So I knew *again*. He
had eyes looked so deep I wanted to shout right
downtown with everybody going by. And he didn't
even have to touch me, he already did some way,
anyway I already felt it. I told him They said I was
like an aberration; even if I didn't know what one
felt like I didn't feel like one. He said Sure, me too,
only I was in jail for it but you're not—how's that?
I laughed *You!* He said We could go to jail together then. This time I set him right: you mean
we could get out, we're *in* one, you could get me out
and me you. He said You just let me out being here
and talking that way, thanks. He said it softer than
any hands ever put on me, he said it like Going
away forever but I'll never forget and I got no right
to ask anything more; and it was asking at the
same time Stay, Don't ever let me go back in jail,
now you let me out. Asking like that. You've got
green eyes just like mine, I said and laughed and
took his arm, knowing all the days I'd go with him
if he asked me.

and
Bette Davis
and
him

I went to the movies—one of the nights I could
feel, remembering every minute, my mother's slaps
that always made me want to slap myself, making
like her. I won't forget: I was so full of being empty

I couldn't hold any more emptiness—sometimes
when I was that way I felt all the air might go out
of me like a balloon and I'd collapse on the sidewalk flat as a newspaper, they could step on me, it
wouldn't make any difference, treat me like dirt anyway, so empty a thing could pass right through my
skin, all of me. The picture was a rerun, an old
Bette Davis movie and she was Carlotta, an em-
press, standing on the balcony and they were playing "La Paloma" and she was dying inside for
Mexico, it looked like, because she was supposed to
be crazy with that wild look and her eyes leaped
out like that, but I knew it wasn't just Mexico and
Maximilian, it was a thing inside her trying to get
out because nobody would come to it, but I knew—
I stood up right there, and said Here I am, and
"La Paloma" was playing real loud then and she was
moving far off now, and I said Wait! because I
wanted to tell her but somebody said Down in
front! and "The End" came on the screen and the
lights came on and everybody looked at me like trying to make me ashamed but I wasn't, I stared back,
I couldn't help it they didn't understand a thing.
And I felt emptier than ever. I hung around the
lobby just watching the people go by, bunches and
twos and kids and sometimes just one, like me. They
put out the lights and the street was dark except
under the lampposts and the cars mostly gone now,
only one now and then, and I went to the corner
and stood on the curb by a car. After a while a man
came for it and said You want a ride? and I said
Yes, I was waiting for you and he laughed and said
Don't con me and I said What's conned? I never
did that to anybody, and he said Where do you want
to go? and I said Anywhere you're going. So we
went to Piedmont and he parked and put his hands
on my shoulder and one on my leg and kissed me
and I thought *Never before* and I kissed him, I

couldn't stop, I thought I'd be sick if he stopped, I
couldn't stand it if he did and I told him I'll die if
you stop, Don't stop, moving like mad, and he said
he wouldn't, It's your first time, hey? and I said Yes,
and I knew I couldn't die, never die now, and
couldn't let him go, only for a while he wasn't there,
it was like I *did* die, only suddenly was somebody
else, *she* was gone and she couldn't come back, no
more Dorothy, never, I knew it. And when he
stopped he said You're sweet, you were so good, and
I said Did you feel me inside you? and he couldn't
say anything and then said Inside you? with a kind
of laugh, bad, and that laugh did it, not a mean
laugh, but I knew he didn't understand a thing, I
was just Carlotta, I wanted to cry, I looked out the
window down across the park where it went deep
into dark like far off it was Mexico and maybe that's
what she was remembering too, Carlotta—how it
was just for a second when a hand got up inside you
right around your heart and squeezed and made you
cry out all alive, him inside and you inside, full full,
and making everything they said at home a lie, I
wouldn't forget that, Maybe he tried, I don't know
or didn't care. I wanted to think he did care; I still
want to after all this time and maybe if I ran into
him again he'd tell me he remembered, it would be
right. I leaned over and put my head on his shoulder
and kissed his neck and said Thank you, I'll never
forget and then got out and he said Hey, I'll take
you home and I said No, I'll walk and went down in
the dark under the trees and sat there all night and
thought Why didn't they ever tell me? And in the
morning I still had to tell somebody so I called and
woke up Mr Farraday, my old English teacher who
always had a good feeling for me, and I said Mr
Farraday, this is Dorothy, I was out all night with a
man who picked me up at the movies and he took
me to Piedmont and had me and he said I was good

and I'm so happy. And Mr Farraday didn't answer
right off, but when he said I'm glad, Dorothy, I
knew he wasn't, he was too sad, and besides it was a
long silence I heard first, before he said anything,
long, and I knew he didn't understand what happened.

and the
psychiatrist

He said Don't you know that—it will kill you? and
I said How do I know if I never was alive all the
way? You have to find out what'll kill you and then
you'll know. And he said Suppose it kills you or
nearly kills you, then what? And I said Then I'll
know the biggest thing—I was alive all the way. It's
the one thing I can tell you I learned from sex only
it's not enough yet—you never came so near dying
as me: when you've been near dying, beat down and
near killed, your body that hurt and worse, you're
so alive, you begin to know the *thing*. What thing?
he said. That's what I'm trying to find out, I said,
but I'm nearer than you are, I can tell—you don't
know anything, maybe you won't let yourself be
wide open, because you know what? You have to
learn it and there's only one way: you have to forget so many things you've been taught—go back
down the same street like backwards and undo it,
like unwinding a spool of thread and seeing it all
stretched out: it's no fun, it makes you feel like the
mess all over the floor will never get back on again;
the one thing is it's all the same thing, not broke
yet, there's that one thing you pray for—you can
keep it all connected till you get it together again.
Look, I'm just a girl and you're a fullgrown man—
you are, aren't you, you know you *are?* you must be
because you studied and got through and have this
office and I'm your patient and I'm here because
you *know*, don't you? And what I want to know is
what is it you know and why you're not telling me?
And I'm telling *you* it's because I'm just a girl, that's
what you're thinking, a girl patient, and that's the

trouble: If I said Touch me, doctor, I need it, you know what? *You'd* be the patient, you're already the patient, because I'm not just a girl, I'm something I don't know what yet the same way you're a patient and not a real doctor, the only kind in the world there can be, that we're all looking for who doesn't need an office and degree and clients, only can know he just has to *say* something or *do* something or not even say it or do it, just make you know you're not alone, he walked right over into it, crossed over so one other in the whole world made you know he understood and nothing could stand in the way, just he'd come without anything holding him back, like he wasn't even a man anymore and you a girl and not even two just one even if they're walking down the street or sitting in the same field, in the salt water, and they never had to say one thing more all their lives, then you wouldn't be a patient anymore and I wouldn't be—go ahead, laugh—a doctor. It's all wrong even now because I'm thinking like a doctor making you a patient, only I'm trying, I *am,* and someday I will make it right: I'll find out. There won't be doctor and patient. If I ever get a doctor who comes and crosses over, just one, that's all, we'll be alive all the way, and we'll be like they're all the time saying, what we keep wanting—to get out, like we're free of skin, free, and we can tell them and they'll see, everybody, and maybe want it too—

and Momma

and got so tired of all that Don't do it, You're too young and you have to be careful, and I had to find out *Careful*—you might wake up and never want to go to sleep again and like it and want more and even love: she never said it came that way or that way helped or anything, just Don't, Someday you'll be sorry if you do. I don't mean I got tired because she *said* it so much, only that nobody in the whole world except somebody sick believes that and you tell from their eyes and their hands and the way they look at each other when they're saying it that just then, while they're talking, they're sick because they're telling lies, I mean half of it's a lie anyway because there's a secret in them wants to tell you Do what I didn't but if you do it'll kill you, only they're not sure it'll kill you either, they never found out, and maybe they lived wrong all this time and make it like it looks fuller than it is and it's like an orange with no juice they squeezed, or the wrong one, and they'd like to try again but it's too late, they make it too late for you too before you even reached for it, that's what's so bad, you don't know the kind of hating all mixed up in them when they say they're loving you, and they do, but how do they know, never trying, they don't know either, poor things, but you can't tell them because you're young, you don't even know anything, there's nothing for you to know they don't know or didn't once, only why do they forget so much? I keep wanting them to remember; if they did, if they only did, everything would be all right—they wouldn't be sick, and I wouldn't be sick, maybe things would happen. But it's too late, it already happened, what they could never stop. How could they if they never felt it, and if they did, how could they ever forget? *How?*

and Dennie And I'd say to Dennie If I held the knife would you push it with my hand? *Yes.* If I cut open the vein and let the blood out, would you hold him? *Yes.* If I held the gun, would you pull the trigger? *Yes.* Would you go all the way, no stopping, no matter what? *Yes.* And not care if my hair fell out and my eyes dried up and all my body rotten, you'd stay? *Yes.* And we'd laugh loud like we'd never stop and didn't care who heard us right there in the park on the grass. And all eaten with disease? *Yes.* And dying too? *Yes.* And you'd come with me when my hands reach the edge and I pull up and I look over and see——? *Yes.* And you don't care what it is just so long as we get there and see it and know because it'll be forever then and you won't be able to change it, it'll be too late, and maybe then you don't even want it or me either but we got to find out, only we know we want it, just we're afraid, like if I opened you up and got right inside and swam in your blood then I'd know you and you me? *Yes.* Or cut your vein and drank all the blood and you'd go with me then, you'd have to, I'd carry you, I'd run all the way, I'd say we're coming together to find out, and maybe I'd have to do that to everyone I could want to go too, drink their blood and carry it up with me, all of it, over the edge and right into——? *Yes.* Maybe you're——you begin to sound like him——Manny? *Yes.*

and the
rehabilitation
man

He said They will send you to school. He said They will help you get the kind of job you want and make money and be respectable and dress well and that will help you get a good man to love you and you won't have to work anymore but bring up the children you're going to have. He said They will help you and you can have a nice house and a new car to drive around in. He said They will help you belong to clubs and the church and organizations that will keep you busy in a constructive way. I was watching a leaf move. I wanted to be a tree for a minute, green breathing green, and going to sky, and feel the earth around it holding good and they couldn't tear me out to put me in any place they thought I should be for my own good, I'd have the place, I'd be going somewhere.

and Wally

I could hear Wally in the corridor, I couldn't move yet——much. The nurse would sometimes crank the bed up, but I could hear him, it was all I heard: Is she going to be all right cause if she's not I'm going to kill somebody, I *am.* Even if I couldn't move I

could laugh in me, hurting all over but not feeling
it anymore when I heard him talk like that, and so
sick of all white and no window I could see green
and blue and houses from. And I'd go—far out, I
can't tell you, a funny trip I couldn't know, and
come back—me not even dead like I thought, seeing the culvert and cement and the cycle in the air
and Wally's hands on my waist, no not even dead
but in the old body, and hearing I don't know if in
the place or remembered, Wally saying that: I
laughed. That'd be two dead, Wally, instead of one,
you'd have that on your hands, they'd put you in
jail with the people who knew how deep in you
could go, for sure. But he was talking in my body.
He was saying I'll keep you alive and me thinking
As long as there's you I'm alive, I have to be, Everybody else's dead, You have to show them how to
keep them alive, Wally, and you're doing it to me,
hear me? I wanted to tear all this white. I called
Wally, but my mouth hurt and a whisper came and
the nurse said Don't try to talk; but I tried anyway,
she didn't know, she was just doing what she was
told, poor thing, didn't know what was going on in
me; if she knew, she'd say You go ahead, Shout
Wally, Don't pay attention to what the doctor says,
Just scream it—

and Boris and
Stack and
Torbert and
Billyjoe and
Hector and
Carlos and

The only way is to use your body, every bit of it
full before you die or you *can't* find it and die:
that's what it is—you've used it up till the only
thing's left is what you can't see, I *know* it and I
want it, and then maybe that day you'll *see*—what
you can't see—it's where I'm going, to see; they can
pull the whole blue sky off that day but first you
have to let the sky in every pore and all the things
they tell you's not living, to find out: and how do
they know, not trying, even if it's wrong and
near kills you and destroys some of you; it's hurting
that way counts, you remember it, you *have* to re-

member—everything—hear? Something in you
doesn't forget when the time comes and you need it
and it makes the next thing more. I've been dreaming it all my life—with my eyes open. See, Boris?
You see . . .

and Lucy

In jail they kept asking what I did. I told them I
tried to live. They said they understood that. Yeah,
but what'd you do? Lucy asked me. Nothing, I said.
Not killed nobody or doping or robbed or nothing?
she said. I said, Why'd I do any of those things,
though maybe I did all those things in a way, maybe
everybody does. Lucy said You sure are the crazy
one. Not about a man? It's gotta be. And I said,
Well, in a way—yes— Well, what'd you do to
him then? or him to you? she said. I said Maybe
we just came alive. Oh, she said, you get caught
screwing on the grass or somewheres in public? I
laughed: we did it but we didn't get caught. But I
got caught and he did, that's what. Only Lucy didn't
understand—not just the thought I was doing
something wrong, like hustling. Maybe you have to
be a special kind to know—I don't know—but
when you get with somebody, you *know:* this is
the one, I can tell *him,* and he'll *know.* They're not
so many, but you have to find them; if you don't,
it's like it'll die, everything'll die, there won't be a
thing with everybody dead, so I got to keep looking. Sometimes I get to thinking about how many,
Russ and Sam T and Will and that crazy Boris,
Stack, Dennie, Torbert, Billyjoe, and Hector and
Carlos and Drake and then Manny, one after the
other like all the others, Manny, Manny, and all just
him all over again only more, I get closer, I got to
keep looking. . . .

and Arthur
Moore and the
welfare repre-
sentative and

Your mother and father came all the way from
home, the welfare man said. How'd they find me?
I said. Arthur Moore found the picture in your
bag, the dog, and the place stamped on it. We

Momma and
Poppa

called the police. Arthur! I said. He's gone—he
didn't want to go—but he couldn't stand it, he
said, seeing you when—now he's done it—he's
ashamed of everything; he said you'd know what
he meant. Besides, the welfare pays him for one,
they're not putting up with you if you have any
money at all and he's getting any, you complicate
it for him, he thinks, you'd have to get out. It's all
right; I guess, I said, he wasn't the one. But I felt
afraid: Momma, Poppa. When they came in, I
knew how they'd look: I was afraid they wouldn't
see me, their daughter, only the girl they knew
and the girl they saw on the bed but not what I
was feeling; maybe if they could see that they'd
just come and sit down and touch me and not say a
word, not just one word, they wouldn't need to
ever again. That was my prayer. But I saw the
minute she came in hard and stiff and shamed,
poor thing, and I felt all hard inside when I saw
her like that, something tightened up, maybe
getting ready already for her words—I'll never
forget them—You have to come back and straighten
up so's the neighbors will see you ain't what they
think, You disgraced us and made us so ashamed
we can't hold our heads up no more, It's hard, Your
daddy has all he can do to keep going, You got to
come back and do the Christian thing by us. I could
see Daddy was wanting to touch me and take me
up like he used to and say My girl and just once
when I looked at him, and he looked at Momma, I
knew he was going to speak up and shout her down
the way a few times he has, but she kept talking
and I said Yes I know, Momma; but all the time
I was far away, the sound was different there, I
was listening like she wasn't talking, and I was
thinking Maybe it'll be Manny, He won't turn
and back down, This time we'll make it all the way.

and Wally

When the nurse turned her back and I was practic-

ing walking, she never knew, and when I could I
went down the corridor looking for Wally. I heard
him calling me like I called him and saying I'm
going to kill somebody, I *am*. They told me there
wasn't a Wally in the corridor, never. I was alone
when they found me and the motorcycle a wreck
and nobody else around. But I knew that was a lie:
he was with me, behind me, I still felt his arms
around me, hands on me, letting me go for all
getout like we'd shoot into the sky over the top
of the hill. So every day when I was walking I'd
go to the corridor and look down it and it'd be so
long and empty and white but I knew they were
crazy. And when the doctor came and said I can tell
you now, You are going to be fine again. I said
Tell me what? And he told me Wally was dead
outright that night and they couldn't find out who
he was or I was, wouldn't I tell them? And I
laughed. By all normal considerations you should
be crying, he said. But I couldn't help it—I *was*
crying, only it was my way: crazy crying laughing
because if they couldn't see who he was or I was,
then I had to laugh crying because what's a name—
I knew—me, at least that, and I had him, Wally
wasn't that dead, and what's a body—he'd be no
good dead, wasn't, just alive, he knew it too. He
left it to me to do, get him where he was going,
not his body, that could stay right here like mine
would when I found somebody else then, and
who's going to cry about that? I thought, crying—
yes I was—but not for dead Wally but him inside
me I had and had to carry and had to find somebody else and start all over again only make somebody see you got another one's life in your hands,
your body, to carry it like somebody'll maybe carry
you when they get to seeing and pretty soon somebody's carrying all of you. I was crying how sad
and glad and lucky I was I could still do it, and

the doctor said to the nurse She should be crying but she's not, but she will, right now she's frozen, it's her type of hysteria. I listened, I watched them, I got out of there the next night. They never found me. I got out. I'm running all the way.

and Momma

If they would only once take me for what I am, I thought, and I felt sorry I even thought it. I know nobody knows what I am because I did not even find out; I had to—in me, not in anybody else, and how was I going to do that? It drove me crazy, but you know what? It was smoking that helped. Momma caught me. She hit me, slapped my face— it burned my cheek, only it was something else: it went all through me, my head got almost dizzy; and when I saw what slapping me did to her—she changed, her face got red, her eyes were shining wet but not like crying, she got bigger too, straight, and she moved fast and it was all that that made me excited. I never saw her that way before—*alive* I mean. She always poked around; she went all day from the kitchen to the bedroom and upstairs and never with energy, a drip, and now the first time I felt something electric in her and me and I wouldn't let it go, I said Yes yes I smoke every day—a lie, I didn't, it was the first time—and she cried You do do you? and struck again. I got afire with her, I laughed at her, and she hit harder this time and kept at it and I said Go ahead, hit me, hit me, hit me, and she did, she couldn't stop, and *I* couldn't, and I was near screaming before she was through and not even knowing what I was saying except I was glad—she touched me, she hit, and she was alive, she wasn't dead, and I was so glad I kept laughing and she didn't know what it was all about, and she said I'll tell your father, He'll give it to you, and I wished she would so he *would* give it to me; but I knew she wouldn't tell him or if she did he'd never get that excited— But I felt a

thing open, like I got a cut, a wound then, from
her and it was ours and I had to keep it open and
let everything in it to keep it open so I'd remember
she could feel and me too—that much.

and Tide

Listen, Tide: Sometimes I'm afraid to look up because I'm afraid behind the sun there will be another sun too big and terrible to look at, but I
want to, even if it destroys me. You just pray one
of us gets through. Somebody has to. You know
what it is to have somebody's life in your hands?

and Troy

He told me I'm glad you don't want to be just like
everybody else, I mean you *do* want kids and a
world, only to make it *for* them so their eyes see
for themselves what it is, not *made* and shoved and
jammed at them, but like you say: like opening a
big door and letting them see it all so wonder-
ful-terrible they got to spend their whole life
learning to hold it the way you should. Only it's
too much, you can't hold it all, he said, and I said
No you can't— It was the first time I saw his eyes
so green they were like the harbor sometimes where
I lived all my life and I saw them yes for the
first time—like *it* was too big. And I said You
mean what you said? Sure, he said, I mean it. And
I was ready to bust I was so happy. It's too big for
anybody, he said, you can't hold it by yourself,
Dorothy. I could scream, I said. Why? he said.
Because it's the longest time, one time somebody
said it, I think it's then, it must be the first time. I
grabbed his hand and put it to my heart. Feel it, I
said. Why's it pounding? he said. Because I could
give it to you, it's pounding for you.

and Manny

I heard him dying, I knew they'd never let him live
—was why I hung around and let him hang around:
cause if they killed him, they killed me too, some;
but I'd have him then all my days—or he'd have
me all his if they did something to me first. We
had to stick together, somewhere near, not far,

close as could be: and if he killed somebody he
couldn't help it—they tried to kill him with a
shovel crossing the tracks, thinking he'd stolen
something, and all the guards after him. And me
waiting: and I heard him, I looked right in his eyes,
I couldn't do anything: only carry him, his words
pushing me all the time. He said Because if I don't
go with her, it's my last one chance in the whole
world to help her, maybe somebody, I don't know
who; maybe I'll even lose the feel of how to help
or even want to because I didn't do it and answer
her, and then maybe even thinking it'll die and
something else, one right after the other, till I'm
just all dead inside—not alive like she made me—
and sometimes I want to take a knife and cut my
arm, slash it wide open to see if there's blood and
how I'd feel or *if* I'd feel when I seen my own
blood running out of me, and I can't forget—
maybe that's why we do it or have to—her lying
there that time I hit her, thinking I love you, you
better listen, and she didn't, and blood running out
of her and me watching and not being able to
stand it and throwing myself down on her and
covering it with my mouth so I'd catch her blood—
crazy now, yes, but not then: *she* knew—you did,
didn't you, Dorothy?—I saw it in her eyes how
she looked at me and her whole body all trembling,
and my tongue and my lips, I can feel it now,
thank God oh Jesus God, I can still *feel* her against
me and the blood hot in my mouth, and her hand
come down just soft on my head and I knew she
knew—crazy now, yes, maybe so to you, not me—
the only thing makes sense, her, and running—
and where to? I don't know, maybe she don't even
know either. Dorothy, where're you? Touch me.
Put your eyes here: when I seen her. How'd *I* see
her, me, Manny? When I seen her, like inside her,
and her eyes, and something she was looking at I

never seen and I know I'd never till I had her eyes
or got the same thing to see where she was seeing,
where it was going—like she said—and where it
takes you, always moving like that my Dorothy, or
me go with her until she finally stopped, and had
to stop, she couldn't go no more. . . .

And I heard him stop. I looked at them, but I
heard him. I turn and run, not even hearing them
behind me. But I heard him, I still do, I always will:
inside me; and I wait for it sometimes to push me,
he keeps at me, and all the other ones too, and
when I get tired and think If he don't come back, I
won't . . . I hear him shouting it to me like he
did all the times. I get up and I run, hearing him
oh Manny, his voice over the hill calling down to
me: Dorothy, keep going. Don't stop. Don't stop,
Dorothy. Don't *let* them—